"Green gives us a layered portrait of the life of a rural working-class southern man, scarred by his fighting in the Vietnam war. In this time of forever wars and festering economic inequality, Green's book does what good fiction can do – shine a light on the meaning and psychology of lives unknown by many."

– **Jay Youngdahl**, veteran, and author of *Working on the Railroad, Walking in Beauty: Navajos, Hozho,* and *Track Work*

"Jack 'Half-Pint' Crowe, reeling from two tours in Vietnam and the loss of his friend on the battlefield, returns to the oil fields and swamps of Louisiana determined to practice nonviolence in a world where a simple act of kindness might get him killed. Mack Green is a skilled storyteller who never flinches in his depiction of the roughnecks and holy men that populate this story, and who never fails to show grace even when describing men's darkest impulses. Frank's Bloody Books *is a gripping tale of resilience and redemption.*"

– **Tiffany Tyson**, author of *The Past is Never*

"As a fellow Vietnam veteran, Mack Green's Frank's Bloody Books *pulled me back to my own deeply-etched memories surrounding that misbegotten war. Green's Jack 'Half-Pint' Crowe doesn't take one step wrong in recreating how so many young men have had to make peace with their wartime experiences as they try to slide back into some semblance of a normal life 'back in the world,' as we would say back then. I was fully absorbed."

– **Dick Price**, *LA Progressive*

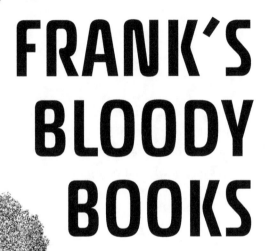

FRANK'S BLOODY BOOKS

A Novel

by Mack Green

Design by Theo Hall

APRIL GLOAMING

©2024 by Mack Green
Design ©2024 by Theo Hall

-First Edition

Publisher's Cataloguing-in-Publication Data

Green, Mack
Frank's bloody books / written by Mack Green / designed by Theo Hall
ISBN: 9781953932211

1. Fiction - General 2. Fiction - Literary 3. Fiction - Southern I. Title II. Author

Library of Congress Control Number: 2023946408

For Kathy Gill Mahan, my wife,
my sister, Paula Jeanette Harvey, and
the memory of Edward Wayman Wisner

PHONE CALL FROM BUSTER MILTON

When I was a boy, my friends nicknamed me Half-Pint because I was a runt. That unsolicited moniker carried with me throughout my days in the Marine Corps and beyond. I am now known as Dr. Jack Crowe, Associate Professor of Religious Studies at a small college nestled in Vermont's Green Mountains. But I got a call less than a month ago that has compelled me to tell the story of Half-Pint's search for meaning and purpose on this earth. Which starts with Frank, who was the only holy man I ever knew. And since it begins with Frank, it begins with the war.

It was last month when I unlocked my office and the phone rang. Sunlight struck my face through the windows and blinded me for a moment. I put down a bundle of class lecture notes on *Religion in the American Experience* on my desk beside the latest issue of *Science Magazine*. Earlier, I'd noticed in the journal's listing of contents an article about the disappearance of three billion birds on the continent. The topic had piqued my interest along with some trepidation. I'd looked forward to reading it in the quiet of my office after the lecture. But the phone kept ringing and I answered it. A new phase of my life was about to begin.

"Dr. Crowe speaking."

"Half-Pint? This is Buster Milton."

A thimble of air caught in my throat. Close to a half-century had swept past since I last talked to Buster Milton. No one had addressed me as Half-Pint since I left the South in the summer of 1973. Outside the window, trees across the campus oval swayed in a high breeze. Mottles of shade quivered across the vast lawn. I braced the palm of my hand against the corner of the desk.

"Buster?"

"Blackie has died. He starved himself out in the final run. He'd been at the Veterans Nursing Care in Alexandria a good year now. Lived in twilight time most of a day. Remembered here and there. He was ninety-four." A brief space of silence came. Buster repeated, as if an affirmation to himself, "Ninety-four. I'm not far behind." Another respite of silence.

1

Then, "You alright, boy?" His voice had an old man's quiver. But within it, there was strength still and a tint of whim.

"I'm alright," I said. "How are you, Buster?" I sought to secure the grounding of my feet upon the floor. I slowed my breath. Blackie was dead. The wild of things further gone. I thought of his fascination with panthers. His certainty that they still roamed the southern swamps and woods. The avoidance of my past penetrated me with shame.

Buster cleared his throat. "Preparing. Practicing kindness, sacrificing wants and needs, looking at truths that cause me to shiver in my bed at night. Every day I hug my blood and bone children and their children that came of my body and that of Beatrice. She is of the memories now. But listen to me go on and on embarrassing you I be sure with my wandering thoughts. To that, I'm sorry. I'm an old man. Don't wish to make you more uncomfortable than I do."

"I too am an old man."

Buster rasped a chuckle. "But I'm an old geezer," he drawled. "There came another pause. Buster sighed. A magical transformation of electrical signals shot through the phone's receiver. "Blackie's dead," he said. My breath stole away. Buster kept on. "Before his senses abandoned him, he permitted me to beckon you. As a favor to me. But only after he was dead could I make this request of you. Blackie's dead and I'm asking. I need you to come here as a favor to me. Will you come, boy?"

An inner part of me, inflexible as an iron bar, held me back. I, the constant student of religions, all these years saying that I was through with the South. A history of violence denied. I knew what I was about to say to Buster Milton, this man who had dwelled in my memories as a wiry cord of muscles and bone perched high on the monkey board of an oil rig derrick, his skin glistening of sweat as he muscled stands of drill pipe into position above the platform floor. I was going to say, No, you damn fool. I won't come back.

Instead, I said, "I'm sorry about Blackie. You know I am." My words floated into the cool office air.

"Revelations await you," Buster said. "You come hither; maybe redemption will finally be served me. Just need you for a day. Even an hour. This old man would appreciate the kindness of your appearance." His voice cracked. Sadness wavered through me though I'd always been quite good at keeping painful emotions at bay.

"Buster, we've entered different worlds. A lifetime has passed. What are you talking about?"

2

"Revelations await you. Please come, boy. Opportunities to pay your debt. The chance to see the truth of it all. Within and without. Please come, boy."

"Buster..." I stopped.

"I'm too close to the truth of things, Half-Pint. Should we be forever protected from the truth? Are we not without the strength to confront the truths? That's the craziness you hear in my voice as you try to read into my supplications. We worship only what is and what isn't these days. I've never been an asking man. To that you probably know. But I believe in truth. In the acknowledgment and payment of debts. I saw in you that need to know and be as well. I remember you, boy, as did Blackie, who always hoped you'd come back despite his hog shit threats. Blackie's dead. Truth calls out. Burdens to be lifted from our shoulders. Please come, boy. Please come."

"I don't know of debts, Buster." I took a long breath. *Damn...damn...damn.* Then, "It will take a few days for me to make some arrangements. School break is coming shortly. I can get away for a while then."

"Come soon, Half-Pint."

"Alright," I said. A hand took hold of my heart. The hand released its grip and everything inside me hollowed out. Can you see the pathetic quiver of Half-Pint's chin as he sucks back the pain? Professor Jack Crowe can't. He's looking out the window, blinded by the overwhelming sunlight.

Come soon, Buster says. Come soon.

I put down the phone. A seminar awaited me in an hour, one I've conducted many times over the decades in my academic sanctuary. The shimmer of sunlight through the trees striking the smooth lawn of the campus oval continues. Frank comes to mind, and I conjure him up into his full material breadth. He rarely speaks to me these days. Just visits in the quietness, sits off to the side, comfortable by our long friendship. He never ages, this young, lithe, swift-of-foot phantom with the enduring smile. I look straight into that serene smile of his and ask, "What do you think?"

There is silence as I expected, but then he fucks with me in the only way Frank could by murmuring gently, "Mysterious opportunities, Jack. Maybe you'll learn something about meaning and purpose. Finally."

"Yeah," I said. "Finally."

THE BLOODY BOOKS IN FRANK'S PACK

Frank was the only holy man I ever knew. He was a Navy corpsman. At first, I shied away from him like all the other grunts. He read books that had incomprehensible titles, two or three always crammed inside his haversack as if they were as essential as a C-ration meal or cigarettes. Disturb him in those quiet moments while he read, he would look up with a sleepy smile, "How can I serve you, Marine?"

A corpsman usually garnered automatic respect from the Marines. Most of us, as jarhead grunts, possessed at most a high school education. Navy corpsmen seemed to exude an air of higher knowledge. They had well-honed powers—the ability to stanch bleeding wounds, treat clap and jungle rot, administer the remedies for heat exhaustion in the jungle and paddies. But the ultimate test was how a corpsman reacted when the shit hit the fan, when enemy rounds clipped through the underbrush, when the distant whomp-whomp sounds of mortars released from their tubes and we hugged the earth and sucked up the Asian soil with our breaths. Those were the times a corpsman would reveal the depth of his mettle. Frank had provided proof of his worthiness too many times. He moved through the brush like some deer's shadow flashing past toward the call, 'Corpsman up!' giving of himself a willingness to die. We Marines afforded HM3 Frank Maudsley great admiration; yet, with such awe came a sense among us that he was an odd kind of animal packed with neurons that lit up in a way far different than the rest of us.

With all that nah thinking on our part came ridiculous rumors. Frank was a Navy experiment. Fear and anger culled from his heart. The wildest story—he carried an unloaded .45, the corpsman's only weapon. Although such gossip bandied through the ranks, we knew it to be bullshit. No one kept an unloaded weapon out here, not even a goofball, saint-like individual like Frank Maudsley.

Frank shit like the rest of us but ate only crackers, cheese, peanut butter, and fruits from the C-rat packs. "Half-Pint, Fuckin' Doc ain't

4

human," Lance Corporal Roman Romano said to me one day while we huddled together in the soft rain, looking out into a blackness resonant with the plaintive croaking of tree frogs. "I asked him for some aspirin and said this monsoon crap is the shits, ain't it, Doc? He pulls out an aspirin bottle from his medical bag, grins at me like he always does, man, and says, 'It's beautiful, Romano. Glorious.' He's a scary motherfucker."

Romano, whom I had made the mistake of allowing myself to become too close, got offed three days later by one spectacular shot through the neck from an NVA sniper. Frank had worked on him, exhausting a pretty bundle of battle dressings to stanch the wound that pumped red with blood. A stone-like stillness had already settled across Romano's face, but Frank rasped into our dead buddy's ear, "I'm sorry, brother." Tiny muscles below his right eye twitched. Yeah, Frank fought the storms of anger and fear and sorrow just like the rest of us. He just had a different way of dealing with it and I grew more curious.

Four months and three days before my time to rotate back to the States from my second tour of duty, headquarters command pulled us out of the field for a week of rest and recuperation in the battalion area. Our decimated and bedraggled company of Marines fed out of the bellies of relief choppers and stood upon a sandy acreage from which you could look west upon the green delta that swept toward the mauve peaks of the Northern Truong Son Mountain range. In this battalion sanctuary of squad-size tents with tin roofs and plywood floors and canvass cots, I felt damn near at peace. These periods of respite always hit me like a warm breath of air but swept my thoughts too far inward. It's ironic now that fifty years later, looking back upon those violent days from the bookish comfort of a departmental office in a minor university, my view is sharp and clear. Far into my second combat tour, I should have been dead.

The war had hollowed me out. I'd seen bad things, done bad things, and spent what goodness I might have had inside me. The myths of war, those promises of glory and heroism that every male child harbors inside his bosom, had been shred by madness and the desire to stay alive—neglected topics on the tasks of war. With all this insight I have now sharpened by the clarity of hindsight, I know that wasn't me back then. It was Half-Pint, a kid far different from the old man looking back upon his life.

During our company's week of rest at the battalion base camp, Frank had claimed a spot in the tent manned by my meager squad. He had stretched out on a cot, his head at rest against his pack. One of his books stood propped upon his chest and held open by one hand. He and I were the only occupants of the tent that first afternoon. Ordered by the Gunny, I'd assigned the rest of my squad to various details. Burning shitters and filling sandbags along the perimeter were the primary tasks. The men went bitching, but underneath it all, grateful for the promise of an ordinary day. Burning a barrel of shit or shoveling dirt and sand into a sandbag didn't carry a high risk of injury or death. On this afternoon, I had the rare luxury of solitude but for the supine presence of Frank.

A side flap of the tent had been hoisted and tied off, giving the interior a steady burst of sunlight filled with floating dust motes. I sat on the edge of my cot across from Frank. I'd just broken down my rifle for cleaning. Barrel, bolt, and bolt carrier lay upon a ragged, oily tee shirt between my feet.

"What are you reading, Doc?" I spoke as if someone spoke for me.

He rolled his eyes toward me and closed the book. "Nothing really." He gave me that sad, loopy smile.

"Shit," I said and began to assemble the cleaning rod.

He kept his gaze fixed upon me. I turned away from it and lifted the rifle barrel from between my feet.

"You'll forgive yourself someday," he said. "Try to take comfort in knowing that, Jack. It'll be helpful for you to know that."

The earth seemed to tilt. He knew of my big sin. My atrocity had been padded in silence and stuffed away in the dark box of complicity. We all shared in sins out here. And he'd addressed me by my first name. No one called another by his first name in the green machine.

"What are you talking about, Doc?" I could hear the seething tone of threat low in my throat.

He kept his sad smile upon me. "Call me Frank. Will you do that? My name is Frank."

"All right."

He lowered the book flat upon his chest. His eyes wouldn't let go of me.

"I know this makes you uncomfortable, me talking to you about this. I hope that you'll be ready to deal with the bad dreams that will come of what happened. The challenges that you'll face."

My heart sped faster. Its beating thrummed inside my ears. My hands had grown clammy as I placed the rifle barrel across the brace of my thighs and fitted the last section to the cleaning rod.

"There's an antidote to what will come, though you can't undo the cross you'll have to bear. You can only make it smaller. You've got a good heart, Jack. I watch you. I think you deserve to prepare yourself for all that's coming."

"All right," I said.

His smile broadened. A small gap in his upper row of teeth cast an almost humorous look to his grin.

"I hold no judgment, Jack."

I knew too well of what Frank Maudsley spoke. Cold fear steeped inside me as his eyes kept penetrating the side of my face. It had happened on a day we'd lost three guys in my squad alone during a sweep near the Hill of Angels. In the aftermath, Romano and a new kid, PFC Duckworth, had drug a wounded NVA out of the high grass by the ambush trail. The NVA soldier had been shot through the hand and right shoulder. The wound below his clavicle had stanched well on its own. Just a dark oxblood patch emblazoned his ragged khaki uniform by the side of his neck. Romano confiscated his rifle and held the soldier's pith helmet in his free hand. Duckworth shoved the soldier to his knees on a mottled space of grass and mud and roped his hands behind his back with comm wire. The NVA's expression had a far distant bearing as if he were listening to some imaginary wind. A bang of thick, dusty black hair curved across his forehead.

This is where I must pause as I describe the event. Give me an angel to prop me up, slap me across the face, make me look upon myself. Goddamn my dispassion. I can't let myself feel, even to this day, so many years after the ultimate shame of my act. I felt nothing when I shot the enemy soldier in the head. In quiet moments, I've tried to examine the hollow depth that accompanied the killing. I've concluded that dispassion and indifference are real marks of evil. When I killed the soldier while he crouched on his knees with his hands bound behind him, I was the embodiment of perversion. It's in me, this propensity to commit violence.

Romano had removed the binding from the soldier's wrists and pushed him over on his side. Our platoon commander at the time, a Lieutenant Jorgenson, came over, crouched low, and plucked through the soldier's pockets, examined the sky, muttered, "Saddle up," and the afternoon descended into evening and evening into night, and I gave thanks to the darkness. Only later, in the deep shadows of the brush did I notice the return of my beating heart.

Now, in the breezeless air of the tent, Frank looked at me from his supine position on the cot, saying he didn't judge me.

"So, you don't fuckin' judge me? Huh, Frank?"

"You'll find your way. I know you will, Jack."

I gave him the full brunt of my silence. My body went numb. My hands went on automatic pilot. Driving the barrel rod through the muzzle, scrubbing the barrel clean, wiping down the upper and lower receiver with an oily rag, breaking down the bolt carrier, swabbing off dirt and carbon . . . just let the hands work, then reassemble. When I came out of that dark and narrow tunnel of consciousness and shifted my vision once more on Frank, he was asleep. The book lay face down across his chest. I stood, holding my rifle by the stock in one hand. My eyes focused through a haze of fatigue on the book's title, *The Upanishads*. I walked out and down the wooden steps of the tent and into the full blast of the Asian sun.

It would be the next day, after a night of fitful sleep laden with dreams forgotten upon awakening, that I would again talk to Frank. He'd been busy in the medical tent all morning. The few men of my squad had sauntered off to the mess tent and had the full scope of an afternoon free of work details or watch duties awaiting them. I perched myself on a shelf of sandbags lined outside the sickbay tent and waited for his exit. The sun blazed at its high point in the sky when the entry flaps of the field tent flew back and Frank emerged. He spotted me straight away and there was a brightness to the smile he gave me.

"Come on, Jack. Let's get some chow."

Mashed potatoes and canned green beans were the only food items Frank accepted along the mess tent's chow line. They were piled into high mounds on his mess kit tray. We left the large tent and its rough-hewn tables and chose a sandbag wall above a perimeter trench to perch our trays. We sat beside them and began to eat. A landscape of vast green paddies and the mountains beyond spread away before us.

I hadn't spoken, just trailed along with Frank as if caught in some gravitational pull from which I couldn't extract myself. But my appetite livened my senses. Hunger was always a gnawing presence back then. I dug into the potatoes and a slab of what appeared to be roast beef. Frank chewed slowly, swallowed, and began to talk. "I'd like to wander through those mountains someday. No one trying to kill anyone. Wouldn't that be grand?" He looked away, shaking his head in wonderment. "Grand, Jack. Wouldn't it be grand?"

Grand? What strange, fucking words Frank used. The muscles of his jaw worked in little undulant waves as he chewed. "What's that book about? The one you're reading," I asked.

He looked at me with his eyebrows raised. "From yesterday? *The Upanishads*, it's about Hinduism."

"Why do you read shit like that?"

A great smile erupted and Frank took a deep breath. "Curiosity."

"About what?"

Then came Frank's loopy grin, a faint emanation of sadness from the light in his eyes. "The meaning of life," he said. Frank fixed his vision directly into me as if to say, it's okay to laugh, but I said with a curiosity of my own stirring, "You can find that in the book?"

He bit his lip and his Adam's apple rolled up then down. "Nah, reading's just one way. Religious writings provide a guide. The Holy Bible, the teachings of Buddha, Mohammed, on and on. Yet, I think the best guide is just living, looking, listening, tasting, smelling, touching. The answer is already in us. You can't believe all the bullshit you read. But it all gets you to thinking."

"You read all that shit?" I said, trying to sound disinterested, but inside myself something moved low in my chest. A worm of interest pressed through all my cautions about this deadly world.

"You want some of that shit to read?" Frank said. "I get all sorts of stuff." His grin spread wider.

"Fuck nah." I looked away and forked potatoes into my mouth. "Fuck nah."

The mountains with their soft crenellations loomed in a milk-white haze against the cloudless sky. I imagined Frank hiking through them as an older man far into the future. It hit me then at that moment. Frank scared me, provoked me, piqued my senses, and caused me to wonder about life in ways that had always been beyond my ability to comprehend.

"Hand over your .45, Frank. I want to check it."

Frank laughed. "You'll find it's empty. There's no need to check."

"You can't do that."

"I'm not going to kill anyone."

"What if I needed you to protect me?"

"I'd do what I could, but I wouldn't kill someone."

"Not using that .45 might get a Marine killed."

"I'm not part of that picture." Frank had that smile. Not a smirk but a sad upturn of the lips. He set his mess kit tray at his side and pulled the .45 from his side holster. It lay flat across his palm in front of me for the taking.

"Put the goddamn weapon back," I whispered.

"All right." He drove the .45 back into the side holster and snapped shut the flap. Then he picked up his tray and resumed eating. A great heron swung low in flight across the paddies as if it were but a shadow at the corner of my eye. The warm, palpable air of the delta lay over me like a blanket.

"Why don't you eat any meat?"

Frank looked at me as if he could hardly contain his amusement. "Vegetables and non-animal organisms are better at tolerating being consumed. Gosh, Jack. Several days a week I fast. Don't eat anything to give homage to all life. Sharpens the senses." He shifted his gaze to the mountains and scooped another bite of mashed potatoes into his spoon. I had the sense he was working extra hard not to laugh.

I shook my head. A little dip and rise of my chin to show I'd heard enough of that nonsense.

"What's an antidote?"

Frank swallowed, answered in a soft drawl. "Oh, it's something like a medicine or a decision you make to counteract poison or wrongdoing. Like when a rattlesnake has bitten you. You take an antidote to help keep you from dying."

"What would be my antidote?"

Frank rested his dark, burning eyes on me. Square-jawed, thick, black hair in need of a cut, several days of beard stubble, an old scratch beneath his right eye, a bearing of anguish invading the goofy smile.

"Jack...Jack...poor Jack. You'll have to find it yourself in the search for meaning you're about to take."

Looking back upon those times through the brighter lens of hindsight, I feel soft movements of lament and nostalgia working through my body. And I often look at the past these days, my body vexed with muscle and joint pain, reminding me that old age presents its own form of Vietnam. Casualties mount with each passing month, it seems. Colleagues, friends, academic acquaintances I've known through the years succumbing to the downward drip-drip of aging. A darker sense of humor has enfolded me, and the truth is that Vietnam has never left me.

That strange day, sitting with Frank on the sandbag wall, the green delta and the mauve mountains flooding my senses, my heart pumping with the vigor that comes from newfound hope, I wanted to change my direction in life but knew I didn't possess the strength. Four months left on a second tour of duty in Vietnam, I had no bloody idea where my life would lead. Yet, I had the vivid sensation of being afoot and the possibility of embarking on a path not taken.

Frank never asked me again if I wanted to read the books he carried. And he always seemed to have a fresh supply coming in by way of small, well-bound packages. He told me in passing that his mother, a history professor, supplied him with his requests. I grew more amused and enthralled by his spirit of peace, mysticism, and grace. In the jargon of military experience, we became buddies. Not just military acquaintances.

As the weeks slipped ever closer to my day of departure from this land of injury, death, boredom, terror, exhilaration, I sought every opportunity to share chow with Frank on patrols and operations, partake in conversations with him that would lead my mind into delightful, confusing spheres of thought. I relished saying, "You're fucking crazy, Frank," in response to some of his wild observations.

"That bug pushing a tiny ball of water buffalo shit past our boots has the spirit of the universe within it."

"Fuck you, Frank."

"We're all part of a great living organism inseparable from the planet upon which we walk."

"Oh, fuck you, man." And then, him grinning, showing his strong teeth, "We're pals, Jack. We'll be friends forever."

His openness always brought me to the point of heated embarrassment. I'd grind my teeth, shake my head, exhale as if sweltering from the sun. "Fuck off, Frank. For God's sake."

And he would prod on, clasping my shoulder. "Admit it, buddy. We're friends. Aren't we friends, Jack?"

"Yeah, yeah, we're friends, you weird motherfucker." Then the motherfucker would laugh as if he'd just hauled in a fish.

One of the most jarring remembrances I had of our conversations was on an evening after our platoon had set up a perimeter during a small-scale operation. We had perched ourselves on a hillside in terrain thick with tall, broad-leaved evergreen and a heavy growth of palm trees. Our cover was dense and filled with insect song. More the enemy that day had been the heat, the dense air, the perpetual burn of sweat into our eyes. It had been a good day.

Frank and I crouched side by side, looking out into the twilight. He supped a cup of coffee he'd just prepared over the flame of a heat tab before the full breadth of darkness descended. In the valley below, a firefight erupted. The orange glow of tracer rounds crisscrossed the land. That's when, for reasons inexplicable to me, I told Frank about my old man igniting himself in flame and dying from fire.

"My old man burnt himself up."

Frank's lips lifted from the rim of the C-rat can. He peered into the side of my face. After a while, he spoke. "I'm really sorry, Jack. Buddy, I'm sorry."

I nodded, mumbled, "Hell, I didn't even go back."

"I'm really sorry, Jack." He paused, flexing his jaw. Drew his voice down into a low, smooth tone. "You need to start where you began. That place we call home. Where our souls first get shaped. You can change the history, buddy. That's where your journey should begin. When you get there, just look around. Something will come to get you. From there, you can start creating another story for yourself." He said nothing for a while. Propped an elbow on his knee and looked out in front of him as if trying to focus on some point just beyond his nose. "And I think you need to go to college, Jack. You got a real hunger to learn."

What I'd needed was to share this strange secret I harbored with someone I trusted, to just hear the validation and understanding in a friend's voice. Frank gave me that, but more. He confirmed that he saw me as a fellow traveler. Sanctioned the odd desires to learn that I know he sensed were just beginning to ignite inside my body. My old man's death is another story in which I'd eventually gain some insight, but at that moment it could not unfold. The magical interlude of twilight faded into darkness. The insects and tree toads went mad, rendering the night into an ebb and flow of electrical buzzing.

On a steamy day, Frank and I stood side-by-side on a mountain trail during a break in which the platoon had trudged its way through jungle brush for the course of a morning. I asked him how he came to be in this ungodly place. Sweat dripped off his nose, and he said, and I can only paraphrase his words in a manner too inadequate, "War is a portal offered by evolutionary design to enter a level of higher consciousness. But filled with lies. I wanted to observe it up close. I was curious. Buddy, it was my choice." And grinning brightly, he added, "Ain't that the shits."

Then I knew for sure that Frank was crazy. Scaring the hell out of me and drawing me toward the flames at the same time. But I liked his craziness.

I will not apologize for admiring his nutty way of thinking. His incomprehensible beliefs. On my own journey—years later—the understanding smacked me in the face that I'd embraced Frank's madness quite readily. It wasn't any more insane than hordes of young men blindly trying to kill one another at the behest of old men rallying them forward in the name of God, Country and Glory.

"Sure, Frank. I hope you make it through. Fuck, I hope we both make it."

But you knew this was coming, didn't you? Frank didn't make it. In that humid, supernatural land, I didn't see it coming. I thought Frank too emboldened with holiness to get blown away.

On a company size operation south of Danang, three days before the 1968 Tet Offensive unleashed its blood across the full breadth of the country, our platoon conducted a sweep across a diverse terrain of rain forest and rice fields that lay beneath spurs of hills jutting down from the mountains. Frank had attached himself to the second squad of the second platoon. The point and five men from the trailing fire teams had passed along a wide path when Frank stepped on the S-mine—the Bouncing Betty. Once the foot's pressure triggers the small prongs of the mine, the body of the device, propelled by black powder, shoots upward at about waist level and detonates, releasing a bevy of ball bearings. Describing the event in technical terms, to this day, helps keep my emotions from flooding. The explosion's effect is devastating at close range. Also, the results are quite deadly to those nearby when the blow comes.

Frank would have died from agonizing guilt if he'd known that his misplaced footstep on the mine had killed the man in front of him and wounded the one behind him. So, there was a bright spot to the quickness of his death, I suppose. Kind oblivion. When I trespassed from two squads back through the haggard Marines kneeling in the brush by the trail and gave witness to the remains of Frank's body, it would be the only time in my two tours of duty that I sank to my knees and fell into blackness. Sometimes I revert to old Marine language— Fuck it. I couldn't see the world around me for a few seconds. When I could see again, there was, at first, blinding light, then the sun breaking through the canopy. I was dimly conscious of radio static, muffled voices, far distant chop-chop sounds from helicopter blades—all those sounds so familiar now in the war movies of that period.

I slung my rifle and unfastened the straps to Frank's pack. Shrapnel had penetrated the rough canvass. Blood splotched over my wrist as I probed the recess of the compartment. I removed three paperback books. I couldn't focus my vision but remember the damp, raggedy feel of the pages against my fingertips.

"Get back to your men, Half-Pint." It was Lieutenant Jorgenson. His natural tone of authority came at me, but something else, the keen, soft edge of compassion. His voice quaked, "Don't you break like that on me again."

"Yes, sir. I'm taking his books."

"Get back to your men."

I turned on my knee, rose, books clutched in the crook of my arm. I'd made a decision that would carry me through the rest of my life. If I make it through the portal, I will try to follow Frank's way. Absolve myself of violence. For reasons well beyond my comprehension, the next steps would begin where I began long ago, where an abandoned house stoked with the residue of another kind of violence would serve as my basecamp, where the reenactments of conflict could be confronted head-on in battle.

A black kid named Harris from North Carolina hissed from his crouched position within a swaddling of leafy vines by the trail as I swept past. "Half-Pint, was that really Doc who got it?"

"Yeah, it was Frank," and only then realized I was sobbing and felt no shame.

ARRIVING

A train cut through the town of Baptiste back in those days before the mills and factories of the upper parishes had shuttered down. The Southern Belle railroad line ran from New Orleans to Kansas City, pausing at the tiny stations to gather small crowds of passengers. Even now, as Mr. Old Man Wisdom himself, I fail to grasp why I chose to fly into New Orleans after being mustered out of the Corps at Camp Lejeune and purchase a ticket on that train back to Baptiste, a place that, as Frank put it, had shaped my soul.

My proneness for self-deceit never stops chugging along. Getting old has only slowed it down. Hell, I know why I took that train on the last leg of my journey back to Baptiste. I wanted to try and relive a short period of happiness in my childhood when I had served as a nine-year-old chaperone to my mother on a visit to the Crescent City.

My mother, Ida, had always longed to visit New Orleans. Throughout her life, it seemed some far-reaching dream. One day my old man bought her a ticket on the Southern Belle and a reservation for a hotel room at the edge of the quarter. Despite his tragedies, both inner and outer, he loved Ida beyond any scope of understanding. But that's the way it is, I suppose, with badass love.

The point is that the ticket included me, her runt of a son, who might secure her commitment to return. That brief time with Ida on the train ride to New Orleans and returning to the upper Louisiana mill town was the happiest of my childhood. And it stemmed from the joy that radiated from Ida on the journey. I basked in it.

Through the Pullman car window, she watched what seemed to us both a foreign land sweeping by. I couldn't take my eyes from the rosiness of her skin, the perfect contours of her face, a light of excitement she rarely exuded. She was a beautiful woman, and I was alongside her, proud and protective.

As strangers in the jungle city of lavish homes, sweeping oaks, tall palms and exotic people, the city did not eat us alive as I'd initially feared. Oh, but it beckoned us to tickle its belly. We gave each other strength. Ida's warm hand clenched mine as if there were a bond between us. We explored the quarter's streets, garnered a table at Cafe Du Monde by the river, ate sugary beignets that coated our lips in powder, laughed together at the sound of bullhorns from the riverboats.

The first morning, we walked along the narrow streets of the quarter to the corner of Canal and Carondelet and took the streetcar down St. Charles Avenue. I didn't ask her where we were going. Having her hand and her smile was enough to sustain my warm fire of happiness. The sounds of the streetcar still resonate in my memory—the clanging bell and screeching brakes at each passenger stop on the oak-shrouded avenue; the groan of metal that came when the conductor swung open the door lever and the doors clapped loose and thumped shut; the strange languages and dialects of the people. I remember the thick scents of perspiration and perfumes and the feel of the hard wooden seats, but overriding all those senses was Ida's warm hand holding mine as if I were her beau.

Only once did my heart sink. We arose from our seats at a juncture near what I first thought was a mysterious forest. Ida leaned into me as we pressed down the steps and past the clash of the door onto the grassy median. The streetcar rumbled away and the air was warm and heavy. On one side of the avenue spread elaborate edifices enshrouded by the limbs of oak trees and surrounded by flower gardens. On the other was the forest. Massive oaks shaded manicured terrains of grass and gravel pathways.

"Ma, where are we?"

"This is where gentlemen fought duels to win my love."

We crossed the street onto what I learned later was the vast landscape of Audubon Park. We eased across the grass and onto a long, circular path. At a point near a bridge crossing a narrow bayou, Ida stopped to point out a spot of terrain that was heavily shaded and sprawling with uplifted roots.

"Two gentlemen of noble bearing dueled by pistol here long ago."

Her shining eyes shot down toward me. "Gallant combat to procure my hand." she explained. Dimples emerged at the corners of her mouth. The word, procure, to my nine-year-old mind sounded foreboding. I took it to mean what it seemed to suggest. They wanted to be the beau of my mom and were ready to die for her.

"I would have fought for you," I said.

She lifted her chin, her smile fixed upon the leaf-strewn lawn beneath the oaks where blood must have soaked the ground. Sweetness grew across her lips. "Oh, I know that."

I shucked my inner tremors of anxiety that the moment had unleashed. Her hand was warm and soft. A dulcet laugh came from her lips. She spoke in her most silken voice. "Don't worry, Jack. I'm not crazy." But, of course, that's what you say when you are.

Those few remaining days we explored the streets of the Quarter as if Ida was searching for something that she couldn't remember having lost. A bemused expression was always on her pretty face. I remember the heaviness that grew in my legs as the day would sink over to twilight, but I was happy. The taste of fried oysters, French fries, as much Coca Cola as I wanted. She didn't care. She was smiling and I was too young then to comprehend the fine wrinkles of sadness etched at the corners of her lips. It's only from my own speculative mind now that I look back and see in Ida's face the recognition that life had too quickly passed her by. The exotic domain of New Orleans would provide no rescue from the quiet desperation that haunted her.

We returned to Baptiste after three days. The inner warmth of contentment had already begun to dim. The train bore north on the rails through the upper parishes. Ida withdrew into the train's rhythmic click-click noise as her vacant eyes fixed upon the swampy terrain of cypress with hanging moss fading away to piney forests. Her hand began to elude me, but damn it all, the journey had been remarkable, like the first time I witnessed a shooting star.

On this train ride, at the age of twenty-one, newly spent from the body of the Corps, I sat beside an empty coach seat. A leaden weight settled across my eyelids from lack of sleep. Hunger built inside me. The woodlands surrounding the outskirts of Baptiste floated past the window of the train. The vast mill appeared from far off, a grey profusion of smokestacks, warehouses, and barren pulp yards. From a good mile out, I could tell it was dead. No smoke plumes curled from its giant body, and a profound absence of human life milled through its cavities. A half-collapsed cardboard box stood as the lone occupant of a broad, chain-linked parking area. When looking back from some fifty years ahead, the brilliant light of hindsight overwhelms. I can see the dead mill now for what it was back then, the beginning of a dying America.

The train slowed as it neared the inner folds of the town. The click-clack of the wheels beat steadily down toward the grinding screech of brakes. It came to a gradual stop in front of a pathetic little station house built of dull-red brick. I pulled my seabag from the luggage shelf and lumbered off down the aisle. The canvas bag was light in my hand. It possessed only a few civilian clothes, my old haversack from Vietnam, and Frank's books all bound together by twine and encased in protective layers of cardboard. There were three fellow passengers, an older gentleman in faded denim overalls and a young woman with a small boy. The sun beat down on the concrete platform and the train began to rumble away. The old man limped off slow and crossed the tracks over to the street that curved toward Main Street. The woman and the boy hurried off to a dusty Ford Fairlane parked in the gravel lot next to the station. A man waited behind the wheel. He never ventured to get out and greet them. The woman and boy got in and the man drove off.

I remained steadfast on the station platform. Let my senses paw the world around me. Look around, Frank had said. Look around; something will come to get you. Frank, you crazy son-of-a-bitch, I muttered to myself. I felt lost. Not the kind of being lost that I've experienced in the dense terrain of enemy territory but that kind you feel deep inside yourself. Look around. No one was around. Radio music from a country music station twanged low behind the depot building's closed door. A weathered bulletin board, thumbtacked with notecards of various sizes, was bolted to the building's facade by the entrance. From the direction of the town came a quiet that signals the encroach of economic impoverishment.

I swung around slow, and my vision rested on the scattered array of notices tacked on the platform bulletin board. One drew me toward it. It read:

Oil Field Work.
Roughneck Wanted.
No Sissies.
Spin Chain Experience.
Inquire, Theodore Blackie Shively, Haiti Cullen Hotel, Room 25.

I plucked it off and shoved the card into my back pocket. Replaced the thumbtack to its spot and slung the strap of the seabag over my shoulder and ambled off down the platform steps. The low pulsing beat of the awful shit-kicking music coming from the depot station faded behind me. I walked down Main Street toward the southern edge of town predominated by homes of mill workers, where Seymour and Ida's empty house would be—if not yet looted and plundered.

The pang of emptiness burdened the old Main Street. Few cars and trucks occupied parking spaces in front of the storefronts. Behind the plate glass window of Robinson's Clothing Store, two naked mannequins stared at me from their dusky chamber. Empty shelves spread backward behind their lifeless bodies. I gave a nod to the deadness in their eyes and paranoia flared up. I kept going.

There came a saving grace. The old Magnolia Theatre that had afforded me escape as a child into other worlds on Saturday afternoons still exuded vibrancy and hope. Bold letters proclaimed the coming of *Butch Cassidy and the Sundance Kid* across its marquee. The hallowed doors next to the glass-encased ticket booth remained burnished by the repetitive press of warm hands.

Near the end of Main, a few blocks before I'd angle through the old neighborhoods toward Roosevelt Street, two men dressed in grease-smudged khaki work attire emerged from the doorway of the auto parts store. Familiar faces dredged up from my childhood memories, but I couldn't attach names to them. The back of my neck warmed as I passed them by and felt their eyes measure me up and down. Heard, or thought I heard, one whisper, "Seymour's boy." But what I heard may have been only the rustling noise in my suspicious mind. It would be a while, a long time, before this ongoing vigilance toward a hostile world would begin to subside.

I walked on through the blasting heat of the day. When I reached my parent's abandoned house on Roosevelt Street, my shirt clung to my skin. The front yard grass stood tall, yellow-tipped, and unruly. It was not without companions of abandonment. Along the way, I'd passed other homes with yards of uncut grass strangled by the influx of high weeds and untended shrubs. Such neglect of lawn and abode back in the days of a living mill on the town's edge would have been the subject of gossip among the citizenry.

Plywood sheets, discolored by assaults of rain and mold, framed the windows. Paint curled and flaked on its exterior. It was now my house or basecamp as I would come to call it. I found the key behind the loose brick at the right lower side of the front stoop. Seymour, my old man, had said it would always be there.

Duskiness pervaded the inner recesses of the house. Enshrouded in the shadows, the museum of my inconsequential childhood posed before me. Sears Roebuck furniture paid off by installment plan. Unornamented yellow walls with their musty smell of mildew. Hardwood floors coated in a film of dust. A blue jay heralded my return with intermittent squawks from one of the tall sycamores outside the screen door. I flicked a switch. No light. Utilities shut down long ago.

I lowered the seabag to the floor and walked softly down the corridor to my abandoned room in the back of the house. Inside the pall of the room, I opened the closet door and swept my hand through empty darkness. Ida had rid herself of my material traces. He, who was never to come back.

I ran my hand across the upper shelf and the back of it struck the metal ammunition case. Supposedly, inside the canister would be Seymour's gift, his treasured handgun from the old Corps, the M1911 .45, bequeathed to his son. Some awkward gesture of love overtook him when the moment arrived for me to part for war.

A muscle spasmed through my stomach. I stepped back and closed the door. Violence would never retake me. I had Frank's path to follow and his books to read over and over until I found my passages to lead me further on the way.

At the doorway of Ida and Seymour's bedroom, I stood for a

moment. A traditional patched quilt lay pulled back atop it. The room's meager furnishings were neatly in place. The vanity dresser's mirror tinted with dust caught my reflection, which followed me across the room to the closet door. Ida's assortment of old dresses, blouses, and slacks hung from one side. The other side posed empty in the shadows. I supposed she'd tried to rid herself of all remnants of Seymour after he'd destroyed himself in fire. On that side, only an old duffel bag lay collapsed upon the floor. I picked it up and brought it out into the brighter light of the room. Unzipped it and pulled what appeared to be a scroll of some sort from within. I unfolded it and read the crude and smudged writing in large, bold letters: *AMERICA, YOU'VE FAILED US*. The other items in the duffel were a hammer and a box of flathead nails. "What story have you, Seymour?" I said beneath my breath and replaced the rolled-up scroll, hammer, and nails to the duffel and dropped it back into the dark of the closet. I left the room and closed the door behind me.

As the sun eased toward the horizon, I rummaged through the little shed built against the house's back wall and found a claw hammer. I wiped clean scrims of mildew from the handle and set about removing the plywood sheets from the windows and stacked them against the trunk of a chinaberry tree in the backyard. Small grasshoppers flew up like ash out of a fire when I waded through the grass. The sun blazed yellow-white on the horizon above the trees and rooftops. Sweat rolled off my face and fingertips. Summer had bent to one knee in its starting blocks.

I made my way up the backsteps past the kitchen door. The late afternoon sunlight now flooded the insides of the place. On a whim that broke through the new brightness, I turned the knob of the faucet over the kitchen sink. Water flowed. A feeling came that I can only describe as that moment of levitation when you doffed your heavy backpack after a sweltering day of trudging up mountainous jungle terrain. Damn, it felt good.

Luck in some rare form graced my presence as I stood in that desolate kitchen. Maybe some field service worker from the water department fucked up the shutdown order; perhaps the big Pilot in the sky waved his hand over me; maybe Frank's spirit idled out of the ether and gave me a little gift for making it this far on the journey to be. I turned around and slid my back down the kitchen counter to the floor. Sat there thinking through the frail light falling over me. I hadn't eaten since the morning before boarding the train at Union Passenger Terminal in New Orleans. It was a good day to fast, and tomorrow, and the next day. Keep the senses sharpened. Strengthen the antidote to my violent tendencies.

I formed a plan on how to utilize the remainder of daylight. I'd draw a bath with the bounty of water given me. Soak and bathe in the cool water. Read into the twilight from one of Frank's almost incomprehensible volumes while I sat outside on the front stoop. Give the hunger of my fast its due.

The sun gradually descended behind the treetops. I felt clean and light after the cold bath and sat on the front stoop's upper step with one of Frank's blood-stained books in my hand. Fatigue drove the words on the pages into a blur of nothingness. Katydid song came from the high tree limbs and enchanted the twilight. I tried not to think of the past of this place. It would confront me soon enough, I was sure.

Frank suddenly was beside me. He looked young and fit and would be forever in my imaginings.

"Somebody must make some money," he said in a dreamy, matter-of-fact way.

"On it tomorrow."

He heaved his breath high up into his chest and exhaled. It was good to hear him breathe, but it saddened me.

"I don't know where this will take you," he said. "You do understand, don't you? I don't know what you'll find."

"It's alright. I'll find out." And I said again, "It's alright. Try not to worry. It's alright," as if to assure this ghost of my imagination whom I held so dear beside me that I was committed to the journey.

Beyond the tall, unkempt grass and the narrow, crumbling walkway across the front yard, the street was quiet in the dimming light, and Frank was gone. After dusk thickened enough around me, I went inside and lay upon my bedroom floor beneath an open window. Dreams that I'd lost my rifle slithered through my slow-to-come and shallow sleep. I woke up often, reaching through the moon shadows for that which was no longer there.

BLACKIE, HIRE ONE KILL ONE

Hunger gripped me but I felt strong. In one hand, I held the notecard from the train station. When I knocked on the old hotel room door, the sound echoed desolately through the dim light of the corridor. A moment passed and the door swung open. A huge man dressed only in a pair of khaki work pants hovered in front of me. He was barrel-chested, hairy like moss on a tree trunk. A thick shock of dark hair curled across his forehead.

"Mr. Shively? I'm Jack Crowe. I'm hoping for a job."

"Blackie," he said, and his ham hock of a fist rotated over his chest.

The click-click of a ceiling fan came from behind him through the shadows. He was sleepy-eyed. A demarcated line of stubble ran from high cheekbones down fleshy jowls. The man's dark eyes hung obliquely onto me. He sniffed the air. If he were angry being awakened by my knock at his door to ask for a job, he hid it behind the languid draw of his breath. He rubbed one side of his chest and looked abstractedly at my feet. The steamy scent of black-eyed peas cooking, cornbread rising hot in the oven seeped up from the hotel's downstairs kitchen.

Blackie's voice came at me with a begrudging drawl, "I need someone who can throw a spin chain."

"I can do it."

"People lose fingers," he said. "Ol' boys die if it ain't done right. Cables snap and iron tongs whip about and break men in half. Did you know that?"

"Okay," I said.

He kept rubbing the flank of his vast chest, looking away. "Seymour Crowe was your daddy?"

"Yes, sir."

"You still go by Half-Pint?"

"Yes, sir. That's what I'm called, but Jack's my given name."

Then he drawled again, "Well, Half-Pint, I can use someone to throw a spin chain." He rotated slowly around, closing the door. "The crew meets out front at 7:00 tonight. You got to learn fast."

The hulk of the man was gone. Staring back at me was the faded number 25 on the door of his room. I turned away and went down the stairs, a strum of joy in my heart for having just landed a good-paying job. I ignored a gnaw of uneasiness at how simple it had been. A summer of oil fieldwork and the G.I. Bill would get me through one year of college if I managed every penny. I'd run the numbers.

Downstairs, the cooking smells went straight to my stomach. Mrs. Gladys Perkins, who owned the hotel, stood with her back propped against the kitchen door, watching me cross the open lobby. Her apron compressed her giant bosom and her hands worked the hem of the cloth.

"Come here, Jack Crowe. Come here, boy."

An old man sunken deep into a worn lounge chair peered up over his Times-Picayune. The first thought was to keep moving and bolt into the sunlight past the glass door. But I swung obediently around and made my way toward her. She placed a warm, fleshy hand on my neck. A puffy ream of bruised flesh, like purple larvae, hung below each eye. At the ridge of her left cheek a tiny muscle articulated below the skin. I saw it as the loss of hope moving inside her that was in all the women sentenced to the darkness of the bayous and woods. Past the door, two black women scoured dishes at a steaming metal basin in the kitchen.

"I haven't seen you in years, Jack Crowe."

"Yes, ma'am."

She dropped the apron cloth and rubbed her nose with the back of her damp wrist. She was looking at me, almost the twilight of a smile.

"Was that not Shively you sought? I knew your mama at Church of Christ. For her sake, I'm telling you, don't work for that man up yonder." She punched her lips out and pointed with them toward the stairs.

"Yes, ma'am."

"Your mama had her demons, but she was God-fearing in the end. The Holy Ghost shined bright all around her when she died. Members of the congregation boarded up the house as best they could in hopes you'd make it back. We prayed for her, and we prayed for your safe return. Our prayers answered. Hallelujah. You served God. Your country. Now I'm telling you, don't work for that evil man."

"I'm happy she found God." I tried to restrain the sarcasm scraping through my voice. I had to look away. "The mill's dead, Mrs. Perkins. I need the work."

"Not with that evil man," she replied.

Mrs. Perkins' face was flush with rising blood either from exposure to the steamy kitchen heat or the Savior's passion that burned within her. A fleeting thought spun by. She'd not mentioned my old man's death. It was as if the horror of it had burned away all traces of the event in the tribal memory of this community.

"Yes, ma'am, I'll have to think about it, though. I need the money."

I stepped back and walked across the lobby floor and out into the summer heat. I began the two-mile trek back to the small shamble of a house on Roosevelt Street that my parents had bequeathed to me. My basecamp.

Evening came with a red sky above the dark piney woods that surrounded the small town. Three other men made up the roughneck crew. We piled into an old Impala that had a faded paint job and rusted out dents and drove away from the old railway hotel's gravel parking lot onto the state highway that paralleled the tracks north and south out of town. Blackie, ensconced in glum silence, sat squeezed in behind the steering wheel. I sat between two in the back on a spring-broken seat draped by an oil-smudged quilt. A blonde-headed kid called Sandy was to my left. His last name, Guillory, suggested Cajun descent. He had blue eyes, a perpetual dumb smile. He chewed gum slowly, stole glances at my neck as if trying to get a read on my pulse. On the other side was an older boy in his late twenties. Blackie called him Buster. He had a white trash look. Hair slicked back into a ducktail, inbred signs, eyes constantly flicking, frenetic fingers tapping on his knee, wiry bands of muscle too tight over his bones. Up front on the passenger side sat Clifford C. Bowles. When introducing or addressing him, Blackie used the full breadth of the man's name.

A few miles after crossing into Arkansas, Blackie turned the Impala onto a gravel road that bound straight through this wilderness of sloughs inhabited by razorbacks, rattlesnakes, alligators, and the skeletal remains of rusted and sealed pump stations. Clifford C. Bowles fiddled with the radio dial.

"Play some of that rock and roll," Blackie said.

"No sir," Clifford said and Blackie laughed. The twangy cry of gospel music came up from the dashboard.

The sandy-haired kid nudged an elbow into my ribs and grinned conspiratorially. He whispered into my ear above the rattle of the car. "Cliffie's a fuckin' ordained minister." Then gave a quick wink of one blue eye.

On the other side, Buster escalated his finger tapping. Blackie drawled in a deep-throated, melancholy kind of way, "Don't nobody be shootin' at my kitty cat tonight. I want no more of that. Poor girl just tryin' to stay alive out there in what she's got left of wilderness."

The sandy-haired kid caught my eyes, raised his eyebrows in mock shock, whispered again close to my ear, "Panther."

Blackie peered back in the rearview mirror and focused hard on Buster.

"I didn't bring my gun. You promised not to call to her." A long vein throbbed on the side of Buster's neck. I smelled fear seeping from the man's skin, the kind that grows, ignites too quick into anger. That fear was shining bright in his yellow eyes. Something about him was off-kilter. He would not have lasted long with us, I thought. Not from where I'd just come. Not long at all.

"All right then. I want no more nonsense about my girl." Blackie looked back to the narrow road, a darkening tunnel through the intertwining overhang of big oak limbs. He switched on the headlights into the dusk.

No one spoke for the next half hour as the Impala rumbled down the road. When Blackie slowed the car to a crawl and eased off onto a rutted passageway into the woods, I saw far down through the trees the derrick lights. Sandy rolled down his window. The raucous song of frogs and cicadas filled the inside of the car, but as the derrick lights neared, the noise of the insects succumbed to the oil rig's generator hum and a strange metallic clanking. We bounced along the rutted ground toward the rig and Blackie parked his Impala beside a metal shed. We piled slowly out of the car. Clifford, Buster, and Sandy, carting lunch pails and thermos jugs, disappeared into the shed. Blackie stretched and looked up at the commotion on the platform.

"Well, they comin' out of the hole." He kept his eyes fixed on the men above who were moving around the derrick floor in what appeared to be an organized frenzy. I'd learn later that coming out of the hole or tripping was the deadly operation of hoisting steel pipe from the bored hole in the earth to replace a worn-out drill bit, then send it back into the hollowed-out ground. Blackie gave me a proprietary squint of his eyes. "Go in the doghouse. Should be a hard hat on the wall you can use." He tossed a pair of new beaded oil gloves at me. Their brand tag still bound them together. He shook his head, some private lamentation given to my lack of gear.

My heart had already sunk low but sank lower. Sweat broke across my forehead. The stupid ones, those most unprepared in the war from which I'd just come, usually died quickly. I'd violated a well-learned rule from the Corps in my urgency to find work. I imagined Frank laughing, "Poor ol' Jack."

Clifford, Sandy, and Buster reappeared, rid of lunch pails, their eyes peering at me beneath the rim of oiler hats, hands donned with grease-smeared gloves. Blackie growled beneath his breath, not once breaking his line of vision from the activity above.

"Goddamn, I sure hired me a Virgin Mary, didn't I?"

"Yes, sir, you sure did," Clifford said.

The crew of men we were replacing peeled away from their positions as we filed onto the floor of the giant rig. Clifford guided me to a spot in which a colossal metal tong hung from a cable. A coil of chain lay in a neat heap off to my side, and a single line of it wound onto a large pulley off an array of motors. Buster shimmied up a ladder toward the upper rungs of the derrick. By the sure way he moved, I pulled back on my earlier judgment of this man. You're always too quick to judge, I reminded myself. Cheerful banter riffled back and forth between the departing crew and Blackie. A thin smile was all I gave these swaggering men and their cuts of dark humor: "Blackie's got fresh meat. How long do you think that ol' boy will last?" The heavy stomps of their boots faded down the metal-flanged stairway as they departed.

A giant traveling block, attached to its steel pulley, descended from the derrick's crown to a cantilevered board where Buster, now strapped into a safety belt, hovered high above like an unhinged electrical wire.

I realized Blackie controlled the block's fall rate by maneuvering an arm-like lever protruding from a lighted control panel. He yelled above the turbine's roar. Aimed his booming voice at me, "I'll show you once then it's you and your God!"

Sandy dove forward. He latched onto the handles arching off the sides of the fast-descending traveling block. Above the engine roar, the snap of the block's jaws resounded around the vertical section of pipe like the blow of a hammer on hollow iron.

Sandy stepped back and stood beside the iron tongs that dangled from cables. Sweat beaded across his face. He smiled at me, revealing a missing incisor. The engines revved wildly, and the first stand of pipe unsheathed from the hole, rising swiftly in the clasp of the traveling block toward Buster leaning out from the plank high up on the derrick. In a few seconds, the strand of pipe rose to the point of its threaded connection to the lower section.

Blackie idled the motors, leaped cat-like at one of the iron tongs that seemed to float at the ends of suspended hydraulic cables. In one flashing motion, the man heaved the tongs onto the lower pipe while Sandy's tongs snapped onto the neck of the section of pipe just above. Blackie skipped lightly back toward the control panel. Through the drumming beat of the rig, his command shot at me, "Grab 'er and learn!"

Without hesitation, I drove my shoulder into the arc of the tongs and clasped the handles. The crunch of metal threads loosening, the oozing, then spilling of mud from the parting of the two pipes, then Blackie shouting, "Unlatch the goddamn tongs!" pounded into me as I mimicked Sandy's actions and slung back the latch.

Clifford C. Bowles materialized out of the shadows, wrapped his skinny arm around the body of the dangling pipe and guided it across the deck to a stacking area as if it were some brotherly drunk. I looked up to see the shadowy figure of Buster, high up on his planking, stretch out and unlatch the head of the pipe and guide it with a loop of rope to its stacking space.

This harried sequence called tripping continued into the warm and humid night. I became an integral part of the maddening flow and felt it smoothing out. In the sweaty blur of it all I glimpsed the stars, remembered how the night sky above Con Thien, the Hill of Angels, opened into dusty starlight after the flares would die. The guilt of staying alive in that fucking war passed through me and I threw my shoulder back into the tongs.

An hour later, when the last section of pipe fumed out of the hole, there at its end gleamed the drill bit, its teeth ground down, posing like a museum piece of medieval weaponry. Blackie and Clifford, the back of their necks glistening under the electric lights, worked like carnivores tearing at a fresh-killed carcass, using cumbersome wrenches to unscrew the worn-down bit, lifting into place a shining new one. Then Blackie lunged back to his position by the controls. The crazed rhythm on the rig reversed. The lead section of pipe drove downward back into the hole, the clamped end coming to rest waist high. Clifford was peering at me beneath the rim of his hard hat. Sandy was steadying the lead tong in his brace, looking nervously away into the darkness beyond the rig lights.

"You ready to die?" Blackie said.

I nodded.

"You ready to die?" He sang again and leaned forward; his elbow propped upon the shaft of bone above his knee.

"Yes, sir," I said.

He leaned back and gripped the lever jutting away from the control panel. His voice scraped through the rattle and vibrations: "Hire one. Kill one. That's my motto. Grab your spin chain and wrap it around that pipe."

I grabbed the chain from the mud-wet floor and wound a hefty length of it around the pipe stem that protruded above the rotary table. A new stand of pipe seemingly began to float from the stack across the floor. Clifford C. Bowles hugged the base of it in the crook of his arm, leading it toward its mate above the drilling hole. A gentle thump echoed up as Blackie levered the pipe into the lower stem. I stood lead-footed with dumbness. The chain shone in my gloved hands. Sandy looked down at his feet. Fear warped across his sweaty face. Blackie convulsed with anger, bound across the floor and knocked me aside, ripping the chain out of my hands. The man seemed to pirouette on his toes, whirling around in mid-air. A snap of his thick wrist and the chain flashed away, clacking into a perfect coil around the upper pipe. He thrust the tail of the chain into my face and leaped back to his position by the control lever.

Sandy's voice rose over the racket. "Hold on, boy, and catch that cattail. That thing's about to fly."

I lowered my shoulder and Blackie hit a lever that powered the chain. The coil of it screeched and the upper portion of pipe spun and thumped, sealing its threads into the lower section, but the chain's tail whipped out of my hand and lashed across the floor like some viper gone mad.

"Goddamn, you goin' to kill us!" Sandy cried. He drew one of his knees up belt high and swung the iron tong in front of him, using it as if some Neolithic shield. Eyes aflame with fear, he drew the tong around and snapped it onto the upper pipe. I swung the second tong onto the section below and coiled backward as Blackie jiggled a switch. The cables attached to the tongs' handles shook violently in the air. The broad clamps of the tongs ground around the pipes, fully sealing the threads.

Blackie howled to the star-lighted sky. "Hire one, kill one!" The stand of connected pipe drove rumbling down into the hole.

I scrambled for the chain on the muddy deck and leaped back to my position. Fear flooded high up inside my chest. Feverishly, I wound the chain around the pipe's protruding collar and looked up to see Clifford C. Bowles guiding the next line of pipe across the floor. With Blackie's deft maneuvering of a control lever, the new section set gently into place. He yelped, "Yah! Yah!"

I flicked the chain like I had seen the son-of-a-bitch do. The coil swirled up and around the upper section then burned into the pipe as Sandy smacked the tong's jaws around the lower pipe collar. The chain smelled hot and acrid as the coil spun violently beneath the guide of my open hand. Then I caught the tip as it lashed off toward the black of space.

"A goddamn natural! Will I get me a finger, Sandy? How long do you think it'll take to get me a finger?"

Sandy and I grabbed the handles of the slip and lifted it in unison from the rotary floor. The black staff of pipe drove downward. The fear began to dissipate in my chest and lift from Sandy's mud-splattered face.

BLACKIE LISTENING, BUSTER BREAKING

Everything fell into a new rhythm—synchronized chaos. I lost myself in the beauty of the teamwork. We sent the long stands of drill pipe down the mile of hole. Mud splashed up and across the derrick floor. The sweet aftertaste of danger lingered in our mouths and met the salty taste of sweat at the corners of our lips. The chain would flash away from my hand and coil in a whir around the standing drill pipe. Blackie would hit a lever that whipped the chain away, spinning the appendage into the lower section that would then be sealed tight by the iron tongs. I was happy.

Early toward morning, when the last section shimmered down the hole, a sweaty haze enveloped me. I'd forgotten my pestering hunger. Sandy and Clifford swung a long hose shaped like an elephant's trunk across the floor and latched it to a device called the swivel. For a moment, the great rig was still but for the vibration of the deck beneath our feet. Then the swivel contraption began to rotate and grind. Across from me, Clifford wiped his brow and looked toward the dark stretch of woods. Blackie faced the rows of dials on the control panel. He shoved his beefy hands into his pockets and shifted his gaze toward Clifford.

"I told you he'd be okay. Now, didn't I, Clifford C. Bowles?" Blackie's chest rose and fell in apparent satisfaction, and he looked upon me. "I'll go listen for my cat now. My girl might be roaming tonight."

"Wish you'd stop that now, Blackie. Buster is all worked up enough as is." Clifford tossed a quick look at me. "You did all right, Jack." He turned away and walked over to the railing and knelt facing the black outline of woods past the rig lights. He lowered his head, eyes shut, lips moving like two little worms warming in sunlight. *To what God do you pray*, I thought, and Sandy shoved the handle of a push broom into my chest. He had a hose in his hands and began to aim a jet stream of water onto the muddy deck.

"Sweep up, boy, and I'll hose her down. Damn, I thought you'd kill us," he yelled jubilantly. "So did ol' Cliff over there. Couldn't believe Blackie hired a green hand to throw a spin chain. Shit, ol' Cliff prays to God 'bout every fuckin' thing. But I don't. Don't nothin' scare me. Hey, me and you need to drink us a cold one and drag us Main Street sometime between holes. You damn good with that chain." He flicked his eyes onto Blackie who was now trundling his way down the metal stairway. "Hell, we can pick us some girls. You're kind of small. Find you a pee-teet one." He laughed as if he'd conjured the finest joke of all time.

The spray from the hose kicked across the floor and I began to sweep along behind it, wondering what the sense of cleaning up was. Blackie had disappeared out into the darkness along the edge of the woods beyond the derrick lights. Sandy, holding tight to the bulky hose, kept grinning in good humor. I guessed it was for having eluded death.

"Blackie's gone out to wood edge to listen for a screaming panther," Sandy yelled toward me and laughed again. He kept tugging on the hose that trailed behind him across the platform of the rig.

Buster clamored down off the narrow derrick ladder. He plopped lightly onto his feet at the edge of the derrick floor where the rows of drill pipe had stood in vertical columns. A wild dog look glazed his eyes. The way he moved like a lit fuse twitching down to its base stirred the meanness in me, hard and acidic.

In my mind, I spoke to the ghost of Frank.

Where does all that acceptance come from, Frank?

How do you get it?

You could've lived, Frank. We could have been friends forever. You could have told me more about these damn paths we take.

I shuddered, catching myself carrying on this silent conversation with the dead. But know it if you must. I've been talking to Frank for over fifty years. And I'm not one damn bit ashamed.

Buster stood over Clifford who still knelt in prayer. He shouted above the rumble of the rig. "He's callin' her up again, ain't he? He promised me he'd stop! Now, I'm hearing her, Cliff! He promised me he'd stop!" Buster pressed his hands against his ears and thrust his elbows forward as if to shield himself from the raucous sounds of the outside world. But I suspected it was inner noise most troubling to him.

Clifford C. Bowles had risen off his one knee. He pointed a knotted finger at Buster. "Jesus is Lord. That's all you need to know. Don't be gettin' yourself all excited."

Then Clifford swung up a long crescent wrench into his hand and slapped his feet down the stairs off the derrick floor. Buster fell in behind him. Half-way down, Clifford turned around and blocked Buster's path. "Don't you make no trouble! You got a wife and three young'uns dependin' on you!"

Sandy had placed his boot on the lower railing and tilted himself over the edge of the deck to get a better view of the unfolding commotion between Clifford and Buster. I kept sweeping the channels of muddy water off the derrick floor, trying to ward off the edginess in the air. Sandy moved down the railing and shut off a valve. The hose convulsed in his hand and the water stopped flowing. He motioned me over. I tried to blink away the sweat in my eyes. My hunger came rolling up, striking me hard. I placed a shaky hand on the top railing.

Sandy eyed the bundle of tremors shooting up my arm. For a second, his vision went inward; then, he flicked his chin out toward the black ink of the woods. "I don't know who's crazier, Blackie or Buster. Talk is that Buster spent most of his younger days in the state hospital at Mandeville." Steady trickles of sweat rolled down the side of his face. "Maybe that makes him crazier, but ol' Blackie ain't far behind. Thinks he can call panthers and all the wild things back but that ain't goin' to happen. Hell, they gone forever. Makes Buster get crazier than shit and ol' Cliffie just gets more religious." Sandy laughed.

I stole in a deep breath to calm the hunger spasms and said, "Anything's possible. Maybe they've come back or will someday."

Sandy snorted a laugh. His big round eyes locked onto the side of my face. "If you hear a panther screaming out here, you're crazy as Blackie and Buster." The electrical droning of cicadas ebbed and flowed above the rumble of the drilling rig.

The acreage around the rig had once been virgin woodland. Now it was moonscape shaped by the blades of bulldozers and the tire tracks of giant diesel trucks. Black woods semi-circled this decimated ground beyond the reach of the derrick lights. Out on the edge of it, Blackie stood as a dark shadow just inside the trees. His head rolled faintly back and forth as if to catch the sounds inside that wilderness. Buster had rushed past Clifford C. Bowles, and his wiry frame tracked across the barren ground toward Blackie. He resembled a piece of rope knotted at the very end, his head bobbing to his hurried pace. Behind Buster, Clifford sauntered along, swinging his arms.

"What's going on here?" I said.

Sandy hung the hose nozzle over the railing, muttered beneath his breath, his voice suddenly solemn. "Buster's got himself riled up, I guess." He turned around. "Claims he hears the panther scream too and there ain't none. Blames it on Blackie. He's shit crazy."

We both looked back out over the phosphorescent glow spreading out toward the phalanx of oak and pine, nettles and briars.

"You're hungry, ain't you?"

"So what?" My anger flashed as if I'd been spotted naked. For anyone to see weakness in me was a violation. I kept my attention riveted on Buster who had begun to lope toward Blackie across the barren ground. Vaguely framed against the woods, Blackie turned around and Buster hurled himself into him and the two men tumbled to the ground. Clifford's shadowy figure now rushed forward, swinging the crescent wrench in hand.

Sandy spun around and shot past me, clamoring down the steps with a terrific banging of his boots off the metal rungs.

"Come on, boy!"

I leaned the sweep broom's handle against the deck's railing and started walking down the stairs. Sandy shot across the clearing toward the commotion at the wood's edge, his gait quirky and bowlegged.

At the base of the metal steps, I halted. Sandy's back grew dimmer. The shouts of desperate men rose from the nearby woods. I blinked and absorbed the dim light and carefully followed Sandy's path across the scarred terrain. The winking of fireflies lit up the darkness among the trees.

Near the wood's edge, Blackie held Buster on the ground, his fist rising and striking with a strange meaty thump into Buster's head. "You want to dive into my chest, Buster! You want to stick me with a knife!"

Clifford traipsed back and forth behind Blackie's hunched-over figure. "Seek of thee thou guidance!"

I came up beside Sandy who shifted from foot to foot like a barefoot man on a hot beach. Blackie kept beating Buster's face. Blood, ink-like in the pale light cast from the derrick, spotted over the side of Blackie's shirt. A bone-handled hunting knife lay beside a pine stump near Buster's feet. Clifford, amid his religious pacing, his beseeching of a Lord that seemed more remote than the eternal dust of this southern heaven, kicked the blade away as if it alone deserved the wrath of his emotions. At the same time, his hands towed upward above his head. He supplicated the dark sky with writhing fingers and a crescent wrench firmly bound within one fist. Sandy had stepped back. "Hell, Blackie's goin' to kill Buster." An uh-uh-uh cadence came up from the back of Buster's throat.

Clifford swung the big crescent wrench down to his side and heaved it up, crashing the flat of its chrome-plated jaw across Blackie's hard hat. Sandy danced backward like a man shot in the chest. "Hell!" he shouted.

Blackie's hat flew back, flipping through the air before striking the ground with an unceremonious thump that sounded over the hum of the distant rig and the croaking of frogs. Blackie spun about. His wild eyes scoped for the source of such a blow. One big fist clung to Buster's neck.

"Stop, you muthfucker," Buster said, his voice a bare rasp.

"Don't let religion ruin your life, Cliff'," Blackie said just as casually as if he had greeted Clifford on some downtown street. He turned back to beating Buster's face. Clifford raised the crescent wrench and sent another blow that whomped across the backside of Blackie's half-bald pate. Blackie shook his head, and his fist grew still.

Sandy gasped, "Oh, hell," and sprang away across the scraped earth toward a trailer set near the tall derrick. I walked the few steps toward Clifford who still held the wrench in both his hands. He chanted, "Je-sus, Je-sus, Je-sus, Je-sus…" I pried the crescent from his clenched fingers and fought back tremors building inside myself.

Blackie rose off the limp figure of Buster. His head cocked to one side; ear uplifted as if in wonder at the feel of blood trickling down the side of his head. He stepped over Buster and turned his broad back to Clifford's chanting. "Je-sus—Je-sus—Je-sus."

Blackie patted a rosy blotch on his shirt. He showed us only his back, assumed the stance of a man who had walked upon a private affair, and with discretion turned to politely face away. Clifford drew silent at last.

"Clifford, don't you hit me again." Blackie shoved his hands into the side pockets of his jeans.

"Yes, sir."

I knelt on one knee beside Buster. Inside the woods, the frogs and cicada refrained to the hum of the rig's turbines and the warm night air was heavy and still. Buster's right leg twitched. He drew his knee up. He crossed over the threshold of consciousness and sought again the travails of this outer world.

Maybe he heard the cries of his hungry kids, the harangue of a frail, overwrought woman he called his wife. He rolled to his side and propped himself up onto the axis of his haunches. My hand reached out to steady him. His shoulder was mostly a plate of clavicle bone beneath my fingers. Buster spat blood onto the clay dirt and staggered to his feet. One half-opened eye peered at me from between puffy eyelids. The other had not awakened. He began stumbling toward the darkness of the woods.

"You need to lie back down, Buster," I said.

Blackie had moved farther into the shadows. His hulk of a body merged into the dark spirals of the trees. "Listen to her. Ain't that the wildest sound you ever heard? Oh, how I'd love to see her on her hunt, slippin' through the trees."

Clifford covered his ears with the flat of his palms. What the hell, I thought. Past my right shoulder, out amid the barren ground surrounding the rig, Sandy appeared at a trot, clenching a shotgun in his hands. Buster swung around and stumbled into the brush and disappeared into the trees. Clifford dropped to his knees; his hands still clasped over his ears.

When Sandy came up, he leveled the shotgun toward the darkness from which came the sound of dry limbs cracking in the wake of Buster's path through the undergrowth. The snapping of dead branches grew dimmer, then was lost. Clifford rose to his feet, but his hands remained stationed over his ears. Elbows shifted toward the front of his face and the length of his arms formed a pathway down which he sighted.

"Damn, Cliffie, you hear her too?" Sandy said. He lowered the gun barrel, one eye on Blackie's back.

"Buster ran off into the woods," I said as if stating the obvious might help make sense of these strange, unfolding events. My heart pumped wildly. Cicada song pitched into my ears.

"Well, goddamn, why did he take off into the woods for?" Sandy said. "That crazy son-of-a-bitch was half-beaten to death."

Blackie swung around and strode toward Clifford. He began kicking around in the weedy brush.

"Where's his knife? Help me find it, Clifford. I want to see what he stuck me with."

"Yes, sir." Clifford dropped his arms to his sides and walked a few steps toward a skirt of weeds by the patch of bare earth where Blackie had pummeled Buster. He stooped and felt along the ground, rose with the knife in hand and passed it handle-forward to Blackie. Then, Clifford wiped his hands on his trousers and bowed his head back into the clasp of his forearms. "They ain't supposed to be no panthers out here anymore," he said.

"She beautiful soundin'. Ain't she?" Blackie said.

"Yes, sir. Scary, she is, but they all gone. She ain't here."

"There's always hope when you can hear her." Blackie held the knife in front of his eyes and examined it in the hoary light cast by the distant strings of rig lights. Blood speckled across the blade.

"Hell, he might have got an inch in me. That's all. If she don't get him tonight, he'll probably want this back." Blackie swiped the flat of the blade across his leg and handed it back to Clifford. He walked over to his upturned hard hat, momentarily inspecting the indentation across its back. Then he fit it on his head and went away whistling toward the trailer.

"What are we goin' to do about Buster?" Sandy said toward the croaking of frogs.

"Our Lord will protect him." Clifford spread his arms apart, pointed the knife blade toward the heavens. "Lord Jesus, shine thou light on this wilderness. Help us be pure and follow thy path. Protect the forlorn who wanders lost in the wilderness before us."

"Shit, Cliffie." Sandy spat, wiped his mouth in the crook of his arm and threw the barrel of the shotgun over his shoulder. A swagger entered his gait as he made his way back to the drilling rig. "I don't hear no goddamn panther," he sang back to us over his shoulder, then laughed and cast a mock howl toward the sky.

An inner chill went through me. I folded my arms across my chest and looked toward the black of the woods where Buster had disappeared. Clifford's arms spread apart against the beams of an imaginary cross.

"Do you hear a panther, Clifford?"

The man rolled his eyes toward me.

"I've heard her, Jack," he whispered. "Blackie thinks he can divine the return of the wilderness. All the panthers are supposed to be gone, but it don't matter 'cause I am shielded by divine light. Stand in its radiance, Jack, and you too will be protected. You'll be washed of your sins."

My hunger snarled up at me. Dizziness circled my head. I left Clifford impaled against his imaginary cruciform and walked back toward the rig lights.

Sandy was leaning against the doorway of the crew shed near the base of the rig. His hands were now empty of the shotgun and he waved me over. In the soft rays from the lights that steepled up the derrick, Sandy's extended hand wriggled half a sandwich at me as I stood before him.

All the weakness in me converged at that arc of crust and rim of bologna. I thought for a moment that I heard a big cat cry out far off and looked over my shoulder.

"It's time to eat, boy. Then we'll get on what chores Blackie's got for us. He'll set the torque low on the bit. Day tower will be takin' the pipe out of the hole. Not us."

We sat down on a wooden bench. Shovels, pipe wrenches, sledgehammers, skeins of chain hung upon hooks on the wall behind us. Sandy opened a can of Vienna sausage and set it next to me. His jaw worked in small, round motions as he chewed, and his eyes were but half-open slits. He rifled more into his lunch pail and pulled out a brown paper sack lush with Ritz crackers. We shared the little canister of processed meat, plucking one wiener at a time from the can and laying it between two round crackers. Sandy poured black coffee from his thermos into a paper cup. I thanked him, just a soft, abstract utterance of the word that did not come easily off my lips.

Clifford stepped into the doorway. He sniffed and seemed distracted by some wandering thoughts that had just arrived. Finally, he cleared his throat.

"We got to stack some water pipe bein' hauled out tomorrow." He scraped the bottom of one boot on the threshold rung, then spoke again. "We didn't see no fight tonight. Blackie said it didn't happen." He shifted his feet and scraped the bottom of his other boot. "Blackie's done bandaged up and changed his shirt." Clifford cocked his head to one side. He said to the frayed light that went out to the dark woods, "That panther won't eat ol' Buster. He'll be all right. The Lord has told me."

"Ask the Lord if I'm goin' to get some pussy any time soon, Cliffie. I'd appreciate the heads up." Laughter choked up Sandy's throat as he chewed and swallowed. Clifford turned away with a proud but somber bearing.

"Blackie's just messin' with people. They're crazier than shit. Especially the likes of that superstitious-minded Buster." Sandy possessed a devilish smile.

It all hit me at once but was like a warm wind passing by, leaving me hollow inside. Everybody is seeking something. Blackie—panthers and wildness. Clifford—the light of the Lord. Buster—an abiding peace. Sandy—fun and pussy. Me—an answer to some meaning in life I couldn't yet define. Everybody seeking something.

GIVE BUSTER HIS KNIFE

The stars gradually rotated and the quarter moon swiftly trekked across the night sky, marking the progression toward twilight. The rig kept up its steady rumble amid this decimated ground surrounded by pine and oak woodland. The electrical buzz of cicada song carried over the heavy mumble of the rig. The occasional hoot of an owl cut through. I kept listening for what might be the cry of a panther but heard none and kept looking for Buster to reappear out of the darkness of the surrounding wood. No one seemed worried.

We worked at a steady pace. Sandy and I hauled long strands of disassembled water pipe to a spot designated by Clifford near the mud pit. Sandy seemed gluttonous with cheer, singing as he trudged along behind me with strands of water pipe wedged between his gloved hands. When we laid the last section out onto the serried mound of iron, he shuffled up the stairs to the derrick platform.

Clifford handed me a broom and directed me back to the crew shed. We stood in front of the entrance. He was silent for a moment looking up at Blackie on the derrick floor. Blackie had his back to us and faced the dials of the control panel by the motor mounts.

"Clean up in here, Jack," Clifford said. He nodded to folded rags stacked in a heap by the doorway. Clifford's jaw worked in small rotations. He rubbed the knuckle of a disjointed finger across the tip of his nose, peered into the starlit sky. "Your mother got right a few years back. She was a good lady who shouldn't have died before seein' you again. Your daddy was a good man. But too willing to die for uncharted causes. Too right about things. Bless his tormented soul. I'm sorry you witnessed this spectacle. It ain't like this every night. Buster and Blackie been fightin' for years. Now, it's about screaming panthers. Blackie's always conjuring up somethin' to fool himself into thinking the wilderness will come back. Makes himself feel better about his part in destroying it. His foolin' around just gets some of us a little

41

uncomfortable. Buster, in particular, he's had inner frailties all his life. I suspect he'll be back about daylight."

I took off my soiled gloves and gripped the broom handle. A bare light bulb lit up in the low ceiling and threw a garish light over us. I kept my mouth shut.

"We're not as ignorant as we look, Jack. It's crazy everywhere on God's earth. Your mama and daddy did the best they could with what they got. You shouldn't be so ashamed of who you are or where you're from. Or what you did over there in that far away country."

He walked away, carrying a grease gun at his side. He began to move along what appeared to be a familiar route among the pulleys, machines, and other gadgets below the platform, pausing to fix the nozzle of the grease can on some remote axle or neglected spigot. With the broom in my hands, I looked up to the derrick floor. Sandy had regained the power hose and was blasting the platform railings. Blackie scrambled down the metal steps. He cursed loudly at Sandy about watching the direction of the spray. His vociferous harangue barely carried over the hum of generators and the rumble of the rotary.

I started to sweep but watched Blackie stride once more across the dirt clearing out into the dim light by the woods. Hands stuffed into his pockets, he drew himself up into the stance of a mysterious sentinel and lifted his head as if to join the screaming of panthers.

I wished I could hear a panther's eerie cry lifting from across the woods. At that moment, I wanted something wild and pure to pierce my heart. Instead, I heard only the steady thrum of the drilling rig's rotary table and felt the imagined weight of Frank's hand upon my shoulder. *"Yeah, we're all seeking something,"* he would say.

* * *

The men of the day tower arrived in the soft rays of dawn in two muddy pickup trucks. The driller of the fresh crew, a short man with cropped hair and huge tattoos of an anchor and battleship on his forearm, stomped heavily up the steps clutching a thermos out before him. Dregs of sleepiness splotched his deep-set eyes. He looked at Blackie. "We passed one of your ol' boys on the way up. Just sittin' on the side of the road. Looked beat up. Didn't want no ride. What the hell, I say."

Blackie folded his hands across his belly, thumbs wriggling together. "He got scared of our big cat screaming last night. Lost his head and went charging out into the woods. We'll pick him up on the way back."

The day driller, named Comeau, shifted his attention to the faint jiggle of the torque dial on the control panel. "Alright," he said.

After we drove away from the rig site, Sandy leaned the side of his head against the car window. He propped the side of his chin against his fist and drifted into an open-mouthed doze. Without Buster, there was plenty of room and Sandy's long legs sprawled across the seat. Blackie and Clifford sat in silence up front. The Impala bounced down the rut-laden passageway through the woods. As Blackie turned onto the remote road, gravel pelted up and under the car frame, sounding like the clatter of rain. The shadows of the trees passing over the cracked window shield drifted across my eyelids. I slipped to the edge of sleep but heard Clifford clear his throat and say, "I'm sorry I hurt your head." And Blackie said from somewhere even more distant, where I envisioned a black panther standing beside him, "Hell, you did us all a favor, Clifford C. Bowles. Friend, you know I need all the help I can get."

Moments later, the car slowed and Blackie pulled off the side of the road. Sandy and I sat upright, peering about, awakened but not quite seeing. Buster opened the door and we moved over for him. One eye was puffed up and blood-red, the other yellow and searching through vectors of oblivion. Bloody scratches reticulated across his face and arms.

"Give Buster his knife."

Clifford did not look back, just lifted his arm over his shoulder, the blade handle extended in Buster's direction. Buster took the knife and slipped it into some clandestine scabbard strapped to his skinny ankle. He muttered thanks.

A calm had settled through him. He seemed to be a man no longer denying his demons but sitting quietly and reflecting at peace.

In my four years in the Corps, I had seen this transformation happen twice. After the men changed, they seemed drawn into another world; they no longer wanted to fight. We avoided them as if a foreign disease infected them until, finally, some corpsman from medical services led them away. Then we all went about being normal again, pretending those men had never been among us. But strangely, sitting beside Buster in the backseat of Blackie's decrepit Impala, I didn't fear the peace that now seemed to possess him. I wanted to squeeze his shoulder, give him some recognition of humanness, but I could not.

"Why did you run off into the woods, Buster?" Sandy said.

"Leave Buster alone," Blackie said.

"Hell, it was sure a dumb thing to do." Sandy went silent with his flagrant grin still etched across his face. I leaned my head back against the musty seat and closed my eyes.

The clatter of gravel released me from sleep as Blackie turned off the town highway into the parking lot of the Haiti-Cullen. Buster was first out and threw his hands high over his head. He stretched his long muscles. His tee-shirt lifted past his navel, exposing a thread work of scratches. Blackie had squeezed himself out of the driver's seat and faced Buster from the opposite side, leaning against the car with his elbows braced across the car roof.

"You're fortunate, losin' your head like that and still bein' alive. She won't spare you next time."

Buster lifted his chin. A corner of an upturned lip shone torn and red. "I survived her comin'," he said, "and found her to be gracious. Forgiving." He didn't blink. "It's—a glorious feeling." Then Buster walked over to a beat-up Ford pickup, got in and drove away. Sandy stood beside me, staring into the side of my face. Light twinkled at the corners of his blue eyes.

"Need a ride?" he said.

I shook my head but thanked him for the offer. Blackie kept his eyes fastened on the two of us.

"See you tonight, Blackie." Sandy looked over his shoulder as he opened the car door of a bright red '57 Chevy. "We got to drag Main sometimes, Half-Pint. You a natural, boy."

Clifford had disappeared through the hotel entrance, his lunch pail swinging at his side, his eyes cast downward to the gravel apron of the front lot. A train lumbered down the tracks across the highway and the dead paper mill stood vast and silent just beyond. I started to leave. A two-mile walk awaited me to the old house that had once been my home, a place now void of electricity and gas but still giving me water and shelter.

Blackie thumped hard the car roof with the flat of his thick hand. He signaled me over with a flex of his jaw and started digging into his back pocket. When I turned around to the hood of his car, three twenty-dollar bills fanned apart between his thumb and finger.

"No, sir," I said. "I got access to money."

"You're good for it. I want you eatin' something. Don't show up without a sack of chow tonight. Some oil rig gloves. Keep hold of that hard hat you got."

I took the money and slid it into my pocket. I kicked at pebbles of gravel between us with the toe of my ragged boot. "Why do you go on about the panther, sir? I expect you know they've been killed out."

"Don't be asking me goddamn questions. I see and hear what I believe. Go on home. Get your rest. We'll be comin' out of the hole tonight." He sniffed, rubbed his thumb against the side of his nose. "Sure you don't need a ride?"

"No, sir," I said. I kicked the gravel one more time. "I need to be straight with you. I'll be leavin' at summer's end to go to school."

"Alright."

I turned and walked away. Blackie hummed. His hand kept tapping a rhythm on the Impala roof. I felt his eyes tracing up and down my spine.

Entering crazy worlds came naturally for me. I'd left the I Corps of Vietnam a short while back, a violent, surreal place, and entered this one with its own unique brand of madness. A sad smile struck upon my face. Within these desperate worlds, I am most comfortable. I am acquainted with the rules. My objective was to unlearn them. Replace the old rules with new ones.

On my route home, I ventured into a shabby little grocery store on the edge of town. I bought canned goods, sliced bread, saltine crackers, bologna (I'd not yet forsaken meat products, despite my newly acquired habit of fasting), a pack of Pall Malls, and one set of beaded oil rig gloves. With a plump sack of groceries wedged into my arms, lightness entered my step, grew lighter across the vacant field where the old bush league stadium had once stood years ago, where I had once shagged foul balls and the night sky burned with a haunting moon beyond the stadium lights. One night of work was past me. Others were coming.

Along Roosevelt Street, morning sunlight brightened. Mockingbirds sang robust songs of life and death, fluttered to the full height of oak and sycamore trees. The door of the ramshackle house opened with a light push of my shoulder. I entered and imagined Ida, ghost-like, swaying back and forth in a drunken dance. Then my mother was gone, devoured by a nimbus of light.

I drew a bath and soaked in the cool water until the flesh of my hands began to wrinkle. With my head leaned back against the tub's rim, my thoughts loomed briefly over the night that had just passed. Though it had reeked with violence and a special kind of madness, I gave it little afterthought. The brightness that comes from years of hindsight behooves me to make admissions to myself and whoever might be listening. Adrift in the luxury of a tub of water, I thought the events of that night to render no particular significance. The bizarre acts of we human beings did little to evoke surprise in Half-Pint, who had been well acquainted with spectacles of tragic folly in his short life. Insanity was par for the course. A knifing, a beating, the haunting cry of imagined panthers fit well within the scope of my personal history. My thoughts drifted instead to Frank's books that awaited me in my bedroom. They were like doorways enticing me to enter.

A grey ring loomed over the porcelain enamel after the water drained. On my knees, I worked to clean the tub and felt no end to cleaning. There would never be. For lunch, I ate three slices of bologna between white bread at the kitchen table, my elbows propped over a constellation of ashen spots wrought from the fallen coals of her cigarettes. *How the hell she didn't burn this place down over the years?*

I salvaged two old alarm clocks out of junk drawers in the kitchen and set the alarm settings five minutes apart. It was past noon when I lay on the bed of my old room. I turned my head toward the limbs of the chinaberry tree outside the open window. A breeze sifted through the rising heat and the limbs swayed gently. I propped my head higher on the pillow. A real pillow. I was still getting used to them. Then I plucked the top book off the stack of three volumes by the rickety side table. A number two pencil thrust between ragged pages marked the spot I'd last read.

I shrugged my shoulders farther up and opened the book. It parted like an old, wounded soul. A few corrugated ridges lined the outer cover from the penetration of shrapnel. Smudges like coffee stains coursed across pages into the book's depth ending at page thirty-five. Beyond that page, the blood had failed to seep. Despite its shredded features, few words were lost to me.

The book's title was *The Bhagavad Ghita*. The other two books that awaited me, that I had already strived to rehabilitate through the careful parting of blood-dried pages, and my own specially designed cardboard sheaves to encase them, included a novel by Somerset Maugham, *The Razor's Edge*. The other book was almost beyond repair. A Christian mystic of the nineteenth century, John of Ruusbroec, wrote it. I'd searched his name in a volume of the Encyclopedia Britannica. Shrapnel had practically obliterated the book's title, but I was able to eventually decipher the mangled print: *The Adornment of the Spiritual Marriage*.

Frank had searched all realms of religious and spiritual thought. It came to me that despite his holy and selfless bearing, he always moved forward, exploring all avenues of spiritual doings with uncertainty about meaning and purpose. We wouldn't have it any other way

MOST COMFORTABLE

Weakness of curiosity had always protected me from questioning the uncertainties of life before I met Frank. He lit the flame.

I was just eighteen, as were so many of us bright-eyed kids who joined the Marines and lived and died in Vietnam. When I first set eyes on Frank, I was almost twenty-one, an old man in that war. I was pretty well diminished by that time, mostly staring within, plagued by blurry questions that wouldn't come into focus. Young folk who are fodder for the cannon do not usually subject themselves to existential questions. The best of those who play at war don't ponder the deeper meanings of existence. Generals don't want philosophers and dreamers in the ranks. They want young souls committed to the myths of glory and heroism. In that regard, now looking back so many years later, Frank was a dangerous element embedded within the troops. May all the gods, imagined or real, bless his renegade soul. I suppose, thinking back on it all with broad enough perspective, his one flaw was being too curious. Wanting to know too much.

After Frank's death, it seemed that I couldn't let go of this need to understand life's purpose. He'd fucked me up by parsing some of his self onto me, inflicting me with an insatiable thirst for knowledge.

Yeah, that sounds pretentious.

But don't we all at some point wonder what the fuck is going on? It's in bone and blood to muse about the purpose of our lives. It's there, innate, just waiting to be triggered. Even cloaked in the comfort of religious belief all your life, haven't there been points along the way when you asked yourself, *Really now, what's all this shit about*? You can't do that unless you give invitation to uncertainty. Uncertainty drives you forward. Gets you to start noticing things and asking all sorts of questions.

Proselytizers seeking my soul, offering me the assurance of their answers, have always pushed my buttons of contempt. "Do you have God in your life, brother?"

"No, thank you."

And when the next pitch would come. "You don't want to know God?"

I would level the ultimate response: "Fuck you."

Frank would have smiled that loopy, goofy grin of his and said something like, "Bless us all," or "Thank you for your heartfelt concern. I'm so happy you've found your path. I'm still seeking mine."

I've always been mystified by what I deemed the unquestioning acceptance of a supreme being, attributing omniscience, that often reeks of contradiction, to an all-powerful Him.

Let me tell you something I once witnessed. A billboard sprung up along Interstate 10 running east and west across southern Louisiana in August 1973. I remember the date because I'd just been accepted into the Religious Studies graduate program at Temple University. I would soon be migrating north to the land of the Yankees. Some years later, I would obtain my doctorate in Religion at the university. The sun had broken red beyond the cityscape and shot a spray of orange hues across the horizon when I first spotted the sign out my car's side window. The large billboard greeting the morning traffic flow read: *THANK YOU, GOD, FOR ENDING THE WAR*. The flaw in such gratitude to a supreme being hit me with wonder. If He had the power to end it, couldn't He have had the power to prevent it? Of course, there would be fine rationalizations from true believers if I'd posed to ask such a blasphemous question. But that was then.

I'm writing this story along a thread of time from which I can conveniently choose points to look back and forth. I'm an old man. I have many vantage points to take a perspective of events that have passed into the forays of dubious memory. It's worth saying from my current position in old age, looking back with the advantage of a comfortable and familiar academic routine, that I do believe there is a God, an entity that embraces paradox and mystery at every level of time and space in this universe or the next. He or She or It or That is known as Unknowable. As Blackie might have called out into the darkness below the vast dust of stars above, "Get it on, God! Let me hear that panther cry out into the night!"

PIGGLY WIGGLY

A week had passed since that first raucous night on the drilling rig. After my third night of work with the crew, Sandy had commenced picking me up at the old house on Roosevelt Street on his way to the Haiti-Cullen. He was that way—generous, bathed in boyish innocence, a perpetual and mischievous uplift to one corner of his lips. On the drive to the hotel, I'd listen to Sandy's tales of carnal exploits. "I had my hand so close to her panty line, my fingers burned." Or, "Oh man, that girl couldn't stop screaming, 'Love it! Love it!' 'til I had to beg her to let me rest."

He'd say things like that and I'd let it go. But then, with that blue-eyed twinkle and a tilt to his head, he'd often admonish himself, "Of course, I might be exaggerating just a bit," followed by a hearty chuckle.

We'd pull alongside Blackie's beat-up Impala in the graveled lot, smoke a cigarette while we waited for Blackie and Cliff to saunter out into the softening light of evening. Buster would wheel in behind us, often right at the edge of being late, that grey aura of life's strains enshrouding him.

From the angle of looking back after decades have passed, I see those times with Sandy more clearly. His boyish innocence drew out my protective instincts. I was only two years older but, beside him, I was a weathered old man and I would bask in his youthful vigor and his imaginary conquests of girls.

Of course, he could fling surprises at me, which in an instant would cause me to pivot in my estimation of his depth of thinking. Such as what happened on the evening near the end of my first week on the job. We pulled into the Piggly Wiggly parking lot to grab sodas to put on ice for the night.

"You don't believe in God, do you, Jack?"

Why he asked me such a spear-pointed question that evening in front of the Piggly Wiggly has always been a mystical echo in my life because a few minutes later, after we'd entered the store, I saw the only other person who'd asked me about my belief in God.

But at that moment, after being hit with Sandy's question, I looked at the side of his smooth jaw and his pinched-up grin and said, "I suppose not," and stared at my reflection in the passenger side window. Then, I swear, he went on about the preferred preference of pussy over an ice-cold Pepsi, Dr. Pepper, or Coca-Cola, if such choices confronted a man on a hot summer day.

The air-conditioned air of the grocery store chilled into me when Sandy and I pushed through the glass doors. I made my way past the produce section. As I walked alongside the bins of fresh fruit and vegetables, a piece of me hollowed out from the display of abundance. What would they have thought, the enemy I'd left behind, who had so little, if they could behold this bountiful array of food? My enemy? No, I was letting go of that already. I tried to kill them. They wanted to kill me—us—but strolling through the Piggly Wiggly and hearing the soft music piped through the ceiling, I was shedding that illusion. My enemy?

After lifting a pack of soda off the shelf, and then by second thought, a loaf of Wonder Bread for sandwiches, I started back up an aisle stacked high with canned goods on both sides. Sandy trailed behind me, his boots making a clip-clop sound that had replaced his mindless banter. He carried a six-pack of Dr. Pepper in one hand and a package of bologna in the other. "Eatin' good tonight," he grinned.

I smiled back at Sandy. "Connoisseurs of healthy shopping we are."

Julie Longo stood at the checkout counter behind the cash register. My heart sped. Her eyes darted between the keys of the cash register and grocery items she scooted down the counter toward the kid bagging the groceries. The body of her youth, now draped in a red Piggly Wiggly apron, had withered, just as mine—hers by years of strip dancing on barroom stages, mine by a couple bouts of dysentery, a few shrapnel scars and one red-welp of a wound from a carbine round in my thigh.

The clip-clop sound of Sandy's boots went silent behind me. He muttered a throaty damn beneath his breath, and I knew he was seeing her just as I was seeing her. The same pounding of my heart struck me as it did when I was a boy hiding inside a sanctuary of shrubs and honeysuckle vines, watching her cross my parent's backyard. Two rows of stacked canned goods now served as my hiding place. The long arcs of her slender muscles seemed to have shortened. Although a heaviness accentuated her body, her skin and hair still glowed. I calculated that I hadn't seen her for ten years.

Remembrances of gossip that had sifted through the town long ago reeled through my mind. The story often went that Julie had dropped out of one of the small business colleges in Shreveport for mysterious reasons, drifted to New Orleans, took up residence in the French Quarter, and danced the striptease in the dives along Bourbon Street. Later, she'd been spotted in seedier bars along the highways from Opelousas to Lafayette. For a while back then, a glut of prayer for Julie arose from the Sunday congregations, beseeching her return to the fold, and then as if a switch clicked, shutting off the light that lit the way to heaven, she'd been forgotten.

Julie's eyes darkened and she glanced away as if searching through some glimmer of an elusive memory when I moved into the checkout aisle. She raked the pack of soda across the counter, deftly clacking the register's keys, and looked up. I said, "I hope you've been well, Julie." I rubbed my hand across my mouth as if trying to pry away more words. All I could say was, "I mean that. I hope you're doing well."

Julie gave a tilt to her chin and stared at me. "Do I know you?" She glanced past me at Sandy with a curious glint to her green eyes. He stood frozen, his mouth agape. Sandy's finger poked hard into the back of my arm. I ignored him.

"You're Jack Crowe. My God, Jack," she whispered. "How are you? You're not a kid anymore."

"Are you still dreaming, Julie? I hope you haven't stopped dreaming. I hope that you never stop." I felt incredible sadness. A sense of kinship with this woman overwhelmed me.

Julie clutched the loaf of Wonder Bread. I smiled at her and she rotated her vision away from me. Her eyes, the almost translucent skin around them crinkling with tiny crow's feet, looked out through the windowpanes of the store and onto the light of the parking lot.

"Nahhh," she whispered. She leaned forward in a slow, surreptitious movement over the counter toward me. "I was La La Longo, Jack. I packed them in. No, kid. I'll never stop dreaming. But they're far different dreams from what they were. And neither will you stop dreaming."

"I'm glad. I'm really glad." My heart screamed at me to reach out, embrace, assure her that I was still her friend, but I did not.

Outside in the warm evening air, I waited for Sandy. Despite the sun lowering toward the horizon, its heat still beat down, humid and fierce, on the parking lot. Memories of my boyhood wrapped around me. Sandy strode out. He stood beside me and stared with unaccustomed silence at his Chevy. He mumbled, "Damn."

We went on to his car and got in. Both of us were still steeped in a thick residue of silence. I set the bag of soda and bread between my feet. Sandy sat behind the wheel with his hands resting on his knees. Lines of puzzlement crinkled across his forehead. "You know that girl? Damn, I think I just fell in love."

"She was my friend." I said nothing of my boyhood infatuation for Julie Longo. When I was twelve, hormonal forces just awakening, she had roamed my fantasies.

Sandy grunted a laugh. "Shit, that's got to be a story." He turned the key in the ignition, and the engine roared in the way of some giant animal proclaiming to the world its dominion.

I pressed the back of my head against the seat and shut my eyes.

Sandy drove west down the main road out of town toward the Haiti-Cullen Hotel. I opened my eyes. The sun had burnt into an orange orb on the horizon behind a scrim of clouds. Sandy's fingers drummed with Gene Krupa speed on the steering wheel. "Damn, Half-Pint, what a mystery. Love and God and that girl, Julie Longo. Man, I'm goin' to ask her out 'til she says yes. You watch."

Memories are vaporous, existing out there along the continuum of time by the projections of our unreliable minds. Ages hence, I write this as the older man that I am, and I try to honor with as much accuracy as possible the events that unfolded. The evening that Sandy and I strolled into the Piggly Wiggly market was and wasn't. That's how stories go; they are, and one day they will be not. But I know I can't move forward with Half-Pint's story until I go back to a faraway summer that includes a portion of Julie's life.

BAPTISM, A GIRL'S SHINING KNEES, AND JULIE

I was barely twelve years old when Julie first materialized in my life. Her legs shone golden-brown in her walk across the sun-scorched grass of the backyard. From inside my jungle of honeysuckle shrubs, I watched her. She looked over her shoulder toward my tunneled hideout in the vines. She raised her hand, wriggled her fingers. Goddamn, I was sure she possessed powers of clairvoyance. She knew I was here, plucking out the slender pistils from honeysuckle blossoms, swiping nectar across my tongue. I pressed my knees into the ground beside the venous network of roots and felt the rush of shame. Her power imperiled me with bouts of dizziness. I looked back through the limbs. She went up the wooden steps at the back of my home and knocked on the screen door. If some great voice from above would have whispered into my receptive ear, *Take heed of that beautiful girl, for she will someday walk along your path once again*, I would have responded into the dazzling light, *Of course, she is the love of my life. How could I not?*

My mother opened the door, partway. She stepped a little forward, one shoulder braced against the doorjamb. Her laughter carried across the sun-burnt yard. Not the familiar, drunken laugh, but the sweet one that would cut through your heart. Julie turned on her heel and faced me, resting her hands on her hips. I imagined a rosy pout exuding from her lips. My mother laughed again. She stepped out onto the back stoop beside Julie, some essential gesture of female camaraderie.

A sagging print dress draped down my mother's middle-aged body and she folded her arms across her breasts. She peered out as if to be a hunter trying to sight game in the undergrowth. I closed my eyes. Light pulsated behind my eyelids. I opened them. My mother slipped back through the doorway, shutting the screen, disappearing again into the darkness. She had had enough of the sunlight and the great mill looming toward the west beyond the roofs of the mill workers' houses.

Julie, though, walked toward me across the yellowing lawn. She was a high school senior who lived with her mother one street over from our own. Her old man had shot himself in the head one morning several years back. The event had kindled an energetic flow of gossip and wonder in the neighborhoods. The town knew Mr. Longo as a pleasant, considerate man, then one morning he takes out his shotgun, walks out into the backyard, and blows buckshot through his head. I remember my old man and I waiting in the barbershop for a haircut days after the tragedy and him saying to those seated around us, "What's going on under is a lot more than what's going on above."

I don't remember when Julie began to invade my fantasies. Or how many times I'd sat in the corner darkness of my closet, imagining her sitting across from me while I held that confusing member of my body.

"I know you're hiding in there. Come out so I can talk to you decently." Her voice was silken but commanding.

I edged out of the undergrowth and straightened myself to full height. Looked away to the rustling of a flock of cedar waxwings that had sought refuge among the upper limbs of a nearby sycamore tree. A threadbare tee-shirt clung to my chest. Dickie's jeans, patched at the knees, adorned my lower body. Keds, oversized due to my mother's foresight about a young boy's growth spurts, graced my feet.

From the corner of my eye, I saw the almost undetectable lift of Julie's breasts. She peered down at me with a scrunched curiosity bewitching her face.

"I'm sorry to interrupt your play…"

"That's all right."

"I want you to help me. Could you help me?" She cocked her head, her chin encompassed within her white hand.

I stood bewildered, not from lack of will to aid this goddess but by limitations of confidence in my ability to accomplish what she might desire.

"So, you'll help me? Your mama doesn't mind. I love your mama. Ida's so funny. We always get along."

I looked up in disbelief.

"Revival's next week. Will you come with me?" A splay of honey-golden hair curled past her ear. "God loves you and through Jesus Christ he is made known. I want to introduce the Lord to you. Revival's at the church, and it's the time of glory and rejoicing. I can pick you up on Thursday morning at 8:00 if you go with me."

Julie crossed her sunbrowned arms and awaited my answer. A collapse of spirit quaked through me. My mercurial mind flashed upon those episodes when my mother would jolt herself into the sober world and frequent the Baptist church's services for two or three subsequent Sundays. She would haul me in tow alongside her within the vise-like grip of her trembling hand. Awaiting me would be the stultification of a rigid church pew, the town's most pious sitting in rows straight and strained, their eyes uplifted toward a supernatural fellow who boomed declarations of hell and damnation at those who dared to be sinners. The aromas of toilet lotions would drench me. Discerning and approving glances from members of the congregation would play upon my mother and me. And me? I'd be wishing in silent anguish to the God outside the high church walls to please fucking get her to drinking again so I could get the hell out of there.

"Yeah, I'll go with you."

"I'm so happy you will." She winked, turned to go. As she shimmered past, her warm hand brushed across my neck. I withstood an onslaught of conflicting emotions that my body was unprepared to manage in the evaporation of that touch. She'd come to me in an act of mercy to save my soul. The realization cut into me, but surrounding this awareness were waves of physical desire that I was yet too young to understand—the craving for a mystical alliance with the opposite sex. I bit hard on the back of my lip and watched her walk away. Her thighs near the rim of her shorts posed to me as an unfathomable part of her body.

"I'll be ready. Goddamn sure."

Julie looked back and I thought there was in her eyes some glimmer of satisfaction as if I could have said nothing better to please her. She strode away. A mockingbird sang from the roof of a neighbor's house. It was then quiet but for the distant, low rumble of the paper and pulp mills, together stretching for a half-mile along the highway out of town.

* * *

My old man sat at the kitchen table with his back to the open window. Seymour bent over a plate of fried chicken, mashed potatoes, and a heap of green beans. He'd said that he'd worked setting pipe in a freshly dug ditch near the pulp mill's sulfur pits that day. Though he'd scrubbed his skin a rosy red in the bathhouse shower, he still smelled of sulphury resins.

I looked at him loading his fork and fought the heaviness that built around my heart when first sitting down at the dinner table. My mother sat across from my old man. At the end of the table, I drank from my tea glass. Chunks of ice against the sides broke through the quiet.

"The Longo girl wants to take him to church?" my old man said, chewing as he talked to some point of curiosity in the air just beyond his nose.

"It's revival," my mother said. "I told her it would be fine to take him. He might get the Lord. Finally."

"It's a contest," he said. "Who gets the most boys like Half-Pint to church wins a prize, a free meal at Dairy Queen, picture in the church newsletter." He looked at me. "Kid, did you know you were a lost soul? You're a valuable commodity to the true believers of our community."

"I want him to go," she said, almost inaudibly. "I don't want him to be a heathen. He's peculiar enough." She reached over and patted the back of my wrist.

I cast my eyes toward my mother's face. She had a sallow pall but still possessed the facial symmetry of what had once been youthful beauty. High cheekbones, deep-set eyes, a firm and slightly dimpled chin remained finely proportioned features despite middle-age encroachment. Dapples of grey blended into her brushed-back hair. Filaments of wrinkles sprouted near the corners of her eyes.

"If he wants to go, that's all right." My old man looked at me. "God lives at the head of a girl's bright and shining knee." His lips drew back in a smile. I squirmed in my chair and speared a cluster of green beans onto my fork.

"I want him to go," Ida said. Her voice rose to a higher pitch.

Goddamn. Here comes the blow, I thought.

"I want him to go!"

"Of course he can go. Didn't I say he could go? You want to go, don't you, Half-Pint? But I know that Longo girl and she gets sex and God and the devil all mixed up." He drew back his shoulders as if sensing the next step he took could trip a mine. "She dated that juvenile delinquent Louie King, telling her friends she was trying to rehabilitate him. After a few weeks, he starts pulling a pair of her underwear out of his pocket and showing them off to all his cigarette smokin' friends at the high school. Her mom found out and ripped his ass. The Longo girl said he stole them from her dresser drawer one night they were studyin' together. Ida, hon', all the guys at the mill hear stories about the Longo girl."

"Jack needs saving," Ida said. A seething tone had slid into her voice. "How do you know such things?" Her fierce stare directed at my old man caused me to latch farther down on my breath. That familiar conflagration of violence was about to explode across the table.

"It was scuttlebutt." Seymour turned to me. "It's going to blow, kid. Get on now."

I pushed back from the table. The dying rays of summer sun hurled through the window across my old man's shoulder, striking bright against the peeling wallpaper. I turned away. The tips of Ida's fingers brushed down the side of my arm when I shot past her, but her fierce, dark eyes remained fastened upon Seymour. I padded on bare feet down the dimly lit hallway to my room, shut the door, and fell back on the bed. The pitch of her cry careened through the walls, "What sex do you know about! Goddamn you, Seymour, why didn't you die over there! In front of the boy! Sex!"

I studied the serpentine routes of the ceiling cracks. Pictured my old man locking into silence, like he and his fellow Marines did when the Japs bombarded them at night with howitzer shells from the narrow maws of entrenched mountain caves and you just had to wait in silence, kid. While it blew. I rolled my head to the side and could hear the beat of my heart inside my head. Hell, I knew the pattern. They'd be making up, "Honey, honey, honey, I love you," in their bedroom tonight.

* * *

Thursday morning came, and I waited in the dim living room. The slatted window blinds were closed. I sank deeper into a Sears-Roebuck reclining chair, my old man's prized possession. My mother had gone back to bed after dropping Seymour off at the gates of the mill. Our mill worker's house possessed a quiet that belied the perpetual stalking of volatile episodes. My heart pounded in my ears, but I dwelled upon the scent of Ivory soap off my fresh-scrubbed skin. I rubbed between my fingertips the end of my clip-on tie. The top button of my shirt gnawed into my neck. My starched and pressed blue jeans seemed to grate against the muscles of my legs. The ceiling fan clicked in a lazy way that rendered longing for a greater understanding of this bewildering world. Two quick beeps of a car horn summoned me from the street outside our house.

As I walked out and onto the spongy St. Augustine grass of the front yard, the churning faraway breath of the mill's colossal smokestack coaxed me onward to the parked Bel Air sedan. I opened the door and slid onto the seat. Julie's legs twisted at a slant toward me. My eyes fell upon her bare knees protruding from beneath the petticoats of her dress. I drew in the fragrance of perfume and the puppy smell of what I could only imagine being the natural scent of her skin.

"You're it today. Just you and me," she said and smiled with lopsided red lips. She crossed her eyes.

"I don't mind."

"I bet you don't," she said.

Although there was no traffic on the isolated lane, she looked intently over her shoulder and pulled the car away.

As we entered the bowels of Center Baptist Church, a fog of stupefaction took hold. A vertical stained-glass window with depictions of a foreign lady clad in colorful robes cradling the Christ child careened upward toward the cathedral ceiling. In another, a fully grown Jesus dressed only in a loincloth and impaled on a cross looked forlornly down on scary folks with big, round eyes, their hands clasped in prayer. Their visions strained upward in witness to the cruel act that had taken place in front of them. I kept wanting them to storm the cross with a ladder and take him down before he died, but I guess that would've ruined the whole religion.

Down the carpeted aisle, I followed the rustle of Julie's petticoats, sighted upon the downy hair on the back of her neck, and turned to shuffle after her in front of a long pew where we halted at its center and sat down. I sat very still, an inch apart from the splay of Julie's dress. The tips of my toes pressed down upon the floor. Clusters of familiar townspeople and those with less familiar faces from neighboring communities continued to stream past and edge their way down the pew aisles, many clutching a small, burnished volume of the New Testament. The wooden bench began to burn into my haunches. The brush of townspeople's glances passed over me like the pelt of flies. The clearing of manly throats harbingered the beginning of some profound event—the preaching of the way into salvation, into everlasting life.

I closed my eyes and let come the drift away from conscious awareness. Julie's breath wisped into the whorl of my ear. "You're a sweet boy, Jack. You do want to please me, don't you? You will listen to the word of God, won't you?"

I would've run through a hail of bullets for her. My eyes clasped shut. I could not comprehend the enormity of the religious protocol that was beginning to roil through the stultified air. Julie's long fingers patted my knee and an electrical charge bolted through me. A great crying of "Amens" burst into the turgid air above the bustling congregation. A tall man in a suit as black as his shining hair rose from the church's gospel side and entered the pulpit. He settled into that sacred space elevated above mortals driven to God by the awareness that one day we shall all perish from this earth.

The man raised one hand into the air, directing the attention of all toward heaven. His voice boomed out, but I couldn't hear the words. I could only stare upon another hand that was retreating from my knee. It possessed a silver bracelet that fell just behind a delicate hummock of wrist bone. Once more, I shut my eyes and practiced what I knew best when this world overwhelmed me. Disappear and float away.

Thunder rumbled along the rim of my half-lit consciousness. The reverend's voice melded into darkening clouds. Inside my daydream state, I was safe from these supernatural forces churning all around me. Minutes must have passed. For a second, my eyes slit apart, stared ahead at the thumb-smudged backs of hymnals supplanted in the pew's book rack. I saw nothing else. Heard nothing but the buzzing of atoms inside my brain, a sound like the automatic pilot of a basement furnace.

Then came a chug-chug chanting of spirits. The earth quaked. I dug my fingers into the muscles of my legs. Julie's shoulder jarred against me and I sat upright in the pew, startled into sharper awareness. The reverend's voice boomed, "Raise your hands, all you who are sinners! If you're a sinner—if you wish to be let through the holy doors and into the Kingdom of God, lift up your hands!"

Julie looked at me in an aura of joyous melancholy as I slumped farther down. The skin of her face was red with the flush of blood. Sweat glistened on her cheeks.

"Are you listening, Jack?" Her lips brushed against my ear so that I might decipher her words amidst the joyous shouts, stomping, and clapping. The earth shook more. The reverend traversed the territory surrounding the pulpit, imploring all those who have sinned to lift their hands and surrender to Christ. It was Julie's eyes that bewitched me. Even now, with so many years gone by, I proclaim that I would have sacrificed my life for her at that moment.

"Is he talking about me?" I slowly pronounced each word so that she could read my lips.

"Yes, Jack, he is. Surrender to His love."

Dazed, as if I'd taken the blow of an iron fist to my head, I lifted my hand into the thickening air above the heads of the congregation and saw then a smattering of other hands up high, fingers clenching and unclenching. My hand stayed timidly aloft. The resounding command from the man pacing upon the stage pitched higher toward the arched ceiling. "Come on down now! Glory! Glory! You who are to be bathed in the light of divine acceptance!"

Julie hugged me. One arm remained clasped around my shoulders. I glimpsed her round white knees projecting past the hem of her dress. I looked back into her eyes. "Where am I going?"

"To Jesus," she said.

Oh hell, I thought. I neared the outer edge of the pew aisle. A heavy-bosomed woman hurled past, arms flailing into prisms of muted light pouring through the stained-glass apertures. A boy, not much older than myself, scudded by in the wake of the rotund lady, his face contorted in pain or rapture. I looked back at Julie. She was radiant, skin aglow with perspiration. A rotund man dressed in overalls and a starched white shirt slid his legs to the side and shoved me fully out onto the aisle.

In this vortex of religious fervor, I stumbled down to my knees on the red aisle carpet. Shouts of "Hallelujah!" seemed aimed directly at me. I sank into darkness. When I regained my sight, I was still on my knees and braced by my outstretched hands on the carpeted floor. The altar, draped in a white cloth emblazoned with a gilded cross, awaited me down below. The cries of God's flock came at me like a cascade of water down a dry riverbed. "Glory! Glory! Arise! Come down to share in God's light!"

I pushed myself up through the thunder and tread on unsteady feet down the aisle. My shoes pinched tight against my toes. At the front pew, reserved for fresh acolytes, I sat down in a crevice between the heavy-bosomed woman and a man my father's age. The man wrung his hands together. Pearl drops of tears flowed down his cheeks to the endpoints of his quivering mouth.

I looked down the row of people who had surrendered to God. They would soon realize that there are no illuminations of divine light in my unworthy body. I breathed and began to tap my feet, chuck my chin back and forth in the manner of a chicken dance.

The reverend's long legs scissored past me in a blur. Out of the corner of my eye, I saw him fall on one knee before a tearful yellow-haired girl at the pew's far end. Polished half-moons flashed from his fingertips as he grasped her head, shook it like some mother dog who had bit into her pup's loose neck and flicked it back and forth into obedience. When he released the girl's head, her sweet face lifted, eyes shut against a seeming brightness she couldn't bear. Her mouth gaped fiercely as if to receive the kiss of Christ. The reverend slid in front of the next person, clasped his hands around the man's uplifted face. I broke apart inside. I turned to the heavy-bosomed woman beside me. I pleaded: "What the hell's happening?"

She looked down at me. Her face, too, was glazed with incomprehension. Then the deep lines across her forehead melted downward into the kindest smile I'd ever felt cast upon me. The woman grabbed me with her fleshy arms and drove my face into her breasts. Amid those giant tits, I struggled to breathe. I succumbed to her powerful embrace. The noisy tumult of spiritual upheaval dimmed in the plush sanctity of her body. Her damp breath struck into my ear: "You are being reborn, child! Hallelujah! Do you understand!"

She released me then. I coughed and froze my vision in front of the space before my eyes. Motes at orbit in a beam of light floated just outside my reach. I awaited the laying of the minister's hands. I prayed. *Give me the steady river of calm that flows in the veins of my father, the man who could sit as still as a stone in the shit and mud while the shells struck and shook the earth, the man who quit believing in You.*

The reverend's sweaty palms squeezed against my temples. He leaned in close. The smell of aftershave lotion shot into my nostrils. His hands slid down, compressing my cheeks. My lips puckered out like those of a hooked fish.

"Are you here to accept Jesus Christ as your savior? Do you surrender to Him, child?" One fleshy palm swept up and sprawled over tufts of my hair. A silver crucifix dangled at the end of a chain around his neck. I knew what I had always known about myself. I was too small to be enlightened, too weak to understand God.

"I'm a sinner for sure," I stammered. "I know that."

"You're a sinner and Jesus loves you. God loves you. Now baptism awaits you and you will be cleansed of your sins." His fingers wrenched over my shoulders, towed my face into the cleavage of his suit jacket. The full hit of male perfume shocked me. Shoved back out of that pocket, I lifted my chin and released a trembling breath.

"Is Jesus your savior, boy?"

"Hell, I don't know," I gasped.

"Do you accept Jesus Christ as your savior?"

Sweat rolled down my flanks. In front of the convulsing congregation, what meager courage I had evaporated around me. I said what he needed to hear, "Yes."

I had surrendered my way out of damnation. I escaped by way of cowardice.

In what might have been a glimmer of recognition about my questionable sincerity, the reverend's jaw slackened. "Bless you in Christ, child." He shuffled away, positioning himself directly in front of the heavy-bosomed woman who rocked forward, anticipating the reverend's long, white hands.

I crossed my arms over my chest and looked, unblinking, straight up into the high ceiling. The reverend arose in front of the jubilant congregation and moved in an effusion of spirit before the nave. He spread his arms high into the air and proclaimed to all the date of baptism for the newly surrendered. I blinked, looked straight ahead, then over my shoulder. Julie looked down upon me out of the passionate faces of the congregation. Her eyes were sober and questioning. I turned back around and drifted into the constellations of motes caught in shafts of sunlight.

On the way back home, I sat with my shoulder wedged against the passenger door. The side of my head pressed hard into the window. The unrelenting summer sun warmed the inside of the car. A leaden weight spread across my eyelids. As Julie drove down the narrow state highway toward the mill end of town, she smoothed the ruffles of her dress with one hand and held the steering wheel with the other. Her attention seemed fixed upon the steady white line that bisected the state highway.

"Did you understand the meaning of altar call, Jack?" She tucked her chin and peered over the steering wheel. "You know you're scheduled for baptism next Sunday night?"

"Yeah, I know." I drawled out my next words with severe contempt. "Now I'll be able to enter the fuckin' gates of heaven."

I rubbed my forehead against the window glass and pushed myself up in the seat. I sighed and studied the tree lines of oak and pine sailing past.

"Have you heard stories about me, Jack? That I'm a bad girl?"

The car rumbled forward, but I felt the world tilt. A movement inside my stomach signaled a transformation in my view of people. We all reach out for a helping hand by-and-by and hope that someone is out there to respond. Sincerity wrenched Julie's voice. I studied the side of her face. The smooth arcs of bone and skin gave me the illusion that she possessed eternal youth. Julie would never grow old, never wither into the ordinary travails of this life, never be drawn down by despair's gravity. Something akin to pain flickered in my chest.

"Yeah," I said. "Dad called it scuttlebutt. I'm sorry. I have heard bad things about you. That don't mean you're bad, though. I think you're swell."

There was a cold wind striking Julie's eyes. Rheumy streams burned down her high cheeks. Her vision remained fixed upon the road. She slowed the car and stopped at the intersection stoplight of the highway and Butler Street. The car idled into a marble-like purr. To the left, down Butler, the road connected to Main Street. Straight ahead the highway ribboned south in tandem with the railroad tracks past the high school football stadium and toward the sprawling paper mill.

"Let's get us a frosty root beer at the A&W," she said. "Mother gave me some change for offerings. Shit, I kept it."

The light winked green, sunlight flashing behind it. She turned down Butler and drove past the few old wooden homes of the street and their carpeted green lawns and majestic oaks toward Main. In the graveled parking lot of the root beer stand, Julie turned off the car's ignition. A profound quiet hung in the air. The mill's drumming and churning sound was cut off from our senses as we sat in the front seat. I thought to myself, *Fuck this world.* I did what I did in those bare moments of my mother's drunken sleep. I took Julie's hand that whitened over the rim of the steering wheel and squeezed it in my own. "It don't matter. You're all right."

On a Sunday night where the evening sky rived with heat lightning but no rain came, I was baptized. Seymour and Ida sat somewhere in the congregational midst. Up there on the baptism stage hidden among the kneecaps of a bevy of the revival-enthused saved, I trembled in a thin tee-shirt and jeans. A clean white sheet, cut down in size to fit my minor frame, a hole scissored out of its center, draped over my runt-sized body. My turn came after the great bosomed woman, whose name I had learned was Eva, pushed herself up from the steps of the water tank. Eva sloshed past me in dainty cadence. She held her head nobly in the air and looked beyond to a place where truth was absolute.

I shuddered and began my short walk across the small stage and stepped unsteadily down metal steps into the vat of water. The reverend awaited, dressed in a white robe that billowed up to the water's surface, his arms extended toward me. Traces of fine stubble glistened on his firmly set jaw, the under rippling of tiny muscles.

Out there in the shadowy darkness of the pews, I heard my father laugh, that same laugh taunting death, taunting resurrection. And my mother's slurred voice, following through in predictable sequence, "Goddamn, Seymour, why didn't you die!"

Hush-hushed came the stunned silence of the congregation. Then, the reverend's voice boomed: "I anoint you in the name of the Father and Son and Holy Ghost, free of sin."

The reverend's thumb and finger clamped down on the brow of my nose. Guided by his other hand over the middle of my spine, I sank back into the body of water. My eyes remained open beneath the surface. I blinked up into a refracting world of zipping light and quavering shapes. I shot up in an explosion of water to witness the minister's overbite of teeth bearing in on me. A smile, a round breath laced by mouthwash, and a passionate utterance: "Bless you, boy. You are now entered into the Kingdom of God."

I shook away the little rivers cascading down my face, and aided by the reverend's deft hands, I shifted myself about and placed my bare feet upon the coarse steps. At the back of the stage, someone wrapped a towel around my neck and hugged me. I recognized Eva's fleshy arms, her kindest of all smiles. She bent over me, holding me in a damp and compassionate embrace, whispering into my ear, "You'll find God someday, Jack. I know you will."

I am prone to be contemptuous—if you haven't noticed. The process of looking back reminds me of this sullied aspect of myself, this disregard I hold toward all those who profess to know the meaning of life, the pathway to truth, to have the grasp of God in their hands. It's always been hard-edged and razor-sharp, this perspective I've held toward true believers, though it's softened in my later years. Frank would have been approving of this gradual maturation of mine. I can imagine his ribbing, "Ol' Jack, getting mellow. You're seeing it, aren't you? All of us need something in which to believe. Respect that, Jack."

And back there in the recesses of my mind, I respond, "Christ, Frank, give me some slack." He would pile on amused, saying something like, "Being aware of our limited time on this world is frightening, buddy. No one should be ashamed for trying to lessen the anxiety of knowing we are finite."

Enough of talking to the dead.

What has caused me to pause and push back my chair in this office, it now filled with moving boxes stacked with books, papers, and photographs from the shelves, and turn to gaze through the window upon the trees and the campus green was the memory of Eva holding me tight. I knew her as a human being of remarkable compassion in those few moments following the baptism. The connection overwhelmed me. Here it is: This gracious woman who had found the truth for herself recognized that I, the weird kid, Jack (Half-Pint) Crowe, had accidentally stumbled into the boudoir of God and didn't have the sense to excuse himself and get the fuck out. Empowered by her relationship with a God from the heavens, real or imagined, and her magnanimity, Eva gifted me kindness despite the deceit that coursed through my pitiful soul.

Back those many years ago, after my immersion into the rituals of the church, I'd spy Eva from afar. She'd beam a knowing smile as if we possessed together a private joke. After eventually managing to fade away from the glory of the church, I spotted her only once. She was entering the corner drugstore downtown, and the heft of her backside caught the force of the glass door. Eva didn't see me. I was thankful. After that sighting, I never saw her again until years later when I witnessed her attempt to touch Blackie's wounded soul and was rebuked. But in my thoughts, my heart, I continued to hold her dear, having known someone pure and kind—the essence of my buddy, Frank.

The summer of the baptism had drawn overly ripe, tree limbs beginning to yellow from the heat, cats and dogs lying together in the cool dirt beneath porches at mid-day, heatwaves curling off the oil-slick streets when I finally shucked the routine of weekly Sunday school lessons. Three Sundays straight were enough. Sprawled out in his reclining chair, my old man peered over the evening paper and chuckled an approving grunt after my proclamation. But my mother sprung out of her chair and clawed her fists around the neck of my shirt. I was usually adept at parrying her lunges, but this time I floundered. My teeth clacked as she shook me. She slapped my face hard and then came the salty taste of tears. My old man's reclining chair thudded down, and newspaper pages ruffled loudly.

"Ida, don't hit that boy!"

I vaulted backward, flying to the floor in a heap. I sat there panting, unable to catch up with my breath. Above me, my mother cried, "I'm sorry, Jack! I'm sorry!" Such exclamations after a wave of assault were always part of the pattern. My mother was bent over in my old man's arms. She wailed, tried to cover her mouth with her hands that my old man kept suppressed at her sides. I saw my parent's bodies rock back and forth, grow liquid like a slow-motion wave.

"Now, Ida. What's it matter what people think?"

I leaped up. Dizziness brushed across my forehead. I padded backward, felt for the doorknob with the back of my hand.

"Go on, boy. She didn't mean to hit you."

My mother sobbed, "I didn't mean to, honey."

My father's throaty voice sounded as calm as the melt of ice in a mountain stream. "Ida, Ida, it's alright."

"Hell with you!" I sobbed and slid out the door into the soft, bold fingers of evening light. At the foot of the steps, I shoved my hands into my pockets, rubbed my bare feet across the cool grass, and cocked an ear into the air. I wiped away tears and chucked deeper into myself an inner pain. Kept down there deep, I could move on.

I hoped to hear the whooping and cries of other boys starting up a game of tin can shinny, a game that would extend from the last violet rays of the evening into the night. Maybe they'd let me join. Instead, I heard only the rhythmic song of the cicadas, the cries of blackbirds flocking into the trees for evening roost. I shrugged, began to whistle, and made myself into a shadow that wandered until the first streetlights burned in the twilight. The bull bats frolicked in the waves of their luminescence. I tossed pebbles into the air and watched their disappointed lunges.

During the remainder of that summer and into the early months of fall when the seasons changed at the tentative pace of a beautiful woman undressing, I experienced a transition in my life that before I would have thought unimaginable—friendship with Julie Longo.

In my sanctuary, nestled in the jungled shrubbery at the boundary of my parent's mill house yard, I watched clouds roll into giant mountains beyond the wavering limbs. I could reach and touch sparrows that flitted among the branches above me. Moving to my back on a niche of soft cool earth, I would half-doze and dream myself years forward where I performed heroic feats as an unassailable warrior. But I, unlike my old man, would remain pure.

During one of those indolent afternoons of dreaming, trying to ignore the march of an itch up my spine and the siren of a mosquito near my ear, I heard Julie whispering my name. My heart began to pound. I sat up, scraping my head against the stouter branches. She stood barely visible through the blossoms and limbs.

"Jack, are you hiding in there?"

"Hush," I said and pushed myself forward and parted the limbs, showing her the passageway. She smiled. I noticed for the first time that she had one crooked tooth in the upper row. It only made my heart beat faster.

"Don't get any ideas, kid, or I'll slug you."

"I won't."

Julie set her hands atop her knees and lowered her back. She wore loose jeans, cuffed above white socks, and bright yellow sneakers. Her cotton blouse tapered snugly against her breasts. She looked askance to the right then the left and edged her way forward, brushing back supple limbs, and entered the cool den. I leaned back against a firm branch and drew my knees up to make room for her. She nestled her haunches into the earth directly in front of me and sat like an Indian. With her smooth jaw uplifted, she scanned the dark recesses of the foliage. Honeysuckle blossoms that had dared to seek life in the latter days of summer drooped against her hair. She looked upward, exposing the faintest necklace of sweat on her neck. I thought that she could hear the pounding of my deceitful heart and was looking for the source of the sound somewhere far away among the clouds that portended a building storm.

"This is your doorway into other worlds, isn't it? I hear you're a strange boy, but I know you're just a dreamer. Someday you'll be somebody that nobody in this town will have ever imagined. Won't you? I will too. You can bet on it."

Her lips shaped into a pensive bow. The honeysuckle blossoms rubbed against the smooth crown of her hair. Julie whispered and her voice became echoes of her breath. She plucked at the skin of a broken twig and told me that someday she would sing and dance before great crowds and star in Hollywood movies, serious films in which her dramatic portrayals proffered to the people new visions of modern life. I placed my chin on my upraised knees. I could feel my eyes glistening, encouraging her to go on.

"And then someday I'll marry a handsome, sophisticated man like Prince Rainier of Monaco. He married Grace Kelly, the most beautiful actress of all time," she whispered. "Did you know that fairy tales can come true?"

I shook my head. I told her that I didn't believe in fairy tales but hoped that all those things would come true for her. At that moment, an errant bee sliced through the limbs and fell upon blossoms clustered above us. Julie laughed and cupped her mouth. She looked around, mocking fright, and spoke into the arc of her palm: "I know it's just dumb dreams." She smiled like a little girl half-hidden behind her slender, long fingers. "I just like to dream and dream and dream."

Julie curled locks of hair through her fingers. She looked straight into me.

"Is God so hard to understand, Jack? You aren't a believer, are you? You don't believe in God, do you?"

"Hell," I said, flicking away an ant crawling over my elbow. "It hurts me to think about all that. It hurts too much."

In later years, adolescence and on into those bloody days of Vietnam, I looked back at the times with Julie in the sanctuary of the honeysuckle hedge and lamented not having kept a journal of the encounters, one in which I would have recounted the march of her dreams, the specter of her growing awareness that just as the body must die and decompose so must our fantasies. I acknowledged, of course, that I would have made copious notes about her varying fragrances, the undulant motions of her muscles when she moved, the satiny sheen of her tanned skin, the variations of her smile. Still, I also hoped there would have been notations in the journal's pages that would have captured my transition from boyhood sexual longing to genuine feelings of compassion for another human being.

Her visits, which probably totaled a mere dozen, were always presaged by a hushed whisper outside the thick foliage. "Are you hiding in there, Jack?" She would enter, parting the lissome branches, descending as if Alice, reincarnated, slipping once again down the rabbit hole. As summer eased steadily into fall and the leaves withered into a superannuated brown, her visits stopped. She had seemed to be far distant the last time she appeared.

On that last visit, she said, "I think I've told you too much. I don't know why." Her hand splayed through her thick hair. She looked straight into me with an aggressive look I'd never seen from her before.

"You've never really told me much about yourself, kid. You just listen."
She cocked her head. The honeysuckle blossoms had withered to brown
specks on the vines weeks before. Julie's eyes fell upon my shoulders
that since the baptismal night had noticeably broadened. Though I was
small for my age and would always be, Ida often complained about my
sudden bursts of growth and the cost of keeping me in clothes.

"Little boy, you're starting to get dangerous," Julie said, looking at
me as if she were speaking to her breath at the end of her nose.

"What is it?"

She twisted her legs around and eased away, pushing up with her
hands. She looked back over her shoulder and then was gone, the limbs
swaying behind her haunches.

"We're good friends," I said to her fading silhouette.

In the fall of that year, I sat in classrooms where my teachers no
longer kept the windows at half-mast to catch breezes coming past the
shade of the school ground oak trees. Autumn had drawn into a full
circle. Budding scents of early decay harbingered the inevitability of
winter's descent. I sniffed my schoolbooks' inner bindings and
contrasted the redolence of stamped cloth and glue with the
remembered scents off Julie's skin. During each visit, as we shared our
visions of the world, she would ask, "Jack, what are your dreams? I tell
you everything. Tell me your dreams, kid." And I would shake my head
and look away and say that I could not.

REMOTE ROAD

The summer days of work in the oil fields continued to pass into weeks, and I felt what I didn't want—the growing of Sandy's friendship. It was difficult to prevent. He grew on you. The kid thread through my defenses with his implacable smile. His life seemed fueled by goofy innocence. In those weeks following our chance meeting with Julie, Sandy continued his mission to pursue her affections. I continued to spend myself deeper into Frank's books, performed delicate page repairs using transparent tape, purchased a used paperback dictionary to help me interpret the snags of foreign-sounding words, and there were shitloads of them.

I learned more about Sandy's life mainly in private conversation with Clifford C. Bowles. Cliffie had a bent for divulging the secrets of others. Sandy's old man had died a few years back in an offshore oil rig explosion in the Gulf. His mother had been "sent to heaven" (Clifford's words) after a defeated bout with breast cancer when Sandy was in high school far south in Plaquemines Parish. Blackie had hired Sandy on his seventeenth birthday. The kid had worked with the crew for almost two years, proven himself to be a steady hand and not easily intimidated by Blackie's bruising bossmanship. Sandy had one known relative, an uncle housed in the state penitentiary at Angola.

During this time, we completed the drilling operation and capped off the hole with the "Christmas Tree," a strange totem pole of valves and spools used to control the flow of oil out of the well. It had been a good hole. We had struck oil. The decomposition of dinosaurs and ancient flora to be siphoned up from over a mile below the earth. Back then, I never imagined the planet as finite of resources, though I'd become quite acquainted with the fragile limitations of self.

A downtime of three days came before we would shift to the next location, a place described by Blackie as virgin woods in the parish's upper realm and noted for rare sightings of elusive panthers. Clifford had told me in private whispers that Blackie's fascination with the big cats had always been a part of the man's history. Yet, he'd garnered a string of obsessions about various disappearing wildlife over the years.

Besides his fixation with the southern panther, an extinct woodpecker had once possessed him. The Ivory-Billed Woodpecker had vanished decades ago, but Blackie had harbored the belief that some must still inhabit the deeper woods. Clifford related with a half-lit grin that Blackie invested in a pair of binoculars. At rig sites by woods edge, he would peer into the vast darkness of a forest. Clifford also shared with some amusement that Buster had been fine with the woodpecker obsession, but somehow, Blackie's shift back to his panther obsession had unsettled him. The conjuring up of panthers from a bygone time considerably rattled Buster's superstitious nature. Reviving my memory of that first night on the rig, I considered Clifford's commentary about Buster to be a significant understatement.

The retreat from work hit me with a surprising breath of freedom, though I lamented the loss of three days' worth of pay. I used the time to continue the necessary cleaning of the old house. Rotten leaves in the gutters scraped out; loose roof shingles nailed down; door hinges replaced; a thorough dusting, sweeping, and swabbing of the old place until I was sure it would pass inspection by any hard-ass gunny of the Corps. On the second day, I washed my two pair of jeans, shirts, and socks (I'd given up underwear during my enlightened days in Vietnam) and cut the front yard grass with what had been Seymour's rusty push mower. Later, I poured a big glass of iced tea and settled down on the steps shaded by the sycamore tree. There, I resumed my pursuit through the ragged pages of one of Frank's books, the *Bhagavad Ghita*.

The language of it struck me as a bit too sweet toward the nature of war, but the flowery dialogue appealed to my mind's ear. I was far into it, slowly peeling back each page that had been stuck together by Frank's dried blood. Though I lacked certainty about the book's theme, an impression formed that there is always a war, and every human being is challenged by how to deal with it. In the middle of a battlefield, a prince named Arjuna has doubts and recognizes that many of the enemy are his old friends, teachers, and even relatives. He looks to his charioteer, Krishna, for advice. Krishna is actually a god of some sort and tells him he must do his duty and act. That is, kill the enemy because it's God's will. Not to act would be shameful and create cosmic chaos.

I imagined Frank reading this by candlelight deep into the night, mumbling beneath his breath, "Fuck you, Krishna, but I'm not buying your God's will bullshit."

I remember thinking, maybe there's hope for me. Maybe I'm seeing that we've been tricked into playing out the will of the bullshitters. I will curtail the violence within me. That's my vow, and it's all I've got for now.

Then Sandy, preceded by the thrum of the Chevy engine, emerged from his car at the side of the crumbling street, swinging a six-pack of Pabst Blue Ribbon in his hand and strutted across the yard. A shit-eating smile crossed his face and stoked him to the brim with innocence. That seeming innocence of his plucked at hidden cords within me. Compelled my desire to protect. In Vietnam, I'd learned it always got you into trouble. The statistics were against you.

"Half-Pint, take a ride with me, boy. Let's scout out the new site. Miss Julie's busy with her mama tonight."

"She still willing to see you?" I said and looked up from the broken pages.

"How can she not be willing? Come on, let's ride."

Sandy stood over me. Droplets of condensation slid down the sides of the beer cans in his hand. A heavy scent of cut grass permeated the air.

"It's our day off."

"What you reading?"

"Nothing really."

"It looks torn up."

"Give me a second, you pain in the ass."

I got up to go inside. Sandy's eyes roamed from the new hinges on the screen door to the freshly mowed grass. "Damn, boy, you making a home."

His comment struck my back. A disquiet rolled over me as I made my way across the bare wood floor to my room. I put the book atop Frank's other ragged books stacked on the small bedside table and stood for a moment staring out the window. Shame pitted through me; this was not home, and I wanted no man or woman to think otherwise.

It was basecamp, a place of shelter while I stored money and goods for the journey that Frank and his books had set me on. I put on a clean shirt and went outside. Sandy had positioned himself on the doorsteps with his legs stretched out in front of him. He'd opened a can of beer. A froth of foam oozed from the openings. He handed it to me. I took it cold into my hand.

"This is no home," I said. "Never was. Never will be."

"All right. Let's go."

The road out of town shot north through the dark woods of the upper parish. Its blacktop surface shimmered with heat mirages that disappeared in a rhythmic, inconsequential pattern as Sandy gunned the Chevy toward them. Though the sun blared, the woods stood laden heavy with darkness. The beer tasted cold and satisfying; the chill of the can lingered on my fingertips. The radio drummed out rock and roll music. Sandy was uncommonly quiet, then, flashing a grin, he said, "Me and Miss Julie drank a Coke together outside the Dairy Queen the other night. She don't drink beer anymore."

I chuckled, picturing Sandy and Julie Longo sitting in Sandy's car, the windows down, the buzz of summer heat coming up from the pavement. "Smitten by an older woman," I said and felt a keen warmth toward the two, but underneath, if truly honest, a lament.

"Yeah, Half-Pint, it's a mama complex I got. Damn." He took a long drink of his beer. His eyes peered down over the uplifted can to the road pressing upon us. I couldn't advise him on love. I knew little about it.

Few cars swept past on the remote highway. Seven miles out of town, Sandy turned east onto a narrow passageway of broken macadam that seemed to have been carved out of the forest by someone's mindless afterthought of exploration. Regular townspeople shied away from this parish area where the most marginal of the marginal chose to live. The limbs of ancient oaks closed in on the road and broke the sun's rays into fragments of light. Through this corridor, Sandy sped the Chevy forward, and I sat in what I felt to be an almost unnatural state of normality. Two good ol' Southern boys cruising through the wilderness of swamp, slough, and forest while shadow and light danced across the front windshield. Barely six months before, I'd not thought such a moment to be possible. A job, G.I. Bill, quiet times to read the books, the dream of college taking form, a cold beer in hand, and a friend. I looked at Sandy. His eyes held to the narrow road ahead in their shining blue brightness. The beer warmed me from the inside, and I grinned. "You're dumb as shit, Sandy."

Sandy nodded and winked and flashed that boyish smile. "Yes, sir, I am that, Half-Pint."

I've risked my life for and fought beside those brothers whom I'd given enduring trust, those I'd called Shithead, Numb Nuts, or Dumb Fuck. I was beginning to place Sandy in good company. Halfway through my second beer, I was a little drunk. A few miles down the rough-hewn road, the trees broke from the embracing darkness and pastureland spread out toward a rim of pine woods on our right. An oil pump, set against the wood's edge, worked tediously up, then down, a motion like some giant dipping bird toy.

Sandy craned his neck a little forward and scanned the woodland ahead. "It's near here," he said. "Pretty sure."

The landscape gave way once more to woodlands, a great inter-mixture of oak, pine, hickory and an underlying hodgepodge of bramble and vines. The road curved. The surface darkened into the heavy shadows of the trees. After less than a mile, the sunlight burst upon us as we approached a bridge, its silver-rust railings, trying without avail to glint in the sun. Sandy slowed the car to a crawl. A creek spread out into a black pool before disappearing into the backdrop of cypress trees. Cypress stumps and dragonflies skirted its surface. Turtles sunned their backs all lined in a row on the grey carcass of a tree trunk that had long ago succumbed to the black water. The snout and eyes of a gator penetrated the surface. It was called Burnt Bridge, named in honor of a minor skirmish in the Civil War when Confederate resisters torched the bridge to slow the march of Union soldiers on their way to Alexandria. At least that was the myth that had built around it.

A pickup truck was parked on the roadside a short distance down from the bridge. A woman stood at the back of the vehicle with what appeared to be a lug wrench dangling in her hand. A boy, thin as a willow switch, stood off to the side, watching us approach. A shroud of glumness crossed his face. The woman, a frail figure dressed in a pink tee-shirt and jeans, did not lift her eyes.

"We're not stopping," Sandy said.

"Why not?"

"You've been gone a long while." He tilted his head and looked hard at me. Muscles pulsated in the side of his jaw. I'd not witnessed this kind of fear in him since I walked onto the deck of the rig and first tried to whip the spin chain around the pipe.

"Pull over, Sandy."

"Shit, boy." But he wheeled the car over onto a low apron of grass just beyond the desolate truck and turned off the ignition. He propped his can of beer on the shelf of the dash and rubbed his hand over his mouth. "That's trouble, Half-Pint."

I gulped down the last of the chilled beer, shuffled the empty can into a paper sack Sandy used for trash, and unlatched the door.

"Hold on, boy," he said. "Listen up."

I puffed a laugh. But as I thumped the door shut, that odd sensation of danger that had been born within jungle and rice paddy tingled in my stomach and whipped up the beat of my heart. I looked toward the dark of the woods, then back across the narrow road. The frail woman, lug wrench still loose in a hand unadorned of jewelry or fingernail polish, stood beside the boy.

I walked around the back of Sandy's Chevy and crossed over through sunlight and shadows. The warm air had a velvet feel to it. A smell of both decomposition and regeneration slipped out of the wood's darkness. I could hear the low hum of violence clicking its way across the terrain. In the early workings of my post-war mind, these kind of signals came as mere vexations of spirit and soul, and I told myself, my runaway heart, my flush of sweat, that it's all residue from those times. Someday I'll be shed of it.

"I can help, ma'am." I offered my hand to the woman. She glanced at the boy. The boy's dark eyes froze on me as I took the wrench. I started to work, loosening the lug nuts on the tire. The woman shuffled off to the back of the truck. There came a metallic scraping sound across the truck bed. The woman came back around and set the jack and its scissor wrench beside me. "Your brakes set, ma'am?"

"Yeah, they set." It was the boy that spoke. Something shifted inside my stomach. The light buzz I'd held from the beer faded out. A sense of foreboding overtook me. I felt like I'd lifted two rattlers by their tail. I shoved the jack beneath the truck frame and rotated the jack handle. Sweat streamed past my nose and drops hit the tar of the road beside my knees. I drug the deflated tire off the lug nuts and lay it on its side. The woman stood with arms folded across her chest. A faint tremor kindled at the corner of her lips, then was gone. She nodded toward the back of the truck.

"Spare's in the back," the boy said. "She ain't goin' to say shit to you. We could've done this ourselves."

"Yes, sir," I said and flashed a bright grin.

The boy spit off to the side and his lips clawed into a snarl. The woman held listless eyes on me. My breath went deep into my lungs and seemed to stay there. I knew the vacant fields of vision behind that look. I got up and went around the woman and boy and drug the spare out across the lowered tailgate. It thumped and crunched hard on loose gravel. I wheeled the tire around the two who stood silent and watching, part in and part out of the shade.

I wanted to do kind acts, think peaceful thoughts, and somehow be forgiven for all the violence I had committed in my life. I wanted atonement for surviving. I wanted to see Frank enter the dreams of my restless sleep and say how proud he is of me.

The boy's row of sharp little teeth beneath the scowl of his upper lip put a rent in my quest to be altruistic. I worked faster to finish up the tire changing, tightening the lug nuts on the spare, removing the jack, tossing the flat tire and the jack equipment back onto the truck bed. Neither boy nor woman spoke as I turned away and walked back to the car.

Frank said to me once on a quiet night of no enemy contact, and we shared a cup of C-ration coffee, and a few stars winked from beyond the rain forest canopy, "Kindness to be kindness must be a selfless act."

He was always saying shit like that, out of nowhere, shit that I rarely grasped, but I understood what he meant that night and muttered back, "That can be hard to find." The conversation seemed eons ago, but only a few months had passed.

Now I was in a different wilderness trying to exude kindness. Sweat drenched my clothes, and the eyes of the woman and boy burned into the back of my neck while I walked to Sandy's Chevy. I realized that true selflessness belongs to those of a higher nature. Me? I hungered for praise and gratitude. The only person I'd known who had shown unadulterated love for others was Frank, and he was dead. Being like Frank would forever be beyond my reach and I doubted I'd ever know another.

I unlatched the Chevy door and slid into the passenger's seat. "Mind if I have another beer?"

Sandy reached behind the seat and lifted the lid of the cooler. His hand broke through the chipped ice and he presented the beer to me with a shake of his wrist. He kept his vision on the rearview mirror. I took the beer and pressed the icy-wet can against my forehead.

"I should've held you back."

"They didn't really want any help," I said and grabbed the church key and popped two holes into the top of the can.

"Those were Whiteheads, Half-Pint. Should've held you back." He looked over his shoulder toward the boy and his mother getting into the truck. "Hell, I guess it's alright. I guess. Her husband's Calvin Whitehead, a man of means, logging money, takes trips up north to grizzly hunt or fish. Can you imagine that? Leaving sportsman's paradise to go north for fishing and hunting." Sandy settled his vision forward once again as the Whitehead truck drove slowly away. "He's been known to hurt people." Muttered more to himself than to me, "It's probably alright." Then again, said, "Yeah, I think it's alright."

"Wouldn't have been right not to offer help to them."

"It's not those two I worry about, you dumb shit."

Sandy turned the key and the engine low-rumbled. Gravel cracked beneath the tires as he pulled away. A burst of sunlight through the windshield blinded me for a second. I must admit to a feeling of uneasiness as Sandy pulled his Chevy back onto the road. This was the South. I thought I knew well its intricacies of culture, the suspicion, fear, and anger that bubble just beneath the niceties. But in the clear, long vista of my remembrances, the uneasiness nagged just like it would before a patrol had gone bad.

BEATING

We began work at the new location by laying a pipeline from a secluded bayou to the drilling rig and its freshly uplifted derrick. The rig's supervisor, or tool pusher, in the parlance of the oil field, had bequeathed the daylight tour (pronounced tower) to Blackie's crew. A sweltering heat embraced us on that first day back. The morning sun burned bright above the lowland forest and swampland. Ancient cypress trees cast a swath of dark shade along the narrow waterway that coursed near the weather-beaten road. Farther away from the little bayou, the woods transformed into a mix of oak, hickory, and pine, and sunlight splintered around us through tree limbs.

I imagined us to be in a forest much like that of the native people who had long ago vanished. Later, in my various studies, I would learn that European diseases had decimated the people who'd once populated this land. The indigenous people had little immunity to such foreign viruses which had slithered well ahead of the white man's main migration.

When Europeans trickled into this region, they looked upon deserted villages and what seemed a virgin hinterland. Possibly that tragic history and ghosts still wandering about caused the anxious twitching of muscles in my belly. I felt myself to be part of an invading force, violating an oath of nonviolence. I shook my head as if to fling sweat out of my eyes. It did no good.

Ahead of me, Buster came to an abrupt halt. "Rattlesnake pilot, hah!" he yelled.

A copperhead sunned itself in a band of sunshine on the forest floor. Buster tossed the end of his pipe to the ground and hastily scavenged a dead limb breached between lower branches of an ancient oak. He jabbed its point at the snake, just scathing its side. The copperhead swiveled for a second through the leaves, then wound into a coil, its head pitched back and ready to strike.

"Now you're dead." Buster drew back his makeshift club.

"Leave that son-of-a-bitch alone," I said. "Ain't hurtin' nobody."

Buster snapped his twitching eyes upon me. For a moment, a fuse lit in the space between us. A strange sensation hit me—sparks sputtering along a slender thread to the point of igniting. I slowed the beat of my heart. Spasms of flesh around Buster's eyes grew still. Sandy stood nearby in the periphery of my vision, holding the other end of the pipe atop his shoulder, shifting from foot to foot. Then a veil peeled back between Buster and me. Something foreign to the man's nature awoke behind those tiny kinetic pits in his eyeballs. He looked askance.

"You're right. It ain't hurtin' nobody." He turned and with the dead limb in hand swished the copperhead on into the foliage depth.

Clifford stood in silence within an overhang of vines. He said to Buster, "Pick up the pipe and let's get on."

An inevitable drop of sweat struck into the corner of my eye. I tried to blink it out and stepped forward through the trees, adjusting the weight of the pipe across my shoulder.

That moment of tension still resonated in the humid air. If Buster had ignored me and drove the point of the limb into the snake, what course would I have taken? Weakness sunk into the regions behind my knees. I didn't know what action I would have taken. I dwelled upon Buster's ultimate act, him swishing the snake back into the wooded depths where it belonged.

By mid-morning, our pipe-laying had reached the crumbling roadside. At that point, a shallow ditch paralleled the road for about half the length of a football field. It then cut a straight path through the trees before meeting an untended field where the tall derrick of the drilling rig rose above dense woodland. While we continued to roust pipe from the flatbed trailer of a diesel truck and set the joints in the roadside trench, Blackie wandered back toward the bayou, inspecting our work.

I'm sure his ear was cocked to the side, always listening for the haunting cry of one of his panthers. I didn't hear the pickup truck lumber in behind us. My half-shut eyes burned with sweat.

Sandy and I had shouldered a length of pipe and begun to tread up the roadside through the mottle of shade and sun. I led the way. We drew close to the next drop-off point. Tiny gravel crunched underfoot.

Sandy said my name in sort of an alarmed whisper. The earth shifted. A wave of dizziness crossed over my brow. I felt something bad was coming, but what it was to be hovered like a blinding point of light.

Behind me, Sandy dropped his end of the pipe. It made a thunk sound when it hit the ground. I wheeled around, sliding my end of the section down my shoulder.

The pickup truck rolled up just abreast me, its side window down, and a man in the driver's seat pointed a gun in my face. The scene lit through my mind like an electrical flash. I didn't believe it was real. The man's right hand gripped the top of the steering wheel. He held the long barrel revolver in his other hand just above the open window.

"You be the seduction," he said.

I tried to blink out the sweat in my eyes, and for a moment, the man's s face came into clear focus. An atlas for a forehead, cropped hair, pinkish, freshly shaven skin, a small mouth with sensual lips that were aflush with the undercurrent of blood.

"Step back now."

I stepped back a few feet from the pipe trench. He had not commanded me, but I removed my oil field hat, dropped it at my feet and clasped the top of my head with my gloved hands, then lowered myself to my knees. A replication of the position taken by the NVA soldier I'd shot in the head.

He turned off the ignition of the truck and unlatched the door. It gave a grated click into the silence that was consuming me. My awareness tunneled onto his bulk, slipping off the edge of the truck seat. The smell of his skin came with him, ivory soap, aftershave lotion, the faint reek of cigar smoke. He wore oversized dress pants, black, spit-shined boots, a Sears-Roebuck-type shirt patterned with ducks in flight. The barrel of the gun kept fixed upon me. I wished at that moment for Frank's wisdom, his voice to explain to me this sensation of deliverance that comes with the approach of absolution coupled with the utter regret of having to die too soon.

"Mister, you needn't do that now. You needn't…"

Clifford's muted voice rose, came through the thick air like a sad song. I shut my eyes.

"Clifford, all of you drop back!" The words coughed up from my throat.

The man struck me with the flank of the gun across my ear and temple. The position of my arms as I held my hands clasped over my head saved me from the maximum impact of the force. He'd had to abbreviate his swing. But I toppled to the ground on my side and for a few seconds entered an ether world that resounded with the harangue of a fire alarm bell.

"You dead if you move!" That's what I believe he yelled to Clifford and the others who stood stunned by the road. I grasped it all through a dim layer of consciousness. The toe of his boot thudded into the side of my neck.

That's how the beating began.

The assault clouded into softness, the world dimly lit, and each strike into my body, whether delivered by fist or foot, softened even more. Adrenalin washed through and absorbed the boot and fist blows like the padded leather of a boxing glove.

My breath had left me with the strike to my throat, but as he beat me it came back in a siphoning whoosh. The pummeling stopped. Like a deflated jack-in-the-box figure with some life still in its coiled spring, I pushed myself back up to my knees and wavered into the position of hands atop my head. Though later, Sandy would tell me that I'd barely managed to raise them to the height of my ears. Of course, there was no thought on the matter in my state of bare consciousness. But upon years of reflection, I've concluded that the absolution that this man was gifting me had to be done right. And to do it right, it was necessary to assume the position of the soldier I'd killed—it was essential to be on my knees. The quest for college, books, learning, and purpose had no relevance in this short stretch of time. The date of payment for my sins of war had come. All else in life dissolved away.

Out beyond the circumference of my vision was a place possessed of tobacco stink, cardinal song, a pair of legs cloaked in baggy slacks, a .357 handgun clutched in a hairy hand wagging back and forth in front of my puffy face. My breath rasped.

Then came Blackie's gravelly voice, "You need to get on down the road, mister."

Even in my half-lit state of awareness, I couldn't help but admire the steadiness of Blackie's voice. Its underlying message demanded that no other option existed. You had to move on down the road, mister.

The man's knee flashed up like a piston pump and struck the side of my jaw. The light that had stayed with me went out then. All the background sounds of this daunting world went with it. When it yawed back, the first sense of my body that sought to reconnect with my surroundings was taste. The grittiness of gravel burned into the corner of my mouth. Voices stirred above me and the back-and-forth exchange between them went something like this (later corroborated by Sandy): "Get on in your truck and git," Blackie drawled.

"This piece of shit dares to tempt my angels." Each word seethed through the man's teeth.

Blackie had moved within a few feet of the man and the gun was now pointed straight at his barrel of a chest, according to what would be Sandy's lavish report.

And then came Sandy's voice, sappy and nervous. "He was trying to be of assistance, Mr. Whitehead."

Whitehead fired off a shot. The gunshot reverberated in concussive waves down the road and through the trees. He'd aimed to the right of Sandy's shoulder and the bullet fed into old-growth pine and oak.

"Git in your truck and go," Blackie drawled.

I lay on my side and winked through a scrim-like haze. A short distance in front of Whitehead's legs, Blackie stood as firm and contemplative as a bull. My vision rested on his open hand, the size of a ham hock, it rubbing his chest in a hypnotic rotation.

"Git on down the road," Blackie said. "Your angels are waitin' for you."

My knee drew up to my waist. I hadn't willed it to do so, but I took its lead and began propping myself back up into that rightful position to receive my sacrament of penance in the form of a gunshot to the head.

"Half-Pint, stay down there," Blackie said.

I struggled up, it being the only time I will have ever disobeyed Blackie.

My chin pointed upward at Whitehead's face, his flesh pinkishly aflame. He had his eyes directed into Blackie, the gun fixed straight into Blackie's chest, and I said, "Here it is…"

I'm pretty sure that's what I said and, again, Sandy later confirmed my pathetic utterance. Sandy stood a few yards beyond Blackie, hands extended in front of him as if waiting to receive a box of groceries. Buster and Clifford were farther down now, sprawled flat on the road's edge.

"Git on down the road, Mister Whitehead," Blackie said. "Git on now."

The latch on the truck door clicked. My vision sharpened for a moment. Whitehead stood tall and wiry beside the open door. His eyes glared down upon me in that sheer angle of righteous vengeance. A wriggling of his puffy lips. "My angels shall not be corrupted. Of that, I swear."

"Here…" I said.

He swung himself into the truck cab and latched shut the door behind him. Nothing hurried in his movements. Bars of sunlight crisscrossed the fading paint job of the truck's body and accentuated a swath of hairline scratches just below the rise of the bed. He switched on the ignition and the engine rumbled low like a taunting predator. The vehicle rolled forward, gravel cracking beneath the tires. Within the scope of three breaths, he dissolved down the corridor of these woodlands, leaving nothing but exhaust fumes to burn into my nostrils. The hollow thumping of a woodpecker and the oblivious, far away revving and fading engine sounds of the bulldozer at the rig site flowed into the hollowness that had taken me over.

Confusion can trek down many paths. On looking back, it's worth mentioning that I came out of Vietnam, as many of us who had engaged in multiple bouts of combat, in malady of having survived. Survival guilt is shuffled around in conversation in well-known terms these days—part of our standard vocabulary of eternal war. But back then, in the late '60s of Vietnam, it seemed a rather new idea. Guilt was a vexation for many grunts having come out of the war on the side of the living. We just didn't know how to describe it, especially when you had taken keen sight upon the evil within yourself and hungered silently for penance.

Looking back, I can clearly see my perverse desire for Whitehead to have put a bullet through my head. Next to that crumbling road, stationed on my knees, chin uplifted, I'd offered myself into the waves of karmic payback. Thankfully, Whitehead let me down.

Blackie crouched beside me. The slow rasp of his breath encroached into my blurred state of mind.

"Lower them hands down," he said softly.

I drew my hands down the sides of my face and planted them flat upon my thighs. I sniffed and managed to raise one arm and rub away drainage of mucus with the back of my wrist. Blackie gripped the top of my head. He applied gentle pressure, cocking the side of my face closer to him for inspection. "All right. You goin' to be bruised up pretty nice. Not bleedin' hardly at all. You want the law in on this?"

I shook my head. Sought to slow my breath. I was too unsure of myself to speak. Dizziness came in jagged waves.

Sandy had rushed forth and hovered over the two of us. "It's my fault. Fuck, I should've known it was coming." He pawed his foot upon the ground like a kid on a hot sandy beach. "Damn, Half-Pint. Damn, I brought this shit on. Goddamn me and my stupid ass."

"Be quiet, Sandy," Blackie growled up at him.

"Yes, sir." Sandy groaned. "Goddamn. Goddamn. I should have stopped Half-Pint from helping out that Whitehead woman. Goddamn."

Clifford and Buster emerged just beyond Sandy's bobbing shoulders. Pained, dumbfounded expressions gripped their sunburned faces. A big smudge of iron-red dirt coated the side of Buster's ferret-like face. I almost laughed as I imagined him diving for cover. In the scope of my blurred vision, Clifford stepped up beside Sandy. He held his oil field hat in both hands, his eyes half-shut, his lips wriggling in prayer. Kneeling there, bracing myself, palms planted against the muscles of my thighs, leaning forward into a scurry of dizzying waves, my heart warmed out to these people. And I drew it back in quick, a reflex learned, at least in part from war. Getting close to others carries dangers of its own to which I'd learned not to abide.

"Clifford, you dumb son-of-a-bitch, run back and pull the Impala up. I'm goin' to set Half-Pint in it for a while."

He turned on his heel and sped away, slapping his hat to the top of his head.

"I'm alright." I started the slow push up to my feet.

"You goin' be alright?" Buster said.

Blackie rose with me and kept a firm clutch on my arm.

"Yeah, I'm alright."

"Goddamn. Goddamn." Sandy kept up his mantra of invectives.

"That bastard shot at me."

The earth slowed its jerky spin. I began to trace the surrounding world in more exact detail. The steadying swirl of leafy trees, the pine smell of southern woods, the cawing of crows, and the firm grip of Blackie's hand on my shoulder. Blackie scanned me up and down. Amid my recollections, I believe that I repeated to Blackie that I was okay at least a dozen times before Clifford rumbled the Impala forward onto the side of the road.

Blackie gripped the back of my arm and guided me across the narrow passageway, its width barely capable of accommodating one vehicle. Clifford held the back door open like a limo driver gone nuts. One hand thrust high toward the sky, broken rays of the sun striking Clifford's uplifted face, and him murmuring prayerful thanks. "Merciful Lord, thank thee for sparing this boy's life. Thank thee for sparing all these men's lives…"

"Get them boys back to layin' pipe. We'll be along in a bit," Blackie said.

"Yes, sir," Clifford replied.

The Lord may be above, but Blackie was right here, and Clifford always respected the proper juxtaposition of the two entities. He shuffled off, giving my shoulder a gentle pat as he swept past.

Standing silhouetted against the trees, Sandy had finally grown silent. A flash of awareness hit me as I slid myself across the warm back seat of the car with Blackie's palm pressed against my shoulder. I'd brought this mortar shell down on myself. Crazy as it might seem, I'd crossed a boundary line, failed to appreciate the aberrant rules of violation that existed for some tribes down here. I should have known better.

What drove deep inside myself as I struggled to settle my head against the cushioned backrest, it redolent with the stale, dry scent of oil field workers' sweat, was shame, and alongside it, my old friend, guilt. I'd endangered Sandy, Blackie, Clifford and Buster, men who were focusing their concern on me. That flash of awareness made the world tremble around me.

"Yeah, you're who I thought you were, alright," Blackie said. He shook his head and for a moment the expression on his face went blank. He had planted one boot on the rocker panel below the open door and leaned forward, crossing his arms over his knee. Deep furrows lined his forehead. Small muscles pulsed at his temples. The perpetual stubble that coated his jaw gave more prominence to his presentation of fierceness.

"Sometimes your mama, Ida, had been known to stray cat around. Seymour was pretty tall and you bein' so short. But yeah, you're Seymour's boy alright. Ready to die to make a statement about nothing. But hell, who are we to know who we are?"

The anthracite darkness of his pupils trained on me like those of a man studying the nature of some curious problem. He drawled out his next words even slower than usual. "Yeah, you were ready to take that bullet." He sucked his breath in real slow, then laughed in his deep-throated way.

I stared straight ahead over the rim of the front seat and through the cracked window shield. Stands of century-old oaks lined each side of the road for about a quarter mile down the corridor. Their limbs swirled out and embraced, forming a canopy that cast a blanket of shade across the tunnel they created. My mind was still not set right; some faint buzzing intruded into my senses. Blackie spoke softly, "I'll check on you in about half an hour, Half-Pint."

"I made a vow to hurt nobody no more." As soon as I uttered this proclamation, it sounded pompous and foolish. The words hung in the sultry air like ash.

Outside the open car door, Blackie straightened himself upright, placed his large, calloused hands on the small of his back and stretched. When he leveled his eyes on me once more, he gave a barrel-chested laugh and said, almost sadly, "Don't nobody give a shit, Half-Pint."

He turned and walked away. I watched him for a moment saunter back across the road, my mouth open, the heat growing thicker around my neck. I pushed myself to the side and slid out the back seat. My feet seemed to be farther away than usual, the woods greener and sharper, and bird songs intruded into my conscious mind in a tinny, metallic way. I steadied myself with one arm propped over the top of the door.

"I give a shit."

PERFECT MEAL AND HOW SEYMOUR DIED IN FIRE

Sandy stayed with me that night at the old house on Roosevelt Street. He made a run to the Piggly Wiggly, hauling back a grocery bag filled with round steaks, russet potatoes, iceberg lettuce, and various accouterments to complete a feast. Julie Longo walked alongside him down the root-buckled walkway. I sat on the front steps trying to read through a persistent fog that had beset me since the gun whipping.

The two may as well have been apparitions. The world still beheld a dark aura whereby distance and shape took on unfamiliar measures and textures. I tucked the book away beneath my shirt, held it in place with the palm of my hand. Twilight edged downward and softened the shamble of the mill workers' neighborhood. Venus, the evening star, was trying to press itself into a steady point of light low in the steel-blue sky.

Julie sat down beside me on the concrete step. Her warmth, and what I can best describe now as an electromagnetic force that pulsed from her body, disrupted my ability to breathe. She wore blue jeans, a loose tee-shirt, and white Ked sneakers. A curl of hair on the side of her face damped down onto her cheek.

"Jack, does your stove work?"

I managed to draw a breath. "Yeah."

"Well, I'm cooking for you and Romeo tonight."

Julie leaned over and touched her lips to the high cheekbone below my eye where flesh had swollen into a purple bruise. She stood and took the sack of groceries from Sandy.

"I'll take care of these. Sit with Jack."

Sandy, tall and sunburned in the softening light, lifted his chin and bore a smile as wide as I've ever seen on his boyish face and said with whimsical cadence, "Okay, Miss Julie."

He lowered himself beside me, taking Julie's place as she disappeared into the house, then whispered toward those first twinkles of light above the sycamore trees. "Go ahead and put your book away, Half-Pint. I'm not goin' anywhere."

I touched the side of my sore cheekbone where Julie had pressed her lips.

Sandy leaned back against the stoop, pulled one knee up. "She's the best thing that's ever come into my life, man."

I mumbled, "I'll never, never, never forget the touch of her lips upon my face." And I wouldn't and have not.

Maybe it was the sensation of mist pervading my consciousness that gave the evening an even greater dimension of unreality. Blows from Whitehead's beefy fist and the butt of his gun had rattled some brain cells and probably given origin to the sound of a narrow wind that slipped through the cracks of the house throughout the evening. Neither Sandy nor Julie heeded the slippage of this odd breeze into the rooms that whispered of Ida and Seymour's shouting and screaming over the most piddling of things. Despite these vague hallucinations, I felt happiness. Such a feeling at that kitchen table in the old mill house on Roosevelt Street was unfamiliar, like terrain possibly laden with tripwires.

While Sandy and I lazed back on the front steps, Julie had scrubbed and tossed the potatoes in the oven for baking. Tenderized the steaks by pounding them on the counter with the mouth of an empty Coke bottle, rubbed them deep with salt and pepper, and began frying them in Ida's ancient iron skillet that hadn't felt the torch of flame in years.

When Sandy and I pushed ourselves up and wandered into the kitchen, leaves of iceberg lettuce lay heaped in three bowls. She'd set the table with paired sets of forks and knives that lay in strict repose beside three plates. The windows were raised to full mast, and the back door stood opened wide to draw out the heat. Her skin glowed with perspiration. She hummed what I thought to be a Sinatra tune, *I've Got the World on a String*. Through the screen door, fireflies began to wink and glow in the dusky backyard. Sandy strode over beside Julie where she leaned with her back against the kitchen counter while the steaks sizzled in the skillet. He draped his arm over her shoulder. "Been neglectful. Anything I can do to help?"

She looked up at him. "Just give me a smile." Then she looked straight into me. "I remember you well, Jack. For a while back then, in those days before I left, I regarded you as my best friend."

Goddamn, I thought while the sound of that low wind kept whispering through the cracks of the house.

What was to come was the best meal I've ever had in my life. That which is so ordinary, the camaraderie of three people sitting together, sharing a meal, and talking about life can seem as extraordinary as the aurora borealis to an ex-grunt freshly discharged from the body of the Corps. As we ate together at the old linoleum-surfaced table with its welts from hot coals of cigarette ash gracing its surface, we talked about the meager past in our lives, the slender present, and the vast uncertainties that lay before us.

Julie placed her fork down and spent a long gaze upon me. She spoke as if from someplace far away. "My dreams are so different now, Jack." She looked down at her plate, at her half-eaten steak and bit into her lip. "Well, that's all I'm going to say about that. I don't know where that came from." She laughed and scrunched her lips.

And I do know where the words I was about to speak came from. They flowed down a channel gone awry between my concussed brain and my mouth, the intoxication of just sitting at a dinner table in a warm kitchen on a summer night, the sense of imbalance stemming from my lack of acquaintance with that which is normal in everyday life.

"When I was a boy, I was in love with you."

I spoke those words without shame, without remorse.

Julie giggled and a rosy flush crossed her cheeks. "Well, I was a lot to love back then."

"You still are," Sandy said.

What a grin that sunburned boy could flash into a room lit by a single ceiling light bulb. Julie rolled her vision toward him. Broke into a smile. Tiny muscles rippled ever so faintly in the delicate cleft between her nose and upper lip. Something hit me then, a blast of awareness. I no longer loved Julie Longo. At least not in the way of he who had been Half-Pint Crowe, the kid that fell in love during the tumbling throes of preadolescence. The war burnt away that skinny runt. Out of the ashes had arisen Jack Crowe who didn't have an iota of knowledge about love.

I sat there, straight and true in the table chair, fork and knife in hand, and looked upon Julie and Sandy as if they were beings from another world. They were young and beautiful. My thoughts went into odd little spaces of my racked brain. Fear for the two sharpened in my chest. I worried that they might trip a wire or die in an ambush. Where was I? Not back there. I was in Seymour and Ida's kitchen of my childhood home. I was worried about Sandy and Julie traversing a terrain laden with booby traps.

Maybe this disquiet inside myself was some dimension of a more altruistic love trying to come to be. I didn't want them to get hurt. I wanted to protect them. Oh, Half-Pint, you asinine fuck, I was saying to myself when Julie's voice drew me back. Her voice hit me soft, sad, and seemed to echo toward me in the warm air.

"Mom saw your daddy die, Jack. I can tell you about it sometimes if you wish. What Mom said to me. You let me know, hon', if you ever want to know."

A dog barked from far off. Another responded, higher pitched in its yelping. A mockingbird, probably a bachelor harbored in the limbs of the chinaberry tree, began to sing through the dusk.

"Okay, Julie. I'd like to hear someday." I squeezed my lips together and looked down at my scraped clean plate. "From you. Someday. If you can manage it." I rocked back and forth and winced a smile. The evening coursed softly onward.

The late Ida and Seymour Crowe's kitchen transformed for a while that night into a small, vibrant enclave. The worn linoleum floor shifted continuously beneath our feet. We finished washing and drying the dishes and listening to music on an old transistor radio that Sandy confiscated from a closet in Ida and Seymour's room. I hold that part of the night in a prism of warm memory. Julie swaying, scuffing her bare feet to the music of Marvin Gaye, *I Heard it Through the Grapevine*, handing off a wet dish to the lanky soul, Sandy, smitten by love, himself swinging to the music, shoulders dipping and rotating, all the while he wiped the dishware dry.

I practiced my mutated version of the Harlem shuffle, spurred on by Julie's giggles and Sandy's hoots. Then my head went south for a moment, and I swung myself over to my chair and sank in surrender and joy and just gave witness to the foreign exuberance. Marvin Gaye sang into the summer night, his voice tinny through the transistor circuits but still soulful.

"This is fun," Julie said.

She stood over the sink, her hips still swaying to the music, and winked at Sandy. He shut his eyes and rotated his head to the side back and forth while he lip-synced Marvin's words into an imaginary microphone. Julie looked over her shoulder at me. Her face glowed with perspiration. She smiled straight into me, and I read her lips as she mouthed the words that now directed her life: *My dreams are different now, Jack.*

I let the strangeness of this moment in time overtake me. Fun was an exotic animal in this place of peeled wallpaper, uneven wooden floors, and broken windows. And I, being the wretched asshole I was, kicked at it like it was some poor, lost dog who wandered in off the street. I stared at Julie for an interminable minute while the music swung its rhythm through the house. My concussed brain unhooked all control from my mouth. "Will you tell me about my old man dying?" My head flopped a little to the side. "What your mama told you."

"You look pathetic, Half-Pint," Sandy said and turned the dial on the radio, the music dimming.

Julie laid the washcloth over the rim of the sink and came over and sat at the table across from me. She stared at me, studying my eyes as if to determine my degree of coherence. I winked at her.

"I'd like to hear. It's just been hanging in the air."

Julie looked at Sandy, then back at me. Her smile was sweet and sad.

"People gathered together like the mill was a dying friend, Mama said. Nobody knew what would happen. I guess we still don't know what's going to happen to the town though we can see everything starting to dry up and blow away around us."

Julie shied her eyes away from me and said her mother, Blanche, had stood among this crowd of curious folk by the state highway near the plant's main entrance. Despite its rough and grimy extremities, the mill had given lifeblood to the community. Had woven opportunity into the parish. Now, it was about to be eternally silenced. The company had broken the union. People faced the realization that forces beyond them were at work. Powers driven by needs for efficiency and profit, though hefty profits still showed on balance sheets. The people, being who they were, accepted it mostly. Even blamed themselves. Somehow, they hadn't done enough to keep it all going.

Townsfolk had come to see the smoke cease its last breath from the monolith smokestack that was as sanctified as a church steeple in the town. Those who arrived stood somberly along the roadside among the weeds and litter of rusting soda cans, Styrofoam cups and candy wrappers.

"Your daddy drove up and parked on the side of the road down from the crowd. He got out holding a big ol' duffel bag in his hand. Mama hadn't seen him in a while. She said he looked worn down and frail. Mama thought he might have been sick, but then she determined he must have been heartbroken. He'd headed up the local chapter of the pipe fitter's union and was taking it hard." Julie looked at me, her face shining in the light.

"I'm alright," I said.

Sandy stood against the kitchen counter with his arms crossed. He looked at me and, for once, was absent of his dumb smile.

"Well, I'll go on then." Subtle dimples of flesh quivered above Julie's lips. "He went past everyone and stepped around the metal barricade by the security gate. He headed across that long driveway that leads up to the big arched door at the mill's main center. Mama said company men had chained it shut the week before, but Seymour aimed for it. Then she heard the gate guard, some fellow in his security uniform garb, yell out for your daddy to stop. He had a shotgun in hand and a pistol sidearm in a holster on his hip. Mama said he yelled louder, 'Where you heading? You need to stop!'

Then the man stepped away from the gate station and another guard stepped out and faced the crowd lined up along the road. The first guard started walking fast toward Seymour and fired off a shotgun shell in the air. He chambered another shell, and he was mad, screaming, 'Now you stop it! Goddamn, I'll blow it into you next time! I don't want to do that!'

Seymour had stopped, stood still, and turned around. Mama said he was shaking his head and heard him yell out, 'Can I nail something on the 'ministration door?'

The guard yelled back, 'Put down that bag and get yourself here!'

Mama said everybody around her, including herself, held their breaths, muttering what the hell is going on, some people even crying. One of Seymour's union brothers called out to him, 'Stop being crazy before you get shot!'"

Julie looked over her shoulder at Sandy. He was unable to offer her anything.

"I need to hear it from you," I said. I smiled reassuringly, and I did want to hear it like I had to get it into me, so I could finally grab hold of it and get it out of me.

Julie shrugged her shoulders into her neck, closed her eyes, opened them, and went on.

"Seymour set the duffel bag on the ground, unzipped it and pulled from it what looked like a large can of paint thinner. But it was gasoline. He'd rigged the spout so that when he turned the can up and onto himself, it flooded over him."

Julie looked directly at me. Her eyes were green, bright, and shining, just like I remembered when she had looked at me inside the honeysuckle hedge.

"The guard started running at him. Mama thought he would try and knock Seymour over and save him from lighting himself with the cigarette lighter he'd pulled out, but the guard got knocked back by the flame. And that was how it came to an end. I'm so sorry I asked if you wanted to hear the story."

Julie was crying. I felt awful for her. For myself, the low wind that whispered through the cracks of the house grew louder in my head. In silence, I asked of my old man, *To what meaning and purpose did you sacrifice?* Smoke blew past my eyes.

"I wanted to hear it. I'm grateful."

"He wanted to hear it, Julie. Half-Pint wouldn't have asked if he hadn't wanted to hear it. I know Half-Pint. He wouldn't have asked if he didn't want to hear it."

Julie straightened her spine against the back of the chair. She drew in her breath and exhaled slowly. "Everything went hush-hush. Like some invisible hand had crossed over everybody's eyes and rid them of its memory. Not even the local paper reported on it. Not even the goddamn local paper."

A leaden weight had built into my eyelids.

"Now it's in your head and I don't know if that's to be good or bad for you. But damn, it's not invisible." She reached across the table and touched the back of my wrist. "Be kind to yourself, hon'."

For me, Half-Pint Crowe, it was a night of Julie's kiss upon my cheek, the warmth of a feast with friends entering my life, a shuffle of dance and moving song from Marvin Gaye, and the strength to hear the story of my old man's death from Julie, my friend. It was at this point a perfect evening, but not finished.

NOT FINISHED

At precisely half-past ten, Julie asked Sandy to take her home. "I told Ma I'd be home early. I'm not into making her worry anymore."

I walked with them to the front door and stood on the lower step as they made their way to Sandy's Chevy parked by the side of the street. The moon loomed as a bright crescent barely visible through the limbs of the sycamore trees. Above the treetops spread the illumination of stardust. My insignificance bore down on me out of that mysterious firmament and, for a second, released me from all concerns about the world. I wished Frank was here so that I might ask him about this momentary sensation of escape. I'm sure he would have said something that I'd been unable to grasp at that time, something like, "It's a paradox, Jack. The smaller we see ourselves in this vast universe, the freer we become."

An ignition switch flicked on, then the sputter and guttural roar of a truck engine broke through the night. The truck crept past along the street in front of the house. Shadows glided across the yard from the truck's headlights. Sandy and Julie stood hand-in-hand in the small front yard and the truck's lights swept across them. The vague outline of Whitehead in the driver's seat materialized in my vision. The orange glow of a lit cigarette floated in the darkness of the truck cab. Sandy and Julie watched the vehicle roll by as if some instinct had risen through their bones and compelled them to be still and silent while the predator slid past. The taillights dimmed in the distance. Shadows cast by the beams of the truck disappeared. Sandy turned around and faced me. I could hear blood pumping through my veins.

"That was Whitehead," Sandy said. "What the fuck, Half-Pint?"

"He's not letting go," I said.

"I'll be back," Sandy said.

"Go on in and get to bed, Jack," Julie said in a commanding, mother-like way. She took hold of the back of Sandy's arm and guided him away to the car. Sandy started his Chevy. Its lights flashed on and broke out more shadows across the grass. As the two drove away, I said again to myself, "He's not letting go." This thought sunk through me—I can't give the son-of-a-bitch much more, and I felt bad for thinking it.

That night I went to the floor. I pulled the pillow from the bed and propped it against the floorboard beneath the window. The side lamp cast just enough light for me to read. I lay fully clothed and stared at the blood-stained pages of Frank's book without seeing the words. They couldn't draw me in. Instead, old forces towed my thoughts inward into primitive spaces. Inside them, the urge to strike back at Whitehead, to act with violence, arose like a cat that had just awakened and begun to lick its paws. The shaking commenced. Wave upon wave of inner chills. Outside, my hands held steadily to the ragged covers of the book. I didn't want to lose my way on this path that Frank had set me on. But it felt too fucking complicated. This trying to understand all the crazy shit. Beneath my breath, I proclaimed to the spartan room, "I'm too weak to resist the temptations of this world."

Outside the window, katydids chirruped with escalating madness. I'd not comprehended one sentence of the page when I heard Sandy's footsteps on the floor outside my room. He stood at the doorway and gave a tilt to his head as he stared at my sprawled position beneath the window.

"I got Julie home okay. You not getting crazy on me down there, are you, Half-Pint?"

"No," I said and closed Frank's book. I angled my gaze on Sandy and tried to dim the fierceness that I imagined burned in my eyes. "I don't think the man is ever going to let go. I think he's of that kind, and I'm sorry for it."

Sandy shook his head. He crossed his arms and leaned against the side jamb of the door.

"Heard that he once tried to kiss a copperhead. Show his faith to the Lord at some big revival gathering. Got bit on the lip. Must have been quite a show but he rode it out and came to say the one and only God had kissed him with new life. His lot was to guard the flock against the temptations of Satan. He's one of those old boys that makes me nervous. Don't tell anybody I said that." Sandy bowed his head and scrunched up his face to emphasize his command.

"I won't." I thought I could hear Sandy breathing but wasn't sure it was my own breath.

"You got to keep it let go, even if he don't," he said.

"You might want to keep some distance from me."

Sandy chuckled. "Distance don't matter in the way of the Lord. Don't be doing anything stupid, Half-Pint. Mind if I use that spare bed you got?" He pushed himself away from the doorjamb, stretched, and made his way to Ida and Seymour's old bedroom.

"Say goodnight to Ida and Seymour for me," I said.

From the narrow depths of the hallway, he called back above the sound of his boots creaking across the wood floor, "Nothing scares me, Half-Pint, and I'm a boy in love." Two slow breaths came and went. "Don't be thinking no crazy thoughts, Half-Pint."

I lay there for a while longer and let the ancient rhapsody of the katydids quell the aftermath of my deafening thoughts. Silence now emanated from the house. I placed the book down by my side and stood up. Soreness shot through my jaw socket. Standing in the lamp's diffuse rays, I cupped my chin in the palm of my hand. The paint-peeled door of the closet called upon me to open it.

On the shelf far back, the ammunition canister that held Seymour's most prized possession bequeathed to me on the day before my departure to the holy brotherhood of the Marines awaited in its dark corner. I drug it toward me and held the canister in my hands, testing its weight before unlatching the lid. Inside, all was the same as on that day of presentation when father presented son the tool of violence, the coveted handgun of the United States Marine Corps that he'd confiscated during the Pacific campaigns.

The .45 lay wrapped in a work rag. A box of shells was wedged into a corner of the ammo box. The rag came easily undone from around the gun and fell away to the floor. I placed the empty canister back on the shelf. Gun in hand, I dropped the magazine from its well, raked back the slide and checked the chamber. It was empty. The .45 remained in my grip for a moment as if it possessed some power of volition beyond my own.

I retrieved the rag, swaddled it back over the gun, and knotted the loose ends together. I returned it to its place of sanctuary and clamped shut the lid and shoved the box across the shelf against the buttress of the wall. The cool floor welcomed me back.

Frank's book, delicate and tender, came into my hands. I parted the pages where I'd reached near the very end and began to read, and there the message within came stalking me: *Calmness, gentleness, silence, self-restraint, and purity: these are the disciplines of the mind.*

Fuck, I had none of these things. No vessel to tote them, no material to build them, not one fucking tool to shape them. The quest I had set upon belongs to a different kind of animal. Those born with the strength to resist the call of their weaknesses. I'm trying not to slip.

I put the book away to my side, a slight tap with my fingertips to give it my apologies for my shortcomings. I arose once more and turned out the light and lay back upon the bare floor. Seymour came to mind, though I tried to push him away. The more I pushed, the more he came. As his son, I knew him not to have been significantly bent on analyzing the complexities of life. My old man had been what my fellow Marines would have called a salt of the old Corps, a true grunt, a bloodied survivor of the Peleliu and Okinawa Island campaigns. I wished Seymour and I might have had time for a simple tête-à-tête over a glass of whiskey to compare our combat experiences. I imagine that I would have been straight with him. "I wouldn't do it again, Pop. I wouldn't go." In the wildest of such fantasies, he grins, clicks my glass with his own and says, "Son, now you fuckin' know." We become not father and son, but brothers.

Though the air of the room was warm and humid and a mosquito sirened near my ear, I trembled as if lying naked on a shelf of ice. Sleep did come that night after all the shaking and pathetic grunting in my throat played out. And guess who wandered into the quirky shadows of my dreams—ol' Seymour, who'd lost all meaning and purpose and lit himself up like some hari-kari soldier of the Rising Sun.

Hell, it was my own damn fault that he'd showed up. I'd willingly taken Julie's offer and asked her to send him to me. It was but a brief visit while I slept, just mere seconds across an unassigned frame of my dreams. Seymour presented himself, swallowed by an effulgence of flames. A sooty duffel bag off to the side. Inside it, a rolled-up sign made of placard paper—*America, You Failed Us.*

TRUCK ON SIDE OF THE ROAD

Blackie's eyes held onto me for long moments during the week that followed the gun-whipping I took from Whitehead. I felt them burning into the back of my neck. When I'd lay down the wrench or the broom or the pipe and turn to face him, he'd ply those eyes deeper into me, dark slits set into his broad face with its high, stubbled cheeks, measuring me, as if trying to unravel a strange problem.

Adding to my vexation with his probing stare would be Sandy's private conversations with the man, his oil field hat held in his hand while he wiped his forehead with the sleeve of his tee-shirt, nodding his head toward me in some half-witted surreptitious gesture.

Come on, Sandy, you numb nuts, I can see you standing there, still, proclaiming your indulgent fears to Blackie that Half-Pint might go crazy and try to kill that motherfucking Whitehead and unleash his demonic vile upon the world.

That week I welcomed the harried tripping of pipe in and out of the hole when I could take the spin chain and whip the hate out of myself and around the pipe with a flick of my wrist. I say again, without embarrassment, I was good with the spin chain. Never could I convey with satisfaction to my professorial colleagues, usually after quaffing a few beers, the exaltation I would feel hearing Blackie Shively shout above the roar of the rig, "Now that's how to fling a spin chain! That's my boy! Y'all working like a team now!"

Sweat would flow into the grins on Sandy's and Clifford's faces, and from up above, high on the monkey board, Buster would howl in unaccustomed glee. And for me, the gnawing desire to kill a man would subside to the size of a grain of salt on the back of my tongue.

On the eighth day after the gun-whipping incident, we finished our day tower shift on the rig. Blackie's stern observations of my behaviors and moods had decreased a fraction with each day, as did Sandy's clandestine, but woefully apparent, consultations with the driller. The roughnecks of the evening tower arrived to take over our shift. The usual good-natured ribbing ensued between the guys on the fresh crew and us as they assumed control of rig operations.

We piled into Blackie's car. I leaned my head back against the backseat and waited for some cool air from the air conditioner vents to break through the oppressive heat. We bumped along the dirt corridor from the oil rig, and Blackie swung the Impala onto the paved road that cut through the parish's remote woodlands.

Whitehead's truck stood parked on a narrow apron of gravel by the road's left side thirty yards ahead. He leaned against the hood and held a rifle or shotgun in the crook of his arms. The boy sat on the open tailgate and seemed intent on studying the motion of his dangling feet. A Doberman sat upright beside the boy, its head uplifted, front paws forward, chain collar loose around its neck.

Blackie said nothing but drove straight down the road in the direction of the truck. He rolled down his window. The rest of us had ceased breathing and fastened ourselves into silence. As we came abreast of Whitehead's truck, the boy's eyes lifted and seemed to take due account of Blackie though he kept his chin angled downward. The Doberman beside him rose onto all four paws.

We rolled past at a crawl. Blackie's eyes fastened onto those of the boy. A sad grin edged up the old driller's stubbled cheeks. The boy crinkled his nose and tucked his chin deeper into his throat. From my seat, wedged against the backseat door, I looked toward Whitehead. He held his head cocked to the side and spied upon the Impala with a sniper's gaze. It was a shotgun that rested in the crook of his arm.

He's looking for a flash, I thought—*something to unleash upon*. We must have enemies to feed our lust. I sucked in my breath.

Once past Whitehead's truck, Blackie rolled his window up. "Get me a rock and roll station, Clifford C. Bowles."

There came a series of long exhalations. Crammed into the middle of the backseat between Buster and myself, Sandy shifted his legs and murmured a seething expletive, "Shit."

Clifford didn't respond to Blackie in his usual quick manner of feigned offense. His jaw worked back and forth. He clutched it between thumb and finger and muttered, "No, sir. There shall be no indulgence of rock and roll. No, sir."

Then the world seemed to flip over. Blackie struck the brakes hard, and though we had been moving at a gradual pace, our bodies flung forward and back. Blackie's hands pounded on the steering wheel. He whipped the Impala to the left side of the road, hit the brake again, and reversed the car back across the road in a mad fling of gravel. My shoulder slammed against Sandy then recoiled into the side of the door with Sandy tossing into me. The smell of sweat, the flare of body heat rushed over my senses.

Cliff released a pathetic cry of protest from the front passenger seat, "No-o-o sir-r-r!"

We swept past Whitehead's truck. Gravel popped beneath the tires, clacking into the wheel wells. The engine ground into a roar. Blackie had shot us into a different world. One riled with contempt. A place rife with the taunt of all things dangerous. In it, Buster yelled, "Goddamn you, Blackie! What the hell you doing?"

Cliff and Sandy had latched onto silence and disbelief and I gulped for air. I looked over my shoulder. Through the jittery frame of the rear window, Whitehead slid into the cab of his truck. The boy and dog scrambled farther back onto the truck bed.

The Impala careened down the flimsy road and a windstorm seemed to engulf us. The trees swept by in a blur. Buster clinched a white-knuckled hand over the top of the seat in front of him. Cried out once more, "Blackie! Goddamn you!"

Sandy's blue eyes flashed into mine for a moment and mine into his, then we looked away, our heads bobbing up and down to the bumpy ride. In the front passenger seat, Clifford sat with his eyes shut. His lips, in undulant motion, implored the protection of some God that the kind, gentle man would never abandon.

Blackie blew the car past the dirt offshoot that led to the rig. The narrow bridge that crossed the creek haunted by tall cypress trees swept past the side window. I knew at that moment Blackie's destination. The Impala hurled forward in the direction of Whitehead's domain where that fanatic's heart had beat the most on this fragile planet. Whitehead's home stood somewhere ahead near this disintegrating artery through the swampland. The realization struck hard into my harried consciousness. Blackie intended to roust Whitehead's madness. Violation of mine moral rules must be met with rabid vengeance, sayeth Whitehead. And Blackie, in his own peculiar way, suffered from a madness just as perverse as the man who now pursued us. Don't fuck with me, sayeth Blackie.

Everyone sealed themselves into a silent space. Blackie didn't let up on the gas pedal. If a deer had leaped onto the road before us, it would have died in an instant of horrific brutality and we along with it. With each glance I managed to take through the rear window, Whitehead's truck did not appear, only the road's narrowing tunnel lay behind us. Maybe three minutes ticked past, then Blackie slowed the car.

In his undefinable way, Sandy said, "Blackie, don't make me late to see Julie." His attempt at humor hung suspended in the car's stale air.

Blackie pulled off the road onto a narrow dirt drive that sliced through a dense grove of trees. A trim house stood at the end of it about fifty yards away. He shifted down quickly and stopped the car. The engine idled and heatwaves rose off the hood. A spine of tufted grass coursed down the middle of the long dirt drive aiming straight at the isolated house that stood back in the shadows of the trees. White siding and red roof shingles. A gallery with hanging pots of various plants. Crepe myrtle shrub, stoked with pink blossoms, stood tall along the edge of its yard. A neatness graced it all.

"That's where the world ends," Blackie said ruefully. Then the son-of-a-bitch sucked on a tooth as if the time for contemplation of universal mysteries were bestowed upon him alone.

Clifford's lips continued to move in their ultimate beseeching of protection from a roaming god. Buster clutched the top of the front seat with one hand, purple veins trying to burst through the sunburnt skin above his knuckles. In his other hand, he clasped a knife he'd supposedly unsheathed from the scabbard around his ankle. For a dire second, I thought he aimed to thrust the blade into Blackie's neck, but his wild eyes twitched back and forth as if seeking to comprehend the approach of predators from outside. I knew something now of Buster. He'd use the knife if he got the chance to get in close to his assailant. When cornered by death, he wouldn't squeal and die of fright but would fight back viciously. Buster could be the most dangerous of all creatures triggered by the fierce desire to survive. I was glad he was here.

"You going to make me late, Blackie," Sandy said.

And I tried to breathe, waiting for what felt to be that final descent of rockets and mortars, humbling me in the harshest of terms. Not knowing if they'll hit wide or close.

Blackie said, "Well, it's about time to head back." The engine rumbled. He shifted into reverse and began to slowly back the Impala out onto the road and aimed the car back down the narrow corridor from which he'd just sped the Impala. Whitehead's truck emerged in the distance. Blackie's foot remained light upon the accelerator and the car crawled forward.

"Let us git, goddamn it!" Buster spat out the command.

The Impala kept up its crawl forward. The approaching vehicle grew more distinct inside a tunnel formed by the overlap of tree limbs from the oaks along the roadside. Whitehead's truck drew upon us and, it also, began to slow. The rumble of its engine lowered to a soft throb. Whitehead's stern face materialized through the truck's front windshield like some bust of sculptured art atop a pedestal. There were no eyes to it, but the man's head turned toward the Impala slowly moving past. No shotgun emerged. Then we were past him, and I saw the boy crouched in the back bed of the truck, his arms wrapped around the neck of the dog. The boy, unlike his father, had eyes bright, round, and shining with fear. Longing was within them, and they fastened beseechingly upon the burly driver of the Impala.

Blackie accelerated the car to a reasonable speed and flicked the air conditioner lever to full blast. He spoke as if giving himself a thoughtful lecture. "That man knows where the fence lines are. Cruel and mean all over the place but just inside his God-given boundaries."

The light whooshing sound of air-conditioned air through the cooling vents spent a false calm into the vehicle's odorous interior. I sank farther down into the spring-broken seat.

"Goddamn you, Blackie Shively," Buster mumbled. The knife was gone from his hand. He'd slipped it back into the leather sheath strapped to his ankle. Buster leaned a little forward with his head turned toward me from his position on the opposite end of the back seat.

"Half-Pint, the law needs to be in on this. That man won't let go. His nature is such." He licked his cracked lips. His voice carried an underlying sentiment of concern meant for me. Buster would always tend to confound my accounting of him.

"I'll take care of it."

From within the rearview mirror, Blackie's eyes flicked upon me.

Clifford's prayer vigil had ceased. He looked over his shoulder from his privileged position in the passenger seat. The sides of his lips carved downward into deep crevices. "Mind you, Jack Crowe. Mind you."

"Half-Pint has made a vow," Blackie said and shifted the clutch. The car sped faster down the road through the woodlands. "Haven't you, Half-Pint? Going to college, get some learning, and make us all proud."

Muscles knotted in my throat. I realized what I'd just said. I'd take care of it? How staunched I was in my old ways. I stuttered, "Yes, sir, I've made a vow."

The back of Blackie's head crinkled into a ridge of crevices. A rusty patch of scab from the wound served him by the blow from Clifford's wrench during my first night on the rig still lay exposed through thinning hair at the back of his skull.

"Don't be suckered into doing foolish things by the likes of such a man," he said.

"I made a vow to take Julie to the picture show this Friday night." Sandy's grin beamed at the side of my head.

"The name of Whitehead's boy is Theodore," Blackie said. "Just like mine. Imagine that. Goes by Teddy."

The Impala continued its jarring route. Sunlight and shadows streamed across the window glass upon which I now rested my head.

Clifford murmured to Blackie, "You've talked to that boy?"

"He's a fine boy. He's heard my panther screaming in the woods past midnight. Swears he saw her once moving through the moonlight. He's a fine boy."

"Well, I guess that's alright. You've talked to the boy?"

"Yes, I've talked to the boy. He's a fine boy. Don't ask me again."

Christ, I thought and pressed the side of my head harder against the warm window. Blackie's nonsense about the boy and the panther rifted through my unsettled state and was gone. Buster sniffed and coughed. Sandy poked my arm with his elbow, gave me that dumb, innocent, shit-eatin' grin that only a good ol' Southern boy can provide, and said, "*True Grit*. Julie wants me to take her Friday night."

I could hold back these urges building inside myself. It would all come to pass, transform into a calm sea. Whitehead knew boundaries. Blackie, in his own deranged manner, was trying to tell me so.

When Sandy and I got back to the house on Roosevelt Street, the summer sun blazed about a thumbnail length above the horizon. The sound of water flowed from the bathtub faucet. Sandy stirred about in his newly adopted quarters that had been the bedroom of Ida and Seymour. I took a cold beer from the fridge. With Frank's book in hand, I went out the front door and settled down on the deck of the steps and leaned back against the wooden railing. It had become my favored reading place whereby the intensity of the day's heat would exhale its last breath, begin to cool around me as I disappeared into the pages. The aftermath of the incident on the upper parish road was receding alongside the descent of a reddish sun.

The book held in my soiled hand was a novel, penned by a man whose name I couldn't pronounce—W. Somerset Maugham. I liked the title, *The Razor's Edge*. Shrapnel shards had partially segmented the faded blue cover. Several letters of the book's title posed as mutilated symbols, the *r* in Razor's, the *dg* in Edge, but enough remained to garnish the title's meaning.

Sandy pushed back the screen door and stepped out onto the narrow concrete stoop. He wore clean jeans and a tee-shirt at least one size too small. His fresh-scrubbed skin glowed in the softening light. He ran his long fingers through his hair.

"I'm not goin' to be late after all. Supper with Julie and her mama. You're on your own tonight, boy." He threw back the metal lid of the letterbox by the doorway and pulled out a light blue envelope. Held within both hands, he stared at it for a long moment. "This is for you, Half-Pint."

He jiggled the letter in front of my face. I reached to take it, but he snapped it back and wove it back and forth beside his ear.

"Just fuckin' with you, Half-Pint." He lowered it again directly in front of my eyes. I took a drink of beer. Set the cold bottle beside my outstretched legs and, once more, reached for the letter. Sandy again jerked it back, flicking it in his hand. Goddamn that boy's effusive smile. I tried not to laugh.

"One more time, motherfucker." I lowered my voice and struck an element of threat through it.

"Damn, you're a scary fucker, Half-Pint." He stood above me. Tossed his arms and shoulders about in mock fright. Then he dropped the envelope into my open hand. His mind, with its ephemeral attention span akin to the flight of a frenetic butterfly, flew away elsewhere. He shuffled past me down the steps.

"I respect her with body and soul, man. Just kissed the girl. Damn, what's a roughneck like me to do? I worship that girl. Don't give a damn who knows."

"Okay," I said to the back of his head and watched him hurry on and disappear into his Chevy. The car's hood still glinted in the dying rays of the sun. He started the engine and rumbled past on up the minor street bordered by simple wood-frame homes, paint flaking off their sides, a few with windows sealed off with plywood, an occasional magnolia or oak tree standing firm in the unkempt yards.

The creep of poverty had begun to twine its way through the neighborhoods of Baptiste. That's what I was thinking with that letter in my hand. I was thinking about the people of this place, about change, about the whim of luck. Does the mill stay or leave? It goes and is gone. Burn myself to a crisp or plod on? Do I step left or right off the trail? A thin envelope was in my hand. My heart sped as if I crouched under starlight and watched shadowy enemy silhouettes easing toward me through a forest of bamboo. The letter dampened between my fingers. My heart beat differently inside my chest. A strange kind of fear settled into my stomach.

I peeled back the sealed flap and unfolded the page within. An official acceptance letter to Louisiana State University hung from between my thumb and finger. Inner chills passed through me— happiness and fear all mixed together. Damn, I thought and folded the letter and slid it within the back pages of the book. I resumed my reading of Somerset Maugham's novel, wanting to take advantage of summer's long light. Only the first few pages, pocked by shrapnel and splotched oxen-red, confounded my grasp of every paragraph.

I discerned early on that it was a story about a young man's search for meaning. Are we all searching for purpose? I asked of myself. Is it as simple as that?

At the end of another strange day, my heart beat slow and steady. The air was soft, warm, and heavy around me. The bottle of beer was cold beside my outstretched leg. Within its forest of tattered pages, Frank's book enchanted me. I was alive at this moment. Never to be tempted again into violence. Somewhere down this road would be purpose and meaning.

VENGEANCE FADING BUT CAME A PISSING MAN AND JULIE TOUCHED

For the next three days the specter of Whitehead's vengeance faded. No one had sighted the man, his boy, Doberman, or frail wife since he'd stationed himself by the roadside with a shotgun in the crook of his arm and levelled hard eyes into us as we passed by, and Blackie flung his contempt at him.

My thoughts had begun to swing easier back and forth like the diminishing oscillation of a see-saw swing. Whitehead was just a human being who must blow and bluster, taste some blood and, at long last, be satisfied with what he got. The man is like any other who eventually will tire of pursuit. Not like the enemy I knew for the last four years of my life, always out there just within the trees or beyond the wire, probing, reaching to grab your belt buckle and knife you. Wiry fellows I'd grown to respect. A bit of arrogance slipped through the cracks. *Fuck Calvin Whitehead*, I thought. *He is nothing, as enemies go.*

The soreness and swelling in my face abated in small degrees. A beautiful letter stating my acceptance into college rested inside the pages of one of Frank's books. At work, I absorbed the energy of the sun and savored the quest for a steady paycheck I'd add to the school fund. Such dreaminess assuaged the storm of apprehension that had been wrought upon me by Whitehead. I liked the sting of sweat in my eyes, the taste of cold water out of the metal cooler, the clanking and roaring of the rig's motors, the demands that came of hard work—then home to read, rest, dream some more, and back at it the next day.

When the half-light of morning brushed against my bedroom window and the alarm clock jolted into my senses, it was like the beginning of any other day during this time. Mockingbirds in the chinaberry trees outside the window mimicked the cries of blackbirds, orioles, and jays. In my semi-consciousness, I imagined them at play with the cresting sun, jesting it to come forth over the horizon.

I shut off the alarm and lay back. This morning was strangely different as if a stray cat had come and curled to rest gently upon my chest. The scent of fresh-made coffee drifted in the air and sank through the aroma of bacon frying in a skillet. Julie stood at the bedroom doorway. She wore blue jeans and a red shirt emblazoned with the emblem of the smiling Piggly Wiggly pig. She crossed her arms and looked toward me but past me.

"Is Sandy a nice boy, Jack?" She spoke just above the rim of a whisper.

I winked, squinted as if looking into the sun that the mockingbirds beckoned to rise and said, "I don't think there's any real meanness in him. Some mischief here and there."

Julie clenched her upper lip with the bottom row of her teeth, seeming to dig her mind deeper into thought. She lifted her chin toward the ceiling. "I've been hurt in my rough times that I don't want to happen anymore. My judgment hasn't abided me well." She leaned her shoulder against the doorjamb. Her eyes were luminescent, looking past me out the bare windows. "The last hurt brought me home, Jack. It was the worst kind of hurt a girl could live through."

"I wouldn't let anybody hurt you. Neither would Sandy." My chest rose and fell. The bravado in my voice sounded suddenly ridiculous.

"Well, he's going to take me to work, then come back and get you. There's coffee and scrambled eggs waiting. Some bacon, too. Don't let it go cold." She lowered her vision but still looked past me. "You sure are an old sleepy head. Sandy said you sometimes sleep on the floor."

I took a deep breath, tried to find some hook of everyday conversation. "*True Grit* tonight. You kids should have fun."

"You can come with us."

"No."

"There's talk the movie house is going to shut down. I like going to the pictures. It seems like too many things are closing down. I didn't mean to go on about my hurts. Is this okay? Me being here, Jack?"

"Yeah, it's okay."

My chest rose and fell. The mockingbirds drove themselves deeper into madness by the rising pitch of the sun's rays. The exhilaration of their songs accelerated the blood rushing through my head.

Julie shrugged and turned away. The wooden floor of the house creaked beneath her steps, and I heard the soft thud of the front door shutting and Sandy shouting, "Half-Pint, be ready when I get back! We running late, boy!"

What is this world that has come to embrace me? I rolled over to the side of the bed and sat up. I dressed, gathered my gloves and oil field hat, and went into the kitchen in which lingered the scents of other beings as well as the nostalgic smell of bacon and eggs and fresh-brewed coffee. A plate heaped with scrambled eggs and three crisp bacon strips rested on the table. I poured a cup of coffee and sat down and ate. The eggs and bacon were still warm, the coffee rich and wonderfully bitter with chicory. I tried not to think; therefore, I thought more.

It was not Julie and Sandy that came to mind but Frank and Romano. Dead buddies. As you might have guessed, they and so many others who didn't make it back have always been with me, stirring around in my head. I'm sure I've implied this notion before…it's an odd luxury to be able to look back from almost fifty years hence. That morning in the kitchen, my survival guilt laced Frank and Romano together.

This is how it went: I was sitting in this old house bequeathed to me by my damaged parents, eating scrambled eggs and bacon, drinking a cup of the finest coffee I ever had, prepared for me by another human being. A college acceptance letter was inside a book on my bedside table. Frank and Romano had released their carbon back into the universe for reuse. Fairness had nothing to do with the whole gamut of staying alive and trekking onward through the course of life. Effort and talent have their honored places, but—here I go again—luck and chance…luck and chance.

Suppose the asteroid 66 million years ago had struck elsewhere on the planet, rather than just offshore of the Yucatan peninsula's northern end. In that case, some dinosaurs might still be roaming around. We're all subject to the whim of an asteroid's path. Was it choice or bad luck that I made Sandy pull over to the side of the road so that I could exercise my vain sense of humanity? If Frank had stepped left instead of right, we might be buddies today. If Romano had not leaned his head back to take a drink from his canteen, would that sniper's bullet not have sliced the carotid of his neck?

I swallowed the final bite of bacon with the last morsel of scrambled egg and pushed back from the table. I filled my thermos with the remainder of the coffee in the pot, made a sandwich of lunch meat and Wonder Bread, wrapped it in parchment paper, and then shuffled off to the bathroom. While I brushed my teeth, Sandy's voice boomed through the house, calling for me to speed it up. I spit, rinsed, smiled. Let this luck stay with me for a while. Is that okay, brother Frank, brother Romano? Yeah, it should be known. I've kept up this talking to the dead throughout my life. Often, these conversations are more meaningful to me than dialogue with the living.

On the ride in the Impala from the Haiti-Cullen Hotel to the rig, Sandy rambled on about his upcoming date with Julie that night to see *True Grit*.

"John Wayne wears an eye patch, I hear," Blackie said and downshifted the gears to turn off the road onto the graded corridor out to the rig.

"What for?" Buster said. Buster's foot tapped madly on the floorboard. I'd grown accustomed to his mindless foot tapping. I knew Buster well enough to understand that he coped against his inner demons in ways that served him best. Without that shaking foot and spasmodic leg, atoms would fly apart.

"I'll tell you tomorrow after I see the damn thing," Sandy said.

"John Wayne is America," Clifford said. "There's no sinfulness in a John Wayne movie."

"Well, I changed my mind. I'm not going then," Sandy said.

From the corner of my eye, I caught sight of Clifford's jaw tightening, a tiny muscle rippling up.

"When was the last time you got some pussy, Cliffie?" Sandy said. I popped Sandy's arm with my elbow and drove a hard stare into his enduring grin.

"Jesus still loves you despite your wanton ways," Clifford said.

The five of us jostled back and forth in our seats as Blackie gunned the car up the rutted corridor to the scarred clearing surrounding the rig. The derrick stood silhouetted against a white haze of sky. Motors, generators, and the rotary's ongoing rumble sounded like what you might imagine being the guttural movements of some meat-eater dinosaur long lost to the world.

We lumbered out of the Impala, stored our lunch pails and gear in the doghouse, bantered as usual with the departing crew as they, with sleep-hungry faces, peeled away from the platform and meandered in the direction of a battered Ford Fairlane, covered in intricate designs of mud and grease.

There would be no tripping of pipe this day. The evening tower crew had just set a new drill bit into the hole. The drilling rotary rumbled on in a monotonous cadence.

Blackie sent Clifford and Buster on missions of greasing and various maintenance jobs around the rig. He ordered Sandy and me to scrape and paint the railings of the deck. Before venturing back into the upper doghouse to monitor the rig's dials and sensors, he leaned into Sandy's face. "Don't be annoying Clifford C. Bowles about pussy."

Sandy's grin winked out. He muttered above the rumbling of the rig, "Yes, sir."

Blackie left as if he'd just snatched a fly out of the air. I greeted Sandy with a flash of my own smile. His grin ignited once more. If I had known a proper word to describe Sandy back then, it would have been this one—irrepressible. It was impossible not to like the kid.

The sun blazed just above the woodlands. Its breath had not yet stolen the faint cool of the early morning. I must convey to myself, and anyone willing to listen, how normal that morning felt to me, how my excessive vigilance of this unpredictable world had begun to lessen.

The grace of the normal, the familiar, glorified the day. The sun rose higher in the sky. Shadows of the trees grew short then lengthened as the day progressed. Cumulus clouds built into formations of great anvils late in the afternoon sky.

After parting from the others at the Haiti-Cullen, Sandy and I arrived back at the house on Roosevelt Street early in the evening. Sandy immediately sequestered himself in the lone bathroom. He drew a hot bath. I could hear him through the walls, scouring himself clean of oil field grime, grease, and paint filaments that clung to his skin. I'd taunted him, passing by the bathroom door, "Wash behind your ears, you numb nuts."

Twilight stood a good hour off. I drifted through the house and took up my familiar position on the front stoop. A tidiness now touched the place on Roosevelt Street. Sandy and I had trimmed the yard during short periods of respite, gathered broken limbs and hauled them to a pile in the back. Using wire brush and sandpaper, we'd scraped the flaking paint from the sides of the house. Washed scrims of grimy dirt from the windows. I took a measure of satisfaction within my gut and felt okay with it.

The Razor's Edge rested within my hands, held in place against the brace of my knee. A giant glass of iced tea beside my leg sweated with condensation. I began to read and gave myself away to the unfamiliar world inside the book.

Sandy eventually emerged past the screen door and looked down at me. The sun had lowered itself below the trees and twilight had begun to exude its chimerical magic on the earth. Such sequences were becoming familiar patterns in our lives. Me on the stoop with one of Frank's books and Sandy squeezing past, bright and clean, on his way to see Julie. Oddly, I was warmed by the easy lilt of the routine.

"You can't find no pussy in a book, Half-Pint." Sandy shuffled past me.

"Numb nuts," I said to his back. "You be good to that girl."

"I will, you fuckin' bookworm."

He hurried down the broken walk to his Chevy parked on the pebbly apron of the street. Tall and lean and almost bounding to the car. In that second, he reminded me of Romano who had been lanky and tall with a great throwing arm. I remembered how Romano had pulled the pins and released the spoons on the grenades, giving his count of one second before heaving them toward the B-40 rocket teams that had moved up just in front of the concertina wires and with whom we dueled. Those memories emerge less now that a half-century has blinked past, but still, they sometimes come in wondrous little clips that are as clear as the day of happening. Always they seem to be but part of a continuum in space and time waiting to be repeated.

The Chevy door clicked open and snapped shut. Sandy drove off, barely scuffling up rocks beneath the tires. I felt like an older brother watching his kid brother drive away into misadventures of the night. Inside my stomach came a tug of caution. Beware the closeness.

My eyes lingered from the book's pages to the limbs of the sycamore trees by the walkway. My ears tuned to the sounds of the insects, the electric zoom sound of a Nighthawk coming out of its dive.

I'm not sure where my mind began to drift that evening after Sandy drove away. Somehow, I remember myself being drawn toward the stars emerging out of the slate-colored sky. I'm sure I wasn't thinking of Whitehead or the whack of his gun against my head.

My lull into complacency went away with one breathless poof. The breeze passing through died like a man snapped down by the strike of a perfectly aimed bullet to the head. Called the quick fuck. No time for remorse, regret, or wonder on the tumble down. Whitehead's truck cruised down the street toward the house. The engine's rumbling entwined itself into the buzz of insects.

"Give me back that breeze," I murmured. My heart sped.

I closed Frank's book. Placed it in what I thought to be a safe position on the edge of the stoop. The truck turned at the arc of the street and pulled off to the side in front of the house. Whitehead left the engine running. It purred in a marble-clicking way. The day had eased deeper into twilight. The chicken shit breeze that had teased through remained flat upon the earth.

Whitehead and his wife sat in the truck cab. I kept trying to slow my breath, letting my vision sharpen upon their indistinct images through the window glass of the truck door. Whitehead leaned forward over the steering wheel, his hands clasped in prayer in front of him across the dash. His wife peered at me from behind his shoulder. In the dim reflection of her face, I recognized the expression of resignation that comes when you look around and see yourself as the sole survivor. That vacant stare that comes from being the one left alive after the proverbial shit hit the fan. After a moment, she looked away and appeared to clasp her hands in prayer.

This will be it. He'll get it right this time. Come on, you crazy son-of-a-bitch.

One thing in which I was sure as I reflect on that desperate moment on the front stoop—I was determined, once again, to take whatever Whitehead had to give. Oh, I complimented myself. See how strong you are. And to Frank, I muttered nonsense. Watch me take this shit. I'll make you proud of me. Half-Pint was going to hold his own against the temptation to counter violence with violence.

The truck door clacked open. Whitehead stepped out, dressed in long-sleeve shirt and black slacks. He curled one arm over the top of the door and set his eyes straight on me. The sun hovered near the horizon and the day's heat was loosening its grip. His wife now sat up very straight. She stared straight ahead. Even from my limited vantage point on the stoop, I could discern the quivering of frail muscles on her face. How haughty of feeling I was at that moment. How magnanimous, how bold and resonant of virtue I was. I, Half-Pint Crowe, had the gravitas to feel sorry for the woman.

Whitehead left the truck door ajar and sidled off the street's gravelly edge and onto the grass. He crossed over the buckled walkway and stood beside the trunk of the tall sycamore, examining me in the fashion of a hunter curious about the game he stalked. His hands hung empty. No pistol shoved behind his belt. No weapon holstered on the side of his hip.

An impulse to rise and meet him came and went. "I'm not going to kill anybody. I'm not part of that picture," Frank once said.

I was not going to kill anybody either. Not even this deluded rope of knotted muscle who leaned with his hand against the flaking trunk of the sycamore tree and crossed one foot over the other.

Whitehead's lips began to move like fleshy larvae coming to life. A short utterance resonated from the bowels, "God despises people like you." He shook his head and spat. Let go his hand from the side of the tree and straightened his spine.

"You should go on, Mr. Whitehead." Those words shaped themselves from my lips in a thin veil of compassion. It was the best I could do. I was hanging on. The edges of the earth cracked, began to break away around me.

He walked a few steps forward and unzipped his pants, pulled out his dick. With a wriggle of his shoulders, he began to piss. A stone glaze crossed his face. Eyes unblinking, lips smooth and straight.

A vast accumulation of debris from the war arose inside me. It rounded off into numbness. My breath smoothed out and synchronized with the hum of evening's approach. He finished and with a dip of his knees pushed his dick back through the fly of his pants and pulled up the zipper. He sniffed. "You a piss ant, boy. Bet you don't even have a cock. The devil you worship is weak. You don't have the manhood to even give me an ass wipe. Do you?"

"Yes, sir. You should go on," I said again.

He stepped forward across the trim grass, barely a scuff sound to his feet. He stood in front of me; his eyes glazed downward. He was outlined softly in the emerging twilight. I could feel the heat coming off him and smelled aftershave lotion.

"I could afford you an ass fucking and you'd squeal like you loved it. Wouldn't you? You are perversion and you will stay away from my angels. I will hasten to kill you."

"I'm not going to bother your angels."

"They are sweet and pure," he said. "By my God-given right and duty, I'll keep 'em that way."

"Yes, sir. I won't bother your angels."

He turned and struck back in a slow swagger to the open door of the truck. He got in. The door clacked shut and he drove off slowly as if intent on inspecting the neighborhood's gradual decay.

I reached for the glass of iced tea beside my leg. The clink of ice cubes accompanied the suppressed laughter moving up my chest. My lips touched the cold rim. I breathed out these words: "Damn if I help a lady change a flat tire again." More laughter spiraled up and built into a fit of coughing. It hit me hard; the man had scared me. Defilement slid down me like shit down a hill. The truck rolled on up the street. Its taillights bloomed into the magic zone of evening's diminishing light.

Pressure kept building behind my breastbone. I fought back another fit of indecent laughter, the kind that might insanely happen when crap built too high around you. I exhaled and soon I was just fine. Or so I told myself. Self-deceit back in those early days was a steady companion. Its velvet voice whispered into my ear, "You'll do fine, Half-Pint."

Dusk encroached. I tried to read, but the words retreated into the darkening pages. The drone of insects pummeled my senses. I pushed up and went inside and flicked on the bathroom light. Gave thanks that Sandy had cleaned out the tub then sat on the cool rim and listened to the flow of water from the faucet.

I knew then, naked and sitting on the edge of the bathtub, that I was close to losing all restraint. I could hear someone far off trying to strike a match. In the back of my skull hummed a tiny blue flame.

After the bath, I pulled on pants and shirt and went into my bedroom. I lay on the cool floor beneath the bedroom window, the position I took when vulnerability became intolerable. Drowsiness finally seeped in—a dangerous point where my brain cried for shutdown. This was the space where vigilance lowered. Enemy movements made difficult to detect, the murky time between the dog and the wolf.

Later into the night, my bedroom door clicked open and I reached for a rifle that wasn't there. The backlight from the narrow hallway cast Sandy into a ghostly outline.

"What do you want?"

Sandy stood unmoving. I'm sure he was giving some thought to the fear in my voice.

"He touched her. Grabbed her by the arm."

I sat up. Gave my eyes time to adjust to the thin light. A line of sweat rolled down my flank and slid to a stop at the waist of my work pants. This is the actual moment where my plan to kill Whitehead began to take shape. I'm quite sure that if Frank had been around, really around, not just in my imaginings, I would have looked away from him. The automatic pilot was lit, not by a gun whipping to the face, a pissing on the lawn, but a roll of sweat and the image of Whitehead's hand clutched around Julie's arm.

Sandy slid his back down the jamb of the door frame and settled into a squat. He didn't look at me anymore but off into some distance right in front of his nose. I wanted to tell him that no answers inhabit that space in front of the eyes. I said nothing but waited.

"I got to run some talk by you. You don't mind, do you?" His southern drawl deepened.

"No, man, I don't mind."

The .45 on the closet shelf came to mind. My mouth had gone dry. A knot had tightened in my belly. And then I was struck by how easy it was to let it all go, this strange quest I had set upon—this desire to shed the snakeskin of violence, to learn and understand the mysteries of our forbidden world. Goddamn, how did Frank come to possess his passion? For myself, the past and my old man's blood were too much in me. I let the vain mission I'd set upon—or Frank had set me upon—slip away like some stone tumbling down a talus field. Another bead of sweat broke and I could feel it on its path across the side of my ribs. "Talk, man. It's alright."

"You know what I like, Half-Pint? The sound of popcorn popping in the lobby of the movie house and the way it smells. The air all filled up with hot cooking oil."

If he had been closer, I would have smacked him. The blood strained to release through the veins of my clenched fist.

"Knock off the lament shit. What happened?" I spoke with so-called Marine mentality—gather information, assess, plan, act.

Sandy drew in his breath. He rolled his gaze upon me through the dim light then turned away.

"I was buying us popcorn and soda at the snack counter. Whitehead came up behind us and grabbed Julie by the back of her arm. Pulled her into his face. Said something like, 'God's eyes be upon you, whore of the devil.' I yelled at him to get his goddamn hands off her and Julie rips away from him, grabs my ass, and hustles me out onto the street." Sandy stroked the tips of his thumb and finger together as if concentrating his thoughts. "His dog-whipped wife was behind him looking on like some mute soul out of an orphanage." Sandy pushed his head back against the doorjamb. "She damn near creeps me out as much as him."

"The boy wasn't with him?"

"That kid wasn't there."

"Who saw all this?" I'd released my clenched fingers and pushed my back against the wall. The top of my head rested beneath the windowsill. The night-calling insects chirruped their songs into the summer darkness. Sandy fixed his gaze upon me. From the muted light shed from the hallway, I could see the studied, sad look on his face.

"A few folks were behind us. It happened quick. No time for a big commotion. Julie drug me out the doors onto the street. Swore at me that if I did anything, she'd have nothing more to do with me. She had me swear, cross my heart hope to die kind of promise. Started crying and couldn't stop. I didn't care who saw. I held her there on the street in front of the movie house until she said, 'Let's git. Come on, hon', no *True Grit* tonight,' and I went."

At this juncture of Sandy's discourse, his eyes cut into me. He said something that ripped the lining from my heart: "You know what's about, don't you, Half-Pint? I'm taking shelter in that promise I gave her. I'm hiding inside it. That man scares the hell out of me."

A moment passed in which only the insects convened in the warm night. The space between Sandy and me was stilted with silence.

"I need to use your car tomorrow night. Is that okay?"

"No," Sandy said. "Don't make me feel any worse."

From far off, a train whistle fused its way into the room. The low rumbling of the engine passing down the tracks sent me into a time far back in childhood when the distant song of that train drifted by the edge of my dreams, giving strange comfort while I lay huddled in my bed.

"Okay, it's no problem, but I'll need your car tomorrow night. You got to take care of Julie." I pushed myself up a little by the flat of my hands. "How is she now?"

"She's alright, man. She's seen some craziness over the years. It's not like she's never been exposed to the wraths of vile motherfuckers, but Whitehead is different. He's got a different kind of meanness. It breaks my heart to see her hurt."

We let the summer night invade the space and take us prisoner with its sultry hand. The katydids and cicadas and tree frogs and some lonesome whip-poor-will calling from woods beyond the neighborhood and what had been the hot breath of the sun cooling down through the open window took us deeper into our thoughts. Pardon the poetic flow of bullshit that sometimes comes from the old man in the professor's chair. That moment of that night is locked in my memory. I'd slipped over the edge back onto familiar terrain. I still revisit that memory from time to time to remind myself how quickly the angels can bare their fangs.

Sandy rose from his crouch. One faint crack of the knee on his way up. He stood square in the doorway and flicked off the light switch. His shadow gave a soft outline in the new darkness.

"You can borrow my car whenever you want."

"Okay," I said. Then his shadow evanesced and disappeared. His footsteps scuffed upon the wooden floor and disappeared into the night.

I sat for a while longer with my back against the wall. I rested my head against the windowsill and listened to the summer sounds of insects outside. Then I performed a necessary rite. I arose and turned on the lamplight. Frank's books lay upon their usual place of repose at the corner of the nightstand. I took them, holding them gently, and placed them inside the drawer. A moth arose from out of nowhere and spiraled up toward the ceiling, spinning little shadows on the wall. I watched it for a second then went to the closet and slid the ammo canister from the shelf and removed the .45 and the cartridge box. Turned off the lamplight and draped myself back into the darkness. The cool floor beneath the open window welcomed me again. I lay on my side with the gun and shells positioned against the baseboard. There is a resonance to the act of detachment, a soft echo.

WILL WRITING

I tracked the sun throughout the next day. It still burned high in a sky streaked with cirrus clouds on this long day of summer as we stashed tools and gathered around Blackie's battered Impala. Our shift on the rig had ended. Blackie had vanished into the woodlands, telling us he'd return shortly. The rumbling of the derrick's rotary table edged far back into my senses.

The metal skin of the car burned into my back as I leaned against it. Sandy stood beside me. He had his arms crossed and stared off as if trying to penetrate the dark recesses of the trees. Eyes barely visible beneath the rim of his oil field hat. Clifford knelt in front of the car; his head bent in prayer. God would never abandon Cliff. Or maybe it was that Cliff would never leave his God. It all worked for him. Buster stood on the other side of the Impala in a space where atoms collided at remarkable speed, shifting his weight back and forth as if he stood on hot sand.

Blackie came up through the trees from the direction of the creek like a silent bear. A smile etched up his stubbled cheeks. He held something in both hands extended out before him like a new father might carry a newborn infant. Sweat trickled down his heavy jowls. He never gave his eyes to us. It was as if he'd wandered through some miasma of swamp gas that left the victim shy and ridiculous. He held a moss-covered stone.

"What's that you got?" Buster said.

"A grinding stone left by those before us," Blackie answered in a song-like cadence. "Some folks call it a metate."

Buster flexed his jaw. Blackie walked around to the back of the car and popped the cargo trunk. He placed the stone in the back and slammed the trunk shut. The corners of his mouth made deep commas. His eyes never sought us. I shook my head and said to Sandy, "Drop me off at the library on Main when we get back. I'll walk back to the house from there."

"The library?" Sandy's eyes widened with irritation.

"Yeah, the fucking library."

Sandy rolled his eyes toward the sky and exhaled a long, deep breath.

"How'd you come to find that stone?" Clifford said. "That Whitehead boy?"

"Shut up, Clifford C. Bowles. I'm returning it to the untainted wild tomorrow." Blackie grinned but still averted his dark eyes from the rest of us. "Let's listen to some of that rock and roll on the radio."

"No, sir," Clifford answered and, with a knuckle, flicked a roll of sweat off his nose.

That interaction was the beginning of the day's descent toward the twilight of evening and my plan to kill Whitehead and anyone who got in my way. Clifford, Sandy, Buster, and I were smeared with dirt, grease, and grime lolling around a rattletrap of a car, waiting for a bear-like driller to come up from the woods. He ambles up and drops some ancient people's grinding stone into the car trunk, ignoring Clifford's questions, tells him to play some rock and roll music like he always does for the pleasure of irritating Clifford. Finally, he looks directly at each of us, giving us time to take him in, his barrel chest puffed out, and says, "It must have been some lady's prized possession back when it was wild all around us. I return it tomorrow, but tonight it's with me."

"We still not listening to no rock and roll music," Clifford said. Sandy huffed a scornful laugh, the most emotion he'd displayed during the entire day of work.

We piled into the car. I didn't give a damn about Blackie's fanciful notion of a time gone by when the land was pristine and belonged to panthers and other wild things and indigenous people. Letting go of everything that mattered in life had deepened into my bone. I was anesthetized. My slide back into a violent mode came from weakness of character, and you know what they say, *Character is destiny*. Let me tell you a short story about anesthesia. It's a bit graphic and may be worthy of skipping past. It entails only two paragraphs.

North Vietnamese Army sapper squads, naked but for black sapper shorts, slipped through the concertina and tanglefoot wires of our hill position on a moonless night. As an old man nearing retirement from his tenured university position, I can say that I respected those enemy ghosts. Oh, I came to terms with the feared enemy of the National

Liberation Front and the People's Army of Vietnam long ago. They were mostly boys like us. But on the night of that assault, I hated them, had transformed them into subhuman forms—gooks and slant eyes. Five lay dead in front of our fighting hole. They had piled up, limbs mangled and jutting off in directions that even a gifted contortionist could not achieve. Somehow, these sappers had slithered through the concertina and past the claymores. This accomplishment was an example of their ghost quality. A grunt named Kennedy, a lowly PFC positioned just down the perimeter line from Romano and me, had opened his machine-gun on the brunt of them and saved our lives.

When the sun's rays cut through the smoke of morning, we pored over the bodies, plucking from their ankles plastic pouches filled with the white powder of some cocaine or opioid substance that numbed your tongue when you tasted of it. Romano said, "Fuck, man, we all need some of this shit." For a second, an insight came: numbness to life allows us to carry out acts of madness. Deadening of the inner self, whether from substances like those in the enemy's ankle pouches or from the shit grinding you down day to day, is a major root of evil. Numb the soul inside the body, and anybody can kill. The revelation came well before Frank had befriended me and helped me look inside myself. Before he touched me with unadulterated compassion I didn't deserve. I stared at Romano for a long time as he tapped his tongue with a fingertip coated with amber-white powder and offered me the pouch.

"I don't need it," I said.

The tires of the Impala struck upon the graveled lot in front of the Haiti-Cullen Hotel. Blackie looked back over his broad shoulder at Sandy. "Carry the metate in for me."

"The what?"

"The grinding stone, boy. Now clear your head and git it."

"Can't Cliffie bring it?"

Blackie's eyes sunk into the caverns beneath his skull. Sandy looked away.

"Yes, sir." Then it was quiet but for the last crunch of gravel beneath the wheels and the flick of the ignition switch to off.

I waited in Sandy's Chevy. The seat was butt-burning hot, the air like that in front of an oven door. I rolled down the window. Buster drove away in his dented pickup and flicked a quick wave at me as he turned onto the highway. I lifted my hand in acknowledgment. Buster, with all the electrons of his cells moving near light speed, and me, so quick to judge. I'd almost come to like the harried man.

I've always been like that. Too quick to judge. I leaned back my head and wished for a cool breeze to pass through. Instead came Frank into my imaginings. He sat behind the steering wheel. An amused twinkle beset his bright eyes. Here I go talking inside my head with the dead again while I waited for Sandy to emerge from the Haiti-Cullen. It was you, Frank, who said go back and start at the beginning, and here I am planning to kill some people when the night comes. Yeah, Frank, I'll kill them all: the boy, the woman, the dog, and Whitehead. Me pitted back at the beginnings of my life, at war with the past, about to leap deep into it. No path to peace, love, and understanding here. Just me tracking through the story already written into my blood by Seymour and Ida and the long line of progenitors before them.

A semi-truck roared by on the highway and trounced me out of my pathetic conversation with a dead man so understanding that he lets me ramble indulgently on. He was gone by the time the sound of the big truck had faded away. The abandoned paper mill with its smokestacks tall and dead against a hazy-white sky stood sprawled on the other side of the highway beyond the railroad tracks. Over the next few years, the entire complex would be demolished and wasted to memory. Over there, somewhere near the rusting chains of the main gate, my old man went up in flame.

The door to the Chevy clicked open and Sandy slid into the driver's seat. "Goddamn, it's motherfuckin' hot."

"What was that all about?"

Sandy shrugged his shoulders. "I'm going to smoke me a goddamn cigarette. I don't give a shit how hot it is."

His profanity quotient had risen tenfold since the encounter with Whitehead at the movie house. He lit up. The cigarette dangled from his lips, James Dean style. He started the Chevy and pulled out onto the highway. A brazen wind blew in through the window and a few empty storefronts streamed past my peripheral vision. Sandy's hand knuckled white onto the steering wheel.

"Tell me what Blackie wanted with you," I said more firmly.

Sandy fastened his eyes upon the road before him and seemed to compose his thoughts.

"He wanted to know if you were about to break over this Whitehead shit and do something crazy. I told him to go ask Half-Pint if he wanted to know about the man's emotional wellbeing. He grabbed me by the collar and pulled me into his face and said, 'Who am I asking right now?' Goddamn if Cliffie didn't save my ass, 'Now Blackie, Sandy's got a point. Let thy hands find the position of prayer instead,' or something like Cliffie would say. Now I'm beholding to ol' Cliffie, which is going to be a burden in itself."

The air thickened as I breathed. "Was that it?"

"I told him I don't know what goes on in Half-Pint's head, much less my own. That's it."

"Thanks," I said with some mocking disdain. "Don't worry about it. It's alright."

"He took his fuckin' grinding stone and went up the stairs to his room. Cliffie said, 'Go on home, Sandy. We'll see you in the morning,' and I told Cliffie thanks for not letting Blackie kill me right there and he grinned and I left, and that's that."

Sandy turned off the old north-south highway and guided the Chevy down the beginnings of Main Street toward the parish library at the northern edge of town. Only a few cars, heat vibrating off their hoods, rested in the diagonal spaces marked by parking meters. I latched onto silence as shodden, yellow-brick storefronts flowed past and an old yellow cur hobbled forth across the street at the stoplight of the intersection of Main and Butler. Sandy idled the car. Its gruff engine marbled and purred. The dog stepped up on the shaded walkway by the corner drug store, sniffed the air, then scurried on as if beckoned by an inner messenger.

"Dogs got more sense in this town than the people," Sandy muttered.

I grabbed Sandy's shoulder and gave it a shake. I tried to laugh. He said nothing. I watched the overhead traffic light flash to yellow and green. Sandy shifted gears and we cruised forward, his eyes drifting slow to his left to take in the front of the movie theatre, its walkway littered with popcorn kernels and a few dead-on-their-side soda cups.

"God bless John Wayne," Sandy said.

I grasped for whimsy, distraction, some humor that might be afloat in the air. I needed to loosen the knots that I knew tightened in Sandy's belly. "John Wayne was a motherfucker pansy that never went to war."

"Don't be sacrilegious, Half-Pint." He shook his head. "You can say the dumbest things, man." He scoffed a laugh at the cigarette smoke circling his head.

"Good luck to you, Sandy."

"I don't know how your mind works, Jack." He shook his head again. "I'll leave the keys on the kitchen table tonight. I will. Be careful, whatever you do."

He pulled over in front of the parish library. I unlatched the car door, eased out of the seat, and looked back at Sandy. Tiny muscles rippled up Sandy's jaw. The heat off the pavement patted my face. I narrowed my eyes against the blinding light of a sun descending above the rooftops. Sandy drove away. I stepped over the curb and onto the sidewalk. My reflection stared back at me from the glass doors of the library's entryway. I pushed through. The scent of books struck into my nostrils. Volumes of shelved books overlooked rows of wooden tables. On the inside leg of one of those tables, a kid named Jack Crowe had knife-etched his initials a millennia ago. I walked through the tables and a maze of bookshelves to a far corner desk in the room. A woman whose hair had been raven-black when I was a boy sat behind the desk. Her hair still fell smooth and straight against her sunken cheeks. It was now tinted with hues of grey and white. She looked at me over the cusp of horn-rimmed glasses balanced low on her nose and hit me with a faint smile and an eyewink.

"Do you have anything on Louisiana civilian law? Or something of that order?"

"You're not going to sit down over there?" She dipped the top of her grey head toward a long, scarred table on the far side of the room. "At that table you branded?" A quirky smile brightened her face.

I looked down upon this demure woman of the books, Ms. Lydia Payne, whom I had known in a distant way early on in my boyhood. The stories of Ms. Payne that I remembered had her arriving in the town as a fresh graduate from some obscure librarian school of a college in one of the southernmost parishes. She had always seemed a foreigner, had never married, and as far as anyone could fathom, had never entered one of the halls of God. Rumors had occasionally arisen that she was queer, some even whispering that she was Jewish, but her modest bearing and her quiet obsession with books dampened the flames of malicious talk.

The truth of her social survival was probably due more to her being just too uninteresting for the town to devour with hearsay and gossip. I realized back then that she faithfully observed the world around her. She, of all people, had noticed a runt of a kid who would station himself with a book at a certain library table on a summer afternoon and leave this world for others more inviting. Ms. Payne had always given me a special smile, a knowing wink.

Her desk chair creaked against the floor as she got up. She seemed so thin and fragile like she might blow away and perish if a hard wind struck her. She walked away as if called by some silent voice in the back of the room. My heart pounded. A desire to reach out. I held my breath and pushed back the riptide of blood pulsing into my temples. The soft feelings backwashed, and I was okay again. Dead enough inside to move on toward the night.

Her thin figure whisked along the shelves of books, fingertips tracing bindings that over the years had become ensconced with her DNA. She came back, clutching a short stack of books. One she plucked away from the others and held it in front of me just below her sad smile. She parted the back cover. "Look, Jack. Do you remember going into the forest?"

In the crude print of a child's hand, my name lay in rows on a dull-yellow library card. The book was *Bambi*, the story of a deer that had enchanted me as a child. I had entered that forest of the animals many times, praying in my own way for Bambi to survive the pursuit of hunters and wildfire and live on.

"It was your favorite book." Ms. Payne laid it aside on the top of her desk. She tilted her head and placed the remaining books into my hands. "This is a two-volume set on Louisiana civil codes. Shall we get you a new library card?"

"No, ma'am. I'm going to sit down with these for a while. Can you spare me a ballpoint pen and a piece of paper?"

At the library table of my childhood, I stationed myself once again. I cast out any wonderment about the circles of life and opened the cover of the first volume on Louisiana Civil Codes. Traced down the table of contents with my finger in which red dirt and drilling rig grime stained my cracked knuckles. It took a while, but somehow I more than grasped the legal stance of will writing in the state of Louisiana. This is what I discerned: A handwritten testament is valid if written, dated, and signed by the hand of the person (the testator). It all seemed simple as if perfectly shaped for the ending of the plight that was to be.

My chest grew light. I looked up. A young girl with blonde hair that hung down to her shoulders stood across the room with her chin cocked upward as she scanned the titles on the upper shelves. From her humble throne behind the librarian's desk, Ms. Payne fixed her vision upon the girl as one ready to pounce, befriend. In a fleeting moment, I imagined myself as a decent man, going forth, standing before this gentle lady, and saying, "Ms. Payne, thank you for being here." And taking another inept step forward. "What have you sacrificed? Are you lonely? What meaning and purpose have you found?" And she'd answer, "Not lonely at all, Jack. I'm happy here. This is my purpose."

The pen rested in my hand; the blank paper lay before me on the table. I began to write, and the words flowed onto the page something like this: I, Jack Crowe, give Julie Longo and Sandy Guillory my house at 102 Roosevelt Street in the town of Baptiste, Louisiana. All the money I have accumulated in my bank account at Baptiste Bank and Trust is theirs for whatever purpose they so choose. May Sandy live to be a hundred and one and Julie live on and continue to tolerate his annoying ways. They are good people.

I dated it and signed my name in large bold letters and complimented myself on the good humor I'd bestowed upon the testament at the end. Then I shut it all off like I could shut it all off back in the war before the shit would hit the fan.

I folded the paper and pushed back the chair. Went silently out the door and did not look back at Ms. Payne who had risen to assist the girl with the long, blonde hair, whose soft voice lulled against the back of my neck, "Come again, Jack."

ENACTING THE PLAN

When I arrived at the house on Roosevelt Street, sweat drenched through my clothes. Sandy's Chevy was parked out front. The sun rested behind the limbs of a sweetgum tree that grew in a neighbor's backyard. A mockingbird mimicked the throaty squawk of a jay from the pitch of a rooftop. What had been the crisp paper of my handwritten will and testament was now damp, supple parchment between my thumb and finger. Strangely, one of the most distinct things I remember as I walked the final steps across Seymour and Ida's yard to the front stoop of the house was how a grasshopper leaped from the grass and clung to the side of my jaw. I swiped it off with the back of my hand and went inside.

Silence resonated through the rooms. On the kitchen table lay Sandy's car keys. I placed my will and testament on the middle of the table and shoved the keys in my pocket. I drank a glass of water from the kitchen tap and placed the empty glass in the sink. For a long moment, the faint sway of the limbs from the chinaberry tree outside the kitchen window held me in a trance. Then I pulled away and went into the bathroom. Splashed water from the faucet into my face and dried off with a towel.

My reflection in the medicine cabinet mirror beckoned me to look upon myself. Mean, cold eyes looked straight back at me. A confirmation of who I really was. I raised my hands, fingers spread apart, palms outward, and examined their steadiness in the mirror. Why do these hands grow steady so when violent engagement is anticipated?

Romano whispered into my ear from what seemed an eon past, when we huddled close in the muck behind a paddy dike during a lull in a firefight before the incoming artillery rounds whistled over. "Why you not scared, Half-Pint? I'm 'bout to shit myself."

I told him back then I was always scared. I gave him the blankness of a mask on my face.

"Fuck you. Fuck you, man," he said.

On that day, the zip-zip of rounds passed overhead and that whoomp sound of shells flying out of their mortar tubes picked up heavier. My hands were always steady back then. Damn if you could read anything in my face.

I'm looking at it now and it's looking cold and pathetic back at me. Inside myself, muscles quake, so terrified I am that some emotion might get through. Me, a walking paradox.

Inside the bedroom, I opened the closet door and slid the ammunition canister off the upper shelf. I set it down where the lowering sun's rays struck through the window onto the floor. I removed the handgun. Unraveled the swaddling of faintly oiled cloth from around it. Released the magazine from its chamber and loaded it with seven rounds. Shoved the filled magazine back into the gun's well with the heel of my hand, chambered a round, then slid extra shells into my pocket.

Get a load of the crazy shit that shadowed its way into my feverish mind: I imagined Romano stalking me from outside by the window's edge, sun-scoured flak jacket across his chest, sweat sliding down the side of his face, a thin grin given to his lips, him shaking his head and saying, "You on your own, Half-Pint."

I looked around and Romano was gone like a shadow passing by the corner of my eye. Frank hadn't bothered to show up, of course. I'd shunned him. His books lay bound together and sequestered in a dresser drawer.

Looking back at the unfolding events of that night from my position forward in time, the drive taken in Sandy's Chevy to the darker regions of the parish seemed a dream. It wasn't. And I will exact the events that followed as clearly as an old man whose most prized possessions are, to this day, three shrapnel-torn, blood-stained books.

When I turned off the main highway onto the graveled road that would lead me past the rig site and on toward the Whitehead place, I should have been closing the pages of the *Razor's Edge*, pondering Larry Darrell's story of ongoing search for inner peace. How the closer he got, the more he seemed to let go of his attachments to the world. And after a while, I would have been thinking of dinner and college, then sleep and the happiness that would await me the next day of toiling in the sun and having dreams of a future. But the .45 lay on the passenger seat, barrel pointed toward the dash. I had tripped over to the other side, that place of being that exists just beneath the surface of our social civilities.

Fifty years later, in the cool office air, while the sun of a summer day beats against the window glass, my hands sweat upon a laptop keyboard and tremors ravage the linings of my stomach. Writing this now, I must confront again the killing animal that exists within myself. I endeavor to look at Half-Pint, smell his inner wounds, touch his youthful skin, hear the gurgitation in his bowels, and accept in trepidation and disgust that he was me.

That half-century before, as I guided Sandy's Chevy down the ill-tended parish road, the sun lay below the dark rim of the woodlands. Dusk hung over the land of swamp and old forest gliding past the car window. As the dim lights of the oil rig's derrick appeared far back off the road, I slowed the car to a crawl and turned onto the scraped passageway that led through the woodlands toward the distant rig and its low rumbling. After probably fifty feet, I turned off the engine. A faint pinging came from metal cooling beneath the car. Darkness converged around me but for the apparitional penetration of derrick lights beyond the distant treeline.

I would wait here until midnight broke over into early morning. Confident no one would pass. The patience of the enemy I'd left ten thousand miles behind me came to mind. That enemy would often strike in the wee hours of morning when heart and soul stand most vulnerable, when the predators that had sought the ancients roamed in nocturnal hunt. I didn't possess the patriotic fanaticism that gave my old nemeses such patience. I had only a burning sensation in my gut that came from hate. It gave me purpose, a far different kind that Frank had tried to instill in me. I rolled down the window and spit. Patience it will be, then the violence.

The serenade of frogs overwhelmed the darkness. A half-moon eased past a cloud and gave a faint glow to the night. No vehicles passed by on the remote parish road behind me. Fireflies lit up the inky recesses of the woods. They blinked on and off like stars birthing and dying. The sounds from the distant rig thrummed on into the night.

This was the waiting period. In this time, I reviewed the details of the attack. The logistics were simple. Surprise promised to be the most potent element. Wreak confusion and exploit it. The objective was to kill Whitehead. Due to his paranoid bearing, I wondered about the placement of tripwires around his property but regarded the likelihood he had confidence in the alertness of the dog. The animal would be the first impediment, then a bolted door, then, possibly the boy and the woman scrambling about in howling frenzy through the darkness, if I made it that far. Whitehead would have time to arm himself, and then what would come to be would come to be, one way or another. If it went the right way, the probability of which I placed as low to none, I would gather myself on the edge of his porch and wait for God, the law, or nothingness to come for me.

I lit a match from one of the matchbooks Sandy kept strewn between the seats. From the light of the flame, I checked the time on my watch. 12:50 a.m. Blew out the match in haste and sat in breathless silence. Lighting a match in the night of Vietnam had been a violation akin to striking your mother across the face. Comes the reassuring voice inside my head: *There are no snipers here. This is a different land. A different enemy.* My breath came back. The rise and fall of my chest grew steady. The light of the half-moon created a surrounding world of inky limbs and vines. I skimmed my fingers across the barrel of the .45 on the passenger seat, then started the car.

Whitehead's place lay about three miles away, set back in the woods at the end of a dirt drive about a football field's length. A few days earlier, when Blackie had taunted Whitehead by driving past the man's place and wheeling the Impala around back on him, I'd caught a glimpse of sunshine glinting off the metal roof in the distance. The house hadn't been the unkempt abode I'd imagined. Even from my meager view of the home during that ludicrous excursion, it appeared as a neat, well-kept property. No abandoned vehicles strewn about. Two lines of pecan trees traipsing partway up the drive. Crepe myrtles, tall and pink-blossomed, in the front yard.

About a mile from where I estimated Whitehead's house to be I slowed the car and pulled to the side of the road and turned off the headlights. Gave my eyes time to dilate and gain as much of the moonlight given to me. Then drove forward at a crawl, able to gauge well enough the meet of the tires along the road's edge.

A few hundred yards from where I thought the long driveway from Whitehead's house intersected the road, I stopped the car from its steady crawl and turned off the ignition. Muscles tautened across my stomach. I waited for the faint pinging of the engine to fade away. Listened for the barking of a dog to come echoing through the woods. Just the croaking of the frogs and then amongst their deafening serenade the disgruntled, hoo-hoo-hoo cry of a barred owl.

I took the .45 in hand and got out of the car and shut the door by slowly pressuring my knee into it. A low click and snap spent into the other night sounds. No retort came from beast or human.

The pale light from the half-moon provided me outlined impressions of tufted grass or broken limbs along the road's edge as I moved forward. A few of the dead branches slithered away in front of my steps, wriggled back into the dense brush with a silence I'd always admired.

Fireflies floated in the palpable air between the road and where Whitehead's house stood draped in darkness, invisible yet to my eyes. I went forward, my steps silent on the smooth surface of the drive path and caught the scent of pine needle sap. The barred owl hoo-hooed again far back in the depths of the matted darkness, then another returned its call from even farther reaches.

"Come on back, Jack. That's not you with that gun in your hand. Come on, Jack."

A smile lit on my face with that lyrical plea from ol' Frank skimming through my imaginings. Ghost voices could come from all angles on a half-moon night filled with the birth, death, and rebirth of fireflies. Frank's supplicating voice faded back into the unknown spaces between the call of the two owls. It saddens me still to remember my smirking disdain for Frank on that night, the ice of indifference in me as I trekked forward to Whitehead's house. But that's the way I went and that's who I was—Half-Pint keeping a steady pace toward the emerging outline of the home, the man's truck parked off to the side of the yard, the shadowy forms of crepe myrtles rising past the porch roof.

The yard grass felt soft and manicured underfoot, and this is where it came to me that the flow of the night was out of sync. The guard dog had not erupted into savage barking, its form heaving toward me with rasping whines and throaty growls. Come on, I thought. Only thimbles of breath reached my throat. I held the .45 out before me as I took the last few steps toward the front stoop of the gallery.

A film of perspiration breaks across my forehead as I look back upon that image of myself with handgun drawn. The sweat comes from shame and disbelief of those distant times. I've not held a rifle, shotgun, or handgun in my hands for close to fifty years. If my colleagues held an impromptu contest to guess who among us had the least knowledge of guns and the greatest aversion to weapons of any kind, they would favor me as the likely choice.

But back then, the .45 was steady in hand and my foot pressed upon the bottom step, then the next, and I stood fully exposed on the floor of the gallery and kept moving forward. In front of the broad doorway an inner hook pulled me back, held me in place.

Through a window off to the side was a slight vertical glow. Light seeped faintly through the crack of a door. My breath released and mosquitoes buzzed into my consciousness. Little things out of place; just like in war, things never quite going the way you planned. So that's what you learned to expect, the unexpected. Where was that hound of hell that should be bounding at me? What is this anomaly of faint light beyond the shadowy depths of a living room?

My hand rested on the handle of the screen door. A drop of sweat cut into my eye. I blinked it out and tried to slow my shallow breaths. With the screen door braced behind my knee, I turned the knob of the front door, and it gave back to me a low click then a pale groan as it swung open about a foot. I edged through, letting the screen close in silence and left the wooden door open behind me.

A stale air came into my nostrils, one that exuded a razorous smell of wretched existence layered over aromas of past-cooked meals that clung to the walls and furniture. The dog's absence continued to burden me. The unlocked front door weighed it farther down. This simple, ill-conceived, suicidal plan of vengeance was not going right by way of no contact, the string of it all being drawn too taut.

Shadowy outlines of furniture protruded throughout the darkened room—sofa, chairs, lampshades, a television set. What seemed to be a clear path led to the rail of light at the crack of what I guessed to be a bedroom door. A few seconds wound past. I tried to absorb the house's heavy stillness against the steady drone of insects and frogs from the outside world. There was a lingering scent of family life. It was composed of the smell that comes off the skin of the man, wife, and child. Licorice-like and smoky. Then I went toward the light and fuck the silence and pushed open the door.

The world bent into the oddest of shape and form beyond that entrance. A small lamp beside a large bed shed muted light across Whitehead's bloody body. He reclined in the way of the dead upon one side of the mattress, very still and naked except for the waist of his underwear drawn comically high to just below his navel. In the soft lamplight, blood pooled in a dark configuration across the pillowcase and the rumpled sheet. A wound, probably from a small-caliber pistol, badged the side of his head. The killer had slashed his throat as well, and stab wounds frenzied across his chest. It was as if the one who had cut Whitehead's throat had not had enough and drove the fury of the moment down the man's body.

It was a mess. Blood thrummed hard against my temples. I could feel it up there, turning into a high pitch ringing in my ears.

Whitehead's wife sat on the opposite side of the bed, facing toward a yellow wall. One side of her thin nightgown had slid a little down her waif-like shoulder. Her dark eyes peered back at me over the wisp of a clavicle, hung on me with a questioning indifference, then turned to face the wall again.

After many years of reviewing the bloody tableau that replayed itself so many times through my mind, there came an insight. The spectacle had shamed me. Oh, I know how pathetic and hypocritical that sounds coming from Half-Pint, half-wit Jack Crowe, standing in a bedroom doorway, .45 in hand, driven to kill Whitehead and any member of his family that posed to obstruct the mission. I'd collected many memories of bloody scenes throughout my days in Vietnam. But the portrait of death beset by lady mayhem in that spare bedroom on that night of my attempted vengeance dizzied me. Looking upon the horror, I reset my footing and took slow breaths.

I've come to determine that it was the context of the event that undid me during those first few seconds. War normalized killing, which helps relieve our soldiers from self-wrath after murdering those on the enemy side. It works for a while. We killed only those who, in our feverish minds, were subhuman and mere vermin. Yeah, it works for a time until the light shines through the bullshit. On display in front of me that night were civilians of the United States, albeit the southern tier. Still, this was America. I leaned my shoulder against the jamb of the doorway and lowered the .45 to my side.

"You fuckin' it all up." The boy's voice trembled out of the shadows behind me.

I looked over my shoulder but kept giving him my back. Underwear hung loosely around his skinny belly and barely covered his crotch. He reminded me of a willow limb, its bark scraped clean. Enough of the muted lamplight reached him to strike a yellowish hue over his rib-lined chest. A double-barrel shotgun homed in toward my face. He held it steady with the stock braced against his thin hip and the barrel cupped in his hand. The dog stood beside the boy's skinny legs. Muscles shimmered through the animal's flanks and its saliva-dripping tongue licked at the side of its mouth. A high-pitched whimper creased out of its throat.

"Get goin' now," he said.

"Fire it on, you little shit. Or else I'm going to kill you and your mother and that fucking animal." That is what I said. An inner chill courses through me as I recall those harsh words thrown at the kid. They reflected the madness to which I'd succumbed.

It was the boy's retort that pulled me back to a degree of sanity just enough to see a place of other possibilities. A great sob broke through and he addressed me by my name. The vulnerability he showed and his tidbit gesture of familiarity released more oxygen for me to breathe. "Jack Crowe, you need to git. Get on now."

Then his mother gave a command that quivered through the dense air. "Get him gone, Teddy. Please, just make him go home."

"Back on out now. You fuckin' things up."

"Wipe the door down when he's gone," the boy's mother said. A high, demanding pitch rose into her voice.

The dog's hackles flared and it pawed a step toward me. The boy gutted out some undecipherable command. Something like a haw utterance that rhymed with the caw cry of a crow. The dog whimpered and muscles slackened down its withers. It gave a quick, shameful look at the boy and placed its burnt-amber eyes back on me.

The overhanging limb from an oak tree scraped against the roof. The wind was picking up due to a heat storm kindling miles away. My breath had grown slow and even. I knew then I was going to walk out.

I looked away from the boy and the dog and set my vision on the thin woman who sat with her legs crossed on the bedside in a pure-white negligee spattered with blood. Across from her, Whitehead's dead eyes didn't stare back at me or the woman he'd called his wife but angled upward at the ceiling as if to beseech the heavens for some answer to a question he'd forgotten. *If it hadn't been them, it would have been me*, I said inside my head.

"I'm leaving," I whispered.

A floorboard creaked beneath one of my steps and the boy said, "Don't remember none of this. Make haste, damn you."

I got out the door and onto the gallery and stood for at least five solid seconds, a tiny gesture of defiance to the boy's command. When I came down the steps onto the grass, the inner quakes began. The warm, humid air was so heavy I could palpate it with my hand, but everything inside myself reacted as if to a feverish chill. Mr. Mean and Hard, still fresh out of the Corps, trembled like a gone-dry drunk inflicted with a bout of delirium tremens.

The heat storm that had drummed up some breezes hung far off toward the south. The belly of it flickered with lightning but no thunder came. Stars lit the sky overhead. My remembrance of that walk back to the car is but of the pounding in my chest, my breath catching in my throat, the urge to cry out, the ongoing wink and melt of the fireflies, the echoing call of the owls from across the woods. Sometimes I think I dreamed this night into my history. When I dwell upon it in quiet corners of time, the images take on unimaginable shapes and illogical sequences. Always, I assure myself—I didn't kill.

I clicked the car door shut to Sandy's Chevy and lay the .45 back onto the passenger seat. I turned the key in the ignition and pulled the car onto the crumbling road. The headlights picked up the shining eyes of a deer maybe thirty yards away. The animal, a young buck, spent itself phantom-like back into the darkness of the trees.

A moment of rational thought possessed me. Had any car passed by in the night to take notice of the Chevy parked by the roadside? Probability favored that no human being had driven down this remote passageway in the last few hours. But instinct pressed me to drive farther north toward Arkansas and not return the way I'd come.

A half-hour later, I came out onto the main highway and turned south back toward Baptiste. On this primary artery that ran north and south through the state's upper tier, only a couple of semi-trailers passed by roaring northward. About a mile out of town, the flashing red and blue lights of a sheriff's patrol car sped toward me. My stomach rose and fell as the lights shimmered past. I tried to unravel the knotted threads of what had happened before I arrived at Whitehead's. But fatigue was a leaded weight across my forehead. Little of this night made sense.

When I turned the car onto Roosevelt Street, I rolled the window down and cruised the Chevy to a crawl. The smell of dew rose from the yards. The stark silence of this dying place imbued me with a lament that drove into my heart. Not even the chirrup of a wood frog out there among the humble edifices of sleeping souls. Just the low, steady thrum of the Chevy engine.

I parked in front of the house, emptied the magazine and chamber of the .45, slid the weapon behind my belt, draped my shirt over it and got out of the car. A faint light burned in the window.

Sandy sat upright on the divan that Ida and Seymour had possessed from the beginning of their marriage. He wore a tank top undershirt and a pair of faded work khakis cuffed up to the bones of his ankles. I stood in front of him and he looked up at me, his head askew, eyes slit and fastened hard onto me. His hand rose a bit into the air and in it the last will and testament I'd handwritten a millennium ago earlier in the day.

"Am I looking at a ghost?" He didn't let me answer and lowered his hand back to the top of his leg. "I expected you to be dead, Jack. I knew what you were going to do. You know that I knew that. I'm not a good friend. I'm confused as all hell. What matters right now is that your puny ass is back and you're alive."

I pulled the .45 from behind my belt and set it on the scratched-up coffee table. I sat down beside Sandy. He was looking at the gun. The quiet of the house gave off a sanctified hum. A throbbing sensation kept up above my eyes behind my skull. My hands, the pores lined with the irremovable stains of oil field grime, rested atop my belly. I had to talk.

"Calvin Whitehead was dead when I got there. His wife and the boy killed him." It was then at that very second that I felt it shift inside, a small fault created, just wide enough for some feeling to slip through. I swallowed hard against it, but my voice quaked. "Everything was simpler in Vietnam. Fuck this, Sandy. I just wanted to go to college. Get educated. Learn some shit. I've got a terrible ache to learn, but I don't know what I need to know. I'm ashamed. I'm too fucked up. I went out to kill a man and get killed in the doing. Too dumb to hold myself back from temptations that call on me." Those words, so close to incoherence, came out of a tide of anguish washing through the hollowness inside myself. Goddamn, I was crying.

Sandy kept unblinking, shining eyes on me. "I'm your buddy, Jack. I'm to report you're doing fine as you can do. I say lick your wounds and keep on moving." He breathed deep. I felt warm toward the kid like he was a brother lost who'd found his way back into my life. Next, he sleepily asked, "Who knows besides us?"

It took a moment for me to trim Sandy's question down to its meaningful intent. I slowly pushed myself up. Wiped my nose with the back of my hand and let my head clear. "Other than Whitehead's wife and boy, I don't think anyone else saw me or spotted your car out there." The gun on the coffee table pressed into my hazy consciousness. A need to place it back on the closet shelf overwhelmed me.

Sandy rubbed his chin and stood up, blocking the path to my bedroom. He held the last will and testament of Half-Pint Crowe next to the side of his face.

"This paper will be burned. We try to get an hour or two of sleep of what remains in this fucked up night. Sell our souls and bodies again to the oil field and Blackie Shively tomorrow just as if the world never stopped tripping along. The kid and his mama did us a favor."

Sandy crumpled the paper into his fist, hugged me for a long moment in which I managed to pat him gently on the back.

"Goddamn, Half-Pint, you're alive."

He let go his embrace and turned away toward the kitchen. The switch flicked on and a bar of light cast itself out onto the hallway from the kitchen entrance. Calmness draped over me. From the kitchen came the sound of a wooden drawer sliding open, then shut. The swift, rough scratch of a match against the side of a matchbox. Even the faint, sulphury fumes of the burning match reached my senses. A moment later, the kitchen light flicked off and Sandy walked past me, moving slow and willow-like with his lanky form.

"Ashes in the sink. Get a little rest, Half-Pint. Long day tomorrow."

He disappeared down the narrow hallway. One footstep creaked upon the metal cover of the old floor furnace. From the house's distant realm, the door of Ida and Seymour's room clicked shut behind him. The world keeps spinning, but in those brief seconds, standing alone in the humble abode of my youth, it had stopped. I looked at my watch: 4:03 a.m. I turned off the lamplight by the divan and walked slowly to my room, letting my eyes adjust to the darkness.

Moonlight through the windows cast shadows over the walls. Without flicking the switch to the ceiling light, I swaddled the .45 once more in its oily cloth and returned the weapon to the ammunition canister on the closet shelf. Dropped the shells back into their box. Moonlight through the windows cast apparitions throughout the room.

It would be the floor that gave me respite toward the dawn. I raised the window to draw in the cooler air from outside and lay down on my side fully clothed. Pulled my knees in toward my chest but didn't deceive myself. I would not sleep. In the darkness, about two inches in front of my nose, was an answer to life's meaning. It's just that it wouldn't reveal itself. It was there, only inches away, drawing my thoughts toward it like some black hole that can't be seen but is evident by its gravitational force.

THE NEXT DAY WAS UNLIKE ANY OTHER
OF THAT SUMMER

The next day was unlike any other of that summer. Contradictions ran through it. The men who usually greeted us with ribbing banter coming off their night shift tour could talk of nothing but Calvin Whitehead's frail boy appearing out of the darkness into the hoary glow cast by the drilling rig lights. Clad only in his underwear, scratched up bad from plying through the undergrowth, bare of foot, he slobbered on in incoherent cadence about two n——s killing his daddy.

The crew's driller, a man named Comeau, set the pressure on the drill bit at low torque and acquired with purposeful haste the shotgun stored in the supply trailer. One of the roughnecks had bundled the boy into a blanket, got him water, and knelt before him on one knee like an attendant vassal. Comeau ordered a roughneck to take one of the vehicles and drive like hell to the nearest phone, probably some house on the main thoroughfare into Baptiste, and summon the sheriff. He left his tool man to monitor the instruments and give proper attention to the boy.

Comeau sped away in his pickup, shotgun at rest across his lap, and bore north on the parish road toward Calvin Whitehead's home. The following is what I remember him saying while we gathered around and listened to how the earth had spun from its orbit in the wee hours of morning: "I caught her in my headlights as I drove up. She was curled up on the porch. Y'all, she was naked. Had her nightgown, blood over it, layin' beside her legs. Big Doberman stretched out beside her. The mus-skeets must have been chewing her up but she wasn't saying nothing. 'I'm sorry, ma'am. Are they all gone? I'm real sorry. I'm goin' in just a minute, try to find something to cover you up.'

"Then I went in. Lights were on through the house. I traipsed easy and found Whitehead laid out on the bed. It was bloody awful and I backed out. Don't mess up anything for the law. I pulled a blanket off their sofa. Thought that wouldn't contaminate much and took it out to her. She wouldn't let me put it around her, but she took it and covered herself with it.

When the law arrived, I just wanted to get out of there. Sheriff Hall and some others from State Patrol hit me with questions. I told 'em what I knew and that was it. They were hauling the boy back to the house when I left."

Comeau rubbed his jaw. "Whitehead looked like he'd seen a ghost. I guess he had, in a way."

The men from the half-dazed crew spoke more of the wailing sirens passing down the distant road in the dark hours of early morning. Had Armageddon begun? Should guns be garnered and drawn?

Soon after the night tower crew had departed, Blackie sauntered over to his Impala, popped open the trunk, and lifted the ancient grinding stone from it. He drifted away with the stone held out before him in both hands and disappeared into the darkness of the woods. Through a haze of consciousness, I spied his route while I scrubbed the deck of the rig's platform, which would be rewashed later in the day. With my mind so addled by lack of sleep, time had lost meaningful consequence, but it seemed he returned only minutes later, emerging from the dark recesses of the trees like the shadow of a bear. It could have been hours.

The day beat on and was made of mist and haze though the sun blazed across a blue-white sky and the temperature peaked at 95 degrees. The air thickened. You could poke your finger into it and see ripples criss-cross the vaporous air. Fatigue scraped like claws under my eyelids, but everything close to me was sharp and fine. I trekked through the day like someone walking on the ocean floor. The scent of pine needles caught in my nostrils and dominated every other smell that emanated from the drilling rig.

Late in the morning, when we tripped the pipe to change the worn-down drilling bit, the spin chain whirred out of my hand in slow motion frames around the joints of drilling pipe. The splatter of mud, the engines' hydraulic roar, the usual course of frenzy and mayhem flowed dreamily through my head. After we had pulled the drill string out of the wellbore from a half-mile down and ran it back in, the sun's heat fell over us like it was poured from a ladle.

Afterward, Sandy and I crowded the space around the metal water cooler by the rotary deck's railing. Sweat burned into my eyes. Runnels of it coursed down Sandy's fuzzy cheeks. His blue eyes seemed only half-lit with consciousness behind them. I doffed my oil hat on the deck and commenced to load another plastic cup to the brim with ice water. I swallowed the contents down in three gulps and repeated the process only delayed at times by Sandy's hogging over the spigot.

"Slow it down or you boys are going to make yourselves sick!" Blackie's voice boomed out over the rumble of the rotary table.

"Paying for their sins, no doubt," Clifford said, almost a note of compassion in his tone. "Sandy, for sure, but I'm surprised at you, Jack."

I filled another cup. Leaned my head back to drink. Buster was still on the monkey board high up on the derrick. He hadn't unlatched from the safety harness and stood with his feet apart looking out over the land like a sailor on lookout atop the masthead. Sandy leaned forward and rubbed his face against the chilled side of the water cooler. He mumbled, barely audible, "Pussy'd make you a man, Cliffie. If you'd just get some, you'd shut up about sin…" He stopped midway through his retribution, stood quickly, and the dim light in his eyes flashed brightly.

A deputy's patrol car rolled out from the wooded passageway onto the barren plain around the drilling rig. It stopped near the platform's metal steps and rested down there with an ominous presence that I could feel and taste in the back of my throat. All our eyes fastened down to the glinting top of the vehicle. A tall deputy got out, holding his hat in one hand. His bald pate shined pink in the sunlight, and he ran his hand back and forth over it, put on his khaki cap, and peered up toward us. Blackie had slipped past the doghouse and was ambling down the metal steps. A warm smile crossed the deputy's face. He greeted Blackie with a handshake.

We watched them below us from our position by the deck railing but could not hear the conversation above the groaning rumble of the rig. A clicking sound started up just behind my ear. I thought its origin to be from the distant woods, but it was from inside my head, growing louder and faster. Cliff said something unintelligible, then something again, chuckling, "The law's done come to get you two for sure."

Sandy shifted from foot to foot. Up on the monkey board, Buster remained steadfast, legs apart, safety harness strapped to his wiry frame, looking away across the tops of the trees that stretched to the horizon.

It was an odd respite, we hovering over the platform's rail and giving audience to what seemed a friendly conversation between Blackie and the sheriff's deputy. It probably lasted five minutes but had an interminable quality. At some point within that space of time, I whispered into the whorl of Sandy's ear, "I killed nobody. It's alright."

I said that to Sandy for my own reassurance. But I knew I was not genuinely innocent. I would have been the one to murder Whitehead or try to murder him that night if Providence had not materialized.

Sandy nodded but kept his squinting eyes on Blackie and the deputy. Blood flushed red just beneath the skin of his neck. Cliff, I'm sure, sensed the nearby lurking of evil. Curiosity and the whiff of sin in the air had enlivened him. From high up on the derrick, Buster kept up his steady vigilance of the distant woodlands as if seeing some unforeseen truth.

Then it ended. Blackie and the deputy shook hands once more. The deputy angled his long frame back into the patrol car. Behind the steering wheel, he pulled off his hat, placed it on the passenger seat, and, for the speck of a second, pried his eyes up to the platform and its small audience of roughnecks. He started the engine and rolled the car back and drove slowly away. I wished that a breeze would stir and afford some relief to the stultifying heat. Breathing was hard and we waited for Blackie who stepped light-footed up the staircase.

"Why the hell aren't you cleaning up around here?" Blackie said, but the inherent threat of damnation that usually accompanied his commands and questions was missing.

"Yes, sir," Clifford said.

"Damn, Blackie. What did the lawman want?" Sandy said. He stood with his feet wide apart. A light tremor lit up at the corner of his mouth. I wanted to give my own instructions to Sandy. *Don't show what's in you.* But there was no space or time for such edification. The heat. My unquenching thirst. The faint, far away chatter-bark of a squirrel. I filled the plastic cup with more ice water and took another long drink.

Blackie shoved his hands into his pockets. "Well, what do you think? They're looking for two n——s that killed Calvin Whitehead last night." Blackie sniffed and contorted his lips. "Just like Comeau said. They broke into Whitehead's house and shot him while he slept. Cut him up good. Quite a mess, according to deputy Hall. Didn't hurt the boy and woman at all." Blackie shook his head and looked away.

I sought release for the electrical tension inside myself that wouldn't subside. My anger discharged like an electrical spark onto Blackie. "Blacks, maybe Negroes, but nothing else. That's who you're talkin' about. I won't listen to such being said, killers or not. Who can trust a Whitehead? Nobody knows shit." The words spat out of my mouth.

Blackie's eyebrows lifted into the deep crinkles of his forehead. A tint of amusement glazed his burly face.

Clifford said, "Are you a n—— lover, Jack?"

"Goddamn it, Cliff. Fought, bled, ate, shit, and slept with blacks. One of the best men I ever knew was mixed with black and Spanish blood. Goddamn it, Cliff, he bled all over me when he died. Enough said. You know how I stand."

I hold the memories of Clifford warmly in my breast. He was a kind and simple man, yet he harbored the vile dimensions of Confederate brotherhood deeply inside himself, as we all did to some degree. He cut me with it that day.

"Well, if you're a n—— lover, then that's what you are and I'll accept it," Clifford said. His tongue worked under his lip. He tilted up the bill of his oil field hat a little on his head.

"The son-of-a-bitch is dead. Don't give a damn who killed him." Sandy stomped off down the metal steps.

Blackie watched Sandy clamor down the metal rungs of the stairway then slowly swung his gaze back to me. "Well then, I told the deputy fellow that we hadn't seen any gentlemen of African descent roaming around out here in the woods or on the roads. He'd have to talk some more to the night tower boys, but they done headed home." He shifted his attention to Clifford, who stood mum with half-shut eyes. "Clifford C. Bowles, let be what Half-Pint said. If he wants to love 'em, it's his business."

"Yes, sir," Clifford said. He started to shuffle down the steps, following Sandy's path.

"Get somethin' to eat, then get these boys to cleaning up."

"Yes, sir," Clifford mumbled back over his shoulder.

Blackie tilted his vision toward me. "Go on. You heard me."

"A couple of black men didn't kill Whitehead," I said. "I know it to be bullshit."

Blackie said, "Do I give a damn who killed Calvin Whitehead? That poor woman and boy are free. I hope they stay that way. And you, goddamn you, better wish that for 'em as well. Don't cross too many lines with me. You ain't got many left."

He turned his back on me. Wandered into the doghouse, to the instrument panels to monitor their needles and gauges, checking for proper pressure and weight on the drill bit...and I lost my thoughts and looked up. Buster was slowly unlatching himself from the safety harness, the sky above him ablaze with reflected light. Buster, his wiry body framed against the blue sky, looked almost Christ-like from that angle. I could not stop staring upward at him in trembling awe.

THE REMAINING DAYS OF SUMMER

An unstable atmosphere besieged the parish's upper regions during the remainder of that summer. It was like being caught in the darkness of a swift approaching storm while walking across an open field, feeling the kindle of electrical energy, the rise of hair on your arms and behind your neck. When and where will the lightning bolt strike?

I sought solace in Frank's bloodied-up books. Perched myself on the steps of the old house after work and read into the twilights of evening, often depriving myself of dinner for penance. I was always seeking small forms of self-punishment in those days.

Within the pages of *The Razor's Edge*, I became more enamored by Larry Darrell's quest for transcendence. A lament stirred by loss hit me on the evening I read the last page of the novel. I wanted to stay in the well-traveled world of Maugham, the man who had recorded Larry's spiritual journey. Crickets chirruped inside the dusky buzz of summer. Wistful pondering took hold. Is the opportunity to seek higher purpose only for those who are privileged the time to read, to think, to question? The seed of such quest is in us all, I concluded. Some Great Spirit or lightning bolt into the primordial muck put it there. But what the fuck is it? Did Larry Darrell indeed find happiness and meaning or was he just a work of fiction?

Evening next, I peeled back the pages to the third book, *The Adornment of the Spiritual Marriage*, and struggled to grasp the dense, 14th-century writings of John of Ruysbroeck, who seemed to believe Christ was like a bridegroom and the church a bride. Let me note my bias straightaway. In this book, I would not have minded if filaments of shrapnel had shredded more pages. It seemed to my addled way of thought that ol' John was saying that a person could lose him or herself in the marriage between God and church and live happily ever after. Just so much bullshit to this ex-grunt of the Corps. A tremendous pang of regret struck into me that Frank was not "truly" around so that I could ask him his opinion, though his ghost did his best to assuage my disdain. *"We're just searching, Jack. Just take the journey."* Since Frank had been crazy, this made complete sense coming straight from his apparitional breath. All this time, my college acceptance letter grew smudged with the grimy imprints of my fingertips as I looked upon it each day passing. This letter I still possess in a space of honorarium on my office bookshelf.

Early on after Whitehead's murder, I gauged the moments when fate might call me out. When black men might be beaten and nabbed from out of the quarters and made to stand before Whitehead's wife and kid to be fingered as the two for sacrifice. Then, I would arise, go forth, and tell my story for what it was worth.

Don't pitch the eyes so disdainfully to the side. I would so have gone before the law, the town of the devout, the unknown God in a heaven far away and proclaimed that I knew the truth about the murder of Calvin Whitehead. I, Half-Pint Crowe, would have beseeched all to listen well to my narrative of that bloody night. How Whitehead's death was stolen away from me by that boy and woman. How I regained my senses and reset my path forward. Ask your God to forgive me of such weakness that I would so quickly kill another being, and by-the-by ask Him to forgive me for all the other bloody transgressions I've committed.

But this was the South where myth and reality have a remarkable capacity to blend. Fate never served to call me out that summer or summers hence.

The blacks of the parish and surrounding regions hunkered down, sequestered themselves in humble domiciles on the town's fringes. They gave time for the great storm to blow through. I imagined Christ setting foot once again on earth, toting a sign heaved across his shoulder, *Love Thy Neighbor as Thyself.* His appearance would have been a fine miracle. But would it have slaked the bloodthirst building in the body of the people? I doubt it. Vengeful passion was popping around like heated grease. Poor Christ, likely, would have been knifed in the ribs and a new religion born. Such is the way of sacred circles. *Fuck my cynical nature. Before Frank came along and hurled me forth in search of meaning and purpose, I was just a smartass. Fifty years later, I'm even worse, an educated one.*

"They hauled a couple more to jail," Sandy would say on our early morning route out to the Haiti-Cullen to meet up with Blackie, Cliff, and Buster. He'd grin, just one side of his lip curled up and talk while gritting his teeth. "And Whitehead's wife and boy said, 'Nah, ain't none of these did it.' Sandy would jive himself into ludicrous mimicry. "Ain't none of them! Ain't none of them! Bring us the ones that murdered my boy's daddy! My husband! Please, God! Give us the justice we so deserve!"

Sometimes I'd laugh. Sometimes I'd draw deeper into sullen repose. I suppose the real miracle that summer was that no one, black or white, died in the aftermath of Whitehead's death. Close calls rife with drama but no death. Drunken members of the football team from the segregated high school packed together in the backs of pickup trucks rumbled down the potholed streets of the quarters, hurling racial epithets and empty beer cans at sun-scoured porches vacant of sane people, then clearing out in wise haste when the barrels of shotguns poked through the windows.

A cross was set aflame on the grassy front lot of the *Spirit of Christ Baptist Church* that rested in an enclave of pine trees on the quarters' southern edge. In the spirit of equal opportunity racism, a cross burned the same night in front of the *Sacred Heart Catholic Church*, a lone edifice on the highway that coursed south out of town beyond the dead mill. Catholicism was viewed with ardent suspicion among the prominent protestant enclaves of the upper parishes.

The blacks of the community went about in pairs and threes like little cliques, practiced deference but with eyes cast straight ahead, and the preachers preached this too will pass. The Chief of Police, a burly man who liked to show his belly scars from wounds received on the fifth day of the Normandy invasion, spoke into the circles of conversation, "If there's to be any n—— killing, it'll be done by me. I don't want any more complications with this mess."

Notions arising from deep inside the communal consciousness began to tamp down passions for some form of racial retribution. Questions of a different nature sifted through the southern air. How did two black assassins get past the Doberman? Why did a man of Whitehead's paranoid bearing leave his door unbolted? The military's special forces undoubtedly trained those black violators of southern sanctity, their skills honed by suicide missions in Vietnam. What a mistake Truman bequeathed to this nation by forcing integration onto the military of the United States.

With each failure by Whitehead's wife and son to identify suspects hauled before them, rumors flurried like dandelion seeds tossed up by the wind. From the din of ongoing gossip through this remote parish, I gleaned the story that had unfolded from the lips of Grace Whitehead and her boy, Theodore.

The two held steadfast to their narrative of Whitehead's death. Two men of color, one tall and high-black, the other, medium in height and of mulatto bearing, killed the beloved husband of Grace Whitehead. Grace had awoken to what seemed the crack of a heavy limb breaking from a tree. She flung off the bedsheet and threw her back against the wall. Drove herself down to the floor. Above the panting of her breath, she heard a man's voice. "Calm, Missy."

The light flicked on. Above the bed stood the tall, black man, the wisp of a mustache above his lip. Her husband's body writhed like a pinned snake trying to twist around a stick beneath the bedsheet. Whitehead kept trying to raise his head, his mouth agape. She saw no blood at this juncture, but the black man held a small-caliber handgun. Her fierce-racing mind factored in quick that her husband had taken a shot in the head. The sharp crack sound of the bullet had been what awakened her. The ribbed handle of a hunting knife protruded from a leather sheath at the side of the black man's belt.

A Yankee accent and a deep, gravelly voice stoked toward her heart. "Want him to live just a bit to see who I am." The man shifted his stone-cold gaze down at Whitehead. "Remember Detroit? I want you to remember Detroit, Mr. Whitehead. It's not about the money."

There came a shift in the flow of Grace Whitehead's blurry consciousness. Everything went from slow-motion to high speed. The dog barked from across the house, shaking the foundations. The tall black man nodded at the other black man, short and stout of build, standing by the bedroom door. This man held a handgun of larger caliber pressed over his heart. He pulled the bedroom door shut. Claws tore across the wooden floors. A staccato of barks exploded outside the door.

"Speak to your boy, Missy," the tall black man said. "Lest nobody be spared."

"Stand down, Teddy!" It blew from her throat. The power of her voice shocked her. The black man smiling. Calvin writhing on the bed like a pupa seeking to be borne from its cocoon.

The boy shouted from beyond the door, "Hout! Hout!" A fragile quiet ensued. The dog had heeled, and the boy apparently stood behind him. Not even a low-pitched whine out of the dog's throat, such command the boy had of this animal. The boy cried, "Mama!"

"Tell your boy to put down what he might hold in those little hands. Stay put."

"Put it down, Teddy!" She cried out and wondered from where the power of her voice had arisen.

"It'll go quick," he said.

The tall black man turned his attention to the dimming light in Whitehead's eyes.

"Vengeance is mine. Is that not something you would say, Mr. Whitehead? Well, I'm saying it. Vengeance is mine. And someday, someone will look down at me and say the same. Someone's always saying it. Yes, sir. Someone's always sayin' it."

He drew the knife from its sheath at his waistband and sliced Whitehead's throat in a swoop of a hand free of hesitancy. May have been a shudder of her husband's body for a second, may have not, but it didn't stop there.

"It went dark," Grace said to those few men dressed in khaki shirt and blue pants, holding hats in hand, beads of sweat across their foreheads, surrounding her on the big, cushioned chair in the center of the living room as she hugged her upright knees against her chest, draped in the sofa blanket and the boy on the floor rested his head beside her feet and the dog lay curled asleep by the boy. All of them now free of blood trace. The aura of shock and innocence aglow around them.

Dawn grey-lit through the windows. A man in a disheveled white shirt and wrinkled khaki pants still wandered the house, scraping, plucking, and bagging so-called particles of evidence into plastic pouches. Outside, a few men still roamed, flashlights lit, scouring the ground for indentations of footprints in the high delta earth. Whitehead's body was eventually lifted from its bloody repose on the bed to a gurney and cast on the short journey through the house to an ambulance dispatched from the small medical center that served the parish.

The weapons of murder would be found around mid-morning, laid side-by-side in flagrant display on a gravel apron by the roadside a quarter mile north of the house. In proper juxtaposition alongside them was the handgun they had confiscated from the boy. The tallest black man had picked up the .38 from the floor beside Teddy's bare feet. It was the gun that always hung inside the pantry door in the kitchen. The black man stepped back and said, "If you loose that dog after us, we kill the animal and you best hide your mama cause we come back to finish it. But we won't kill you."

Then the two killers went silent out the room and through the front door, closing it softly behind them. In the vernacular of crime scenes, the phone lines had been cut. The .22 caliber was a ghost gun, without a serial number, cartridges removed. The knife, a commando combat Ka-Bar. Both scoured of prints and minute debris as though drenched in battery acid. It was as if they'd garnished a message to the deputies who found them, 'We are done with nothing more to say. But with courtesy we present ourselves to you.' On the handgun taken from beside the boy's feet, a collage of the boy's and his daddy's fingerprints lay smudged across the barrel and grip. Only Calvin Whitehead's fingerprints were found on the casings of the unspent rounds in the revolver's chambers.

Some reasonable myth emerged from the rise and fall of rumors that thrived in the humid summer air, dispelling suspicions that woman and boy committed murder. Calvin Whitehead loved that boy and had given him license to keep the dog in his bedroom at night. The animal appeared to be the boy's one true friend. Calvin Whitehead believed that God protected them from evil out there in the remoteness of swamp and woodland. He also held confidence in his reputation of one best given a wide berth. Sanctioned by a wondrous and beneficent God, Calvin had beaten close to death a few men that he deemed of unfit character, white and black alike. His proneness for righteous violence hung on him like the dank scent of a fox's den.

A new wrinkle of thought, wrought with fascination and mystery, drifted through the rumor clouds. Hadn't Whitehead been known to disappear on hunting and fishing trips up north without the accompaniment of the wife or boy or friend? Hell, did the man have any friends? No one called himself or herself the friend of Calvin Whitehead. Did this man of God have a penchant for visiting the brothels of Detroit on his trips to and from the upper peninsula of Michigan?

I could almost hear the ruminations echoing back and forth off the inner walls of people's skulls. Every man had a secret; every man had a forbidden desire that itched inside him. People's imaginations flourished and took on wondrous shapes and forms. Calvin Whitehead had drawn the wrath of a black pimp out of Detroit. Whatever Whitehead had done, whether it was some sadistic act with a black girl that went tragically wrong or a guilt-fueled beating to some prostitute after lust was spent, it had been enough for two Detroit black men to find him, shoot him in the head, cut his throat and stab the hell out of him.

This narrative of what happened took solid hold. So juicy, exciting, and horrendous it was that it had to be the truth. It had its benefits. The story released pressure for retribution toward the innocent blacks of Baptiste. As time crept past, I heard spoken the same story repeated and it seemed to satisfy the populace. It came from the checkout aisles of the Piggly Wiggly, from the men of the evening tower as we took over their shift, from the gas station attendant leaning into Sandy's Chevy window: "They were northern n——s that slipped down among us and killed ol' Whitehead. Ours know their place. Thank God for that."

Out of this muck of mind and spirit, I went forth into the remaining days of summer. I had not killed Whitehead. The path forward that Frank had revealed still lay before me. Luck, happenstance, step left or step right. The vagaries of war and cosmic unfolding influence our days.

My thoughts went inward, too deep inside myself for one so ill-equipped. We are strange creatures whose heads poked through the garden walls of Eden into self-awareness, and, alas, we realized our finiteness. The angst of knowing our impending death confused the fuck out of us. So, we created stories of Gods, super beings to explain our origins. Rules came out of these tales that helped us keep social order. Without our stories of origin, we're little more than organismic specks consuming the lifeblood of a tiny blue ball in an infinite universe. Of course, some of us shuffle around with cynical smugness and wonder about the absurdity of it all.

No matter, It's all a story.

On an evening at least a week after Whitehead's killing, two State Patrol investigators pulled their vehicle onto the side of Roosevelt Street in front of the old house. I looked up from my tattered book and spied upon them as they strode down the narrow, broken concrete walk toward me. I closed the book and palmed it over my stomach. From the oak and sycamore trees, Katydids burst higher into their chant of katydid-katydidn't through the softening air. A waxing moon peered down at me from above the housetops.

"Evening, we're looking for Sandy Guillory. Might he be here, or might you be him?"

The one who asked had a tall, lean bearing. He introduced himself as Officer Bill Petrie and the man with him as Officer Steve Hadley. He had a stern face with lines etched deep across his forehead and up the corners of his mouth. It appeared to me that he wanted to spit. The other man possessed a warm smile that curled up stubbled cheeks. He was also tall and skinny, and his pistol belt fit tight around his waist.

I said, "He's inside with his girlfriend armed and dangerous. You might want to lock and load."

A harsh glare struck across the face of the stern officer. The lines etched deeper across his forehead. But the one who carried the warm smile said with a chuckling taunt, "Why, we're always locked and loaded, Half-Pint."

He knew me somehow. I wondered about the drift and flow of whispers through the air of Baptiste.

I said, "Yes, sir," and rose from the steps, opened the screen door, and yelled for Sandy. The two men brushed by me into the shaded recess of the living room and the stern-faced one's hand palmed over his holster. The one with the warm smile said, "It's okay, Half-Pint," as if to cast assurances toward me, and I said, "I know that well enough."

The smell of ground meat scalding in a skillet tinged the air. Radio music from the Shreveport AM station played from the kitchen. Julie poked her head outside the kitchen doorway. She said, "Y'all come in," with a heavier than usual southern silt to her voice. Sandy walked past her with a can of Pabst in hand. He'd bathed earlier and was dressed in a white tee-shirt and patched jeans.

"Mr. Guillory? Can we visit a moment? A few questions to ask."

"I'm guilty as sin," Sandy said. "Y'all have a seat."

I closed the screen door. Resumed my position upon the steps. I could hear the soft chant of my voice inside my head reaffirming that I hadn't killed Whitehead and nobody else was dying. Not anyone. The bound writings of St. John of Ruysbroek remained closed within my hands. The cusp of dusk was wrapping around the old house. The insects spiriting into the descent of the day. A few minutes spilled away. The gentle smiling deputy came out, stood above me, and I didn't look up.

"Mind if I sit a moment?"

"Sit away."

He lowered his lanky frame beside me. The stale scent of cigarette smoke lilted off his clothes. He lit a cigarette. Took a long drag from the fag held between nicotine-stained fingers and exhaled the smoke.

"Your old man burnt himself up. I'm sorry about that." He shook his head, took another quick drag on the cigarette, and went on. "I got a boy over in Vietnam. You made it out okay?" He didn't pause to catch a response, though I had no plan to provide one. "I worry about him, but he's serving our country. Honoring his God. Liberty." He looked at the cigarette between his fingers and the smile never left him. "Probably get into law enforcement when he gets out. Are you doing okay? Now that you're back." He looked at me sideways with his eyes squinting against the smoke. "Sorry about your ol' man. He was quite the character."

"Yes, sir. I don't plan to pick up guns anymore."

"What's your shoe size, Half-Pint?" He swallowed and his Adam's apple went up and down. His smile shifted to an embarrassed grin. My thumb rested between the closed pages of Ruysbroeck's writings where I'd been trying to make sense of his dense language.

"Do you think two n——s out of Detroit came all the way down here and killed Calvin Whitehead?" He emitted a husky laugh. "Hell, we don't give a shit about your shoe size, Jack. That's your given name, right?" His words sped on. "Ol' Bill in there don't care about Sandy's little encounter with Calvin Whitehead a while back. And we don't care about the ass whipping Calvin gave you. Or you drivin' around in your buddy's souped-up Chevy on the night of poor Calvin's demise."

My heart sped and a coldness spread inside myself.

"I don't understand what's in the hearts of people," he said. "Look at me, Jack. Give me that due. We know the woman and boy killed that man. Don't fool yourself into thinking that the world just goes round and round with folks looking only into themselves. Some of us have the power of deduction, ears tuned to the wind, eyes fastened upon the tiny movements around us. The residue of our lives falls all around us, Jack." He took another drag on the cigarette, blew smoke out toward the dusk settling around us. "Appreciate the steps you take forward, son. Appreciate the light that shines upon you, the delicacies of truth. I'll take a guess. Your skinny ass got saved that night. And you chose to keep it all to yourself."

With that, I leaned forward as if to press the warm velvet of the evening air around me. A slew of dogs that wandered like a wolf pack through the town commenced barking from far off beyond the neighborhood. Summer was fully ripe, and the cicadas buzzed like electric drills. At this point, my weaknesses mounted, and I opened my mouth: "If you already know so much, why are you here?"

Steve Hadley, the smiling cop, riveted a dumbfounded look upon the side of my face and I swear to the heavens, the gods, the limitless universe or whatever is worth swearing on, that he kept a genuine expression of astonishment and said, "Why, to maintain law and order, Marine."

"Yes, sir," I said and bit into the inside of my cheek. And my goddamn mouth couldn't stay shut. "What's going to happen to that boy and woman?"

Officer Steve Hadley spit away a flake of tobacco from his lip. "Why should anything happen to them? They'll do fine, I suppose. Ol' Whitehead had means and old money, though not well graced with love and compassion in his wilted heart. They should take benefit of it. Hell, maybe someday we'll catch those Detroit n——s and we'll all be satisfied." He winked at me.

I bit deeper into the inside of my cheek. "Your son is trying to stay alive with black folk of whom you speak, sir. I'd take note of such."

He lifted one eyebrow and looked at me as if taking aim. He laughed and I turned away and looked straight ahead wishing dusk would thicken more into night. Then he gave the evening and me a long moment of silence. He was very still and I was aware he was studying me with an intensity that burned.

"Do you think my boy will be alright? He's everything to me and his mama. Do you think he'll come back okay?"

It hurt bad when he asked me. My mangled wits couldn't fathom much more about what was right or wrong or real or fake in this shadowy southern world in which we roamed.

"I don't know, sir. It can go either way. I hope it goes well enough for him. I truly do, sir."

"I know you do, Half-Pint. I know you do."

The two State Patrol officers left soon after, lithe and shadowy figures crossing the small yard to their patrol car. Sandy and Julie came out as the men drove away, and the patrol vehicle's taillights flashed into the dwindling light.

Julie sat between Sandy and me. The scent of Prell drifted up from her hair and a warm radiance came off her skin. Such smells stirred dull longing inside myself, but I knew what it was and shame came with it. Julie was like kin and always would be. Sandy, despite his abundant flaws and despite my restraints upon closeness, had become a brother.

Oh, there will come a breaking of the heart, but not in the way you might imagine. I don't mean to be a coy old man holding back tidbits of information about what's to come. It's just that I'm not ready to touch upon the irony of Sandy and Julie's life together. I'll get to it down the road. Soon enough.

"It was mama that told them you borrowed Sandy's car when Calvin Whitehead was murdered." She put her hand on the back of my neck.

"That doesn't matter," I said. "Nothing came of that night. We're all innocent."

"I know that," Julie said. "Innocent, innocent, innocent." Her hand slipped away and she leaned her head on Sandy's shoulder.

Sandy was unusually quiet. After about three long breaths, he spoke. "Half-Pint, I think those sons-of-bitches know who killed Calvin Whitehead."

"I'm giving you two this house," I said.

Julie raised her head from Sandy's shoulder. I felt both her and Sandy looking at me through the soft light. Finally, Sandy spoke: "No more of that. We don't want this piece of shit of a house."

"Maybe you'll let me stay here summer next if Blackie hires me on again."

"Stop your nonsense, Half-Pint. I've had enough of it."

"Be quiet, hon'," Julie said. Then she turned to me. Her breath hit against my cheek. She whispered, "Thank you. I understand." She laughed in a demure way. "It'll make mama happy for me to have a place of my own."

The pinpoint light of the evening star broke through the darkening sky, and bull bats flicked themselves into the radiance of warm air rising off the street. I was happy. I felt full, as if giving away a bit of myself left more room for new hope. I told myself I couldn't be happier than this moment on these little concrete steps. Then Julie said, "Come on, let's eat those hamburgers I cooked."

"Just potatoes and rabbit food for you, Half-Pint," Sandy said.

And yeah, I was happy. Summer was waning. The sunlight at the end of the day grew more oblique in its slant. I'd killed no one. I felt the strange warmth of intimacy toward people. Just a few more weeks of work lay in front of me before I transitioned into another world far different from the oil fields of this swampy, piney land and the battlefields of Vietnam. And this is an admission I give to myself looking back over my arthritic shoulder. Going forth into the bloody gauntlet of Vietnam and the dangerous tidings of oil field work gave me less fear than heading into the unknowns of college.

A few days passed and came the quick slap of a reminder across the face that life cuts its own course in front of you. John Lennon wrote in some song years later, 'Life is what happens when you're busy making other plans.' The words have always seemed to hold true. The direction that I thought Sandy's, mine, and Julie's lives were heading changed in the breath of a second back then. Sandy chose an odd moment and place to pull the government envelope from his back pocket.

We shared a chicken sandwich and stood in tree shade at the edge of the scraped-out clearing that surrounded the drilling rig. The derrick protruded toward an azure sky in the distance and the rig rumbled low like some sleeping beast. Blackie's broad back outlined itself on the platform's deck. Buster and Cliff were sequestered in the doghouse eating a thrifty lunch and drinking iced tea out of a thermos.

Sandy handed me the brown envelope folded over on itself. A sudden pressure built behind my breastbone. The envelope was addressed to Sandifer Guillory. I opened it and drew the letter out and unfolded it while I held the remains of the sandwich between my teeth. The first lines of the draft induction notice shot into me: *You are hereby ordered for induction into the Armed Forces of the United States...*

I took the sandwich from my mouth and swallowed and let my tongue roam over my teeth.

"You'll declare yourself a homosexual. Me and Julie will verify it," I said. "Maybe your kin can write something up. Julie's mom. Goddamn, we'll get everybody on the rig to declare you're queer. They'll back you up. Blackie'll think it's a lark. He's not going to want to lose you anyhow. Buster and Cliffie will do anything he tells them."

It was those days when being gay was regarded as a medical disorder in the ethereal realms of psychiatry. My mind churned to find any possible way for Sandy to escape from military induction and the bloody gauntlet of Vietnam. Damn, my heart was pounding and he was standing there like a dumbass without a care in the world. There it came. That southern boy grin lit up. The heat of the August day drove down on us. The air was dead but bore the faint scent of pine needles from beyond the stand of hardwood trees.

"Nobody would believe Sandy Guillory to be a homosexual, you dumb shit," Sandy said. He dipped his chin. Contemplated the sandwich held in his rough hand.

My thoughts kept speeding forward. "We can load you up with drugs. Acid or uppers. I've heard of guys going in for induction physicals hyped up and crazy as shit and the medics shove them out the door. Damn, man, you seem crazy half the time anyway. It should be easy for you."

The bastard took a lazy bite of the chicken sandwich that Julie had made and packed into his lunch pail. His jaw rotated slowly. His eyes held onto me. The urge to smack away that glint of amusement rising into the tiny muscles high up on his cheeks came, but I didn't smack him. Instead, I kept on: "There's Canada or Mexico. Julie would go with you. I know it."

"No, she wouldn't." He shot a sideways look toward the rig. Blackie's frame still held motionless on the broad derrick platform, his usual stance when studying the gauges, monitors, and dials on the instrument panels. Sandy looked back at me. The smooth lump of his Adam's apple drove up and down as he swallowed. The glint of amusement had abandoned his face. "The hell with being drafted. I'm going to join the Marines."

"No, you're not going to do that." A knife went in me. "No, that's not to be done."

He laughed. "You did it. You turned out alright."

"No, I didn't, you brain dead motherfucker."

Silence wedged between us. Sandy held the remainder of his sandwich in both hands like it was a book to be read. The retinal gleam of his eyes pierced me. "Yeah, you did."

My breath slipped away. It hammered into me. The bastard admired me. Half-Pint, the murdering, talking to the dead son-of-a-bitch that I was. Somehow, the role of gravity had shifted and I'd, without will or volition, influenced Sandy's life. He'd walk down a different trail than the one that had been ordained for him because of our introduction to one another in this life that happens when we're busy making other plans.

"Admire me not, you stupid motherfucker. I'm one damaged piece of shit."

"I've decided, but yep, you're a piece of shit alright, buddy." He was gleaming that smile that would melt you.

My fist clenched, shook as if gripping a string of electrical wire.

"I've decided, Half-Pint." His grin overtook the speed of my heart, and I muttered the name of the woman that held my last bit of hope. "Julie. What about Julie?"

"She'll be proud of me, brother."

"Damn you, Sandy."

Angles of light shift. Dreams ignite. Journeys begin. After exposure to Frank's holiness in the last months of the war, after the turbulent summer on the drilling rigs, after friendships formed with human beings least likely, there came a shift in the angle of light. Half-Pint stepped into a different world—a place of noble edifices harboring lecture halls and libraries. A university awaited Half-Pint. The war awaited Sandy.

UNIVERSITY AND SANDY

Sandy left for Marine Corps boot camp in San Diego late into August, and on that same day, I left for school in Baton Rouge. Happenstance had tacked us together for a while. Waterways coursing side-by-side, but then the streams diverge.

There is little to no fanfare in the comings and goings of oil field workers. For both Sandy and me, it was something else, the firm shake of rough hands, and I'll be damned, the liquid sheen of eyes adrift from Blackie, Clifford, and Buster on the day we said our goodbyes.

A section of me tore away that day. I saw it ripping away inside Sandy as well. His lips scrunched together and his usual flippant retorts to Clifford escaped him. It hit me hard that these men whose rough hands I shook had adopted Sandy and now the bejeweled son of the South was heading into the winds of war. And they had accepted me into their own as well. So, it went. Later in the day, I helped Sandy drape a canvas cover over his cherished Chevy after he'd stationed the car next to the house.

The next morning, Julie drove Sandy, who had never been on a plane, to Shreveport Regional Airport in her Fairlane for his flight to San Diego. That same morning, I tossed my seabag into the storage compartment of a Continental bus. I found a window seat and rested my old haversack that held Frank's books across my knees. The bus rumbled to life. I closed my eyes, elbows propped on my pack. The bus tracked south down narrow highways. At some point in the haziness of my slumbering consciousness, it crossed a silver bridge on the Mississippi River into Baton Rouge.

I eventually rented an upstairs room in a fine old house near the university. It had access to a small kitchen on the second floor. Oak trees lined the street outside. A concrete walkway, buckled by tree roots, led to a road that wound toward the sprawling campus.

A widowed woman named Rita Kendricks owned the house. Her

hair was short and white. She smiled often. I suspected the breadth of her smile belied loneliness. She had a love and fascination for bird watching. As I grew to know her, I afforded her time listening to stories of wrens, flycatchers, cedar waxwings passing through the trees and shrubs in her backyard as if they were old friends come to light and say hello. She loved most the wood thrush's song, how it lifted her into the heavens at dawn and dusk.

Inside this tranquil domain, I shied away from my fellow students. They shined too bright, unscarred. I watched them through a different angle of light as they tested pathways in their lives, going happily, nervously, rebelliously along. They seemed to know something that was always beyond my reach—how to have fun. Although, even back then, I suspected that inner struggles inhabited us all—the beautiful, the plain, the ugly.

I kept a polite distance from all these young folks. Swaddled myself into a disciplined indulgence of learning that I attributed to the molding given me by the Corps. When lonely, I talked to Frank or Romano. Here's a quirky note about my conversations with these two dead friends. Sadness always shadowed across Frank's face when Romano appeared and he'd shimmer away.

"Come on, Frank," I would try to say. "No one could have saved him." But Romano's presence reminded Frank of his limitations back in those war days and he would drift away to wherever he might have come.

"Not even Jesus could have stanched that wound, Doc," Romano would implore.

An odd current of energy ran through me while I sat in classrooms of hallowed halls of learning. Algebra, biology, English composition confronted me. Basics of academia that I'd shunned through my early years in public school but now consumed my passions and interests. I learned that I could survive and walk among normal people and mastered the art of blending in with the civilian population. Hair grew on my face. I used a pair of scissors to cut back drooping locks. I kept my few clothes clean. Books were in my hands, more often than not, while a flame burned within the scope of my vision. All the while,

Frank's bloody volumes rested as silent companions atop a night table beside my small bed—in which I sometimes slept. The pallet of a throw rug beside a small antique desk provided a more familiar spartan comfort for me to rest.

Distinct memories prevail of the years that led to my eventual professorship following that long, hot summer of oil field work. Early on, while Sandy was in Marine boot camp, I wrote to him at least once a week. I knew well the assault upon body, mind, and spirit during the gauntlet of Marine Corps recruit training. Mainly, I gave to him encouragement in my wise old man way. "They want to see if they can break you down. Show them that they can't. Walk the fucking line. Imagine Julie's smile. You will not let them break you down." Yet, in the deeper recesses of my damaged soul, I wished them to wash him out, send him home.

I would tell him about the pretty girls on campus and how they would have swooned over the likes of him. (He thought all girls swooned over him.) And I would tell him about the new world that surrounded me and give him as much news as I could about Baptiste, though it was very little that I knew but what Julie shared in her occasional letters to me.

On a crisp fall Saturday afternoon, I was about to make my ritual weekend trek to study at Middleton Library near the university's quad. Mrs. Kendricks called me down to the parlor room at the bottom of the stairs. "You've got a phone call, Jack. Don't be long. I've messaging left to do."

It was near the end of October. Sandy had graduated from boot camp less than an hour earlier at the Marine Corps Recruit Depot in San Diego. The next phase that awaited him would be four weeks of infantry training at Camp San Onofre in Camp Pendleton. But for this afternoon, following the traditional graduation ceremony, he and his fellow head-shaven graduates had been granted the liberty to roam designated areas of the recruit base or commune with family and friends who'd come to witness ceremonial graduation. After each platoon's ritualistic dismissal on the parade grounds, a favorite destination was a row of phone booths near the depot cafe.

Sandy's voice resonated through the receiver. "Half-Pint, stick those books up your ass and have a cold beer tonight. Julie's going to marry me. You're my second and final call. Do you hear me?"

The door beyond the parlor was half open to welcome in the autumn air. On the front lawn, the limbs of a willow tree shuffled in a light wind. I said, "You made it. Oh-h-h, my gosh. Yeah, I hear you."

"You're as intelligent as ever. Nothing gets past you, man." A slender gap of quiet slipped between us. The inhalation of Sandy's breath eased through the phone's receiver. "I made it, Half-Pint," he said in a lowered voice. "It was harder than I thought. Damn, I just got off the phone with Julie. We're getting married in five weeks when I get a ten-day leave. She said it's got to be private. Except you, her mama, and the boys. Blackie, Buster, and Cliffie have to be there. You're going to be standing off to my side. Best Man. Promise me you'll do that, Half-Pint. It'll be near Thanksgiving."

What could I do? I didn't say what I wanted to say, that I'd wished he'd have washed out, bungled it up in his Sandy fuck you way where they would have strait-jacketed him, stuffed undesirable discharge papers in his back pocket and tossed him to the side of the road at the front gate. The ghosts of Vietnam stirred somewhere off to the right of my shoulder like they'd just roused from their sleep and were hungry. I bowed my head away from their wavering images.

I laughed. Sandy Guillory and Julie Longo to be married. How did it feel? It felt good, all that light shining through from different angles. I stuffed myself with well-being. Marked myself through with paw prints of self-congratulation. You see, in an almost perverse way, I heaped the outcome of their pending marriage onto my shoulders. By magic or good fortune, I had brought these two people into proper alignment, had given them a home and the opportunity to transform it. I took a deep breath.

"This is damn fine, Sandy."

"I love that girl, Half-Pint," he said as if in wonder of his words.

"I'll be standing off to the side. You can count on it."

Sandy's breath hit like an ocean wave through the phone's receiver. "You're a light in the darkness, dumbass."

"Dumb fuck," I responded loudly and caught the cut of Mrs.

Kendrick's eyes upon the side of my face. She stood in the doorway a few feet distant. Frail and lumpy in a cotton dress. A notepad of phone messages held within her bony fingers.

"Sorry, Mrs. Kendricks." I turned away and whispered into the phone. "That's damn fine, Sandy. Go well with it. I'm telling you straight out of my heart this is good news. I'm happy for you and Julie. I'm telling you I love you, man. I love you and Julie. What you're both doing. I want you to know that."

"You gone queer on me, boy?"

I rolled with it. Lost the hush-hush of my voice and yelled into the phone's receiver, "Who could resist your pretty little ass, you savage son-of-a-bitch!"

Sandy's satisfied chuckle came through the hollow of the line. I glanced back over my shoulder. Mrs. Kendrick's grey eyes pierced me through half-slits as if trying to spot a warbler in one of her backyard trees.

"Joking around, Mrs. Kendricks. An old buddy of mine with troubles. I try to humor him." Her staid expression remained fixed and I turned away from it.

I lowered my voice again. "I'm happy, man. I'm happy for you and Julie."

"Yeah, Half-Pint, I'm happy. Thanks, man. Yeah, thanks."

We talked for a few moments longer. Logistics. He would complete infantry training late in November and if the gods still smiled upon him, he'd book a flight from Lindberg Field in San Diego to Love Field in Dallas, then a short hop into the regional airport in Shreveport where Julie would gather him up. A few days later, I would take a Continental Trailways bus from Baton Rouge to Shreveport, the nearest drop-off station to Baptiste. He would meet me at the bus station in the Chevy. He'd marry Julie the next day or a few days later when the time came together to make it fit. The operator plied into our conversation, announcing Sandy needed more change to continue, and we let it go... We said goodbye. I placed the handset back onto its hook. Rubbed my nose and turned around to ease the weight of Mrs. Kendrick's presence.

"I'm a gay, old woman, Jack. Please restrain your usage of such language in this house. Son-of-a-bitch and dumb fuck are unbecoming descriptors of a person's character. Such terms of usage are well beneath your grit."

"Yes, Mrs. Kendricks. I'll watch it."

She chuckled and shook the soft, white locks that fell around her ears. I liked Mrs. Rita Kendricks, and I liked her more at this moment.

This was the era before book packs became the basic means for students to tote their books around a college campus. I'd secretly copped my haversack when discharged from the Corps, professing it lost after stuffing it low into my seabag. Hell, it was a part of me. My blood and the blood of others resided within its coarse threads. Thus, a strange sentimentality attached me to it. The meager trappings of my life had been carried in that blood-drenched compartment during a total of twenty-six months in Vietnam and then Frank's books at the end of the last tour. It made practical sense to use it for carrying my books, papers, and pens while in the peaceful domain of academia. I have sometimes mused jokingly to my colleagues that I'd been a visionary of how to lug books around on college campuses. The use of book packs did not fully materialize until the 1980s.

Still aglow in the throes of Sandy's news, I gathered my books, slid them into my haversack and set off to the main campus library. Out on the green expanse of the quad, young men clad in shorts and sweats hustled around playing bouts of touch football. Young women and men strode past the vast playing field along the walkways and sought the shady paths beneath the trees toward the dormitories. Autumn's edge besieged the air. Leaves had fallen, turning yellow-brown from the sun. They made a crunching sound beneath my feet that was like a grumpy retort to the mockingbirds' delirious songs. Frank came up beside me, striding in his slow, comfortable way, and I was happy for him to join my trek. He looked straight ahead, that wan, easy smile alight. "You look very happy, Jack. Watch out for trip wires."

My heart was too filled with song to delve into his cryptic bullshit. I laughed. Then threw at him one of his highfalutin words, "Grand, Frank. Ain't it grand!"

"Yeah, it is that. Grand." He drew silent, cocked his head, and scrunched his smile. "But I'm one to know about trip wires."

Then he was gone and just as well. My usual careful discretion when in repartee with my dear, imaginary Frank had lowered itself in the afterglow of Sandy's news. I glanced around to see if someone had taken notice of me while I'd muttered nonsense to no one there. No eyes of students trailing toward the library past the stalwart line of oak trees shot toward me. Frank's bullshit gnawed at me for a moment, but I swatted it away as if it had been a mosquito buzzing near my ear.

Within the hushed chambers of the library, my mind fought not to drift. Into the late afternoon and evening, I studied my assignments among the silent camaraderie of other students, their faces so smooth and innocent with the sap of youth. At 8:00 p.m. I gathered my books and notes, lifted myself up, and retreated from the quiet halls out into the chilled edge of dusk.

On the walk back to my room at Mrs. Kendricks, I set a detoured course and stopped at a small liquor store several blocks from the sprawling campus. I bought a bottle of beer and slid it amidst the books into the bottom of my pack. In soft darkness, I wound back through the neighborhoods, their streets and yards laden with oaks, magnolia trees and well-kept gardens. The beer still held a nice chill when I popped the cap with a church-key, propped my feet on the windowsill, and looked out the window through trees that contained bits of starlight in the crevasses of their limbs.

Sandy arrived home on Monday, November 24, 1969, for a ten-day leave before deployment to Vietnam. Joe Morgan, the store manager at Piggly Wiggly, gave Julie the afternoon off. She drove Sandy's Chevy from Baptiste to the airport outside Shreveport to pick up the newly sculpted Marine. It was a day engulfed by sunshine, blue sky, a pleasant feel to the November air.

As told to me by Sandy, he and Julie held each other for an hour before walking hand-in-hand to climb into the Chevy. Julie said it was two minutes, but he was handsome in his khaki uniform, and she would have held him tight forever, but the Shreveport courthouse would close soon enough at 5:00 p.m. They had to hurry on to buy a marriage license.

Sandy drove and lucked upon a parking space two blocks from the courthouse off Texas Street. Later, he would say to me, "It was the happiest short walk of my life past the Confederate Memorial and those big oaks on the lawn. Squirrels running around on the grass. Pigeons cooing. Me and Julie up the steps. She payin' for it cause I didn't have the cash." Sweet is that remembrance of Sandy telling me about his arrival home after his days of gruel in Marine boot camp and infantry training.

Two days later, on an unusually warm autumn day, Sandy met me at the Continental Trailways bus station in Shreveport. I stepped off the bus in front of the station beneath the metal canopy. The caustic scent of hydraulic fumes struck into the linings of my nose. Sandy stood outside the terminal canopy in the sunlight by Fannin Street. He'd shucked his uniform and was clad in civvies—jeans and a black tee-shirt. But his bearing revealed the indelible marks of a boot Marine. Cropped hair, burnished at the sides, a hint of gauntness in the cheeks, a ruddiness to the skin. Yet, there was the same perpetual, good ol' boy smile, and I wondered quickly if the DI's had tried to quell it forever with the spit of their abuse. Well, there it was on his dumb, sweet face. The rough, vibrant idling of the bus filled my ears. Sandy spotted me. Two hands shot into the air like a football referee signaling a team's successful field goal attempt. I did a silent prayer to God, whether I believed in Him or not. *Don't let this kid get killed in that Asian war. Please.* The bus trappings continued to rattle while its motor set to idle, tossing noxious fumes into the day's heat. The side panels of the storage compartment lifted with a hiss. Sandy and I shook hands, embraced, nothing said, marriage and war before him. He saw the drifts of smoke cross my eyes.

"Don't worry, Half-Pint. I'll be a hero."

"I know," I said and hoped it would be true.

His deployment orders were WestPac, Ground Forces. He would be an infantryman replacement for those Marines wounded or killed. I gathered up my duffel and we set off to the Chevy.

That evening, Sandy, Julie, and I sat on the living room floor around a low, round coffee table Julie had acquired from her mother. Floor sitting had come into vogue throughout the culture of the younger generation. Even in this remote, outlier region of the upper parishes, Julie had grasped the currents of change. We sprawled on the floor like hippies. Three cans of beer, sweating with condensation, stood perched at the edges of the table on small beermats. Everything was softer about the room. Julie had painted the walls an ochre yellow. Plants in clay pots stood abreast on a shelf by the windows on the house's southern side. A couple of braided throw rugs graced the wooden floor. The little mill house had become a far different home from what I knew as a child.

Reviewing that evening around the coffee table, the lamp lights dim, Sandy's long arm around Julie's shoulder, the sheen of youth upon their faces, hope flowed into me like sunlight on the buds of trees. It was one of those moments in time you hold and seek to preserve. In it, you bask and wish it would always be this way.

Julie rolled her head against Sandy's shoulder and looked up at him with a scrunched smile. "Mama's making Thanksgiving dinner for us. I'll have to go over early tomorrow to help." Then she looked at me. "Friday's the day of no return. Clifford Bowles officiating. The grass is trimmed and raked in the backyard. Planted a couple of sawtooth oak saplings." She pointed her finger at me. "Someday those ugly honeysuckle shrubs you used to hide inside have got to go."

She sighed deeply. With her head still on Sandy's shoulder, she rolled her eyes back up at him. "Are you sure?"

The enduring smile on Sandy's face, as it was bound to do, broke wide. "Yes," he said. "I've never been so sure of anything in my life."

ROOSEVELT MARRIAGE

On Friday, Sandy Guillory and Julie Longo married in the backyard of the house on Roosevelt Street. Clifford C. Bowles conducted the unpretentious ceremony at the chilly edge of sunset. Clifford was solemn and proud in his heart's duties and held his Bible shut upon two fingers of his right hand, clasped against his side. It was to be simple, quick, without chafe or gush as had been directed by Julie. The sun pitched low behind the trees on which only a few leaves, fighting the change in seasons, clung to their limbs.

I remember: "Do you, Sandifer Guillory, take Julie Angela Longo to be your lawfully wedded wife?" To which Sandy said, "Hell yeah, I do, Cliffie."

Clifford's right upper lip winced upward, but otherwise, his solemn bearing never abandoned him. "Do you, Julie Angela Longo, take Sandifer Guillory to be your lawfully wedded husband?"

Julie replied softly, "I guess I do."

I handed off the ring to Sandy and he put it on her trembling finger. A chill infused the still air. The last glint of the setting sun filtered through the trees.

Gathered semi-circled behind Julie, Sandy, and Clifford stood eight other people—Julie's mother, myself near Sandy's side, Blackie, Buster and his wife with their three kids. Sandy kissed Julie, smiles upon their lips. Sandy looked back at me with his good ol' boy smile bursting. I grinned and looked at the short grass around my feet. The world keeps spinning. We are of little significance in the undecipherable expanse of time and space, but at this moment, it was okay to hang on and act like it was forever. It was a good day. I said that to myself. It was a good day.

Sandy was dressed in his service uniform, green coat, green trousers, khaki shirt and tie, and a garrison cap, better known as the "piss cutter." He stood plank-board straight next to Julie. The percussions of imagined drumbeats merged into the pounding of my heart. I avowed that I was afraid for him, but I ignored the ominous drum roll in my head. There is sometimes a time not to think. Julie wore a green dress, cut just below the knees. The bodice swept snugly over her shoulders where her long hair curled across the collars.

The ceremony was quick as Julie had requested, or rather, demanded. There was little difference in the manner of her requests and commands. Her mother, Blanche Longo, was dressed in a blue full swing dress that must have hung aloft in the recesses of her bedroom closet for several decades. She was a trim woman, a bit of blue in her hair. A light aura of physical attractiveness still rose off her skin. When garnering surreptitious looks at others, her glances had a suspicious edge as if many threats inhabited the world beyond her immediate touch. A husband who had abandoned her by blowing out his brains and an only daughter who had sought adoration and love as an exotic dancer in grueling stage venues of south Louisiana dives probably drove her to such vigilance. She hovered mostly in the kitchen overseeing an array of foodstuffs, beer and wine, and dispensing paper plates and plastic eating utensils.

I'm not a warm person, as you may have deciphered over the course of this writing, despite my lifelong quest to achieve a more affectionate bearing. But in the kitchen that special autumn evening, I pulled Blanche Longo into my arms and hugged her. She patted the top of my spine. When I stepped back, she said, "You brought him into her life. He's a nice boy, isn't he, Jack? Julie said you told her so. Say it to me out loud."

I said, "He's a decent human being." Then some rope tugged on both the fear and truth in me and I said, "But I don't know if he'll make it. It's…a hard war." The pain that suddenly wrenched my face must have astonished her.

She flicked her chin up. "He'll make it, Jack. He's a nice boy."

"Yes, ma'am."

I nodded and left it there. Struck down and emptied by my crudeness, my fears suddenly moved inside me uncontrolled and silent like Blackie's panthers in their dark swamps.

The men I'd worked with during the sweltering heat of summer were transformed this evening by hot baths, fresh shaves, and Sunday-style attire. Clifford wore a dark suit, about a size and a half too large, a tie looped so tight around his neck that it seemed to cut off his oxygen and reddened his face. He held himself straight and kept a regal glaze across his face and kept his old, weathered Bible tucked inside the crook of his arm. When Ms. Longo tried to cater him a glass of wine, he lofted his nose and spoke gently, "Not of this temple does he partake."

To which Blanche Longo replied, "You ought to try a glass, Cliff. It might frisky you up," and pinched his cheek. The blood beneath the skin of his face flushed redder, though Clifford never relinquished his stately demeanor.

Buster dwelled in a kind of awkward isolation. He drifted through the commotions in the house like a long stick pushed along by unpredictable currents in a stream. Then he'd settle in place again, silent and awkward. The difference between Buster when I first met him and the Buster I knew now was the stillness. It was as if his inner demons had drained of energy and lain down, giving him time to study them from within.

Early in the evening, less than a half-hour after the backyard vows, I stepped outside the front door onto the narrow steps to take a smoke. The sky had gone smooth and dark and again beheld the lights of other worlds. I struck the match to light the cigarette. Buster slid sideways out the door and stood beside me. He positioned himself within six inches of my shoulder, his stillness almost palpable, and looked straight out into the darkness. I offered him a smoke. There came a slight shake of his head.

He finally spoke. "It is with sincere hope that you will not be lettin' us down."

I let what he said move slowly through my mind. "I'll be back next summer. I've promised Blackie. There'll be no letting down if he's got a job for me."

"Blackie will have a job for you." Silence again roosted on his wiry shoulders.

I took a drag from the cigarette and blew the smoke away from us into the near darkness.

"That is not to which I speak," he said.

"To what do you speak?"

"Going to school and being somebody else someday. You lookin' for something. Escaping to places that be gentle and kind."

"It's important to you for me to do such?"

"Not really. Not to me."

"Goddamn, Buster, you will forever be a confusing son-of-a-bitch."

He laughed, but kept it looped tight deep in his throat. It hit me that this was the first time I'd heard the man laugh, even if it was just a choked-off chuckle.

"It's Blackie that's invested in you...and if he be so, then I must share in it."

"I don't know if books and learning are goin' to get me anywhere. I can't comprehend the likes of Blackie Shively. I just know he's willing to hire me back next summer, and I'm goin' to need the money. Your wife and kids seem nice, Buster." My cordial comment seemed hollow and emptied out into the vague outlines of houses down the darkened street.

Buster scuffed the bottom of his shoe against the step as if he might be scraping off a chunk of mud. "Thanks, Jack," he said. "I don't know nothin' about books."

Buster rotated slowly and went inside the house. I felt bad for a reason I couldn't fathom. That similar feeling when it seemed I was letting someone down. In the Corps, you didn't let the other guy down. The willingness to self-sacrifice for the other was hallowed. And somehow, I felt that I was letting that goddamn Buster down and Blackie and Clifford and, for sure, Sandy, whom I should have kidnapped and crossed him over onto Canadian land months ago until his senses cleared. I put out the cigarette and that *fuck it* feeling pushed away the other feelings and I went inside.

Buster's wife stood at the kitchen doorway looking in on her young ones at the dining table. Radio music played from an FM station out of Shreveport. Aretha was singing, *I say a little prayer for you*, and it was sweet and hopeful with its words and melody. I was sure such a hopeful song was tolerant to Clifford's sin-sensitive ears.

Buster's wife, Beatrice, called Bea by her friends, was short-haired and plump. Spider veins crisscrossed her cheeks. Her eyes sparked with command and authority when directed toward her three boys, whom I guessed each to be a mere year apart in birth. Earlier in the evening, they had trailed near their mother like skinny magnets, never deviating beyond her presence by more than a few feet. Their astonished eyes burned into everyone as if before them was one of the most amazing spectacles on earth. I felt a gladness—and an odd kind of sadness—when Ms. Longo set slices of wedding cake and a heap of ice cream before them on paper plates at the kitchen table. Using plastic spoons, they ate shyly and shared warning looks among each other to show proper etiquette.

Blackie, Sandy, and Julie created a small triangle in the short hallway that led to Sandy and Julie's bedroom, the old room of Ida and Seymour's. What clicked in my mind in that second was the dizzying way time could morph and how it never stopped shaping into different realities. Blackie's back was to me as he faced Sandy and Julie. Sandy's shining eyes caught me, lifted with a beckon to come forward, so I went. Julie's shoulder pressed against him below the uplift of his arm over her shoulders. The drab green of his service jacket formed a somber contrast to the velvet green of her dress. Past Blackie's great hulk, they were beautiful. I wondered again how these two came to be. How could such be possible? I held a cold bottle of beer in my hand, but I was warm inside. Blackie looked at me askance, winked an eye dark as anthracite at me and went on talking in his low, gravelly voice.

"I did see one once. Near Poverty Point along Bayou Marcon where I hunted as a boy. She had sprawled out on a low, broad limb of a water oak. It was mid-fall, still a lot of leaves on the trees. I didn't raise my shotgun. Wouldn't have, even if she would have climbed down and come at me. Her eyes glowed just like you read about 'em in storybooks. She'd been watching me for a good while. I could sense it."

Blackie was in a faraway and time-distant place inside that strange brain of his. His coal-dark eyes sank inward toward his giant skull. They, too, burned bright, just like those of a panther. My thoughts tied together. Blackie was sharing the most joyful moment in his life with us.

"I stood the shotgun against a tree and squatted down quiet and respectful. Her and me just kept lookin' at each other. Long, bountiful moments." Blackie's face transformed, smoothed out into an expression I'd never witnessed before, like some mysterious crinkle of the universe had opened itself unto him.

"We visited inside each other for a while. When she had enough of looking around, she pushed up from the tree limb and leaped down to the ground. Silent as still air. She was gone. I've been looking for her ever since. She's seen me a few times, I'm sure, but as of yet hasn't chosen to show herself again. Someday she will." Blackie pushed a row of knuckles against his nose, sniffed, and caught himself into awareness like somebody just awakening. His ham hock of a hand went inside his suit jacket that fit so tight on him the threads might blow apart at any moment. He handed Sandy a plump envelope.

"Two-hundred dollars for you and Julie in Hot Springs. Spend it on yourselves for your honeymoon."

Sandy looked at it as he held it between fingers and thumb. "Hell, Blackie."

"Thank you, Blackie," Julie said.

Sandy cast his lips into a half-smile. Julie's mouth shaped into an oval like she was sipping wonder.

Blackie's elbows came together in front of him and his arms thrust up when Julie moved to hug him. He cleared his throat and shuffled backward. "No, Ms. Guillory, I ain't to be hugged." He shook his head and averted his eyes from all who might behold his vulnerability. "Y'all excuse me."

He walked away. I stole my eyes into the tautly stretched threads on the back of his coat. It was strange to have witnessed Blackie's shyness of intimacy. As I often do to this day, I pondered the sealed away secrets we harbor in ourselves. And I wondered then what the panther saw when she went into Blackie that day near the Bayou Marcon. And what had Blackie seen in the inner domain of the panther?

Sandy choked a laugh and looked straight at me, then at Julie. He said with a shake of his hair-cropped head, "Last time Blackie gave me somethin' it was a sock in the nose. Semper Fidelis, brother Jack. Life can't get no better."

Julie's smooth neck glowed as she tilted her chin upward and looked at her Marine husband. Pain winced around her eyes, conveying distrust of anything that promised to be good in her life. Her hope hung from twine, not sailor's rope, but she was holding onto what she had, as fragile as it might be.

"We'll stay at the Arlington Hotel, take long walks. That's what I want to do," she said. She was crying. A faint stream of tears rolled down her cheeks. I turned away, held my breath. Figure out the man I am. I could give cold witness to the bloodiest of the wounded, the most silent of the dead, but here before me, I could not bear to look upon the tears of a woman.

Sandy pulled Julie into him tight and held the side of her head against his chest. "Hell, hon'. Hell."

"It's okay. I'm happy," she said.

The ceremony had been a humble but profound affair. This small contingent of souls from out of the oil fields with whom Sandy had worked for all his short adult life would leave early into the evening. Oil men who had scrubbed themselves clean right after their tower run and adorned themselves in rarely worn Sunday clothes. Men of rough skill and hard labor who knew the soon to come call of the wee hours, the drumbeat that heralded the will to survive into the next day.

Blanche and Bea took on the duties of kitchen cleanup. It was the year 1969. Such separations of domestic labor between males and females unfolded during these times without a questioning flinch. Julie parted from Sandy's side to offer kitchen help. Through the kitchen doorway came "shoo-shoo" cries from both Ms. Longo and Bea Milton. The small fry Milton boys chortled as their mother yelled, "Back to that handsome man of yours, honey! You need to save all the energy you can!"

Bea Milton seemed to possess ten times the life and humor in her as her husband. The thought slipped through my mind that a significant purpose in her life was to keep Buster from spinning off the face of the earth. She adored the man whom I'd judged during my first days on the rig as being too mentally brittle to endure life's travesties. Surely, she saw goodness in him. Who is to be the judge of another's chosen quest if it does no harm?

Clifford was the last to leave. Blackie waited for him in the Impala parked along the street and shielded by the shadowy darkness. Clifford stood just inside the screen door and, as he had done throughout the evening, clutched his Bible against his side. Julie and Sandy stood hand-in-hand in front of him. I sat in a heavily padded wing chair that Julie had scrounged from her mother to replace what had been Seymour's broken-down lounge chair. My third beer sweated in my hand. I thought this was a grand evening. Hear that, Frank? Grand. And I thought I should not be here on their first night of marriage, but this was the way they wanted it.

Clifford's voice came rolling through the soft quiet of the living room, "I wish you weren't going off to this Vietnam war. With the light of the Lord upon you, no harm shall come your way. You shall find your way through the gates of heaven when you are old and finally wise of ways."

"I plan to be the meanest motherfucker around, Cliffie."

Julie shot a hushed retort to her husband. "Damn it, stop that."

Clifford lowered his head into his chest, then raised it slowly along with the uplift of both his hands, one in the clutch of his Bible. The bibled hand fell over Sandy's shoulder, the other over Julie's. Sandy grinned. Clifford's eyes shut. His face was as serene as that of a new full moon. He held the two before him in silence.

"Thanks for marryin' us, Cliff," Sandy said.

Clifford nodded and turned away into the darkness outside.

I will speak of what happened next and then I must shine the light of remembrance away from this point of time. A few minutes after Clifford exited into the night, Sandy told me to hold out my hand and close my eyes. I said I don't close my eyes to anyone, much less a Marine fresh out of boot camp. Julie told me to shut them and not be stubborn. I closed them.

"Now stretch out your hand, numb nuts," Sandy said.

I did and felt the rigid shape of car keys fall across my palm. "Don't be driving off to kill somebody with a handgun." He handed me a folded document next. It was a power of attorney paper duly notarized, giving me the authority to utilize his beloved vehicle.

"I don't want this. You'll need the Chevy."

"No, I won't, numb nuts."

"To get to Hot Springs and back."

"We're using my car. It's fine," Julie said. "We want you to keep it safe, Jack. You'll take better care of it than me."

"You'll make sure she's in good shape when I get back, Half-Pint. I know you will."

No ascent of the heart took place. Instead, there came a descent. To those able to appreciate good fortune that comes so easily, savor well that remarkable capacity. For those of Half-Pint's ilk, the smooth, round feel of such good luck was foreign territory. I sighed into the jumble of my emotions. "I'll take good care of it. You know I will."

They left the next morning when the sun's rays broke through the twilight of dawn. Sandy threw two bags into the trunk of Julie's car. The cool air pressed upon us as we stood beside the Ford Fairlane, another gift from her mother who had relearned the meaning of hope for her wayward daughter. Sandy wore a light jacket and faded Levi's jeans. Julie wore a sweater and a pair of oversized baggy khakis. Her hair was damp and covered with a red scarf. Youthfulness and something called love spirited into them. No dark cloud of Sandy's eventual combat duty loomed over them. There was just the weightless sunlight feel of happiness that morning. I can't say what we said to one another. I don't remember. I stood alone in the yard, watching through the naked limbs of the giant sycamore as their car drove up Roosevelt Street and was gone.

I remained at the house for three more days and left the day before Julie and Sandy returned from their honeymoon foray in Hot Springs. Sandy would have a few days remaining on his authorized leave before departing for Camp Pendleton. At the sprawling Marine base, he would begin steps for deployment as a troop replacement in Vietnam. It was time for me to be gone. No restatement of goodbye.

I spent most of those few days sequestered in the small public library of Baptiste with coursebooks I'd brought from the university. Ms. Lydia Payne welcomed me with a side glance and a nod to the books I carried in both my hands, "It's started now and will not stop," she said.

On the day before I was to return, I took the .45 still housed in its ammunition canister down from the closet shelf. I walked out the front door with the ammo box to Sandy's Chevy and placed it on the floorboard in front of the passenger seat. I drove north through town and crossed the state line into the remote woodlands past the old rig site and toward Burnt Bridge. When the bridge's railings came into view, I slowed the car and pulled over above the creek. Cypress stumps ghosted out of the dark water below.

I dragged the ammunition box out with me into the sunlight that was crisp with winter's approach and flung it over the railing. A frothing splash and a gulp came up from the creek. Crows cawed loudly from a far distance in the woods. The cold of the day went through my thin jacket. I felt very lonely, but I didn't seek visitation from Frank or Romano. I drove back to the house on Roosevelt Street and let it be quiet around me.

The morning of the day that I headed back to Baton Rouge, I arose early and drove to the Haiti-Cullen's gravel parking lot. I shook hands with Blackie and Clifford and the two young men Blackie had hired to replace Sandy and myself. They were tall and gaunt and had hungry looks. I wished them well and hoped they would last.

Buster stood alone off to the side and murmured a soft, "Hello, Half-Pint."

I kept glancing toward him, waiting for his eyes to blink. He was here but somewhere else. He wore a thin jacket zipped against his Adam's apple. Its collar stood up around his neck. Finally, his eyes winked slow and long. The fire that had lit up his swirling atoms now seemed burned down to coals.

Blackie never looked at me but scanned the feet of the men, the pebbled ground of the parking lot, upward then at the V formation of geese overhead, tracking south. But on that stubbled, square face with its atlas forehead was a dumb smile. I knew it pleased him to see me. An inner glow came up from my stomach and spread into the lobes of my ears.

When I shook Clifford's hand, he said, "I pray the lord divines upon you the knowledge that is worthy of His light, and you resist the devil's temptations of dance."

I glanced at Sandy's car keys in my hand and said, "Dancing's not my greatest fear, Cliff."

"I miss ol' Sandy. Don't you?" he said.

A few minutes later, just as the sun's rays began to arch over the vast skeleton of the decaying mill across the narrow highway, Blackie's Impala rattled away from the gravel lot, heading to a new drilling site in remote, swampy wood. *How long can this world last?*

ANGLES OF LIGHT SHIFT I

Before Sandy enlisted in the Marines, I had tried to explain that the passion thrumming in his breast, enticing him into the bowels of war was a fucking ruse put there by quirks in nature. Yeah, me, old man wisdom, tried to enlighten him. What lay ahead in war? Besides the madness, there would come whimpers, whines, grunts, growls, and horror. If he managed to survive gauntlets of combat, he'd leave the battlegrounds malformed. The battle-hardened soldier is a misnomer. Speak to those who startle to the sound of a loud knock, stare too long into distant vistas, shy from the crowds, drift but to the edge of sleep, rage at someone's contemptuous glance, or question the meaning of all things. My pleading was useless. The myths of glory and heroism had been lit aflame inside him, turned on by some biological and evolutionary-designed switch. I could only hope that good luck might attach herself to him and he'd come out the other side not totally spent.

Sandy's last letter came written on the torn-away back of a C-ration carton. It didn't surprise me. Long days during field operations in Vietnam rendered it difficult, at times, to replenish luxury supplies like writing stationery. There wasn't much to the note, just Sandy reaching out in some small way to a brother.

I don't think I'm going to make it. Hate to admit that being the southern wonder boy that I am. If I don't make it, look after things all. We're moving out soon. The rains don't stop. Lost two guys from my squad yesterday. Same old story goes on and on, but you know that, Half-Pint. There's an eerie quiet comes through the trees here. We'll have to talk about that sometimes. But anyway, I'm just on a downside for a while and needed to unburden myself on you, man. Forgive me for that. I'll write you again when I got more time. Saving the good paper for Julie.

It was, as said, the last letter from him. Still have it, of course, like all his others. They have rested between *The Razor's Edge* and the *Bhagavad Gita* on a bookshelf of honor for all these years.

The news of Sandy's death came in a phone call from Blackie on a day near the end of March 1970. Spring break was approaching. Rita had summoned me down from my upstairs room, her high-pitched Southern lady voice proclaiming with a hint of disdain that I'd received another phone call.

Blackie's deep voice through the phone line jarred me. And then the wonder of how he got my phone number. I grew very still with phone in hand and was thankful Rita had skirted off to some back region of the house. Blackie addressed me as Jack.

"This Jack?"

"Yes, sir."

"We heard news Sandy's been KIA over there. Miss Julie requested I call you. She ain't able to do much right now. Her mama's with her as far as I can tell. A couple of men in military uniform dropped in on her at her shift at the Piggly Wiggly. Gave her the news. She wanted me to call you. Tell you." He cleared his throat. "Now, you know. I don't have more to say."

Silence carved out its place as I stood with the phone pressed against the side of my face. The quiet was so pure that the sound of my pumping heart echoed in my ears.

"I'm sorry, Jack," Blackie said.

"Thanks, Blackie. I got to go now. Thank you, sir. Tell Cliff and Buster I said hey. I got to go now." There was to be no sobbing shit coming from me.

"I'm sorry, Jack," Blackie said.

The phone clicked.

I must have stood there for a long time. Rita crossed the pathway of my blurred vision.

"Jack, are you alright? Why you're crying. Come here, hon'." Something miraculous occurred. I let her embrace me. She held me close, unashamedly, patting my back. "It's okay, child. We all got to cry sometimes. You go on now. You go right ahead." And not once did the woman damn me with questions. Just accepted me as one suffering into the moment and gave me her unconditional compassion. And I let her.

Sandy had been killed three months and four days into his tour of duty. To be clear, I haven't carried on surreptitious conversations with him over the years. There was only room for Frank and Romano to talk to in the space of my private fantasies. It's not to say that I don't think of Sandy often. I think of him every day, for that matter, but he had his own part of the war. Frank and Romano and I had ours. I often hope that some Marine brother who groveled with Sandy in the shit of combat as the days passed gruelingly by now gives him company in long conversations of the spirit.

Even after the news of Sandy's death, I planned to return for summer work in the wildness of the oilfields. I'd take up room and board at the Haiti-Cullen. A sense of indebtedness to Blackie and the essential need for money to pay for school and board infused the grief. But, also, in an odd way, getting back into the oil fields promised a sense of being close to Sandy again. And after the tranquil indulgence of a year immersed in study, I was sure I'd want to imbue myself in the pseudo-violence of the drilling rig. In those days, we gave no thought to notions of pillage and pollution as we sucked the hydrocarbons of ancient marine plant and animal life from our little mother planet.

No memorial or grand funeral for Sandy came to be. Julie didn't want it, didn't want the folded flag, nor desire the warm pat of hands upon her shoulder, the soft clamp of embrace from those condolent. In the *Baptiste Press and News Journal*, a front-page piece appeared with Sandy's picture in camouflaged helmet, the standard military photograph taken of all Marines just born from boot camp. In it, he was handsome. A clear demarcation of the jaw, a shine in his eyes, just the faintest detection of amusement on his lips. The first line read: *Local Marine killed in action by hostile fire while operating in the province of Quang Tri, South Vietnam.* I would turn my eyes away from that sanitized quip beneath the photo. Such words, so clean and straightforward, are meant to shield us from the gleaning of shit, mud, toil, and terror behind the death. What would prevent a war? If the old men leaders had to fight it. Change the fucking rules. Send the politicians and their children to the battlefields. That would stifle the siren songs of war.

The morning after Blackie's phone call, I awoke from my bed on the throw rug beside the antique desk to the rattle-chime of a wind-up alarm clock by my head. It was 3:00 a.m. Darkness enshrouded me. I listened into it for enemy movement, then remembered where I was. I showered, took a long piss, brushed my teeth. When I turned on the light to the upstairs kitchen, a patrol of cockroaches shimmied fast across the linoleum floor and through cracks in the wall to nether worlds. Hail to those who might inherit the earth, I thought. I drank a full glass of water and took two bananas I'd sequestered in a kitchen cabinet.

Sandy's Chevy awaited me on the side of the street beneath the overhang of oak limbs, pale lamp light aglow over its muscle-car frame. I had no elaborate plan other than to go to Julie and be with her a while as during that summer within the honeysuckle shrubs where I listened to her speak of girlhood dreams. Guilt clawed around in my gut. Strange in its form, but guilt, nonetheless. I'd drawn Julie and Sandy into alignment. Helped weave together their lives. I thought myself to have brought her the heavy onslaught of anguish that comes from loss.

I crossed the Huey P. Long Bridge over the Mississippi River, eventually skirting the Atchafalaya Basin along Highway 190 before bearing north toward the upper parishes. Dawn came in fine degrees through the bug-spattered windshield. Woodlands and swamps along the road emerged more clearly, enticing me to disappear into them as if they were cousins to that jungled land in Asia that didn't get me.

But I drove on, and what do I most recall on that road trip north with my books left behind? The flight of a great heron. She swung her wings slowly up and down alongside the car, following a low path against the backdrop of ghostly swamp in the breaking rays of twilight. Then I passed her and what I recall most from then on as I drove north to Baptiste was a piss stop or two and a refill of gasoline at a small pump station on Alexandria's outskirts. The wrinkle-faced man behind the gas station counter who took my money wore a hat crooked atop his crown and smiled with a bevy of missing teeth. Funny, the things you recall most clearly when looking back through the shadowy windows of time.

Grey clouds hung low in the sky while the mid-day sun kept trying to break through them when I reached the house on Roosevelt Street. A blue Buick, sleek and polished, stood parked on the grassy curb. Somewhere in the back recesses of my mind came a discomforting twinge of familiarity about the car. The sight of it fueled an edginess building in my stomach. I turned off the Chevy's engine. Through the car window, naked limbs of sycamore trees laden with soft green, leafy buds spread against the sky, but I felt no sense of spring in the air. I got out of the car and made for the house. The front door opened for me as if by a magic breeze. Joe Morgan, the Piggly Wiggly store manager, stood abreast, holding the screen door ajar.

"Hello, Jack. I saw you coming up. Julie's sitting in the kitchen with some coffee. I was heading out." He spoke in a hushed whisper as if to respect the dead, wherever they might be. "I'm sorry, Jack. It's hurtin' us all." He shook his head and studied his feet. "We'll do everything we can for Julie. I swear by that."

He had a finely proportioned face, smooth skin, small nose and chin, sensitive eyes, and I knew him to keep a shy smile at the ready for the customers in the store.

"Thanks, Joe. Appreciate it." I stepped past him, kept my hands at my sides and looked toward the kitchen door.

"I'll be going. I am truly sorry."

I nodded but kept my eyes trained in the direction of the kitchen. The front door pulled shut, and I tried to loosen the hard edge that had come so quickly into me.

At the kitchen table she sat, bundled in an over-sized grey sweatshirt, unbrushed hair spilling down her shoulders. A yellow tablecloth draped the table. She stared into a coffee cup held between her fingers, looked over it at me with dark and liquid eyes. Another cup rested at the head of the table close to her. She said, "How goes your search for wisdom, college boy?" Then, she said, "Oh, Jack, please come here."

She stood up, her arms outstretched, and I went into them, realizing it was me come to get comfort, not to give. Her body shook. I wanted badly to cry, but the numbness that came of my own traumas callused over me. Her body trembled. I patted her spine with my otherwise awkward hands. A swath of sunlight streamed momentarily through the window above the sink. Then it was gone.

"Well, I thought that was all out of me," she said. "Thanks a lot for dropping by." Julie sniffed and laughed. "Sit down now."

I sat down. She rolled her eyes toward the window where the light had come through and departed like a broken promise.

"I keep hoping the sun's coming out. I've ordered cremation for Sandy. This grey weather is the shits. Mama went back to her house last night. Thank God. Blackie Shively and Clifford Bowles standing around dumber than Laurel and Hardy. Bea Milton was here, leaving her boys with Buster, who she said was too grieved to come, which I said was fine. Nobody wants to leave me alone. But that's what I want." She touched her coffee cup on the table but didn't pick it up. "Not you, Jack. I'm glad you're here. It's the first you've been back since Sandy left. Not even Christmas you came. Why is that, Jack? I've liked your letters. I've tried to write to you as much as I could. I'm not good at writing. You want some coffee?"

The rush of her words spun past me. A dull throb had settled into my temples. "No," I said. My thoughts compressed harder together. I struggled to untangle them. "I could have made time. I should have. Without Sandy here, it didn't seem right..." A vaporous quiet settled between us for probably thirty seconds.

"I'm alright. Don't worry. I know you love me. I know you always will love me. And you'll always love Sandy."

"Are you truly alright?" I asked her and I heard a voice in my head saying, *How feeble-minded and hapless you sound, Jack Crowe. How stupid of a question can you ask?*

Julie looked at me like an amber-eyed cat able to decipher the depths of my mind. "You're reading the air, sucking in the smells of wont that's come into this home since you and Sandy left, wrestling down suspicions invading your sorrow. I see it in your face. You took note of Joe when he left, didn't you?"

I said nothing. I went empty inside, nothing left but the chill of fear.

"Don't judge me. It hurts too much," she said.

"Then just shut up then. Just be quiet," I said softly.

"Loneliness has always broken me down. Don't judge me." She raked her knuckles across her chin. Lips pressed tight together. A caustic sound pitched up from her throat. "Women in men's worlds. You'll never understand."

"I'm not judging," I said, but I was judging. Seconds rolled over me in which I didn't care. "He's got a wife," I said as if I was using that observation like the point of a bayonet to cut her some. I felt dirty inside after saying it.

"He's a gentle, kind man. Kindness in a man has always been rare to me. I was lonely. Vulnerable to my longings. Don't punish me. Joe has always cared for me. I'm hurting too much."

Inside the length of ten minutes, my sense of right and wrong had buckled, as it would do from time to time over the years, assuming new angles of perspective, always drawing my awe on the complexity of we human souls. Frank ghosted behind me. Without shape or form, he pressed the afterglow of his apparitional hand against the back of my head, reminding me of the forgiveness he'd given me, the executioner that I was. I said to Julie, "I, of all people, have no right to judge you."

But I did judge and kept judging. Here again, Half-Pint's shortcomings lay exposed, the inability to forgive others who seek absolution. Compassion, inherent in one Frank Maudsley, would never galvanize inside the likes of one Half-Pint Crowe. I could merely pantomime motions of sympathy. I touched Julie's wrist. Gave her a tired, pained smile as I ripped myself apart inside. "I'm not to judge," I whispered. Currents of tiny muscles rippled over her chin. Her lips pursed tightly together.

"Oh, Jack," she said. "Just be shut up. I'm not asking you for anything."

Moments later, Julie's mother rapped lightly on the front door and called out Julie's name. She carried a casserole dish wrapped over with tin foil.

"Mama, I'm not in need of more food."

"I'm doing something," Blanche said. "It's good to be doing something."

"Thank you. I'm going back to work tomorrow. I don't give a damn what anyone says."

Blanche looked at me and leaned her back against the kitchen counter where she'd placed the casserole dish. A long frown sealed her lips. Web-like, red veins etched over the whites of her eyes. She said with the softest of utterance, "Hi, Jack, I've made a chicken casserole. Won't that be good? You must have just got in."

"Yes, ma'am." I got up and hugged her. It always seemed easy for me to embrace this woman. It was as if her history of tragic loss gave us ready kinship.

Blanche pressed her warm palm into the softness of my beard. "He was a nice boy," she said. "How does this come to be? You're looking like a beatnik with all that hair, Jack."

The kitchen floor kept shifting beneath my feet and the spinning of the world which had seemed to accelerate when I first passed through the door of the house sped even faster. Julie's fingertips caressed the yellow tablecloth beside her coffee cup. She studied the movements of her fingers as if they were wondrous creatures separate from her being.

"I'm out of smokes. I'm going to run out and buy some cigarettes," I said. I'd quit smoking in early November. Amidst my nose buried in books, I'd gradually shed the urge. But now I needed to find some solid footing and I turned to go for a pack of cigarettes. I felt Julie's vision rise and center on the back of my neck.

"Have I lost you too?"

It stopped me. I looked around. Blanche first came into the scope of my vision. A haunted look had cast itself over her face, deepening the fine wrinkles around her eyes and lips. She rotated her gaze between Julie and me.

"I need to get some smokes. I'll be back in a short while. Don't be thinking crazy stuff." I went on across the wooden floor, the sound of my feet softened by the braided rugs strategically placed along the pathways of the house.

I bought a pack of cigarettes at a grimy convenience store on the main road past the mill's sprawling skeletal remains. Never minded the harsh squint of sunken eyes given me by the leathery cord of a man behind the checkout counter. I knew the names of most in this town, but his face was sullen and unfamiliar. A low feeling passed over me and it came from a sense that the spirit of hope in this town was flickering out. He scoped the spill of hair over my ears. "Are you a girl or boy?" he drawled.

"Give me the damn cigarettes and change." I hoped he'd pitch this sorry moment higher into the stale air of the store. He sniffed and placed the pack of cigarettes with some coins on the counter and turned away.

When I got back, I didn't immediately enter the old house but sat upon the front steps, my familiar place of inner study and contemplation. I pulled a cigarette from the pack, lit it, and went into the smoke where I found Frank.

Come on, man, he said in his gentle voice. *You'll disappoint others and they'll disappoint you. Whereby we achieve some opportunity for grace is in dealing with all that disappointment.*

I raised my knees and clung my arms around them. I didn't want to be sitting on these steps listening to dead Frank spout his bullshit cryptic pearls of wisdom. But still, I couldn't resist the draw of interchange. I said back, "Goddamn it, you never disappointed me. Not once." And, my God, what came next through the delirious air that thickened over my wrinkled brow was his laugh.

Who stepped the wrong way off that trail? Come on, man. Who stepped the wrong way? We all come to disappoint, you jackass.

I took off my shoes and slept that night on the floor of my old bedroom beneath the window that looked out on the backyard. Outside the panes of glass, the chinaberry tree limbs were almost bare of leaves but plump with their yellow fruits. I think I slept an hour or two. Such was the haze that persisted over my mind like mist rising across the jungled slopes between dawn and day where you never slept and never woke.

I heard Julie rustling in the kitchen. I sat up and placed my back against the wall. Dawn was breaking into the room, gradually clarifying the shapes of bed, desk, and chair. After a while, I pulled on my shoes and got up.

In the kitchen, Julie wore her Piggly Wiggly vest and a baggy pair of new jeans. She stood, looking at me sad-eyed, with coffee cup in her hand. She said, "You won't be coming back. I know you, and you won't."

"Nah, Julie. I'll be back." I didn't feel it to be a lie. My judgments were still tossing about to and fro. Nothing that I could understand had lit upon the earth. "I'll be working with Blackie this summer. I got to make money. I'll be back. I'll see you. It's okay, Julie. I understand." And I didn't. There was the lie. I walked out the door.

I profess that when people most dear disappear from your life, lament lies buried in the tissues of your body. Abided by time's trickle effect, the pain sinks deeper, although new experiences with different people coming into and out of the world around you gradually lessen its intensity. But its residue stays there deep inside the tissues.

Driving back to Baton Rouge that morning, I pondered the complexity of being a human on this planet. Too many flaws burdened me. No saints materialized out of thin air to counsel me and the only holy man I'd known had gone silent in his ghostliness. The swamps and woodlands swept by on the journey south. Currents of fate carry us along more forcefully than our individual will. Hours later, crossing the Huey P. Long Bridge over the Mississippi River once more into Baton Rouge, enlightenment still eluded me, and does so today.

ANGLES OF LIGHT SHIFT II

Rita Kendricks had warmed to me in the sultry landscape of Baton Rouge. She was the only person with whom I shared my penchant for talking with the dead. Rita and I would sit at a small table in front of her sunroom's broad windows downstairs and sip an inexpensive white wine. These casual get-togethers had become something of a weekly ritual that usually took place on a late Sunday evening when I'd divested myself of book study for a short while to breathe the air of natural life. Her initial invitation had been more like a command. "Have a glass of wine with me, Jack. It will keep you young."

During these warm interludes, she shared that she'd loved her husband of forty-two years before his death in a duck hunting accident. She did not elaborate on the details of the tragic accident and I didn't inquire. He had been a respected banker in town and an active member of the Baton Rouge Chapter of the Audubon Society. They had raised a son who had been a talented football player and a brilliant student. He had died of leukemia in his second year of college.

She often spoke of songbirds and liked to tell me about the flight paths and eating habits of the various species that came through seeking the lush sanctuary of her backyard. Once, while a bit tipsy, she shed from the golden light coming through the windowpanes that she didn't believe in a God-like being. "I go to church because it's a good habit for an old woman to have in the southern world. Especially an old woman of my ilk." She narrowed her violet eyes at me. The aura of a soothsayer overtook her and glowed around her head of sheer white hair.

"You're looking for some meaning to it all, aren't you? Some answer to what we're all about. You're studying the visions of everybody everywhere, hoping to find answers and truth. Your problem is you don't believe most of what you're told. Cynical and suspicious you are. You'll be searching for ages and ages hence, tasting disappointment along the way. Welcome to the human race, Jack Crowe."

"Will I ever find it?" I asked.

"Of course, you will," she said, accompanied by a chuckle. "Just like everybody else."

I laughed with her and told her that I coped with my confusions of existence by talking to my dead friends, Frank and Romano. Somehow, my dialogues with these two, one holy, the other as coarse and ordinary as myself, calmed my vexations. Helped me get through night and day. She only added that she'd noticed me mumbling to myself from time to time and cautioned me to observe myself better, lest others begin to think of me as pixilated.

On one afternoon, she, with the grace and poise of a true Southern grande dame, told me that I was very religious though I possessed no belief in God as she. In the twinkle of that second, she suggested I pursue a career in religious studies, though I'd likely find no stable source of employment in that field of academic endeavor. For some intangible reason, her suggestion piqued an intense interest. I leaned forward across the table, almost knocking over my wine glass. "Will I find answers there?" I asked as if she were herself the Delphic oracle.

"You'll find them there no less than anywhere else. It seems to be what you're interested in, so why not go that way? Maybe you can teach. Find sanctuary, if nothing else."

And I did choose that path, and she was right.

Less than six weeks after the news of Sandy's death and my discovery of Julie's betrayal, another phone call came to me from the upper parishes. I knew of it by a note left by Rita on my bedroom door. It read: *Call Julie. Urgent. Don't worry about paying for the call.* Julie had written me several letters since I left her in the kitchen that morning, but I had not answered them.

It was early evening. I'd finished a day of classes, unloaded my books onto my desk, and went down the stairs to the parlor room with note in hand and made the call. Dusk was pressing through the house. I switched on the small table lamp beside the phone. Rita was out and I had the parlor room to myself. The quiet of the old house deepened. When Julie answered, she began to sob softly. She stuttered my name twice, "Jack—Jack." Then she managed to say, "Clifford Bowles was killed yesterday. Where is all this death coming from, Jack? Where?" Her words struck through me like chunks of shrapnel.

"How?" My voice crumpled up in my throat.

"My God, I'm crying as much about Clifford as Sandy." She continued bawling, catching her breath along the way. "What's wrong with me?"

"How, Julie? Can you tell me? Please."

"Something about a goddamn blowout preventer. They were installing one on the drilling rig. He got crushed between it and the rig infrastructure. Does that make any sense to you?" She spoke with greater calmness. She blew her nose and sniffed.

Nothing made any sense to me now. I clung to that hard, practical side of myself. "Was anyone else hurt?" My fist clenched the phone's receiver. I leaned my shoulder into the wall.

"No," she said. "Bea Milton said Blackie's taking it awfully hard. Won't speak to anybody. Buster Milton's staying close to him." She inhaled deeply; her breath was as clear as if she stood next to me. "It's all I know. His funeral is Tuesday at New Hope Baptist. Are you coming home? You should come home now. Please. Will you do that?"

"I'll be there. Yes, I'll be coming up."

At 2:00 a.m. on the day of Clifford's funeral, I awoke from a three-hour stretch of sleep, washed, pulled on a pressed, white shirt, freshly washed jeans, a pair of shined shoes, and fastened a clip-on tie to my collar. I would reach the country church called New Hope just in time for the service if my logistical planning proved accurate. Immediately afterward, I'd depart with haste and resume my life in the academic world before that crucial need to make more money through oil field work rose before me.

On the drive, I pulled out the old tricks of not feeling or thinking. I drove the roads to Baptiste in Sandy's Chevy that I now claimed as solely mine and be damned to those who might try and take it away. The specter of spring final exams loomed before me, but I was one emboldened with confidence. Possessing interest of the most intense kind—and studying—led to excellent grades. Semper Fidelis. The Marines had built something into me. Discipline.

It had been five weeks and five days when I'd last traveled to the northern parishes to see Julie after Sandy's death and discovered her to be an adulteress. The pain of her betrayal atop Sandy being killed continued to echo through me, and I thought it would forever be within me. I lacked the strength to forgive. Now, the loss of Cliffie wrenched my inner confusions tighter in my gut. My tricks to ignore such grief failed. On the long road trip up through central Louisiana, the highway tunneled into my blurred vision like a passageway into other worlds. Goddamn, I thought. Goddamn this uncertain world.

Midmorning, I drove through the village of Caney near Baptiste. The secluded place possibly had a hundred residents who lived in small wood frame houses along a few narrow and crumbling streets. Most of the simple abodes had screened-in porches to allow the residents escape into cooler evening air and protection from ravenous mosquitoes.

The crossing of two narrow roads marked the village center. A tiny post office and a general store stood cater-cornered from each other at the intersection. It was a place that seemed devoid of life but for two sleeping cur dogs on the steps of the general store. Above the village's piney woods, a few clouds were puffed up and adrift against a blue sky.

New Hope Baptist was off a narrow thoroughfare less than a mile away, nestled within a grove of pine trees and live oak. When I arrived, a vast collage of cars and pickup trucks were wedged across the grassy terrain in front of the church and through an open pasture nearby.

I pulled Sandy's Chevy to the roadside and switched off the engine. Fatigue burned into my eyes. I swiped my face and suddenly was conscious of the hair over my cheeks and got out of the car. A short burst of cardinal song broke the quiet of the place. It came as three similar flute-like notes— birdie-birdie-birdie—and all quiet again.

I went on up through the parked cars toward the church. It was a simple but sturdy structure, built of broad, thick planks. Strands of black mildew invaded the white walls. Concrete steps led up to a wide portico and two large doors, side-by-side, propped shut. I went in.

Before me, the pew rows teemed with people. Others sat upon chairs lined along the walls. My lateness warmed into my ears. An old white-haired fellow in sharp, crisp overalls lifted his hand and pointed to an empty cane chair beside him. I made for it beside the door and sat down. The heavy fragrance of lotions and ointments hit the linings of my nose.

I blinked my tired eyes and beheld the surroundings. Simplicity in form and structure characterized the inner body of the dwelling. Large, unadorned windows lined the rough plank walls and permitted a bounty of sunlight to spill over the people seated in the pews. A baby cried, quieted quick. There came a faint rustle of shoes against the floor and shifting of buttocks on the hard pew seats. Guitar music plucked into the warm air. A giant of a woman began singing Amazing Grace. It was Eva who had drawn me into her bosom after my abysmal baptism as a boy and assured me, "I know you'll find God someday, Jack. I know you will."

In the back of this simple church, it came to me as it would in recurring beats along the journey we all take, that life is a series of circles, one going into the next. Eva's dulcet voice rose through this timbered chamber, cleansing it of any trace of impurity. Her eyes lifted to the ceiling and she saw beyond everything else.

I felt happy for this woman who had passed briefly across the path of my boyhood before I'd come to be a murderer. Odd questions rose in front of me as the old gospel song progressed. Would she have forgiven me of my horrific sins as Frank had done? Should such forgiveness be warranted? Because I, one Half-Pint Crowe, could not forgive himself. Weariness of body and mind lifted as her song continued to ply into the heavens imagined. I was sure that if we all sang our thoughts to one another, ill will toward each other would dwindle. Her song ended, replaced by quiet, then a rustling of bodies, soft *Amens*.

The back of Julie's head entered the scope of my vision. She sat in the middle of the congregation. Beside her, Joe Morgan leaned his shoulder against hers. The world spun on, wobbling to and fro. I could do little more but look down at my shined shoes against the rough floorboards. Eva and the guitar player seated themselves down front. A black-suited man of heavy bearing with rosy jowls got up and began to position himself by the casket in which lay Clifford C. Bowles' broken body.

Do you recall such times when you've looked out across a far-stretching vista toward the horizon's edge, and there comes the roll of thunder or the collapse of sunlight? Here it comes. Blackie Shively arose from a seat by the aisle near the nave. He strode like a living tree stump to the head of the casket. The black-suited minister, his Bible grasped between both hands, stepped back. A burst of perspiration glistened over his pink face. A roll of murmurs passed through the congregation.

Blackie swung himself around and faced the people frozen now into the pews and outlay of chairs against the walls. He wore a white shirt that stretched across his enormous chest. A solid black tie hung just past his sternum. It seemed to serve more as a garrote than a decorative piece of clothing. His face flushed red and aligned in horrific contrast to the beard shadow across his jaw. Thick, black hair atop his atlas head slicked down over his ears.

I said in a bare whisper, "Blackie, please don't do this shit." The old fellow beside me rolled yellow-tinted eyes toward me and shook his head. Through the turgid church air, Blackie began to speak.

"My name is Theodore Blackie Shively. I'd known this man whose body lies in this fancy box most all my life. He was my best friend, and among friends, I have not many to count."

Blackie's voice cracked. He cleared his throat and sought the distraction of the floor at his feet. Then he lifted his head and shot fierce eyes out at the congregation of mourners. His voice thundered. "I killed Clifford C. Bowles as sure as the world might turn another day! I depended on him too much. Drove him too hard. Gave him no quarter and poked him in the ribs with my senseless raillery. He had no meanness in him. Was always forgiving of my heathen pursuits. I cared about the son-of-a-bitch. Hell, I loved him. And I killed him with my cruel ways."

Blackie drifted his vision over the funeral congregation like the rotation of a submarine periscope. His barreled chest heaved up and out, and as he'd done so many times before to those who might accost him with disdain, he thumped his fist over his heart and cried out, "If you want to jump into this, here it is for you! Nobody's holding you back! Come get it if you want!"

Stuck in the calcified rhythms of his life, Blackie presented himself for retribution in the only way he knew how, an invite into violence whereby pain and grief explode into bits. He stood in the nave beside the closed coffin, one shoulder slightly tucked like a boxer, ready to throw a counter punch. A fiery glint lit up his dark eyes. I knew what Blackie Shively wanted. He wished all of those before him—men, women, children to hurl themselves over the backs of the pews and fall upon him and rip him apart. Then the wildness of his soul could be summoned. He'd know how to be.

"Bless you, brother Shively," someone said softly. Blackie's eyes twitched toward the voice. The black-suited minister had gravitated toward the sanctum of the pulpit. He held his Bible aloft and looked toward the ceiling fans whose blades were still and silent.

"Come sit among us, Brother Shively. You are welcome unto us."

"Amen," came an old woman's cracking voice.

The old fellow in the chair beside me drawled, "Amen."

Amen, amen arose throughout the little church, heads nodding, the baby again crying, a chorus of *Sit among us* building higher.

How can this be described? Perhaps it should begin with the actions of my heart. It broke inside me. Watching Blackie stand bewildered and helpless, his great hands clenched, panicked, burning eyes like those of a trapped panther, the man stepping left, then right, no place to escape, his chest heaving higher with each drawn breath. I knew him to be as wild as those creatures who still roam the dark woods and swamps. Bringing him out of that wildness would kill him.

Eva, huge and glowing in her purity, rose and went to the hapless giant. She reached to embrace his great shoulders. He shoved her back. In unison, a gasp and groan rolled up from the people. Eva stumbled, corrected her stance as well as any prima ballerina might. Blackie wobbled in place like a man struck by an electrical charge. The man's unseeing eyes pierced into the rows of astonished people in front of him.

"Here it is! Goddamn you!"

From a pew on the church's left-hand side, Buster Milton stood up and began to slide his way toward the center aisle. His wife, Bea, clutched the sleeve of his jacket, but her hand fell away. Muscles of her throat worked up and down as she watched him go. I rose to my feet, helpless and frozen.

Utterances, desperate and hollowed out with softness, kept permeating the atmosphere: God forgives all. *Amen. Amen.* But came a smattering of other retorts:

Escort the sinner from this house of the Lord.
Escort him.
The Lord is all-powerful in love and forgiveness.
Escort out the sinner. Bless him on the way.

Buster reached the aisle and straightened his back. He looked down the center of the church toward the old driller. His hand reached out and gave a beckoning wave. "Come on, you dumb shit. It's time to go."

Blackie once more struck his fist against his chest. "Here it is if you want to jump in it!" He drew in his breath and went up the aisle and brushed past Buster. His square jaw bristled forward. Fiery eyes fixed straight ahead.

Down front, Eva opened her eyes into the light. Her glossed lips moved, and I read what I'm sure she said to Blackie's back, "God loves you, Mr. Shively."

There goes evil, someone uttered. The sanctum of the church grew hushed. I stepped over and swung open the door. Blackie swept past me. Buster trailed close behind and I went out after them into the bright sunlight. The scent of pine resin hung in the air.

A hymnal song began to rise behind the church walls. It was a chorus of many souls conjured up probably by the black-suited minister and led by Eva. Its supernatural bearing swirled higher. *The angels beckon me from heaven's open door, and I can't feel at home in this world anymore.*

Blackie swung his body through the maze of dust-coated trucks and cars toward his old Impala parked on the roadside. The scent of decaying pine needles hung in the air. I followed the two men, unsure of the aim of my pursuit. A squirrel high up in some limbs of an oak barked and fussed.

Buster called out, "Blackie, hold it on now. Nobody's to blame. Nobody's to blame, goddamn it. I'm weary from sayin' it."

Blackie turned around and faced Buster by the rear end of the Impala. He stood in place, his head slightly cocked to the side, and peered through dark slits at Buster standing before him. Blackie's fist spent into Buster's gut faster than what seemed light speed. Buster collapsed to his knees. At Blackie's feet, Buster choked and wheezed pathetically. My own breath went out of me for a second. I lunged in front of Blackie, both arms raised, palms out, gasping, "Blackie, Blackie, stop this, man. Blackie, man."

He said, "Don't fail me."

I didn't see the fist but remember the blow flared as a purple-red light behind my eyes. When I next blinked, I tasted the dust of the road. I pushed up to my feet fast and stood on unsteady ground directly in front of the huge man. Everything was spinning and I kept trying to blink Blackie's face into sharper focus. The trees rotated in the periphery of my vision.

Buster still held to the earth with his knees, his head bent toward the ground. He gasped as if amid some asthmatic fit. I could hear bees buzzing in the clover some distance off the roadside. Blackie spoke once more, "Are you goin' to fail me, Half-Pint?"

He hit me again, this time high up in my chest. The blow knocked me back. I backpedaled but didn't fall. My lungs worked and recaptured the flow of my breath. I sighted on him through a film of mucous.

A twitch below Blackie's right eye signaled the plea for me to come on and I hated him for it, the gall to seek this of me. I threw myself into him, snapping my fists into his colossal face. I was a runt, but I could hit hard and fast and have held my own against jarheads a hundred pounds over my weight.

I pummeled him, giving him his penance, losing myself in the rage that had taken me over. No, I wasn't going to let Blackie down.

He stood there, hands to his sides. An ever-increasing glaze of repose set into his dark, deep-set eyes. Buster finally gathered himself up to his feet and hauled me back. Our breaths together siphoned the rich air.

"Buster," I gasped. "Goddamn him!"

Blood pooled at one corner of Blackie's mouth. From it, a thin, red line disappeared into the black stubble of his chin. His high cheeks shone puffy red. Fleshy muscles around his eyes had already begun to swell. His breath passed easily into and out of his chest. Buster held me tighter. Both of us were bent and unsteady like two wobbling drunks. Blackie stood erect and serene. The blissful aura he now exuded sickened me.

"Half-Pint wouldn't fail me, Buster. He's a fine boy."

"You have no call to be this way," Buster rasped. "Nobody's to blame."

"Go on, Jack. Don't come back looking for death in the oil fields." Blackie spat out a little blood. The satisfied grin that possessed him never wavered. "I don't aim to kill nobody but Buster now since he's pickled in the head and wants to stick with me." His chest heaved higher. "Stay away from here. Stay away from me. Good luck, boy."

Blackie turned and strode the last few feet to the driver's side door and lowered his hulk into the dented-up Impala. He started the car, the motor rumbled, and he drove off as carefully as someone's wary grandmother. Sunshine burst across the back window and distorted the outline of the back of his head.

I would never see Blackie Shively again. I felt it, knew it. My heart pumped with the truth of it. Hymnal music resounded from the insides of the old church building. Eva and the minister were probably offering more placations of song to cast out the evil that remained like some toxin floating in the air. If I'd been a mystical sort, I would have imagined Cliffie lying broken in his casket bed, mumbling something like, "Now, now, Blackie's alright."

For Buster and me, it was mockingbird song that let some peace drift into us. Their fanciful banter lit into our clouded senses and reminded us that this was a world that didn't stop to dwell upon our nonsense. We stood apart, now upright. Blackie's car disappeared into the underpass of overhanging tree limbs down the road.

"I got to get back in. Bea don't like this behavior." Buster's breathing had smoothed out. He straightened his coat and ran one hand through his oil-slick hair. "You coming back, alright. There'll be work. He don't mean what he says. Summer's close. You're coming back and he'll hire you."

"I'm not coming back. I'll find work somewhere."

"Someday, you'll have to come back. Can't be no other way." Buster sniffed, cleared his throat, and started walking back to the church building. He was a wiry pole around which beans could grow, one long string of sinewy muscle who wasn't whom I thought he was and was still becoming whom he might become. I am not fit to judge.

Joe Morgan stood on the church portico. His head craned a little forward. He pushed his eyeglasses farther back upon his nose. He seemed to be watching Buster amble forth through the parked vehicles, and then he sighted on me and raised his hand into the air. I was sure Julie had sent him to review and report on the spectacle outside. In a strange way, it comforted me seeing him standing up there in front of the broad door of the humble church, checking to see if all was alright for Julie.

I lifted my hand into the air. Gave a wave. Buster went up the steps, nodded at Joe, and they went back into the church together. As the door swung open, the sound of gospel song rose higher over the tops of the cars and into the surrounding woods.

With the pain of a broken nose seeping more into my consciousness, I turned away and walked with a minor limp to Sandy's Chevy parked down the road. I began my drive back to Baton Rouge and the end of a year in school. Final examinations loomed but a few weeks ahead.

The ache from broken nose cartilage radiated down my cheeks and into my jaw as the highway south opened in front of me. Little towns, cotton fields, marsh and woodlands swept by the side window. I thought of Clifford and Sandy and in other ways Julie, Buster, and that goddamned Blackie and I felt another ache, that of tremendous loss building in the pit of my stomach.

As was my usual habit, I tried not to think, so thought more until it hurt so bad I turned on the radio and played rock and roll music at a volume so loud Cliffie must be frowning on the descent into his grave and in the mist, Sandy is happy.

My mind spent on what I'd need to do to make enough money for the next school year. The G.I. Bill wasn't nearly enough. Money was running low. But options lay before me. I could take an entire year off, get work on an offshore rig, if lucky; maybe join the merchant marines for a few years; or travel north and hustle my way onto an assembly job at an auto plant or, hell, wash dishes and scrimp into the next decade, but I'd make it.

It's just small shit in the way, Jack. Nothing's going to stop you. There was assurance in Frank's voice. The beat of rock and roll flowing from the radio. He could sense from his dead spot that I was on a path to some answer about what it's all about. There are so many paths and all we must do is find one.

MONEY AND BLOOD

I'd finished the last of my final examinations on a late spring day and walked back across the campus to Rita's house that had been my home for almost nine months. The exam had been for an introductory course titled Religions of the World. The instructor was a young graduate assistant with thinning hair across his scalp but wild strands falling over his ears. He had a lazy smile and sported thick, wire-rimmed eyeglasses.

I liked listening to his lectures, which he struggled to keep very objective and academic and suggest no favor for any of the various religious practices. He loved to ask beneath his breath, *Are there many paths to God? Or only one?*

I was pompous and self-assured, which is both dangerous and ignorant. I thought the answer quite evident. In one of the compare-and-contrast composition questions of the examination, I had written, *All the religions are trying to explain and verify the existence of a God or Gods. They all believe themselves to be right in their explanations and offer rituals and moral guidance to gain salvation of some sort. They have all garnered followers who have readily enough accepted the explanations and, in return, receive due comfort in knowing the true meaning of their lives, whether it's true or not. In this sense, they are all winners.* Later, when I reviewed his remarks on my paper, I noticed he'd placed a checkmark beside my notation, underlined it, and drew an arrow to a quotation of his own in the margins, *Walk cautiously upon this earth, brother.*

But on this day, following the exam, I walked across the campus green and through the trees and up the shaded street to Rita's comfortable old home. Entering through the front door, I noticed a blue envelope addressed to me on Rita's small table for the stacking of mail. I slid my haversack from my shoulders and held it in one hand by the straps. I picked up the envelope and walked through the house and out into Rita's backyard. It was pleasantly cool in the shade. I sat down in one of the wooden chairs and dropped my haversack beside it.

Imprints from my sweaty fingertips emerged upon the envelope. I looked for a while out across the place Rita called her bird sanctuary. A weathered plank fence bordered the yard but was barely visible because of the dense foliage. A bounty of flowering shrubs and vines lined the fence. The faint scent of sweet olive blossoms lifted across the grass, carrying sadness with it. A giant magnolia tree lorded over the center of the bird sanctuary. Its white blossoms budded fiercely. I kept holding the envelope and finally opened it. A check for ten thousand dollars made out to me and signed by Julie Guillory rested within the letter's folded pages. Only the faintest of tremors in my hand exposed my angst as I read.

Dear Jack,

The money is real. It came from Sandy's Servicemembers' Group Life Insurance that all you boys in war are covered by. Now Sandy's life is given some to you so that you can go on. I know you would have gone on anyway, somehow finding your way, but this will make it easier. Sandy would not have wanted this to be any other way. And you damn well know it. He admired and loved you more than you will ever know. Always carry that with you. This will not be argued about, though I wish I could hear from you and fight with you. Then it could be like old times, but it never will. Will it?

I am okay, Jack. I know you still love me and worry about me though you're mad and disappointed. It's horrible of you just to hide it. But I say this despite what you might think. Joe is a decent man. I love him. It happened, so it happened, and I'm tired of trying to understand why it happened and so is Joe.

We're leaving here and moving near San Diego, where Joe will be working in the Kroger chain. He's very ambitious. He knows we got to get from here. After his divorce, we're going to be married. There's been hard parts, but it's how it has come to be. Many people are still nice though some won't look at us. Like we're too shameful to be near them. And they're probably right. Mama's okay with us now but was hurt and crying all the time for a while. Will you let me know if your address changes? If you reach your goals in life? Please, Jack. Let me know. I'm not asking you to forgive me. I'm done with that.

Love,
Julie

I sat there and lost the scope of time curving around me. Serenading of mockingbirds lit dimly into my consciousness. Flitting around in the tree limbs, they pronounced with shameful accuracy the notes of any songbird passing through the garden. Inside myself came an inner battle. A violent tossing about to and fro. I damn near threw up. Slowed my breath to smooth everything out.

From a softer perspective shaped by fifty years of hindsight, I understand that I was reacting to the temptation of easiness. Like from high tide to low in a nanosecond. Forgiving was a struggle in those younger days...and still it is, brothers and sisters of the journey. Having the ease of money to pave the way forward required personal adjustment on my part. Especially that bequeathed to me by Julie who in my pathetic sense of allegiance to Sandy could not forgive. Oh, I see me well on that late spring day at the edge of Rita's bird Shangri-la contemplating how best to destroy a ten-thousand-dollar check.

After a while, the screen door creaked open and Rita came out carrying a tray with two glasses of iced tea upon it. She set the tray down on a table beside the chairs and put one of the chilled glasses into my hand.

"My Lord, Jack. Hope you did better on that exam than you look."

"I did alright."

She lowered herself into a chair. Her chin lifted and her eyes narrowed into the dark recesses of the jungled sanctuary. Her presence released a flood of words from my mouth.

"The wife of my dead friend gave me her government life insurance money. Her husband died in Vietnam. That's where I was for what seemed a lifetime. I should have died over there more than enough times. Ten thousand dollars for Sandy Guillory's life. Somewhere there's a meaning to it all and I got to find it though it eludes me for now. I loved him more than I could have loved a brother. I loved his wife more than I could love a sister, and probably more than that. She betrayed Sandy. And I'm sitting here with a passage ticket forward that just arrived signed in her name." I let the pathetic feel of it all seep through me.

Rita cocked her head a little to the side. Her eyes squinted into mere slits as if to accentuate her quest to comprehend this ineffable world. "Don't be such a small-minded dumb fuck, Jack." Her vision slanted toward the backyard foliage. Her eyes gleamed brightly. "Did you hear her? A wood thrush. Oh, listen. Her song makes my heart fly away." She patted the top of my hand, the one that held the check. Her fingers were warm. "Don't be any sillier than you already are."

Whether it was due to weakness of spirit or strength of will, I kept the money. I sent no thank you card or acknowledgment letter to Julie. I sucked it up as tragic irony. But this part I know, weakness kept me from reaching out to her as time slipped by. I shut off all avenues of communication with Julie, and, eventually, her attempts to contact me waned. The light of connectedness grew dimmer and went out. Although the power to search for people who we've lost to time came to be so easy through the eventual technological revolution of the internet, I resisted all temptations to type her name into search engines in those years to come. The internet steals away too much mystery. Beguiles us with answers to everything, whether be the answers right or wrong.

I wanted to keep Julie's life forward mysterious. Fill it with my dreams. Over the years, I imagined her to be forever happy with Joe in San Diego. But I, being Half-Pint, would never enter back into her life. I wanted not to read of her obituary or know of some divorce or tragic ending that might have come to be. Mystery is best when like a purring cat asleep by the fire.

Ten thousand dollars carried a long way back in those early '70s, especially for an ex-Marine grunt who needed little food, few clothes, and who worked diligently to constrain his lustful wants. In my second year at Rita's house, she asked of me during one of our wine tasting tête-à-têtes, "I've never caught you having fun, trying to shoo a girl into your room." She dipped her chin and peered at me over the rim of her glasses and said to me with grandmotherly concern, "I know the wants of young men, Jack boy. I've always had a mind to look the other way."

I'd become very comfortable with telling Rita the truth. Even took some delight in shocking her with lurid and comical stories of Marine Corps hijinks, though nothing about the blood and terror. In this vein of openness, I told her that when desire burned incandescent and disrupted my studies, I might occasionally seek prostitutes who worked out of the hooker hotels in the run-down quarters of the town. She didn't give me the satisfaction of even a crinkled brow. Instead, she said, "Some suppose Mary Magdalene to have been a prostitute. Even married Jesus."

I took on a pedantic air, a bit sodden with my recent extensive readings of the life of Jesus. "Mary Magdalene was more likely to have been a woman of prominence, who possibly had epilepsy or some psychotic disorder. But a devoted follower of Jesus the Messiah, nonetheless. There's no valid proof she was married to him." Then, smugly added, "No valid proof about a lot of things for that matter." I drew back and took a sip of wine and suddenly felt a wave of self-loathing work through me. "Those women I've paid for the use of their bodies have suffered a harsh world. They are not Mary Magdalene."

"And you, Jack boy, are not Jesus Fucking Christ."

It didn't even sting. I'm not sure Rita meant to cut me with her comment but merely observe a fact. It hit and wrapped around me in a perfect fit.

"Yeah. You don't know the half of it."

Ten thousand dollars sat in my once meager account at Whitney Bank of Baton Rouge. A small G.I. Bill stipend at the end of each school month and the small amount of money I earned from a work-study program shelving trundles of books back to their proper places on the library shelves of Troy H. Middleton Library sustained me quite well through the remainder of the baccalaureate years.

Julie's last letter had beheld a San Diego address. She said that she and Joe had bought a house in a neighborhood with palm trees and smooth green lawns. Joe had found an excellent job as an assistant manager at one of the Kroger stores. After training to become a dog groomer, she rented a space in a shopping mall and started her own dog grooming business. She and Joe were happy. She had put the house on Roosevelt Street up for sale, but property was not selling in the dying town. Julie wished me well and the best of luck and said goodbye. I held the letter for a long time. Drew it close to my nose in the hope that I might detect her scent but could not.

With more money available, I accelerated my class loads. My last semester started in the summer of 1973. Graduation with the baccalaureate in religious studies loomed inside my grasp. Rita saw the approach of the end to this phase of my search. She asked a simple question one night. What did I plan to do after I graduated? I told her that

I had applied to graduate schools across the country and would pursue a higher degree in religious studies. I was quite aware of how such study afforded little practical use in this utilitarian world. But obtaining a doctorate might enable me to teach within the field of religious inquiry and thus sustain myself with sufficient income of which I'd need little.

Rita stared at me. Awe pressed through the lines around her widening eyes. "Why you're a fellow with plans, aren't you? How impressed I am."

I smiled, beamed haughtily. Mimicked the low, rough voice of a Marine lifer. "Marine Corps training, ma'am. Situation, mission, execution, administration, and logistics. Semper Fi, do or die."

Rita rolled her eyes. The ceiling light above the doorway shone directly on her face. It was then I realized how the skin over her cheekbones had grown more translucent. Tiny veins shown through beneath her eyes.

"Therein, at the end of the day, will you get the answers you're looking for?" she said.

A little something gave way in my chest and my heart sank within. The translucence of her skin continued to hold me in some odd suspension of thought. Finally, I mumbled, "It seems logical that I will someday find the answers to my questions."

Rita laughed softly. "I can tell you that the answer will be where you least expect it." She patted me on the side of my arm as she'd become accustomed to do during moments of support and reassurance.

I gave her a wink. "Rita, the mystic."

She threw nothing back in jest. I kept looking at her and wondering where had come this cloak of frailty upon her. I touched her shoulder, which was narrow and thin.

"Rita, are you doing okay?"

"Why, yes. Just old and dying." She gave me a coquettish look. "Haven't you noticed?"

I hadn't noticed, of course. In the quick dawning of that second, I recognized that my so-called quest for meaning that possessed me, carried with it the danger of unadulterated self-absorption.

"I must run. Well done on your foresight of planning, Jack. It truly is admirable. I'll be pulling for you."

She left and I went upstairs. By the time I sat down at my desk, emptiness had taken over. I pushed through it and slid the books from my haversack to the surface of the desk. Into late evening, the translucence of Rita's face slipped in recurrent passage across my vision.

That night, not Frank but Romano entered the realm of my half-woke consciousness as the ceiling fan clicked above my bed. He sat at my desk chair with one arm draped over the backrest. "You one pouty, dumbass white boy, Half-Pint."

"Frank wasn't selfish," I murmured toward Romano's shadowy presence. "You're brilliant."

"What made him? What made Frank the way he was?" Sleep held the bottom of my feet, tugging me down.

"That dude was born with pure kindness. Something you and me and a shitload of others didn't git. He was our freak, Half-Pint. Not wantin' nothin' in return. Can't find many like that, can you?" His laughter carried through the shadowy dark. How I missed his laughter.

Romano had enough of me. He was gone. I slipped off the final slope of consciousness into somewhere else in which I had no dreams, no recollections. A kind sleep.

For the remainder of that last summer, I tried to give more attention to Rita. Short walks together along the quiet neighborhood streets beneath tree-limbed awnings, visits to local gardens in Sandy's Chevy, more tipsy evenings of wine-sipping, more bird spotting and song recognition as we sat together in the backyard.

Once on a late evening walk, she said, "What saddens me is that I appear to be your only friend."

"I got all the friends I need."

"I'm not talking about dead friends. I seem to be your only living friend. And here I am, an almost eighty-six-year-old woman."

I shrugged and waited for her to finish her litany of grandmotherly concerns.

"And girls, Jack. I know you like girls. Dare you not give up your occasional dalliance with a poor prostitute to find a girlfriend? You think mine old eyes haven't taken notice of your eyes undressing lovely girls in their mini-skirts walking past?"

"Rita, come on," I coughed. She'd developed a sharper knack for embarrassing me. Seemed to relish the joy of watching my cheeks flush red.

This time, I whacked back at her with as much honesty as I could summon. "Something got blown away inside me during the war. Yeah, I get lonely. My wants overcome me, but it doesn't seem to matter much in the bigger picture. Do you ever see the smallness of ourselves? Not just regular small but infinitesimal small. We're on a mote of dust. It's gigantic to us. Then look out past the stardust and you realize we're less than the size of a needlepoint that just keeps getting smaller the farther away we look. Finally, we're nothing and something at the same time. I'm beginning to think God is unknowable, and it just makes me..." I felt suddenly foolish and reigned in the workings of my effusive tongue.

"It makes you excited," Rita said and gave me a wry squint of her eyes.

"Yeah," I said. "How did you know?"

"Lucky guess."

We strode on along the walkway beneath the trees. I wrapped one arm around Rita's frail shoulders and gave her a gentle hug. She was so thin and fragile. "You're my buddy, Rita."

"And you're my good friend. It saddens me you don't have more."

I left the South for good in the late summer of 1973 at semester end. I'd been accepted into the religion program at Temple University in Philadelphia and would start classes in the fall. I thought it then, as I had thought it until eight days ago when Buster's phone call rang into my office, that I would never go back. My plan had been to leave Half-Pint behind to wilt and die in the unbridled heat of a venomous past. Jack Crowe was going north.

All my possessions fit into Sandy's Chevy. A few clothes, boxes of books, including Frank's three volumes, and a Mr. Coffee automatic drip coffeemaker that I'd lavished upon myself after graduation. It was early morning. Songbirds sang with rhapsodic intensity from the tree limbs. Rita stood with me on the sidewalk beside the car. She handed me what was obviously a book neatly wrapped in red wrapping paper tied off with blue ribbon fluffed into a bow.

"I've bought you a graduation gift," she said.

"A book," I said.

"It seems that's all you've eaten around here for the last three years."

"Can I open it?"

"Obviously."

I pulled the ribbon back and rifted off the tape and paper. The sheen of the book's cover overwhelmed me. I folded the wrapping paper and held a copy of the *National Geographic Field Guide to the Birds of Eastern North America* in both hands.

"When the birds die, we're done. Never forget what I just said. When the birds die, we're done." Her emphatic tone stole away my steady footing. She nodded at the book in my hands. "I thought you might enjoy it from time to time."

"I will."

"This will probably be the last time I see you. Let's be honest," she said.

Rita was much more capable of directness than I. "Come on, Rita. I'll see you again."

She patted me on the side of my arm. I wouldn't let her get away with just that habitual minor gesture of affection. I pulled her thin body into mine and held her gently and could smell her frailness of being. Rita went away up the walk to her front door and disappeared inside without looking back. That was that. I was tough and grizzled as they come. Pull the bodies over. Stack 'em high. Zip the flak jacket. Get ready to die. Semper Fi. Semper Fi. Semper Fi.

I got into Sandy's Chevy and placed the book on the front passenger seat. Somewhere, well outside of Baton Rouge, going east on Highway 190, the sun rising higher above a bank of clouds, I quit crying. That was that.

I received word of Rita's death from Rita herself, so to speak, in February 1974, less than a year after I'd crossed the southern boundaries and settled into Philadelphia's gritty, bustling center. Rita and I had kept up occasional letter writing to each other. Her penmanship grew smaller and more frayed during that short time. The news we had shared was mainly of ordinary things. She had a new lodger, a serious girl who was a graduate student in the psychology program. Rita wrote: *She appears not to talk to herself. What a disappointment.* She said: *Oodles of cedar waxwings migrated through in the fall. Oodles and oodles.* She never mentioned congestive heart failure, diminishing strength of limbs and breath or the sweet breaths of angels upon her cheek.

I wrote that the library at Temple was as grand as I could hope; that my fellow students possessed intimidating intelligence and had unimaginable vistas of what is possible in human life; that the city of Philadelphia pumped a blood of grime and diversity. I wrote to her about a winter day that chilled the bones and how I watched an old homeless man who squatted on concrete steps outside 69th Street Terminal. Wrapped in soiled layers of clothing, a giant plastic bag of his possessions stashed beside his legs, people flowing past, he struggled to place the point of a safety pin through the sideways edge of a dollar bill. His brown, nicotine-stained fingers shivered in the cold, but he kept trying to probe that damn needlepoint into the dollar bill's edge. I watched and did nothing as if there were some unwritten rule fiercely etched in the air that demanded, *Leave it alone, lest you toss akilter some delicate balance of the way things are.* A transit cop roused him up. The homeless guy wobbled off and was gone with his plastic bag swaying by the side of his leg. I tucked away my shame and went about forgetting.

Rita's last letter came forwarded to me by a member of her church. The letter had been sealed, stamped, and addressed to me and placed within a larger envelope that contained a brief note on church stationery. The church member's handwritten message simply explained that Rita had requested the enclosed envelope be mailed to one Jack Crowe after her death. I still retain Rita's message of final goodbye in my memorabilia. It reads,

Dear Jack,

I thought you would find this note from me quite amusing because you are so accustomed to hearing from the dead. Since I count as one of your friends, and now since I am no more, you should be rather comfortable hearing from me. Let me put my macabre humor aside. You are indeed my dear friend. There is much good in you. Much kindness. If you find some answers to the meaning of your life, our lives, I suppose, well I say, fine work. But if not, do not be too disappointed and forget not to appreciate the moments of quiet in any given day. Keep a sense of humor.

Love,

Rita

That letter left me wounded in ways far different from shrapnel or enemy rounds. Sadness drenched my soul. To those who maybe had some college experience, do you ever look nostalgically back upon those days and think fondly of friendships formed? Well, Rita was my pal, my friend who came from those days of study and intellectual exploration. The pain of her loss sinks deep into the body tissues and remains until entropy completes its work.

After I had arrived in Philadelphia, the first days whipped speedily past me. I found a cheap room for rent that possessed a sturdy desk and good lighting in a worn-down, three-story house on Aspen Street. My fellow residents in the dwelling were mostly students from the art academy on Broad Street. They all seemed to be pleasingly eccentric, searching in their own creative ways for truth and understanding. Over the next few years, I came to know a few of them well enough in that casual, 'What's up, man?' kind of way, but always I maintained a proper distance. From out of their mysterious tribe, I was eventually ascribed the moniker of Hermit. It carried an affectionate tone when they addressed me as such. It seemed to fit, so I rolled with it.

Two miles separated the house from Temple University, but the pad's price was so wonderfully cheap I held on to it through my six years in the city. A clunker of a used bicycle served as my primary means of transportation. My navigational skills biking through the streets of Philadelphia sharpened quickly out of desperate necessity. I've joked to myself over the years that I had almost as many near death experiences biking up Broad Street to the university as I had plodding through Vietnam's rice paddies.

Most of the time, Sandy's Chevy remained sequestered on the street curb in front of the house between two giant ginkgo trees. I informed my fellow house residents and street locals quite seriously that Sandy Guillory's ghost kept watch over it. Never was it vandalized. (To those who might be or once were denizens of these inner-city streets and may cast doubtful looks upon the last statement, it is the unadulterated truth.)

My warm acquaintances in the religion department at Temple knew not of my time in war nor of Half-Pint Crowe. What would I have said to these exceptional colleagues of mine about the war? And Half-Pint? That I had murdered, walked among the dead and drew the stink of death onto my flesh. That within the shit of that war, I came to know a true holy person, a simple Navy corpsman who forgave me my sins, befriended me, inspired me to seek answers to questions of existence I'd never fathomed possible to explore. So here I am among you, terribly fearful you'll discover me as the charlatan I am. Was I to share this part of my life, that was the life of Half-Pint Crowe, with these gentle people. Shit no. I was to be known as Jack. Later, the nickname of Hermit would permeate up from the realms of Aspen Street and into the religious studies department of Temple.

Despite these tribulations, I thrived in this land of the Yankees—I loved Philadelphia. Though meager, another money flow came when I received a graduate teaching assistantship in my second year. I found it stimulating to stand before young and eager students, look upon untarnished faces and share the rhythms and rhymes of religious teachings.

It was like taking up the spin chain once again to flick into the air and let it whip around the pipe. It is trite to describe it thus, but here it is—I felt ten feet tall when I commanded a classroom of searching souls and guided the way into topics of religious diversity, the religions in America, or the evolution of world religions.

I was careful. There was protocol given to outlines of course material, but occasionally, no matter the topic, I'd slip off into the story of a true holy person and describe, as best I could, the nature of pure selflessness and ask, Is such a person born with holiness? Or, shaped by the vicissitudes of life into holiness? How has that person come to discover the essence of God? What does that essence truly look like as that person walks the earth?

When I finished at Temple, a rare teaching job had opened in a small Vermont college situated near the Green Mountains. With the advocacy and encouragement of my closest professors and a well-received doctoral dissertation about the "efficacy of saints and prophets and the saint-like to inspire the knowledge of God as illustrated by historical events," I was awarded the position.

I went to Vermont not in a vast burst of enlightenment but into the softer light of sanctuary. And there I've been. Until Buster's call.

THE WHITEHEAD BOY

I opened the door of the rental car into a vault of heat that blasted into my face. Autumn is a slow traveler to this latitude of the South. Steamy air radiated up from the parking lot pavement of the McDonald's. Far south toward the Gulf of Mexico, beyond the restaurant's rooftop, cumulus clouds built like puffy anvils along the edge of the stratosphere. To the north, the contrail of a jet airliner traced across a blue sky. The image of the jet was but a faint pinpoint at the head of the trail.

The air was cool inside the McDonald's. I ordered a coffee and sat down at a booth and waited for Buster. Fatigue settled through me from the flight and then the drive down from the Bill and Hillary Clinton Airport in Little Rock. In our last conversation, Buster had said he would meet me here, at this time, at this place so well identified by its golden arches across the planet. It was mid-afternoon. Only a few people occupied the clean rooms, bright with sunlight.

Two teenage girls sat at a nearby booth. They drank from large plastic containers while they appeared to study scribbled notes inside spiral notebooks. Several grey-haired, heavy-set white ladies resided at a window table on the opposite side of the dining area, paper coffee cups before them, carrying on with muted conversation marked by smiles and nods. I thought them old. Trapped by the staid conventions of their lives. Then I reigned in my arrogance. Acknowledged they were probably younger than me and no more trapped by convention than fossilized professors.

A faint lift came to my eyelids as I drank the coffee. It wasn't bad. I'd become a snobbish connoisseur of fine coffees along the course of my academic career. I knew well the meaning of my coffee snobbery. When Professor Jack Crowe dwelled upon his coffee fixation, he fully shucked Half-Pint from his life. Half-Pint Crowe was incapable of such appreciation of a coffee beverage. And right now, as I draw my vision to the sun-swept world outside the plate glass windows of the McDonald's, I admit that I'm in Half-Pint's territory—the South. He's close. He's me.

"You must be Half-Pint Crowe."

A man of average height dressed in a pale-blue medical smock and baggy khakis, belly overhanging his belt, stood next to the booth looking down at me. He beheld a shy grin across his sleepy face and held a plastic soda container in one hand. His cheeks were rosy-red from a fresh shave.

"You're Jack Crowe, alright. I recognize you. Oh yeah, I do." He shook his head. His smile beamed wider. Faint wrinkles beneath his eyes vanished. I saw the boy in him. That little piece of wiry flesh that I'd once planned to kill along with his mother and sorry old man.

"Buster Milton said you'd be here," he said and looked around. "If I might, I'll sit with you for a while. I'm Ted Whitehead. You got time for revelations?" He reached out his hand and I shook it.

The world had stopped and begun to spin in a different direction. A drift of smoke passed quickly across my vision, like the disorienting haze of battle that you'd striven to forget. I pressed my shoulders against the backrest of the booth. "Sit down. Please. You're not someone I expected."

He slid into the seat across from me. His lips puckered around the straw from the soda container. I remembered him mainly as a scowling and dangerous boy. But here now was a grown man who seemed to possess a cavalier, undaunted bearing. I held back on the questions forming fast inside my head. Old cautions borne of instincts honed long ago emerged. I waited but uttered a quick note of truth to this man who sported upon his medical smock a name tag, Ted Whitehead, Registered Nurse.

"I take it you're doing well," I said.

"I'm well enough." He looked at me over the tip of the straw. "Call me Ted. It was impolite to address you in such a familiar manner. You're a professor up in Vermont, I hear from Buster. He studied finding you mighty hard. You can find anybody these days. My familiarity with you means no disrespect. Doubt you go by Half-Pint these days."

"I was waiting for Buster. You've thrown me off balance. Call me Jack or Half-Pint, for that matter."

"Buster Milton planned this shindig of sorts. I am the messenger. Not Buster, I'm afraid. I know he beckoned you. He can be quite the imploring one, I tell you. If you choose to see him later, he will ask forgiveness for manipulating you to meet me in this hallowed hall of dining. He'll say some crazy shit like sermons never end, but life sure does. Hell is regret. Heaven is doing what's right. Oh, how many times have I heard him say that?" Ted shook his head. He looked at a spot on the table beside my coffee cup. For a second, his smile transformed into a contemplative frown. The faint smile returned and he went on.

"He'll not implore you to be as him, but he'll practice kind acts in front of you. 'It's the only heaven there is,' he'll say and give you everything he's got if you're in need. Never stops. Sets up voter registration, drives into the poor town sections, especially the old black quarters, though he won't call himself political by any means." Ted's eyebrows lifted. "Yet I know that his wife Bea had a picture of Franklin Delano Roosevelt hanging on their bedroom wall. For Bea, he'd have given his life ten times over. Two masters he had. One was Blackie Shively and the other, Bea." Ted took a drink through the straw of his cup.

"He and his freaky followers will walk down the downtrodden streets of the parish towns handing out paper sacks of groceries 'til they got no more to give. Then they'll sand and paint houses of folks needing upkeep when they can afford the paint, and then Buster will be off to rustle up cash to pay Mrs. Lopez's utility bill or repair old Junior Washington's broken-down truck."

Ted Whitehead laughed low and rough. "He's made the clergy and powers that be in the parish nervous. Pissed off their better natures. They call him an apostate masquerading as a renegade disciple. Truth be told, Buster Milton does upset the balance of things. He ain't normal, Professor, but a lot of us love that old man. Never tries to draw people away from their regular lives or their congregations, but more than a few have followed him. Buster don't say much. Never talks about God. Won't blame nobody for what is or isn't. Just says heaven is decency. Hell is regret."

Ted stared into the circumference of his soda straw. "I respect that old man, but I'm not a follower of his kith and kind. It takes too much. That's one of my flaws. Buster's alright with who I am. He places no demands upon me."

"Following along behind him?" I said more to myself than Ted Whitehead but couldn't subdue my astonishment. To what place have I come? It's the South. Across from me sits a middle-aged man who as a boy held a shotgun on me, now staring at a cold soda drink in his hands and waxing on about the spiritual oddities of Buster Milton, a ghost from over fifty years gone by. I'm home, where it's difficult to tell the difference between reality and illusion. My lips are dry. I'm trying to understand what's coming at me. Ted Whitehead is aflame with an aura of secrets. I leaned back as if to take a hard blow to my head but left one hand clasped around my cup of coffee. I managed to comment on that which was obvious.

"Buster took a course in life far different than I'd imagined," I said. "As did you, it appears."

"Our imaginations can limit us." Ted grinned, seemingly proud of his comment. "Would you have imagined yourself sitting across from me in Ronald McDonald's so many years before? Got any words for it, professor?"

"No. Much less imagined a McDonald's around here." My fingers plied the coffee cup in small rotations.

"A major heating and air conditioning company moved a plant here back in the eighties. Put some blood into the spare commerce of the parish for a while. Golden arches came in about that time. But three years back, the plant moved on to Mexico. Same old story. But the golden arches stayed. God bless 'em."

"I'm glad I didn't kill you," I said. "Or get killed by you."

"It wasn't written to be that night." Ted appeared to press his tongue against the back of his teeth and search for some new line of thought. "I know Buster has informed you of Blackie's recent passing. We all come to the endpoint, don't we? The man was ninety-four. He was steady on his feet 'til the stroke hit him about a year back. Before that, Buster and Bea looked after him some. Got him into that old house that belonged to Julie Morgan on Roosevelt for a while when Blackie could still manage his affairs before the stroke."

I held my breath, grew still as if a little bird had lit on my shoulder. I hadn't heard the mention of Julie's name in many, many years and was surprised by the anguish that struck through me and I heard my voice;

it seemed so far away, asking Ted if he knew about Julie Morgan. Do you know? And I waited for the little bird to fly away.

Ted looked at me, his eyes unblinking and lit with a bright curiosity of his own. He said, "I didn't know much of her. Buster's wife had some friendship with the Morgan lady who gave over that old place to Bea and Buster for Blackie to live a good while back. Buster mentioned she had passed away somewhere in California. He spoke well enough of her. I take it you knew of her."

I was breathing again. "I once lived in that old Roosevelt house. She had been a good friend."

Ted waited for a moment, expecting me to say more, but I had no words. Just a strange heaviness that comes to the heart when regret and sadness strike together. He paused a few seconds more, then with a deepening of his breath, went on.

"Bea had always been tolerant of Blackie and kind to him alongside Buster. But she was gone when Blackie got hit with his stroke. Buster got him housed last year in the Veterans Nursing Home down in Alexandria. I helped some, but it was mostly Buster."

Ted looked up and fixed his eyes straight into me. "Cliché coming at you, Jack—Blackie lived a long, interesting life. Of course, he had many faults, but don't we all? One of his was not asking for help unless he bought it from you, or you owed it to him somehow. Buster, his kids and grandkids, and my family kept vigil as Blackie starved himself out while he was at the VA home. He had nobody but us. We owed him. When Blackie died, Buster said let all truths be told. It could be no other way."

I was still struggling to grasp the news of Julie's death and withstand the turbulence of feelings running through me. After all these years, the past confronts me. Vertigo kept trying to attach itself to my head. Ted Whitehead exuded an easiness that kept throwing switches in my aging brain, releasing memories of this man as a spiteful reed of a kid destined to abuse or maim or kill others like his old man. But here he was, like some Alethian messenger of so-called truth.

Ted drew quiet and stared at my hand clasped tightly around the coffee cup before he spoke again. "Spin chains," he muttered. "Blackie said you were the best with a spin chain that he ever saw."

"What did Buster want from me? Why are you and I here talking?" I tried to speak softly, but there was anguish in my voice.

Ted lowered one shoulder to the side. "Buster is afflicted with the belief in purity. Something was left undone back in those days. A violation of truth, the gall of deception. He wants you to know the truth." Ted's eyes drew half-closed.

"What the hell are you talking about?"

"Blackie was always looking for me during that time of which you know I speak. Or I was looking for him. He found me a few times out on the road late in the evening when Daddy would be out of town. Blackie asked me if I'd ever heard a panther scream out in the deep woods and I had. Like some lost soul crying for help in the wilderness. He seemed pleased and said it was the cry of a dying earth. I knew he was trying to scare me, but he didn't.

"I showed him my treasures of arrowheads and a grinding stone I'd found on our land. Looking back on those days, I sometimes think he was testing my merits."

Ted stole a few glances around the sunny dining room. The four older women at a far table by the long window laughed together pleasantly. Ted cleared his throat.

"A summer evening came. The sun was red and low behind cypress trees by the creek at Burnt Bridge. The light of day mostly spent." Ted's eyes widened. He peered at me again as if to signal that he knew I was still there across the table from him. "I rarely fished off Burnt Bridge. I always set up my pole down along the banks beneath the cypress, but I fished for perch off the bridge that evening. Hoping he'd pass by in the wanderings he took after you boys came off work at the rig. My dog Beau sat near my feet." Ted's eyes went half-shut.

"I knew he was looking for me. Twilight stalking through the woods. Fireflies blinking all around. Blackie drove that junk car of his up beside Beau and me. He rolled down his window and went straight to it. 'Are you wanting to talk? 'Cause I got some talk for you.'

"I pulled up a string of perch and set 'em in the bucket. He said that you, Half-Pint Crowe, were building up to do something bad. That you were going to try and kill my daddy. He couldn't let that come to be. Know what I said, Jack? I said, 'Why not?'"

The words of Ted Whitehead hit like the bullet that had chunked through my leg a millennium ago. It also struck me that I hadn't thought of the war in a long time, and here I am down South remembering the burn sensation of the bullet. Everything went still and silent but for the movement of Ted Whitehead's lips.

"Blackie sat in his car a while longer, then he switched off the motor and got out. We stood against the railing, looking out into the redness of the sun setting behind the trees. He said, 'If anybody passes by, all I'm about to say will be null and void.' I said, 'Yes, sir.'

"Blackie roughed up my hair. 'We can take care of two problems with one big stone. We'll need to talk with your mama.' He kept looking at me. He was waiting for me to say something. I said it: 'Mama will listen to what you got to say.' That's when I choked up. I let nobody see me cry back in those days and hardly now. But I choked up on that bridge in front of Blackie. I repeated it, 'Mama will listen.'

"He said that you had a life to fulfill and me and Mama would be free to choose a new one of our own if it all went right. It was to be mine and Mama's choice. It would require recognition of evil in us as well as the evil and prejudices of others who'll believe what they already hold in their hearts. 'People see what they believe. Not the other way around,' he said. I think I understand what he meant, but back then I just wanted my daddy dead and Mama alive. I've come to terms with that."

"It never stops," I said. I uttered these words to start my breathing again and affirm that I was listening despite the chills running through me. Ted was looking far away into some dark places and was loose upon his history.

"Daddy was up in Little Rock that evening with some timber company and its lawyers. Blackie said he knew that and told me to grab Beau and pile into the back of the car. We drove to the house. Not trepidation nor hesitancy nor a calling by all that is holy to pause and question what I was bound to do. I was going to kill my Daddy.

"Mama and I sat in the porch swing. It was good and dusky by then. We were like shadows to one another. Blackie sat on the porch edge, just like he'd dropped by for a casual visit and iced tea. He said when the time came it would come mighty fast. He would do the killing and Buster Milton would be backing him up if things went wrong. His eyes were on Beau. I told him I can control Beau. I can keep him quiet. He just sniffed and said, 'Alright then.' Each night after Mama and Daddy went to bed, I was to unlock the front door. Mama was to do nothing but act herself. The night of the killing did come fast. It happened that week, a day after Daddy took Mama to the movie house in Baptiste. He called those occasions airing her out." Ted scrunched his lips together, cast his eyes downward, and went on.

"On the porch that evening, Blackie spoke to us of one of Daddy's indulgent habits. It would be the meat around the bones of our story. Daddy solo tripped to Michigan in the upper peninsula to fish every year. Had said he'd take me with him when I turned twelve, but that never came to be." Ted gave a quick shake to his head then went on.

"Blackie laid out the story that was to be the killing of Calvin Whitehead. Two black men came down from Michigan to seek vengeance. Mama was to say she heard one of 'em say the killing is revenge for Daddy's misdoings in Detroit. That was to be her job, to say vengeance was uttered by a black man from Detroit who had a northern accent. Nothing more. Vengeance, he said. Over and over. Vengeance."

Ted's chest rose and fell. He seemed to examine the arches logo on his soda container before he continued.

"Mama had one demand if it was to happen." Ted pulled off the lid from which his straw protruded and took a drink from the container. Ice slushed along the insides. He lowered the drink back to the table. "She wanted to stick Daddy with a knife."

"It's alright," I said.

"You know not what that man did to her. Look upon thyself before you judge."

"I'm not one of any worth to judge."

"Blackie shot my old man in the head with a .22 while he slept, then he cut Daddy's throat. Buster Milton stood by in the hallway tasked with keeping an eye on my bedroom door. Wasn't no need. I had Beau well-minded and kept him quiet. I was to take off for the drilling rig an hour after Blackie and Buster left. You showing up that night came close to messing up the whole affair. Mama had taken the knife but stuck Daddy in the chest more than a few times, which pissed Blackie off, but she couldn't stop. He had her wash down. Said to tell 'em she was out of her mind trying to get blood off herself after the northern blacks left. Just leave her gown as it is. We knew there'd be thinking that mama or I did the killing somehow, but all that slipped past eventually.

"Years ago, the law quit sniffing around Detroit whore houses for two black men who might have had cause for retribution toward a white man named Calvin Whitehead or some alias. Privacy of customers was a major creed among the houses of prostitution around Detroit. But stories would crop up of rednecks with southern accents who had passed through that would get fed to the authorities. The scent always led to the emptiness of greater mystery. Our local law enforcement went around smiling in awe, believing me and mama pulled off a clean killing. Sheriff at the time didn't probe too deep for the truth. He enjoyed the story that Blackie had concocted for us better than what might have been the truth. Blackie gave us the parts to hand out and everybody wrote what they wanted to see in their own heads. I believe the law back then wanted us to get away with it."

Ted looked straight into me. "Do you want to know the one request Blackie made of me and mama for killing my old man?"

"I'd like to know."

"Keep our land wild. Never to be sold, plowed, mined, or drilled." Ted pressed his lips together in an assured grimace. "That promise has been kept." He fixed his eyes straight onto me. "I'll pose a question to you. When you showed up that night, would you have gone to kill all of us?"

"I would have tried to kill anyone who got in my way. That's the sorry truth as I know it." I had my eyes locked into Ted's. "I didn't expect to be coming away from your house standing upright that night." My thoughts spun away from that long ago memory. "What came of your mother?"

"Ovarian cancer some fifteen years back. Life was good for her up until then. She was as her name suggested, filled with grace. Lived at the house on her own until she went on to heaven. The old place still stands. Me and my boys use the land for hunting." He shook his head. "We'll never use it for anything else." Ted held the near-empty soda container between both hands, pressing it with his thumbs. He studied it with sudden interest.

"If I hadn't told Daddy about you helping Mama change that tire for us, life would have probably taken a different course. I'd be different now. Maybe, you'd be different. How our lives come to be is all a mystery to me. Like God's hand thrusts into the water and we're the ripples. All I know is I'm pretty happy. I got a respectable profession. I got a good wife and kids grown. Sure, the town's always dying. Crawls a little forward, slides back even more. Change is always coming. Mostly backward these days. But I got Friday night football. A Saints game down in New Orleans once or twice a season. I love to grill burgers in the backyard. Heading down to the Dairy Queen for ice cream with my wife. A deer hunt late fall on my land. All of that makes it worthwhile for me to get through the day." Ted's breath heaved high up in his chest.

"But more often than not, I wonder about evil in myself. What I did as a boy I do find hard to imagine. I know what horrible acts I can commit. That it's in me. Sometimes, I sit on the front porch in the morning with a cup of coffee in hand and ponder the badness inside myself and how I neglect the cries of those in need. I can't hold onto it for long because it scares me. Then I head on to work at the clinic. Another shift. Another day. I try to do a decent job and then I feel alright."

To Ted Whitehead I said, "I only know of one person who I would deem as having been of true holiness. Selfless and as untouched by evil as he could make himself. He was only here a short while. He no longer walks this earth. I've tried to discover his path, but it eludes me. It will forever elude me, and I've come to accept that."

Ted looked at me with a keen squint to his eyes. The straw from his plastic cup jutted toward the space between his lips. "Well, I too have known only one true holy person." He had an inward perspective as if mulling deeply his thoughts. "That would be Buster Milton. I can tell you where he is right now if you wish to seek him out before you head back home or wherever you'll be heading."

BUSTER, DRESSED IN SUN-SCOURED OVERALLS

I parked the car on the curb of a crumbling asphalt street but left the motor running. I was in a neighborhood laden with forsaken homes ensconced by the overgrowth of weeds and grasses and unkempt shrubs. Dead tree limbs lay atop roofs. Discarded newspapers flung themselves across yards long uncut.

A motley crew of people, some young, some old, some white, black, and brown worked upon a wooden skeletal frame of one of the abandoned houses. I recognized Buster quickly through fifty years of hazy time gone past. He dressed in sun-scoured overalls that clung to his body like the saggy-baggy skin of a malnourished elephant. Bare arms brown as tanned deer hide. A ball cap topped his head. He stood at the end of a long wooden plank set upon two sawhorses.

Behind him stood the shambles of an old house. A frame of sills, studs, and joists arose out of it. The wind of old age hit Buster, rendering his movements slow and careful. The sound of hammering ramped through the hot day. He leaned over low and appeared to guide the blade of a circular saw across the plank's end. The whine of it lifted over the high grass of the yard toward the rental car.

That old man who was Buster Milton cutting the plank scared me. I remained sitting in the air-conditioned car. Let the engine smoothly rumble. I thought of driving on but kept looking at Buster who had been transformed by the wrenching pressures of time, who stood off in the distance with a power saw in his knotted hand. I tried to understand the speeding beat of my heart—the dryness of my mouth. Fear swirled around like two dark holes a trillion light-years away, each moving toward the other.

I turned off the engine and got out of the car. Pain shot through the hinges of my arthritic hip. The blazing sun slapped into my uplifted face. The heat of a long summer, reluctant and stubborn, holding on. A narrow ditch, high in Johnson grass, littered with empty beer and soda cans and a mélange of cellophane wrappers, ran alongside the street. A wraith of a girl, probably ten years old, if that, moved slowly down it, tugging a large garbage bag. Braided pigtails hung past her neck. Beaded oil field gloves engulfed her hands. The whine of Buster's saw died in the air and the beat of hammers rose higher still.

I could hear the girl breathing, singing some nonsensical tune, *They said, get back, honky cat, Better get back to the woods* above the ongoing knock-knock of the hammering. She gave me a curious look up from her bent-over angle and kept plucking trash from weeds to sack.

I said with some good humor, "Watch out for snakes down there."

She giggled, said, "You watch out," and kept on.

I said, "What's your name?"

She giggled again. The hammering kept on. She said, "What's your name?"

"Jack Crowe." That odd fear, that son-of-a-bitch fear drained, and I felt relaxed.

She said, "Jack Crowe."

"So, what's your name?" I said.

She giggled more, scooped a crunched-up Budweiser can into her hand, and sunk it into her bag. She said, "So what's your name?"

"I told you, it's Jack Crowe."

"I told you, it's Jack Crowe," she said.

I rubbed my nose. The heat wrapped around me. The girl's bright, dark eyes shined up at me.

"Are you going to tell me who you are?" I said slowly with feinted seriousness.

"Are you going to tell me who you are?" She said slowly with feinted seriousness.

I grinned wider. The sound of hammering beat through the air. Lightness drifted higher up into my chest.

The girl smiled wider. Eyes vast and bright with anticipation.

"Well, I'm going to go over and talk to ol' Buster Milton," I said.

"Well, I'm going to go over and talk to ol' Buster Milton," she said.

I gave her a wink and stepped over the shallow ditch. Buster's saw remained silent. A tall, skinny kid beside him, about as broad as dock rope, carted away a cut plank board. Behind me, the girl spoke to my back. "Mister, are you going to help us?"

I stopped and looked back at her. Downy hair beneath her pigtails tamped down with sweat against her ears. I said, "Mister, are you going to help us?"

Her smile flashed and her eyes beamed into me. She pointed a gloved finger at my head. The thumb of her hand cocked up like the hammer of a gun. She pulled the trigger and giggled.

Buster called out through the backdrop of hammering, the mimicry song of mockingbirds, the palpable heat, "Jack Crowe, come over here! Get away from that great-granddaughter of mine. She'll drive you to distraction. Come on, Jack! Come on over here so I can see who you are!"

ACKNOWLEDGEMENTS

Thanks to the wondrous Laura Pritchett and Barbara Richardson for their valuable critiques and guidance. Tremendous gratitude to readers John Schluckebier, Joe Arnold, Tom Courtney, Steve and Cindy Kestrel, Max and Judy Elliott, Rob Roy, Sally Swartz, Bill Angle, Julie and Dan Eakin, Judy Hibbard, Diana Shelton, Marvin and Sheila Morganstein, and Paula Harvey. As always, great appreciation for the existence of Lighthouse Writers in Denver, Colorado.

at Saint-Esteve

Mack Green is a member of Lighthouse Writers in Denver, Colorado and a retired neuropsychologist. As a young man he served two tours of duty in Vietnam with the U.S. Marines and received two purple hearts. He is a member of Veterans for Peace and lives in Colorado.